# Crisis

Best Wishes!

This book is a work of fiction. Names, characters, places and incidents are products of the author's imagination or are used fictitiously. Any resemblance to actual events or locales or persons, living or dead, is entirely coincidental.

Copyright © 2005 Erik Qualman
All rights reserved.
ISBN: 1-4196-1561-0

To order additional copies, please contact us.
www.american-novel.com
equalman, LLC

Published by BookSurge LLC
An Amazon.com Company

Erik Qualman

# CRISIS

# ACKNOWLEDGEMENTS

This book would not have been possible without the love and support of many individuals. A special thanks to the following:

To my loving parents for always supporting everything that I do. My brothers for being the best friends anyone could hope to have. My sister-in-law's editorial brilliance. The priceless wisdom and guidance received from my Grandparents. Finally, to countless family and friends whose interest, assistance and encouragement mean the world to me! Thank you and Live Free.

*This Book Is Dedicated To The Extraordinary American Heroes That Humbly Traverse This Great Nation. God Bless All Those That Have Selflessly Sacrificed To Ensure Our Children Are Wrapped In The Blanket Of Freedom For Centuries To Come.*

*By Purchasing This Book You Are Benefiting Numerous Charities That Help Provide A Better Life For So Many.*

*Thank You For Your Selfless Action And Contribution.*

# PREFACE

Mrs. Downs made her way across the Avenue of Americas. Accustomed to the bustle of Manhattan, she effortlessly made her way through the crowded street. The distance between her and the glistening glass of the eNetwork Building was diminishing with each step. Zar Kumbadi watched the middle-aged woman closely. When she was about forty-yards from the eNetwork building, he began his approach to the doorman who was standing attentively beside the series of revolving glass doors at the entrance.

"Excuse me sir, I was wondering if you'd be so kind as to drop this package off with Mr. Tom Morgan," asked Zar in perfect English with a nasally New York accent. Zar extended a brilliantly decorated package. A crisp fifty-dollar bill was also flashed in the direction of the frail, 55-year-old doorman.

"I'd like to help you sir, but I'm afraid it's against company policy since 9/11 for me to deliver any type of package. You will need to complete the necessary paperwork at the processing desk, just like all the other carriers. The processing desk is located inside the lobby and to your right," replied the doorman in a Bronx tone. This was his canned reply and one that he'd phlegmatically dole out all morning. His anemic appearance suggested that he could use the extra cash, but he couldn't afford to lose another job. Having to forgo a quick fifty-dollars made his tight green uniform all the more uncomfortable on this unseasonably warm fall morning.

Zar was unfazed by the doorman's rebuttal and quickly set his alternate plan into motion. However, it wasn't really an alternate plan at all. Earlier in the week he'd sent a scout to perform a dry run and thus knew what to expect. Copious research was the key to Zar's success. In this instance, he'd paid a kid off the street thirty-dollars to deliver a package directly into the eNetwork building. The kid had been unsuccessful. He received the same stonewall reaction that Zar just experienced. If asked by authorities, the street kid would describe Zar as an old lady with an unsightly wart. Zar left nothing to chance.

In reaction to the doorman's response, Zar purposely paused as if in deep thought allowing time for Mrs. Downs to reach the entrance. Now that she was within earshot, he broke from his trance and continued his conversation with the doorman.

"Oh, come on. Can't you just look the other way, just this once? I'm late for a meeting, and I want to surprise him with a birthday gift. Tom Morgan and I go way back," pleaded Zar while accentuating the Tom Morgan portion of the sentence for Mrs. Downs' benefit.

Mrs. Down's heard Morgan's name and turned in his direction. "I'm sorry, but I could not help overhearing your troubles. Did you say that you have a birthday present for Mr. Morgan?" she asked politely. Of course, everything sounded polite in her cheery English accent.

"Why Yes, I do," responded Zar.

"Well, I happen to be his secretary, and I would gladly take it to him, if you'd like," suggested Mrs. Downs.

"Oh no, I couldn't ask you to do that, this package is pretty heavy. I'll just check it at the lobby as this gentleman suggests," replied Zar.

"Don't be silly my dear. I may not be as young as I used to be, but these muscles raised four hearty boys," she proudly stated. "Carrying a package upstairs isn't going to hurt this body a smidgen."

"If you don't think it would be too much trouble, I'd really appreciate it. You're so kind. I can see why Tom speaks so highly of you," said Zar.

She blushed slightly and secured her bulky purse strap on her shoulder before taking the box from Zar.

"This is beautiful gold foil. Did you wrap this yourself?" gushed Mrs. Downs.

"I must take a vow of silence on that one, however please be careful, it's awful heavy," said Zar.

"Trust me, it's a lot lighter and calmer than a 2-year-old who's teething. If you don't mind me asking, sir, what's in here?" inquired Mrs. Downs.

"Oh it's just a couple of pictures from our college days that I had blown-up and framed," Zar found amusement in his secret pun and had to suppress a sinister smile.

"Oh, I can't wait to see them, I bet they look lovely. Do you want to come up and help us surprise him? Mr. Morgan should be in around nine o'clock," said Mrs. Downs.

"I'd love to, but unfortunately, I'm already late for a meeting," said Zar as he glanced at his watch. "Besides, I don't know how happy he'll be when all the people in the office see the wild hairdo and funky clothing he's sporting in those pictures," said Zar, again glancing at the gold Rolex. The Rolex hung loosely around his right wrist giving the impression he was left-handed.

"It's too bad you're in such a hurry. I bet Mr. Morgan would like to see you. Come to think of it, I don't even know your name," said Mrs. Downs as she extended her hand, "I'm Linda Downs."

"Oh how rude of me! My name is John Krafton," said Zar. "You can tell Tom that the Kraft-Man stopped by," Zar used his fingers to mimic quotes for his nickname. "Kraft-Man is an old nickname of mine and it's the only thing he's ever called me." His painstaking research of Yale's residency records and yearbooks had revealed the information he needed regarding Morgan's college life. The alias of John Krafton would buy Zar time if necessary.

Krafton was on the debate team with Morgan in college. He was currently a successful stockbroker for Goldman Sachs. Observing Krafton the last two days was all Zar needed to play his character this morning. Zar even went to the hassle of mimicking Krafton's unique swagger. He had also noticed that Krafton was left-handed.

"I'll give him your regards as well as your present Mr. Krafton," said Mrs. Downs.

"Oh, please call me John. You're much too kind. It's been a

pleasure meeting you and thank you again for all your help. Have a nice day," said Zar, who walked briskly to the corner and hailed a cab. Acting the part of a peripatetic stockbroker, he constantly glanced at his watch.

---

About twenty minutes later, Tom Morgan entered the elevator and emphatically pressed the button for the top floor. He waited impatiently for the brilliant chrome doors to close. Silence filled the vast elevator. Being alone in the express elevator wasn't unusual. For security reasons there was limited access to the top floor. Those that did have access to the 88th floor shied away from the laboriously quiet ride with Morgan. Although Morgan was generally gregarious, it was well known around the office that he preferred to ride the elevator in solitude. This peculiar behavior was probably because it was the only peaceful time he could enjoy during his hectic business day.

Just four months ago, *Newsweek* had proclaimed Morgan as the most influential businessman in America. After all, he was founder and CEO of the most profitable and powerful communications company in America, eNetwork. eNetwork was founded shortly after he left SBC's Broadband Division. Morgan had become increasingly frustrated by SBC's lack of progress in creating the nation's "information superhighway," as it was called at the time. His technical knowledge and business acumen allowed eNetwork to quickly become the leader in high-speed communications. Morgan had done the impossible by defeating communication giants AT&T, AOL, Google and Microsoft. His ascent to the top of the business world was unparalleled. *The Wall Street Journal* tabbed him as a jocularly witty and handsome Bill Gates.

Morgan had aggressively acquired assets and technologies from all the failed dot coms while the competition just tried to fend off bankruptcy or accounting scandals that claimed the likes of Enron, MCI WorldCom, and many more.

Success did have a price however, as Morgan's wife of fifteen years and two children grew tired of playing second fiddle to bytes, fiber optics and microchips. Mrs. Morgan, along with the 12-year-old twins, Ashley and Alexis, had left him six months ago.

Morgan eyed his reflection in the elevator's plasma screen. The high definition plasma was running through the day's top stories. Out of habit he patted his salt & pepper colored hair down on both sides. The long hours had taken a slight toll, but he was still handsome and in great shape. He was listed as one of the Top Ten Most Eligible Bachelors in the July issue of *People Magazine*. He was still in love with his wife, but he was more in love with the challenges his career offered. To help fill the void left by her absence, he devoted any spare time to charity along with annual donations.

Today was his 40th birthday and he was truly indifferent about it. He wasn't planning on doing anything special for his birthday, but he assumed his coworkers had planned something elaborate. He appreciated the thought and effort toward giving him a special birthday, but he'd prefer it to be just another day.

Allocating time for fun was always difficult for him to justify. Time was too precious a commodity to waste, especially with the pending merger with Yahoo! set to occur in three weeks. This merger would enable the development of a new technology that would be more breakthrough than the telephone. Morgan truly hoped there would not be a birthday party waiting for him when he got off the elevator.

Across the Avenue of Americas, Zar Kumbadi patiently sipped his black coffee from a Styrofoam cup and read the morning edition of the *New York Post*. His appearance was completely different from his John Krafton character just twenty minutes ago. Zar had removed the black wig and thick mustache. He'd also changed out of the navy blue double-breasted Armani suit and red silk tie. The fake potbelly that had been strapped around his naturally svelte waist had also been removed. The makeup that had added six years to his smooth face had been washed off in the subway bathroom.

Zar was now wearing faded blue jeans with well-worn white tennis shoes. His University of Syracuse hat nicely accented the blue and orange of his Mets satin jacket. The hat rested loosely on his shaved head. He also was wearing a pair of wire rim non-prescription glasses. The glasses were just part of the show; he had 20/17 vision.

Zar calmly glanced at his tattered Fossil watch, and was pleased to see that Mr. Morgan had arrived at his usual time, nine o'clock. Zar had monitored Morgan for well over a month, and found he arrived at the same time every morning, only once being late. He knew that it would take Morgan approximately three to four minutes to reach the top floor. Morgan always rode the express elevator, straight to the top with no stops. Zar didn't need to be this close to Morgan at this moment, in fact he knew he should be on his way out of the country, but he wanted to see the fruits of his labor.

Mrs. Downs glanced at the gold package resting on the round, butterfly-mahogany coffee table. The table was in front of a large brown leather couch in the center of Mr. Morgan's immense penthouse office. She couldn't wait to see the pictures inside the gold wrapping, as well as Mr. Morgan's surprised reaction. She had worked for Morgan the past five years and had never met anyone that really knew him outside of his business dealings.

Mrs. Downs also liked the gift she'd selected for Mr. Morgan, a gift certificate for a full body massage at a spa in Estes Park, Colorado. He was traveling to Boulder for an international convention where he was the keynote speaker, and it would be followed by a few intense days of meetings. Mrs. Downs thought her gift would be a good stress reliever for him that week. However, she also knew that he probably wouldn't take time out for it, but she thought it was worth a try.

The elevator chime signaled that Mr. Morgan had arrived at his destination. His subordinates giggled as they attempted to remain quiet. The workers crouched behind their desks. This was one of the few situations where it was permissible to have fun at the office. Mr. Morgan demanded that his employees work hard, but he also made sure they were well compensated for their considerable talents and dedication. The employees respected Morgan because he, in turn, treated them fairly and with genuine respect.

A banner reading "Lordy, Lordy, look who's Forty!!" hung tenuously above the door leading to Morgan's immense corner office. His two tallest employees had painstakingly placed the sign there earlier that morning. They attempted to hang it with string routed through the ceiling panels, but eventually gave in and stuck it to the wall with duct tape all the while joking that they needed to have an MBA class on how to hang a sign.

Morgan was watching CNBC's "Morning Call" on the elevators plasma screen until the doors parted. He led with his left foot, which was concealed in a pair of expensive brown Italian loafers. As his foot landed on the carpet, his fellow employees sprang from their hiding places with a boisterous and less than harmonious "Surprise!" Mrs. Downs quickly greeted him with a hug. It was obvious that he was uncomfortable with such a display of public affection. His discomfort didn't last long. The clock electrically attached to the powerful plastic explosive in the gold package struck 9:05 am.

No one on the birthday welcoming committee or Morgan felt a thing. They were killed instantly by the awesome puissance of the blast. The bomb also blew a thirty-foot hole in the three floors below. Sheered metal and splintered wood thrashed in every direction. The 23rd floor immediately collapsed onto the 22nd, which crumpled onto the 21st. The occupants on the three floors didn't stand a chance. They were either killed by the explosion or by the falling debris.

Hundreds of feet below, onlookers stood horrified on the Avenue of Americas. Survivors still had their ears covered from the incredible sound of the explosion. Most were in shock for several seconds, before eventually scrambling to shelter in panic. This location was eerily close to where the horrific events of 9/11 occurred at the former location of the World Trade Center. These people still remembered that day vividly just as most Americans would for the rest of their lives. As a result, people weren't waiting around to see what was going on. However, several pedestrians were too slow to react and as a result they lay victimized on the street. A 16-year old bicycle courier lay crumpled over the handlebars of his twelve-speed.

A well-dressed and previously harried businessman was motionless on the crenellated cement of the street. He was wedged between a fallen chunk of concrete and the asphalt of the street. A woman shrieked uncontrollably as she couldn't locate her husband. The incessant horn of a yellow cab filled the smoky air of the tragic scene. The cab driver was face down on the steering wheel and breathless. Zar Kumbadi glanced at the death and destruction that surrounded him and satisfied warmth filled his body. There was just something about the smell of death that invigorated him. A slight grin slinked onto his face. Black smoke dispersed into the morning sky, casting a dark shadow over midtown Manhattan and beyond.

*USA Today*:

*New York City was rocked yesterday morning by an unexpected disaster and its tremors are being felt across the nation. At approximately 9:05 yesterday morning a new type of plastic explosive, with the power of a 15-ton bomb, exploded on the 23rd floor of the eNetwork building. The eNetwork building is located on the Avenue of Americas in downtown Manhattan. A major rescue effort has been underway since the tragedy occurred. At this writing, 105 are dead and 20 others are missing. Among the victims are 23 first grade children from the local Sacred Heart Elementary School. The children were participating in a new interactive media program for elementary schools sponsored by eNetwork Inc. and their philanthropic CEO Tom Morgan. The class was being conducted on the 21st floor when the explosion occurred. Five pedestrians on the street below were killed by falling debris from the explosion. 31 persons were also critically injured. The cause of the explosion is still unknown and no group has claimed responsibility for the bombing. Speculation is that it is the first terrorist attack on American soil since the tragic events of September 11, 2001. Authorities agree the death toll could have been much greater, but since the eNetwork building was built under the new guidelines and standards for all buildings since 9/11 the specially designed steel was able to withstand the intense blast preventing the structure from collapsing like the World Trade Center. One current lead that authorities are checking into is John Krafton of Goldman Sachs. Krafton was detained for questioning from his SOHO townhouse late last night.*

*Democratic Presidential Candidate, Robert Parkhill, was scheduled* *to meet with eNetwork CEO, Tom Morgan, later that afternoon. Parkhill was hosting a $1000 per plate breakfast campaign fundraiser at Rockefeller Center and wasn't available to comment. Morgan was at the epicenter of the blast and has been identified as one of the dead. The Dow Jones Industrial average plummeted a record 758 points. Experts speculate that Tom Morgan's death will put a hold on eNetwork's merger with Yahoo!. eNetwork and Yahoo!'s stocks were also down dramatically on the news.*

# CHAPTER 1

# FIVE YEARS PRIOR, ROCHESTER HILLS, MICHIGAN:

"Twenty-nine! Thirty! Thirty-one!" The chant of the crowd abruptly changed to cheering as Paul Tipton quickly removed his mouth from the tapped keg of beer.

"New Record!" shouted an extremely fat and drunk Fred Weeks. Fred was presently stuffing his face with a burnt microwave pizza.

Two husky Brother Rice hockey players held Paul Tipton by his legs and slowly lowered him to the ground. Struggling to gain his balance, his head felt like it weighed a thousand pounds and was acting as his center of gravity. He knew his body wasn't going to appreciate the recently concluded keg stand. A keg stand was a popular recreational form of drinking that entailed doing a handstand on the keg while sucking the continual flow of beer from the tap. At this point, the majority of the partiers had already taken more than one turn on the keg.

Paul was not going to pull away from the keg until he beat the record; he couldn't deny the burning drive inside of him, a drive that wouldn't allow someone to beat him at anything, even a mindless game. Everything in life for Paul Tipton was a game, a game for him to win at all costs.

This type of competitive spirit had enabled him to be an All-State selection in hockey the past three seasons. It also helped Paul lead Birmingham Brother Rice, a prestigious Birmingham, Michigan parochial school, to consecutive State Championships. Every college in the country had recruited him, along with the Detroit Red Wings and Boston Bruins of the National Hockey League.

Today had been the best day Paul could remember. At his press conference earlier that morning, he declared his intention to attend and play hockey for the Maize and Blue of the University of Michigan. The constant barrage of phone calls would end. The unwanted advice would cease. The recruiters hanging on his every word would vanish. Best of all, he'd never have to answer the question "Where are you planning to play hockey?" The weight of the world had been lifted from his shoulders and it was now time to relax. It was time to reap the benefits of his hard work.

Of course his father, David Tipton MD, couldn't let him enjoy the day. His father's words still echoed in Paul's ears, "You didn't call the other coaches about your intentions before the press conference? How many times did I tell you to do that? Don't you have any consideration for anyone? Don't you feel any responsibility toward the other coaches, the other schools!? That's just plain irresponsible, selfish, and rude." He was upset that Paul didn't have the courtesy to inform the coaches at Boston University and Harvard of his intentions to attend U of M prior to his announcement. Paul had narrowed his choices down to these schools about a month ago. In verity, it was really a two-institution race between Boston University and the University of Michigan.

The only reason Paul placed Harvard on the list, was to humor his father. The elder had received all of his schooling at Harvard and had even met his wife, Jennifer Endreas, at a Wellesley College mixer. His father was also a member of the Harvard President's Club: the highest honor any Harvard Alumni could receive. Despite his busy schedule, he always found time to make it back for Harvard's homecoming. He also occasionally made a special trip to watch the annual crew race between Harvard and archenemy Yale. A race he used to compete in when he was captain back in '71.

So what if he didn't tell the other coaches, thought Paul. He was sick of informing everybody of his every move. Just like every other high school senior, Paul wanted to relish his remaining days there.

# CRISIS

He attributed his dad's anger and outburst to the fact that he hadn't chosen his alma mater. His dad was really upset when he mentioned the party scheduled for that evening. "What party? What is it with you? You're going to college in a couple of months and you can't even remember that you promised to baby-sit your sister for us tonight? Your mother and I are attending a banquet, and there's no way we can get a baby-sitter this late in the day. When are you going to become more responsible and start living up to your commitments? You're not going to that party tonight, young man and that's final," were his father's last words that evening. Paul may be the king of everything else, but not in this house.

Paul's beautiful girlfriend of three years, Stephanie Rison, had insisted Paul be at the party. After Paul confirmed that he wouldn't be able to attend, Stephanie revealed that it was a surprise party in his honor, and he had to make an appearance. Her parents were on vacation in Aruba, celebrating their twentieth wedding anniversary.

Paul felt guilty about forgetting his baby-sitting obligation. However, he wasn't worried about his little sister Allison being able to take care of herself. In fact, it often seemed as if she was taking care of him and keeping him out of trouble. He was also sick of his father's lectures pertaining to his irresponsibility. He couldn't wait to be in college where he could finally be his own man.

The Tiptons left for the banquet around seven o'clock. Paul, disobeying his father's request, left for Stephanie's party soon after. Four hours of liquor shots, keg stands, and general partying put him in his present drunken condition.

He stumbled his way across the family room toward Stephanie, where she was seated on the sofa, reminiscing with her girlfriends about high school. Her supple legs were crossed right over left. To the naked eye, it would appear she was wearing nylons; her skin was so smooth and flawless. This optical illusion resulted from four years of cheerleading at Rochester Adams High School, and three summers of life guarding at Thelma Spencer Park. She went to great lengths for her health and body, and it showed. She enjoyed being tan, but knew that if she wanted to extend her modeling career, she needed to make sure she didn't cause unnecessary skin damage. She was careful to apply liberal amounts of sun block, especially on her face, whenever she was life guarding. The end result was a body that anyone would envy.

The summer humidity and congestion of the party caused tiny beads of perspiration to form just below her graceful neck. One of the more adventurous perspiration beads left its resting place and began to slowly funnel down her firm and well rounded breasts, which were framed by the neckline of her azure-specked sundress.

Paul attempted to walk naturally as he approached Stephanie on the couch, yet his efforts to appear sober were made in vain. He knew she hated when he was inebriated and it was going to be difficult to hide.

"Hey, what do we owe the pleasure of the guest of honor gracing us with his presence?" Stephanie asked as she stood up and wiped the beer residue from Paul's mouth.

Satisfied that his mouth was clean, she proceeded to give him a moist kiss on the lips.

"Congratulations, my big Michigan Wolverine," she said with a twinkle in her brilliant blue eyes, which were partially blocked from view by her flowing auburn hair. She was too happy at the moment to be upset with Paul for being drunk.

He put his arm around her waist, more for support than as a display of affection. She enjoyed this type of attention. She liked everyone knowing that she was dating the local superstar. She had insisted that she be present for his press conference that morning, and made sure she was real close to him when the television cameras were rolling. All along she knew she would be attending U of M, yet she didn't announce this decision until two weeks ago. The delayed announcement was simply because she truly enjoyed the attention from the other schools trying to persuade her to attend their respected institutions.

The hockey coaches at these schools thought that if they could land Paul Tipton's girlfriend, then he would soon follow. There was some truth to this logic, since it would be difficult for Paul to be apart from his first crush, Stephanie. Stephanie had thrown this party more for her sake, than for his. Being the center of attention pleased her the most, even if it was at the expense of others. Paul didn't see this selfishness in her, he was blinded by love.

He was lovesick the moment they'd met at a Western Michigan summer sports camp in Kalamazoo. She was attending a cheerleading camp, while he was competing in a hockey tournament at the Bronco Ice Arena. It was the summer before their sophomore year and he hadn't looked at another girl since.

The beer in Paul's system was really kicking in now, and all he wanted to do was be close to Stephanie. They had yet to make love. She wanted to wait, which was fine with him. He figured he could wait until they were married and he had every intention of spending the rest of his life with her. Prior to their courtship, he'd had sex with two other girls. One was his girlfriend at the end of his freshman year. The other was a 26-year-old woman who was the manager of the movie theatre he worked at during the summer. He'd had a passionate fling with this older woman, mainly in the back of the empty theatre, but it fizzled out once high school resumed.

He wanted to pass out in Stephanie's arms tonight. It was a rare treat for him to stay over in her pink bedroom, affectionately coined the Pink Panther Playhouse. As a joke, he had given her a Pink Panther stuffed animal for her birthday last year. He'd won it doing one of those rigged carnival games that nobody wins. Nobody that is, except Paul Tipton.

The large and soft Pink Panther currently resided on the pillows of her queen-sized bed. He loved to just spoon with her near flawless body. These pleasant thoughts and images of Paul's were rudely interrupted by the reality of the moment.

"Paul, we've got to get you home, it's well after eleven," insisted Stephanie.

"Oh, why did that stupid banquet have to be tonight, of all nights?" said a highly frustrated Paul.

"Oh yeah, make sure you tell your father I said congratulations and that I really enjoyed reading his latest article," said Stephanie.

"Don't worry, I will. I'd better get going before he gets home, although someone's gonna have to give me a lift, I'm in no condition to get behind the wheel. I'd be like an elephant wearing high heels trying to tightrope-walk on dental floss," said Paul, who hadn't intended on getting this smashed. Apparently his pent-up stress was more than he thought.

"Could the hostess please give me a ride?" Paul asked with his glossy, bloodshot eyes starring down at Stephanie.

"I'd love to give you a ride home, but I'm the caretaker of this zoo," Stephanie said as she panned the house with her left hand. "I'm sure there's someone else who would gladly give you a ride. I'll go ask around," she said and headed toward the living room.

Paul slouched down into the flint-blue leather of a nearby recliner. One of Stephanie's intoxicated friends began badgering him with questions about his decision to attend the University of Michigan. Paul didn't want to be rude, but he couldn't stop his eyes from slowly closing and the tiresome questions and ramble of the surrounding party slowly faded into the distance.

"Paul, Paul, get up, come on. I found someone who can give you a ride. Give me your keys," insisted Stephanie.

"Who's driving?" he asked groggily. It appeared to him as if there were two or three images of Stephanie. More of her was fine in his mind. He decided to focus on the middle Stephanie, because the other two were pretty blurry.

"Fred Weeks is going to take you home in your car, and then he's going to walk home from your house. It's twenty of twelve, so you should easily be home by midnight. You said your parents would be home around quarter after, so you guys better get going, oh and don't even think about stopping off at Taco Bell on the way," Stephanie stated matter of fact.

"Are you sure Fred's okay to drive? He was pretty tanked earlier, wasn't he?" hiccupped Paul.

# CRISIS

"Fred stopped drinking a while ago, and besides, he puked it all up about a half-hour ago. That big boy is a fish, I read somewhere that someone his size can consume like six beers an hour and still blow under the legal limit. Besides, everyone else that lives by you has already gone home, so Fred has to take you," persuaded Stephanie.

"Stephanie, I can wait for you to give me a ride home instead of going with Fred. My father's pissed off enough already, it can't get much worse. But, if you say Fred's all right to drive, I'll take your word for it. I'm nooooo smarty smarty...hey that rhymes with party! Oh boy standing up is going to be tough...I'm so frickin' housed," blurted Paul as he pulled himself up and out of the chair, grabbing Stephanie's arm for balance. "I'm just joking grabbing your barm...I mean arm...I'm fine baby."

"You don't need to go at it with your father again. Your dad will like, go berserk if he finds your sister home by herself. We've already wasted like too much time talking about this. Now please be a good boy and give me the car keys," insisted Stephanie. Paul reluctantly handed over the keys, which were attached to a plastic Nike icon. He created the key chain using the tag from a pair of running shoes he purchased last summer.

"Good luck beating your parents home, congratulations once again, and I'll give you a call tomorrow," Stephanie quickly gave him a smooch. She hoped he would beat his parents home, not for his sake, but for hers. She didn't want a blemish on her record-her perfect record. Stephanie Rison was, after all, the perfect girl. She was the captain of the cheerleading team, a straight A student, President of the Student Council, and girlfriend of the state's prized hockey player. Stephanie didn't think she could be more perfect if she tried.

"Freddy, the Fredmiester, wheeling Tipton's drunk asssssss home," Paul said as he hopped into the front seat of the black Trans Am convertible with Ram Air induction.

"Hey the only reason I'm giving your sorry butt a ride home is so I can drive your beautiful graduation present," Fred bellowed as he turned on the ignition. Like many other residents in the Motor City, Fred was a quintessential gear-head. He knew the Trans Am could do zero to sixty miles per hour in five seconds flat and had a top speed of over one hundred and fifty miles per hour. Fred was a big fan of the Trans Am's of the early 90's and when General Motors brought the line back recently he couldn't be happier. Fred had been hoping to drive this car since the day Paul got it. He also found it impossible to turn down the gorgeous Stephanie whenever she asked for a favor and if she said he was okay to drive, who was he to question? Fred and Paul had been friends since the fifth grade. It was inevitable when you live on the same block. Fred, like many kids his age, wanted to lead Paul Tipton's life.

Fred lowered the power convertible top and pulled the Trans Am out of the Hawthorn Hills subdivision, heading southbound on Adams Road.

"This car has the greatest throaty exhaust rumble in the world, feel the power baby! NICE!!!" Fred shouted.

"Mmmhmm," was the best Paul could muster, his thoughts where elsewhere. He was thinking about what his father had said, and it upset him. His father's words hurt, because he knew his father was right about him being irresponsible. His father was always right. Tip tried so hard to be as good as his father, to live up to his high expectations. However, it was a tiring and trying task attempting to be perfect all the time. He was proud of his dad and loved him dearly, even though it seemed they rarely got along.

---

As he cruised eastbound on Walton Boulevard, Dr. David Tipton gently eased his sterling silver BMW 540i into fourth gear. He thought the next car that he'd purchase would be a Seville or Park Avenue or some other General Motors car. It would lessen some of the tension he felt visiting his GM executive friends. However, none of the American makes offered a manual transmission, and he had to have that. Driving an automatic didn't give him the sense of control he desired.

# CRISIS

Dr. Tipton listened carefully to his speech from that evening's banquet. Jennifer, his wife of twenty years, slept peacefully in the passenger seat. Jennifer was extremely attractive and active for a woman her age. An All-American tennis player at Wellesley, she was still one of the top twenty-five players in the country for her age bracket. Dr. Tipton was pretty good at tennis in his own right, though they never played mixed double together. They'd tried it in the past, and invariably they ended up feeding on each other's competitive throats. They found their marriage was better off if they didn't play tennis together.

Dr. Tipton recorded all of his public speeches. Listening to the speeches enabled him to detect and eliminate any flaws, which were few and far between. The local medical association had just honored him for his essay about why socialized medicine would undermine the foundation of American Medicine. Originally published in the *Oakland Press*, a local newspaper, it had been picked up by a few medical journals and eventually *Reader's Digest*. This recognition was just one in a series of accomplishments for the esteemed Dr. Tipton. He was proud of his achievements, but nothing made him more proud than his son and daughter.

He was upset with himself for losing his temper with Paul. The fact was, he couldn't be more impressed by his son. He probably loved him too much and consequently he didn't want him to settle for anything but the best.

Dr. Tipton was glad Paul had selected U of M because it meant he'd be close to home. Despite his hectic schedule, he would be able to attend all of his son's home games. Ann Arbor was a fifty-minute drive from Rochester Hills. U of M also had one of the best medical programs in the country. He did believe that it might be better for Paul to attend Harvard, where he could concentrate on academics and just be another student. U of M treated their athletes like demigods. The pressures on an athlete at U of M were enormous, and often the academics suffered as a result.

Dr. Tipton also understood why it would be difficult for Paul not to take his talents to U of M. His girlfriend was going there, they had a great medical program, and he'd have a much better chance of playing professional hockey when his college career was over. Paul would be better prepared for the National Hockey League and he'd receive more national exposure.

Michigan's program continually ranked in the Top Ten nationally, and everyone knew about their successful football program. U of M was also located in Ann Arbor, one of the great cultural towns of America. Its diverse student population, art festivals, and affluent residents provided a great environment for broadening young minds. The cultural aspect of Ann Arbor was accentuated by having the highest percentage of persons holding graduate degrees in the country.

Dr. Tipton excelled in almost everything he did. Yet he was dreadful in one particular area: expressing his emotions to his son. This emotional deficiency would change tomorrow, thought Dr. Tipton. Tomorrow he'd tell his son how proud he was of him and how much he loved him before he left for college, and it was too late.

---

Paul slept soundly in the passenger seat. He couldn't wait to get home to bed. Fred Weeks took advantage of his newly found freedom and opened up the powerful V8 engine on an open stretch of road. The throaty rumble of the engine felt great and Fred felt even better. The speedometer climbed to eighty mph, well over the forty-five mph speed limit. The ride was so smooth and steady that he didn't realize he was well over the legal limit. The seatbelt around his plump midsection was becoming irritable and he promptly removed it so that he could thoroughly enjoy the ride.

He wasn't worried about getting pulled over. After all, he'd thrown-up thirty minutes ago and he figured those recent three shots of Jagermeister wouldn't hit his system until after he was safely home. If he did get stopped, he'd just grab a penny from his jeans pocket and suck on it. His second cousin, Timmy, told him that the copper in the penny would scramble the results of a police Breathalyzer. He also knew that if you blew hard at first and then tapered off it would help his odds. This unorthodox technique helped because alcohol is stored in the back of the throat and the Breathalyzer takes awhile to get a reading. Hence, he would blow out all the alcohol from the back of his mouth before the Breathalyzer had a chance to record. By the time the Breathalyzer would start to get a read it would only be picking up clean air. This wonderful knowledge was also obtained from Timmy, the same Timmy that didn't graduate from high school.

Fred gripped the leather wrapped sports steering wheel tightly and howled with delight. He was having so much fun that he didn't notice the streetlight had turned red at the Adams and Walton Boulevard intersection.

The explosive concussion, blinding headlights and flying glass jolted Paul awake. A three-ton Ford Excursion violently 'T'-boned the low-slung Trans Am's driver side door. The refrigerator-white Excursion, the industry's largest sport utility vehicle, had been heading west at fifty mph on Walton Boulevard. Terror gripped Fred's face and Paul let out a vicious yell an instant before the Ford's bumper smashed into them. The high riding bumper overrode most of the Trans Ams' side impact protection. The cockpit was instantly crushed to half its original width.

The Trans Am hurtled diagonally across the dew-covered median, directly into the path of eastbound traffic. The Trans Am's brief journey came to a quick halt as it collided at a forty-five degree angle with a Chrysler LHS Sedan. The combined speed of the two vehicles was one hundred miles per hour. The front of the Trans Am made a horrendous sound and crunched up like a beer can in a trash compactor. It was the Trans Am's best attempt to damper the deadly force. The LHS also incurred severe body damage; the left side molding was stripped as a result of the intense friction of the clashing metal.

Upon impact with the Chrysler LHS, Paul launched forward with magnificent force. Fortunately, he was abruptly restrained by the passenger airbag, and his seatbelt clasped painfully down across his chest and flung him back into his seat. His head snapped back over the low positioned headrest of his black leather seat.

What had been so excruciatingly loud a second before was now deathly quiet. Paul's hearing was gone, but his other four senses were operational. He felt and tasted the churned-up grit and grass. He felt the residual propellant powder of the air bag as it settled over him. The overly sweet odor of steaming anti-freeze stung his nostrils. Paul looked across at his motionless friend.

Sound erupted into Paul's consciousness as the volume of the horrific scene descended upon him. The pain across his entire body became excruciating and Paul Tipton's world went black.

---

"What's the problem honey? I wonder why the traffic is so bad. Was there a concert tonight?" asked Mrs. Tipton. She was referring to the Meadowbrook Music Festival on the right, a venue for concerts and theatrical performances during the summer.

"There must be an accident or something. No one's exiting from the concert outlet and it looks like there are police and ambulance lights up ahead. I'll just swing through Oakland University and proceed onto Adams Road," said Dr. Tipton as he took a sharp right into the Festival entrance. The drive took them through lush acres of forest beautifully complemented by a series of meticulously landscaped Tudor buildings. The centerpiece of these buildings, Meadowbrook Hall, lay just over the rolling grass hill from the Theatre.

The majestic early twentieth century mansion lay beside a fastidiously maintained golf course. Horace Dodge of Dodge automobile fame originally built the estate and John Meadowbrook donated the land to the community with explicit directions that the land could never be sold for commercial gain.

Mr. Tipton wasn't thinking the campus was too beautiful tonight as two yellow blockades deterred his shortcut. "Oh nuts, there is a goddamn concert. It just hasn't let out yet," Dr. Tipton said, rolling down the window as he approached a pimple-faced teenager

# CRISIS

donned in a bright yellow traffic vest. "Excuse me son, I'd just like to cut through here to get to Adams Road," said Dr. Tipton.

"I'm afraid I can't let you do that mister. No one's allowed on this road till the concert lets out. Although, you're the fourth person that's asked me that since the accident happened. Rules are rules even if there's an accident," said the teenager dryly in a pre-pubescent voice.

"It must have been a fairly large accident," asked Mrs. Tipton oblivious to the fact that it involved her son. Do you know what happened?" Mrs. Tipton was genuinely curious, but at the same time wanted to befriend this teenager in hopes of changing his mind about the cut through. She knew how irritated her husband could become when he didn't feel in control of the situation.

"I'm sorry ma'am, but I don't know what happened exactly, but someone said a truck broad sided a car which then caused it to run into another car going in the opposite direction. It must have been real bad, because it was loud as hell and it's shut down both lanes of traffic. I could easily hear it over the concert, and that Rod Stewart guy has been playing damn loud for an older dude. The police don't want us to let the concert out until they get all of the mess cleaned up. The cops said it would take at least two hours," said the teenager.

"Honey, since Squirrel Road is closed, why don't we take the great circular route home," suggested Mrs. Tipton. "We can turn right, go through campus, take University Drive back out to I-75 South, and M-59 East back to Adams Road."

"That's what I'm gonna have to do," said the disgruntled doctor as he shifted the BMW into first gear and shot the kid a somewhat displeased look. Mrs. Tipton thanked the teenager with an understanding smile.

The BMW hummed along at 10 mph over the legal limit of 70 mph on the rain-slicked pavement of M-59. The dark, mysterious skies opened up and spit its fury on the earth in a combination of rain and sleet. Dr. Tipton wanted to get home as soon as possible.

He had to debrief his staff the next morning and he still had some final comments to complete his report. As usual, M-59 was very poorly lit. The city of Rochester Hills had just passed an ordinance to correct the poor lighting situation on this stretch of freeway. Construction of one hundred new streetlights would start in a few weeks.

Silence filled the BMW as the recording of Mr. Tipton's speech ended. He leaned forward and pressed the eject button for the SM card. The SM player proceeded to belch the small card onto the floor. "Remind me to get this stupid thing fixed tomorrow," said the doctor to his wife as both of them simultaneously reached down to pick-up the tiny blue data card up off the passenger side floorboard.

By the time Mr. Tipton looked back up again, it was too late. A 1994 Buick LeSabre, driven by an 80-year-old man, entered the highway going Westbound at thirty-five mph with his headlights off. A travel-weary truck driver slammed on his brakes and swerved to the left in a desperate attempt to avoid rear-ending the Buick. The semi-truck's twelve-wheel trailer swung violently across the median and both lanes of oncoming traffic. Smoke emanated from its giant tires. This evasive maneuver caused the cab of the truck to unhitch from the trailer. The heroic effort of the truck driver prevented a massive collision with the Buick. The cab went over the shoulder of the road and came to a stop in a grassy ditch.

The detached trailer continued on its deadly path across oncoming traffic. Dr. Tipton had no chance of reacting to the trailer's unpredictable movements. The BMW cruised underneath the trailer at a speed in excess of seventy mph. Sparks sprayed as the car's head was severed from the body.

# CHAPTER 2

# COLLEGE PARK, MARYLAND

Students quietly shuffled to their morning classes, peacefully exchanging stories of the weekend's activities. Most of these students were freshmen and they still considered eight o'clock classes as late for school to start. They were accustomed to getting up at six in the morning for high school. Making an eight o'clock was a breeze. However, these students would quickly learn that classes starting after eleven o'clock would be more conducive to the nocturnal nature of college life. The upperclassmen were asleep in their beds with no intention of moving a muscle for some time to come.

The trained eye easily spotted freshmen: showered, map in hand, fitted head to toe in Terrapin paraphernalia fresh from the student book store. They would soon comprehend that only dorky alumni wear the school colors during the week. The first few weeks were spent being overwhelmed by the nation's seventh largest campus.

The fall breeze gently rustled through the brilliant orange, red, and yellow of autumn. There weren't many places quite as beautiful this time of year. It was a time of year when the forces of nature combined to put on a spectacular show of colors that no artist's rendering could compare. However, Barbara Fernandez's thoughts were far removed from the brilliant hues of the season.

Barbara fidgeted endlessly with the oversized pewter ring on her middle finger. Her fingers were like twigs in comparison to the gigantic ring. If the pace kept up, she'd be through her skin and to the bone by noon. The waiting was unbearable, she wished Valez would look at her and get it over with, instead of letting her become a nervous wreck fearfully lying in wait.

Ricardo Valez's ominous figure methodically paced over the plush burgundy Persian Carpet. His presence was almost as suffocating as the smoke emanating from the long brown Cuban cigar pinched between his fat fingers. Barbara Fernandez, his secretary, waited fearfully on the edge of the leather chair. She sat in the shadow of his imposing walnut desk, which over the years had bared witness to many terrified faces.

Oh how she hated the silence and the waiting, the only sound being the heavily constricted breathing of the grotesquely obese Valez. He took another puff from his cigar, adding to the already prominent blue haze and distinguished smell of the sunless room. The shades were forever drawn in his office and some wondered if they ever did open. He slowly placed his massive figure into his equally immense burgundy leather chair. The chair's back was facing Barbara and all she could see was the occasional cloud of blue smoke rising from behind it.

She had become immune to the obnoxious cigar stench over the last twelve years, although her dry cleaning bill still pained her. The smoke was one thing, but the hair on the back of her neck still bristled whenever he called her into his office. The twelve years had taken their toll on this once attractive woman, and she looked much older than her forty-five years. It wasn't so much the gray streaks in her black hair, but rather the prevalent veins and tired eyes making her look close to sixty. The physical sacrifice was small in comparison to her generous paycheck. No other job could come close to paying her what she made working for Valez. Lacking a high school diploma, she still made close to six figures during a good year.

Barbara had messed up before, and had been reminded of it, but she'd never come close to making a mistake of this magnitude.

"How does something like this happen?" Inquired the deep and raspy voice of Ricardo Valez. Very easily thought Barbara. If he wasn't so paranoid, he'd hire an assistant to help her, and this would never have happened.

She recalled having a thousand things on her mind last Friday, when he threw that document on her desk and told her it was very important that it be mailed that day. She was in the middle of a telephone call and his request was definitely heard, but somehow didn't register. She proceeded to tediously stuff the hundred outgoing envelopes on her desk, in hopes of somehow getting out of work before six o'clock. She had fallen into a rhythm stuffing the envelopes, much like the daze she experienced when driving down the highway, seemingly on autopilot for hours and not consciously paying attention, but somehow steering safely. It was during this time period that she accidentally stuffed the now infamous list into one of the wrong envelopes. A potentially disastrous mistake.

Although all of these reasons were accurate, she knew better than to express them to the intimidating mountain mass before her.

"You know what I had to do because of you," rhetorically asked Valez interlocking his chubby fingers and starring through Barbara. The cigar did not quite cover up the smell of the pastrami and onion sandwich he'd enjoyed at breakfast, "I had to send someone to Michigan to clean-up the mess that your incompetence created. If *we're* lucky, the least that will happen is it will cost us twenty thousand dollars, and not the whole operation." Barbara knew that even though Valez used the term *we* he meant *her* problem. She would gladly pay the cost of twenty thousand dollars if he would forget the entire episode. She knew this probably wasn't an option. "Now Barbara you've worked for me a long time, so I know it isn't necessary for me to explain my general disdain for sloppy execution," Valez sighed as sweat beaded on his bald forehead.

# CHAPTER 3

# MICHIGAN STATE UNIVERSITY (EAST LANSING, MICHIGAN):

Joseph Garcia's and Victor Sanchez's blood shot eyes were concealed behind their matching black sunglasses. Despite having shaved the previous day, Garcia was almost sporting a full beard. He hadn't had time to shave before they'd left on the first plane out of Las Vegas. His conversation with his contractor at six this morning seemed like days ago. The rented Lincoln Town Car remained silent. Both men were tired and irritable, especially Garcia. Their attention was fixed on the big white colonial house across the street. The Greek letters for Chi Theta were proudly displayed on the front of the house.

Last night, Garcia had a date with his first love, Vodka. Vodka and gambling weren't a good mix for him, and last night was no exception. Taking the early flight to Detroit was the furthest thing from his mind when the annoying ring of the telephone awoke him this morning. His body wasn't happy with him at the moment, but his wallet would be happy after he completed this job.

"He said ten thousand a piece, right?" Garcia asked Sanchez. Garcia desperately needed the money since the dice had not been kind to him lately, especially last night. He still owed a pimp money for some girls last weekend, a position he didn't like being in.

"Yep, all for a stupid little red envelope. Whatever the hell's in there must be pretty important, and hey speak of the devil, here's Mr. Mailman now," said Sanchez.

Garcia quickly got out of the car and crossed Abbott Rd. The mailman was at the front of the enormous fraternity house with two separated piles of mail in his hands. The mailman, Tom "Scooter" Reynolds, was an alumnus of Chi Theta and understood the hassles of living in the fraternity house. He also knew the perks. He separated the junk mail from the pertinent letters using large rubber bands. The brothers of Chi Theta appreciated Scooter taking the time to do this. They also enjoyed his company.

Garcia could see the burgundy envelope that had been so vividly described to him. It was resting near the top of the pile that the mailman held in his right hand. Garcia tried to remember the name of the person it was addressed to. Although he couldn't remember the first name, he was sure the last name was Hamilton. This was too easy thought Garcia, he'd simply grab it from the large brass drop box right after the mailman left. Ten thousand dollars would not be a bad day's work for so simple a task. It was money Garcia would gladly accept and he would have rolled the dice a little more last night if he'd know about this windfall.

But wait, what was the mailman doing? Scooter dropped the pile of junk mail into the drop box, and entered the house with the remaining pile of mail, including the burgundy envelope.

Scooter still wasn't used to the idea of having to use a key to get into the house. Back when he lived in the house, the door was never locked and was even propped open on sunny days. Due to some recent burglaries, including the theft of the big-screen television from the "cave" in the basement, the house remained locked at all times. Intuitively, robbing fraternities would seem like sheer suicide. But the contrary was true. Most fraternities had their residential rooms upstairs while their expensive television and stereo equipment were downstairs. It was difficult for residents to hear activity downstairs when they were sleeping. As a result, fraternity robberies were on the rise. However, when fraternity members did catch the burglars, it wasn't a pretty sight. They usually handed out their own justice before turning the offenders over to the authorities.

Scooter headed around the corner to the individual wooden mailbox slots and proceeded to quickly insert the mail into the correct spots. He wasn't required to do this, but he enjoyed it. It was a break in his otherwise monotonous mail route and there were usually some guys downstairs that he could talk into playing a quick game of pool, or preferably foosball. No such luck today, everyone must be attending class, so he headed out the backdoor to continue his route.

# CHAPTER 4

Chris Hamilton heard Scooter singing "The Freshman" by The Verve Pipe as he headed down the back stairwell and exited out the back door of the fraternity house after having delivered the mail. Verve Pipe was started at Michigan State University in the early nineties and they still dropped into town for an occasional bar concert.

Hamilton pulled the envelopes from his pale oak cubicle and efficiently sifted through his Monday morning mail. His stack of mail was once again five times the size of anyone else's in the fraternity. He received most of this mail because he was the fraternity's treasurer. More importantly, he was the treasurer in charge of a $350,000 dollar budget. Marketing professionals weren't stupid, they knew who controlled Chi Theta's money and made the house's financial decisions. If Scooter didn't sort out the junk mail, Hamilton's mail would never have a prayer of fitting into his mail slot, thank God for Scooter, thought Hamilton. The last thing he needed to do was waste his time sorting through junk mail.

He had only sifted through half his mail when he heard his roommate's voice slice through the air, "Hamilton, you've got a phone call up here, it's your wife checking up on you," said his roommate, only half joking. Although Hamilton wasn't married, he was involved in a very serious relationship.

He discarded the unimportant mail, and stashed the remaining unopened mail behind a framed sports poster hanging on the adjacent wall. He proceeded to jaunt up the two flights of stairs to his corner room. The corner room, Room Ten, was not only the largest room, but was also the most impressive of the Chi Theta house. Since Hamilton had the most seniority of anyone living in the fraternity house he had first pick of the rooms.

Hamilton headed toward the phone resting on the low coffee table situated between the two giant bay windows. These windows overlooked North Campus. He picked up the black cordless Motorola phone. His roommate glanced at a hole in the room's ceiling. The ceiling came to a point twenty-five feet above the floor.

"Hello Eileen. Yeah I'll be there. My exam got postponed till Thursday because the Professor was sick. I won't be able to pick you up until nine o'clock, because I have that Philanthropy dinner tonight, remember? Okay I'll see you at nine o'clock. I love you too," Hamilton said as he replaced the receiver.

Hamilton was always pressed for time. He was always involved in something. His roommate was amazed at how busy Hamilton's schedule was on a daily basis.

His time was either being consumed by his heavy class load, duties as Treasurer of Chi Theta Fraternity, or the twenty hours a week he put into coaching and tutoring the girls basketball team at the local Christo Rhea Youth Center. The latter was a volunteer job he had performed for the past two years without compensation. Hamilton would be the first one to say that he'd never accept money for the job. "The joy I receive from watching those girls succeed is worth more than anything money can buy," was a statement he'd often make. A comment like this from other students might sound insincere or hollow, but his words genuinely came from the heart. He truly coached and taught life to these girls for the sheer intrinsic value. Monetary compensation would only cheapen the pleasure derived from it. Hamilton believed he should be paying for the privilege of the job.

The truth was that if the youth center wanted to pay Hamilton, they would never be able to afford his talents. The Lady Monarchs of Christo Rhea had only lost one game during his two-year tenure, and that was on a fluke last-second half court shot. More important than the winning record, was the winning attitude he was able to give these deprived and disadvantaged kids. Most of these kids were from broken homes, many having been abused since birth and placed into the protective hands of the State. He was able to give these girls hope and instill in them the confidence to pursue their goals in life. Several had received academic or athletic scholarships to private parochial schools during his tenure.

Hamilton's roommate knew how precious time was to him. Thus, he was surprised to hear Hamilton was going to a party on a Monday night. However, when he found out it was for Eileen's brother he understood all too well. Hamilton had a difficult time turning down any request from his girlfriend, Eileen.

"Are you going to Mike's Birthday party tonight?" Hamilton asked his roommate.

"I wish I could, but I've got that International Tax exam at eight tomorrow morning. I've got to ace it, because I bombed the last one. On top of that, it's 25 percent of my grade," replied his roommate Tip.

"I guess I'll have to take on your share of all the underclass hotties that'll be there. It's a dirty job but someone's got to do it," jokingly mocked Hamilton.

"Yeah, it'll be an especially difficult job with Eileen pulling on the thick chain around your neck," said Tip. Tip liked Eileen, but she did have a short leash on Hamilton. She definitely wore the pants in the relationship.

Hamilton was just a nice guy, maybe too nice, if that can be considered a character flaw. Hamilton and Tip were so opposite that it was comical. They were nicknamed Fire and Ice by their fraternity brothers. Tip was very introverted, preferring to keep his emotions to himself, while Hamilton seemed to know everyone on Michigan State's 5,263-Acre Campus. Although there were over forty thousand undergraduate students at the University, Tip could swear that all of them knew or had heard of Chris Hamilton. His popularity was due to his involvement in almost everything: playing co-ed softball, forming a campus recycling committee, entering a 10K charity run, writing a guest article for the State News, or meeting with the

Board of Trustees. It was inevitable that he'd meet new people at these events.

Although he was constantly meeting new people, he rarely forgot a name or a face. This skill contributed to his popularity. It made everyone he met feel significant. This trait is what Tip liked most about Hamilton. There was a time not too long ago that the only one in the world who felt Tip, a.k.a. Paul Tipton, was significant was Chris Hamilton.

# CHAPTER 5

Barbara Fernandez briskly walked up the ten cement stairs to her modest brownstone apartment located on the outskirts of Georgetown. She was surprised that her cat, Muffin, wasn't sitting on the tiny cement windowsill. Muffin, a gray tiger-striped feline, always sat on top of the windowsill for Barbara's arrival. Barbara usually got home between five and six o'clock, depending on traffic. Muffin had a sixth sense, a natural internal watch. Barbara glanced at her watch; the thin gold hands read 5:40. While checking the time, she noticed her hands were still shaking from her meeting with Valez four hours ago.

Inside the brownstone apartment, Valez calmly rested in an antique rocking chair. With a vapid stare, Muffin lay beside him; her nine lives had been exhausted. Strewn about Valez was the chaotic mess he had just created in order to make the scene look like a robbery. Barbara's valuables had already been carted away by one of his goons. The remaining items of clothes and trinkets were haphazardly thrown about the cozy apartment.

Barbara closed the brown metal door behind her, and headed for the tiny kitchen. Valez abrasively stopped her path. His powerful left-hand forcefully tightened around her frail neck and her eyes bulged with fright as he raised the shiny Phillips head screwdriver over his head. She tried to let out a scream, but his enormous hands and ever tightening grip silenced her attempt.

With tremendous force, he rhythmically stabbed her fifteen times. The weapon easily entered and exited the soft flesh of her upper body. The only sound heard was the soft last breath of life exiting her body. The entire struggle lasted less than thirty seconds. She lay unmoving on the worn wooden floor; a pool of blood quickly forming around her corpse. Her eyes would be forever frozen wide with fright. The screwdriver lay imbedded in her still heart. Valez made sure no one was outside before casually walking out the large front door, leaving it slightly ajar.

---

Garcia waited patiently for the mailman to come back out the front door of Chi Theta. He glanced at his watch and noticed that ten minutes had gone by and decided that the mailman must have gone out the backdoor of the elephantine house. He approached the massive red double-doors. He tried to enter, but the doors did not budge. He tried them again before concluding that they were soundly secure. He cursed under his breath. Just before annunciating the K at the end of the curse, he was startled by the doors suddenly swinging open.

"Can I help you?" Asked a 20-year-old student with a green backpack slung over his broad shoulders and both hands on the handlebars of his metallic blue mountain bike.

Garcia hesitated before answering, "Yes, is Mr. Hamilton here?"

"You don't have to call him mister, mister, we just call him Ham. I'm not sure if he's here or not. I'm sorry, but I've got to run, I'm late for class. Dude, if he is here he's probably in his room, which is like room ten on like the third floor," shouted the student in a breathless rush as he jumped on his bike and rode off.

Garcia closed the door, and proceeded to walk around the enormous first floor. He was surprised to find that he was the only person downstairs. He rapidly covered a large area, checking everything as he went. The house was tasteful inside and relatively clean for a fraternity. The house had just been renovated. This renovation was made possible by a generous donation from an affluent alumnus. The oak woodwork, leather couches, grandfather clock, and immaculate pool table impressed him. The hardwood floor creaked under his footsteps. He wasn't at risk of being heard. Loud music was booming upstairs. Some ancillary rough housing was going on up there as well.

## CRISIS

Garcia saw a magenta blinking light out of the corner of his eye; it was the hold button on the fraternity's telephone system. More importantly, he found what he was looking for, the member's individual mail slots. He walked over to the recessed cove and began scanning the more than eighty boxes. The majority of the boxes were marked by masking tape with the individual's name written on it. These labels were dispersed in order of room number as opposed to being arranged alphabetically. Garcia quickly read these to himself: Norkus, Kern, Czerwinski, McCarthy, Fitzpatrick, Slazinski, Tipton, Prylow, Morrissey, Rouleau, Drehime, Dorocak, Hamilton...There it was, *Hamilton*, but it was empty. How could it be empty, wondered Garcia. It had only been fifteen minutes since the mail was delivered. Despite this logic, staring blankly back at him was an empty mail slot, almost mocking him.

Garcia cursed under his breath again, and headed toward the poolroom. Lining the walls of the poolroom were twenty large composite photographs comprising of portraits of the Chi Theta members. If Garcia weren't here on business, he might have laughed at some of the clothes and hairstyles these young men featured during the seventies. It was obvious that big hair, big ties, big mustaches and big lapels ruled the fashion world. However, he wasn't on a pleasure trip. He quickly moved around the room, looking for the most recent composite. There were two noticeable blank spots on the wall. These blank spaces where usually occupied by the two most recent composites.

The ladies of Kappa Kappa Gamma sorority had taken the liberty of "borrowing" the composites earlier in the week with the intent of decorating them. The sorority girls would detail the composites with slanderous comments, clipped from various publications, before returning them to their rightful place. The brothers of Chi Theta enjoyed reading what the girl's put under their names, which tended to range from "Man of My Dreams", to the not so flattering "Reason for Celibacy."

Garcia wasn't aware, nor did he care, about this little game. He wanted those damn composites. Glancing upon the nearest composite, he eventually found what he was looking for at the very bottom. Two pictures in from the left was a small picture of an attractive young man. The name Chris Hamilton was printed beneath the photo.

Hamilton was now about twenty pounds heavier than the photograph portrayed. A much needed weight gain. This robust "freshman fifteen" was the result of the starch-laden food in the Akers and Wonders dormitories. Hamilton's blonde hair was also no longer parted down the middle in butt-cut fashion, rather, it was more contemporary; closer to a Princeton. Despite these differences, Garcia would now have no problem recognizing Hamilton in person.

"Are you looking for something, or someone?" asked a voice from behind Garcia.

Garcia's heart skipped a beat, and he stood up and turned to see a stocky student wearing cleats and a red Chi Theta football jersey. The jersey was torn on the left shoulder and had mud streaked along the tattered bottom.

"Um, yes I was wondering if Chris Hamilton was around?" asked Garcia.

"Oh, I'm afraid you just missed him, he left about five minutes ago, would you like me to tell him who stopped by?"

"Oh that's too bad, I'll just stop by again later. What time do you think he'll be back?"

"Well he's pretty busy and isn't here very often, but Ham's usually here for dinner around 5:30. He should be here for sure tonight, since it is Mexican Fiesta night and the Chi Omegas are coming over," said the football player.

"Are the Chi Omegas pretty good looking or something?" asked Garcia playing along.

"Well, let's put it this way. There will be about fifty girls here tonight that could professionally model if they felt like it. In fact, they are so good looking that everyone on campus knows who the only two ugly Chi O's are," boasted the student.

"Well that ain't half bad. Okay, thank you very much and don't have too many tacos if you know what I mean," said Garcia as he headed for the front door.

"No worries!" shouted the student as he turned toward the backstairs.

The football player didn't find anything unusual about Garcia's presence. Random people were always stopping by the fraternity to talk to Hamilton about some committee or organization he was on. The student was more concerned with getting a good workout at the gym so that he'd look prime for the evening's festivities. He had a crush on a blonde-haired sophomore Chi Omega.

# CHAPTER 6

Tip and Hamilton vividly remember the day they'd first met, four years ago...Tip and Hamilton were just completing their first year at Michigan State University, and were enjoying the warm weather of the last Spring term at MSU. The Michigan State Board of Trustees had decided to switch the class programs from the quarter system to the semester system the following year just like they had back in 1992. The University was going to semesters in an attempt to reduce the school's escalating costs, noting that most other schools were already on the semester system. The Trustees were also concerned that MSU students getting out of school in June were at a six-week disadvantage in interviewing for jobs and summer internships.

The students didn't quite have the same viewpoint as the Trustees and were saddened by the implementation of the semester policy. Students liked the opportunity to take a wider variety of classes and professors during the school year under the quarter system. They also liked the short ten-week class period, because it lessened the chance of boredom or the eternity of a nightmarish class. Most importantly, spring term was the most exciting and joyous time of the year for a student at Michigan State. The students universally agreed however, that it was nice to only schedule classes and purchase books twice during the year under the semester system as opposed to three times.

Knowing it was the last spring term in school history, most students were taking full advantage of it.

Tip was earning some much-needed money umpiring intramural softball games at Munn Field. It was good money and easy work. However, it was difficult for him to sit back and watch everyone else compete. The doctor had instructed him that he was not to compete in any sport of any kind for at least another year. On this memorable day, he had been assigned to diamond number three on Munn field. His only game to umpire that night pitted fourth floor North Wonders Hall against Chi Theta Fraternity.

Tip recognized some of the faces on the Wonders' squad. He had lived in Wonders for two quarters before being kicked out of the dormitory for fighting.

Late one night, a couple of freshmen hockey players, players he had abused on the ice in high school, had pushed him too far. The players had returned to the dorm after an exorbitant amount of cocktails at P.T. O'Malley's Bar and Grill. Tip returned from a night at the Land Shark Raw Bar and Grill, where he too, consumed his share of beers and also a couple of infamous Shark Bowls.

A Shark Bowl is the Land Shark's trademark drink and its contents are almost as secret as the prestigious Coca-Cola formula. The base of the drink is definitely some form of tequila and it is combined with several clear liquors and a maddening cerise fruit punch. The drink is presented in a large concave glass bowl with gummy sharks circling the perimeter. The only way to properly drink one of these ridiculous concoctions is with a group of friends sucking vigorously from their respective straws. Drinking out of a straw gives the drinker a bigger buzz because there is less intake of oxygen. It usually takes three people to drink one of these bowls, and yet Tip had consumed three by himself on this evening.

Tip and the hockey players were both equally "loaded" when they arrived simultaneously at the entrance to the dormitory. The players, upon seeing Tip, began teasing him. They began chanting "boozer, loser." After years of being humiliated and playing in the shadow of Tip during high school, these players now possessed the upper hand over him for the first time. They, not Tip, were on the nationally ranked Michigan State hockey team. They, not Tip, were having their tuition paid for by the University. Tip, not them, had a drinking problem. Adoring girl fans surrounded them, not Tip.

All of them respected Tip as a player, but they were still jealous that he had taken their spotlight during high school. Individually, none of the players would dare say anything derogatory to Tip. However, the overriding group mentality and liquid courage had them teasing him incessantly.

Tip had been drinking heavily every night since the tragic death of his parents. In fact, the only time he was sober was when he visited his little sister, Allison, at the Cranbrook Boarding School in Bloomfield Hills, Michigan. Even during these visits he would have a fifth of Jack Daniel's waiting for him in the car's glove box as soon as the visit was over. Allison was the only pure and good thing left in his life and it was a struggle for him to lay off the liquor for these two-hour visits. He was a raging alcoholic and it truly spoke to his love for Allison that he was able to maintain a two-hour respite.

Tip was going to let these immature hockey freshmen have their fun. Besides, he thought, they were correct, he was a drunken loser. He was going to let these guys sleep it off and so he lowered his head and shuffled his feet toward the waiting elevator. He was halfway inside the closing doors when one of hockey players made the mistake of bringing up the automobile accident and accompanying death in their teasing. "I've thought about killing my parents, but to actually go through with it, you've got bigger balls than me, Mr. Michigan." Mr. Michigan was in reference to Tip, since he won the award for being the best hockey player in the state his last two years of high school. Tip was the first player in the state's history to win the award more than once.

After hearing his parents mentioned, Tip saw nothing but red from that point on. Despite having lost thirty-five pounds since the accident, Tip was still someone you didn't want to mess with. He was immediately on top of the antagonist and quickly split the player's nose wide open with a vicious fist to the face. He then proceeded to break the stocky player's jaw and gave a sharp karate kick to the remaining player's chest, snapping at least two ribs in the process. He was wrestled to the ground by the Resident Hall staff, a feat that took the strength of all five Resident Assistants on duty. The three MSU hockey players lay strewn about on the dormitory's linoleum floor, wallowing in their own blood and lamenting their woes. They were surprised and displeased by the outcome of the confrontation and also the accompanying pain that was quickly filtering through their alcoholic haze.

Tip was kicked out of the residence halls the next day and was almost expelled from school for the incident. The hockey players received a light tap on the wrist for their involvement.

Although the incident occurred over a month ago, Tip was still looking for a place to stay and hadn't been having too much luck. He scanned the entire Wonders softball team and it didn't appear that any of the aforementioned hockey players were present. This wasn't surprising, since the hockey coaches discouraged their players from participating in intramural activities. He also didn't know or recognize Chris Hamilton, the left fielder for Chi Theta fraternity.

Tip, as always, was hoping for a mercy so he could go home early. A mercy occurred if one team was ahead of the other by ten runs or more after five innings of play. A mercy ruling was a good possibility in this game. Chi Theta was an athletic powerhouse. Tip's squeeze bottle contained a mix of Captain Morgan's Spiced Rum and a Michigan brand of especially svelte ginger ale, Vernors. The supply of liquor in his bottle was dwindling rapidly, so he wanted to get home soon. He watched, in dismay, as the North Wonders squad kept the game surprisingly close. The game was tied-up at two apiece entering the seventh and final inning. A short stocky North Wonders player, nicknamed Loaf, hit a towering shot down the left field line. Chris Hamilton chased in vain after the hurtling white sphere, but watched helplessly as it sailed over the left field fence, just barely in fair territory. During his pursuit of the ball, Hamilton's back had blocked its path of flight from everyone's view, including Tip's.

Tip, although wanting to go home early, didn't want the game to be decided on such a controversial call, and thus called it foul since he couldn't really see it. After making the call, he watched in disbelief as Hamilton came running in from the outfield waving his arms frantically and explaining that the ball was indeed fair and should be counted as a home run. Tip had no choice but to rule the ball a home run, giving North Wonders a one run lead. Chi Theta eventually won the game in the bottom of that same inning by virtue of a two-run double by the honest left fielder, Chris Hamilton.

Tip remembered approaching Hamilton after the game, furious at him for showing him up like that, especially in front of the North Wonders team. He demanded to know what the hell Hamilton's problem was; he could have cost his own team the game for a stupid stunt like that. Didn't this guy, Hamilton, want to win? He was amazed when Hamilton calmly explained that, yes, he wanted to win just as bad, if not more than anyone else, but if he had to cheat to win, then who was the real winner? This was a revelation to Tip. He had always been taught by all of his coaches to win at all costs, no matter what the price.

Hamilton had heard "all-costs" philosophies like Tip's before. Hamilton told him the problem with an "all costs" belief is that the people who taught it to him and those cheering him on for practicing it, wouldn't always be there. But, you'll always have to live with yourself. He suggested that Tip should try to perceive himself not based on how others perceived him, but how he perceived himself from within. If Tip did that, than everything else would work itself out.

That Sunday, Hamilton invited Tip over for rush at his fraternity, Chi Theta. Tip accepted the invitation, mainly for the free food & booze and also because he wanted to talk some more with Hamilton. Hamilton intrigued him and it didn't hurt that the only friends Tip had confided in over the past year were Jim Beam, Jack Daniels and Johnny Walker.

Tip thought he'd never join a fraternity, besides he would never be able afford the membership dues anyway. He was surprised to discover that he got along well with most of the guys and actually shared many of the same beliefs that the fraternity stressed: Academics, philanthropy, athletics and brotherhood. He even encountered a few students he'd competed against in high school. He didn't always recognize these students, but they sure remembered him for his unmatched tenacity, high school fame and hockey skills.

He joined the fraternity, because among other things, he could live in the house while he pledged and also receive two meals a day. This was worth well more than his semester dues. It solved his housing problem and gave him a cheap supply of food and beer. However, the overriding reason Tip joined Chi Theta, whether he liked to admit it or not, was because the words Chris Hamilton spoke were so clear and true. It was the first shed of light Tip had seen since the horrendous accident...

Tip awakened from a coma a week following the automobile accident to discover the horrifying fate of Fred Weeks and his parents. He remembers being in an even larger state of shock upon reading comments by his "supposed" friends in the local newspapers. The comments that really stung the deepest were those made by his girlfriend: Stephanie. Stephanie didn't once visit Tip in the hospital. Instead, she sent a get-well card stating in terse words that their relationship was over.

Stephanie told authorities she'd begged Tip to stay at her house after the party, but he wouldn't listen to her. In fact, he wouldn't listen to anyone, since he was very drunk. Her story stated Tip was yelling incessantly about having to get home so he wouldn't get in trouble, because he was supposed to be baby-sitting his little sister. She'd realized too late that Tip had clandestinely talked Fred Weeks into driving him home, although everyone, including her, knew Fred was in no condition to be behind the wheel.

The authorities and press believed every word Stephanie said. Why wouldn't they? She was president of her class, valedictorian, captain of the cheerleading squad, and daughter of the most prominent banker in Rochester Hills. No one besides Fred, Stephanie and Tip heard their conversation on that fateful night. The time when Tip needed Stephanie most, she had abandoned him, as did everyone else. It was a lesson he wouldn't forget.

Upon word of the auto accident, the University of Michigan

hockey staff quickly revoked Tip's full-ride scholarship. U of M stated the revocation was based on ethical standards. The true reason for the scholarship nullification was the medical report stating Tip would never be capable of playing ice hockey again. It was in the school's best public relations interest to release the ethical standards story. This further sullied Tip's name in the national media.

Extensive ligament damage and hemorrhaging in his right knee would prevent Tip from playing on the college level. The MRI indicated that he had completely torn his anterior cruciate ligament and had severely chipped his patella. U of M was entitled to revoke his scholarship under the rules of the National Collegiate Athletic Association. Tip had only made a verbal commitment to attend U of M and, thus, it wasn't binding to the University. He was scheduled to sign the letter of intent the day after his announcement, but the accident intervened. If the letter had been signed, then Michigan would be obligated to fulfill their scholarship offer.

Who could blame the University of Michigan? They couldn't afford to "waste" a four-year scholarship on a hockey invalid. There is no room for charitable action in college athletics in the modern era; rather it's big business. Tip laughed when he thought of the words of Michigan's coach, Ray Fisheman, a man he liked and trusted. He told Tip that as long as he was in the Wolverine program, he'd be taken care of like a family member. What he failed to mention was that family members weren't allowed to be sick. To be fair to U of M, none of the other schools that'd begged on their hands and knees for Tip's skills were calling anymore either.

The well-wishers, backslappers and boosters seemed to disappear instantly. Tip's classmates regarded him as the scapegoat for Fred Weeks' death. Most of the students at the party had seen how smashed he was and took Stephanie's story as gospel. Tip was unable to defend himself by telling his side of the story because he was in a coma.

The only person who was by Tip's side during all of this was his little sister, Allison. Tip thought it ironic that his only confidant was his 10-year-old sister. The same person that he was suppose to be taking care of on that fateful night. She was the one hope in the world that gave him a desire to continue living. His doctors believe he would never have pulled out of the coma if it weren't for Allison's big blue eyes and rosy red cheeks being at his bedside day after day. Tip was still a participant in the game of life, although he wasn't sure if he still felt like competing.

Complicating matters further was the composition of the Tipton's Will and Testament. The Will stated that all of their worldly possessions be bequeathed to the only two remaining Tipton heirs, Paul and Allison. All non-personal items were to be liquidated at market value and placed equally into two separate trust funds. Each separate fund was worth over one million dollars. Allison's trust fund stipulated it was to pay for tuition, room and board at Cranbrook boarding school in Birmingham. Allison would also be allocated two thousand dollars a year for additional expenses and could withdraw one hundred dollars on her birthday. Upon reaching the age of majority (eighteen), Allison would become fully entrusted with the fund to do with as she pleased.

Unfortunately for Tip, his portion of the Will was scripted under the assumption that he would have a full-ride scholarship. He would only be allocated one hundred dollars a year for his birthday and a hundred and fifty dollars a month spending allowance. He would gain control of the trust upon receiving his college degree.

It was important for Tip to earn a degree so he could properly take care of his little sister. Given his financial situation, his choices narrowed to those schools in the state of Michigan. The out-of-state tuitions at other schools were just too expensive for him. At the time, he didn't have a penny to his name. He finally decided to attend Michigan State University due to its inexpensive living facilities for students, good student loans, and an excellent undergraduate business school. *U.S. News* ranked the business school the eighteenth best in the country. He couldn't afford to go to medical school; moreover, he didn't know if he liked medicine or liked it because it pleased his father.

He selected accounting as a major. He'd always been good with numbers, and MSU had one of the top three accounting schools in the country. MSU accounting graduates had a 90 percent placement rate, tops in the country. In order to receive full custody of his sister, the court stipulated that Tip needed to have gainful employment when he graduated.

His decision to attend MSU was a decision that turned his life around. It enabled him to meet Chris Hamilton on that fateful day on Munn field. After a long struggle, Hamilton finally got Tip to join Alcoholics Anonymous, and also made sure Tip was always the "safe driver" at parties. The "safe driver" was required to stay sober at parties and helped everyone make it home in one piece.

Before meeting Hamilton, Tip was also doing poorly in the difficult accounting curriculum and was well on his way to flunking out. Most of the business classes convened before noon, and this was a problem for him. He usually passed out stone drunk at four in the morning and his heavy eyelids couldn't muster the strength to lift themselves much earlier than noon.

Hamilton also helped him deal with the tragic automobile accident. Tip never would overcome the guilt of believing he was responsible for his parents' deaths, but Hamilton helped explain that it was just fate. Even if it was his fault, feeling sorry for himself was doing him and his sister no favors, and, in fact, it was being selfish. Tip came to understand and agree with Hamilton's reasoning.

Tip and Hamilton soon became inseparable during that first year and roomed together for the next three years. Tip and Allison even spent the summers at the Hamiltons. For Tip, it was easy to see that Chris had learned his kindness from his parents, Jackie and Thomas. The Hamiltons went on to officially adopt Allison. She was miserable at the Cranbrook Boarding School, so the Hamiltons pulled her out and put her in the local Catholic school. She was placed into the same school Chris had attended. Most of the teachers remembered and enjoyed Chris and also knew Allison's sad story, hence they went out of their way to give Allison special attention.

Since Allison's trust fund stipulated that the money could only be used to fund Cranbrook tuition, the Hamilton's had to pick-up the cost of Allison attending the Catholic school. Tip objected to the Hamilton's paying the tuition, but the Hamilton's simply said Allison could repay them when she graduated. Tip knew however, that they'd never accept a dime from him or her.

It was good for Allison to have a stable family life. The same could be said for Tip. The Hamiltons were thrilled with the new additions to the family. They had always wanted to have a large family, but Jackie Hamilton wasn't able to have any more children following complications that occurred during Chris' birth.

Thanks to the AA meetings and the support of Hamilton, Tip hadn't had a drop of alcohol since joining the fraternity. He had also managed to pull his grade point average up to an A-minus, consistently making the Dean's List. He also became good friends with several of the guys in the fraternity, although he still stayed to himself most of the time. He only really opened up to Hamilton. His fraternity brothers did know one thing for sure about Tip; they wanted him to be in their corner. The members of the house often told the story about the time a drunken defensive lineman from the football team began shoving around a Chi Theta pledge.

The gynormous African American lineman from the football team was calling the African American Chi Theta pledge a "sell-out" for joining a predominately white fraternity. The lineman continued his harassing until he was pushing the much smaller and intimidated pledge around the bar. Tip, witnessing this, calmly told the lineman that he'd had his fun and that it was now time for him to back off and go his separate way. He had been careful to avoid physical altercations since the incident in the dorm with the hockey players his freshmen year. He knew that another mark on his record might number his days at MSU. The lineman also stood six-foot-seven and was close to three hundred pounds.

The lineman wasn't used to being told what to do and refused the request. In fact, he began giving the pledge an even harder time. As a result, Tip had no choice but to shatter the muscular lineman's jaw with a swift elbow. He also whispered something into the lineman's ear as he lay on the floor holding his face. To this day, only Tip and the lineman know what was said. Despite constant requests, Tip refused to talk about the incident. A lesser man may have boasted of such heroics.

Although he kept to himself, the Chi Theta brotherhood liked Tip. They also wondered about him. He paid little or no attention to the opposite sex. However, the opposite sex paid real close attention to him. His two hundred pounds of chiseled muscle were perfectly distributed over his six-foot-one inch frame. His body, by itself, easily garnered female attention. Add the dark complexion that he inherited from his Corsican mother, wavy black hair, and striking emerald green eyes, and you had one of the most desired men on campus. Hamilton couldn't keep track of the number of Eileen's friends who asked to be set up with him. But, Hamilton knew all too well the familiar words: "Thanks Hamilton, but no thanks." Hamilton would have grown tired of these girl's requests, but he actually enjoyed watching them not get what they wanted for once. Most of these requests were from incredibly gorgeous coeds. Tip's denials made them want him even more.

Hamilton was the only one of Tip's friends who knew the story about his ex-girlfriend Stephanie, but even he thought it was time for Tip to get over it and move on. He often told Tip that Stephanie would still be winning unless he got over it. And didn't Tip think he was better than that?

Despite the persuasive advice from Hamilton, the fact remained that Tip only truly trusted the Hamiltons, Allison and himself. He would never be able to repay the kindness of Chris Hamilton. A lot of people owed a debt of gratitude to Chris Hamilton, but none greater than Paul Tipton.

# CHAPTER 7

Hamilton parked his black Jeep in front of the Sigma Kappa Sorority House. At the base of his shiny passenger side door was a green wooden pole extending from the grass. On top of the post was a white sign exclaiming in bold crimson lettering: NO PARKING FROM HERE TO THE CORNER. Hamilton had already amassed over a hundred dollars in parking tickets since the semester started three short weeks ago. He despised the Department of Public Safety. He was not alone. A student illegally parked for more than ten minutes was almost guaranteed a citation on their windshield. MSU students joked that DPS was probably the most efficiently run program at the University.

His expensive Grand Cherokee was a surprise twenty-first birthday present from his parents. He was overwhelmed and delighted to receive such a generous birthday bounty. It wasn't startling that the Hamilton's could afford such luxuries for him. Mr. Hamilton was a successful stockbroker for Dean Witter, and some sound personal investing in the past would allow his family to live very comfortably for years to come. Besides the Grand Cherokee, however, it was difficult to know that he was from such a well-to-do family. The Hamilton's didn't like to flaunt their good fortune.

Hamilton originally became interested in finance because he looked up to his father and wanted to spend more time with him. One day, he too would be a prominent stockbroker.

Hamilton's girlfriend Eileen was always late, but he thought she might be on time tonight, since it was her brother's birthday. Her inconsiderate practice of being late was the one thing he would love to change about her. That being said, he would soon forget about her tardiness the moment he gazed into her eyes. He was putty in her hands, and she knew it.

He had never been in love like this. Countless nights were spent lying awake in bed thinking how great it would be when he married Eileen. But, this glorious day would have to wait until after graduation.

The positive side of her less than punctual behavior was that it gave him an excuse to go into her sorority house. He loved everything about the Sigma Kappa sorority house: The tidy green lawn, the purple and pink geranium garden encircling the front, the white rectangular pillars, the semi-circular red brick driveway, and the prodigious wrought iron Sigma Kappa letters.

Most of all, he loved the sixty-five tanned and toned women that lay behind the big white double doors. The sorority girls' physiques and spirits were always in great shape as a result of such daily activities as in-line-skating, studying, mountain biking, walking, jogging, and step-aerobics.

The tall and slender 21-year-old who quickly answered his rapid knock on the door home confirmed his image of a celestial home. The girl politely welcomed him and he casually stepped into the foyer. The girl's 5'9" frame was almost equal to his. He hadn't previously had the pleasure of meeting this radiant creature. But, with the advent of the school year, there would be many fresh faces, and he relished the thought of it. Even though he was thoroughly in love with Eileen, he still appreciated other feminine beauty. This thought reminded him of some quotes he'd heard in the past. "Just because one is on a diet doesn't mean they can't look at the menu" and "Just because one may own a Monet doesn't mean they can't appreciate the beauty of a Van Gogh."

His eyes were drawn to her meticulously decorated hot pink toenails that rested on the charcoal marble floor. The gaze continued up the tan and seemingly endless legs. The legs finally disappeared beneath a skimpy pair of navy blue and forest green check-patterned flannel boxer shorts. Embroidered on the lower left leg of the shorts were the gold letters of Sigma Kappa ($\Sigma K$). There was a faint trace of soft blonde peach fuzz over her smooth and firm skin. A gray cotton baseball jersey hung loosely over her slender shoulders. The word "Spartans" was scripted in dark green across the front of the jersey. It was difficult to read the lettering at the moment, for the top three buttons were open, revealing the upper portion of her voluptuous chest. Her left shoulder was almost completely bare, revealing the thin white strap of her second skin bra. The effulgent white material was in stark contrast to her golden skin.

Eileen would kill him if she knew how much his eyes were enjoying the statuesque female before them. "Can I help you?" asked the breathy and erotic voice, a voice rivaling that of Kathleen Turner's.

He tried to be as smooth as possible in his reply, "Yes, could you please page Eileen Swanson." His attempt at coolness was foiled by his voice cracking on the word "please."

The girl seemed to like this. "Sure," said the girl as she turned and headed toward the phone. Walking toward the phone, the girl's jersey slipped even lower, revealing more of the maple colored skin. Framed by sandy blonde hair that barely brushed the shoulders, her dancing sienna eyes were stunning. Her hair was naturally vibrant and its shine would look just as enticing if it were dried with a waffle iron.

It became quite obvious that she hadn't mastered the telephone paging system. Hamilton waited patiently as she cutely continued to struggle. He knew how to use the page system, having visited Eileen many times. Just press the intercom button, followed by the 6, then 1 and say "Eileen you have a caller in the informal room." He also knew that if the guest were a girl then she would be labeled a "visitor" instead of a "caller." This tradition of labeling men "callers" and women "visitors" began in the fifties. The reason for this code system was simple; the women wanted to look more presentable if a male companion was paying his respects.

Hamilton didn't mind the girl's ignorance. He decided it would not be his place to instruct her on the system. It would only cause her to be embarrassed. Her left hand rested on the large brass dinner bell beside the pager. This position exposed her slender lower left side and a slight hint of her black underwear. The black panties were difficult to discern since her skin was so tan. Her left foot was flat on the floor and her other foot was resting on its toes, causing her calf muscle to tighten into a billiard ball. Hamilton hoped he'd be able to see those legs in a high pair of heels at a formal date party later in the year.

The name on the back of the baseball jersey read Wilkens with a block number one directly underneath. Yeah she was number-one, thought Hamilton. He knew he'd better stop looking, but he couldn't resist. He wondered how many relationships had ended due to predicaments like the one in which he currently found himself. He was going to suggest to the MSU Board of Trustees that there be a campus law passed deeming it mandatory for the sorority housemother to answer the door for visiting boyfriends. This law would be especially effective at the Sigma Kappa House. The current housemother was extremely homely and also very bitter.

The familiar sound of Eileen's footsteps on the stairs broke his trance. He was a bit startled and hoped Eileen didn't see him "eye drooling."

"Oh good, there you are Eileen, I can't seem to figure out this stupid phone. Your friend's been waiting patiently," said the goddess, as she adjusted her jersey to cover her shoulders and bra, much to the chagrin of Hamilton, but it was probably his saving grace.

"Don't worry about it Kelly. That thing is ridiculous," came the expedient reply from the stairs.

Hamilton's disappointment with the girl's name was evident. He was expecting the goddess to have a name like Aphrodite or Athena, surely not plain old simple Kelly.

"Have a nice evening you guys," said Kelly, and before he could get a final look, the goddess had vanished.

Eileen Swanson was in full view now and possessed as much beauty as the goddess, yet an entirely different kind of beauty. She wasn't as sexy as the goddess, but was equally as pretty, a wholesome beauty. Her sandy-blonde hair was pinned by a red bow with white polka dots, revealing the smooth skin of her petite face. A brown, leather strapped, Gucci purse was slung across her body causing the only wrinkles on her red Polo oxford. Unlike the Hamilton's, the Swanson's did enjoy showcasing their wealth. The Polo oxford was efficiently tucked into her tightly fitting light denim jeans. This tight fit was made possible by her efforts at aerobics class five nights a week. A set of thick and compact gold hoop earrings accented the gold strap atop her white flats. Red lipstick was spread so perfectly on her tender lips that it looked like their natural color. But it was the beautiful auburn eyes that constantly reminded Hamilton why he was so mad about her. He was starring into these eyes at the moment.

"Sorry I'm late Chris," said Eileen as she leaned up and gave Hamilton a small "hello" peck on the lips.

Hamilton felt Eileen's soft cheek brush against his slightly stubble one and smelled the usual scent of strawberry-vanilla shampoo in her golden hair. The familiar smell caused him to quickly become aroused. Even though they'd been dating seriously for over two years, his heart still skipped a beat every time he came into contact with her tender skin.

"It's my mom's fault I was late. She called in her "panic-mode" while I was getting ready. She's been trying to reach Mike all day, but she can't reach him. So, she wants me to relay a happy birthday message to him.

The image of Eileen and Hamilton standing together in the hallway was almost comical. People continually mistook them for brother and sister, and rightfully so. Both had sandy-brown hair, brown eyes and slender builds. Tip dubbed them the Osmonds after the popular singing duo. Everyone in the Chi Theta Fraternity soon began to refer to them as this, which Hamilton took as a good-natured jibe. However, Eileen didn't care for the nickname, but Hamilton's fraternity brothers weren't her biggest fans anyway. His friends resented the way she wanted every waking second of his day. Didn't she realize that there wasn't enough of him to go around? They knew, deep down, that she was a good girl, they were just jealous that she got so much of Hamilton's time.

Hamilton could only laugh to himself when he saw the fresh traffic ticket flapping in the wind beneath his driver side windshield wiper. Well at least it wasn't a DPS ticket. Rather, it was an East Lansing ticket, his first of the year. The Department of Public Safety (DPS) was affiliated with the University and thus could revoke certain student privileges such as scheduling, registering, and even receiving one's degree. The state, on the other hand, could "only" impound your car or throw you in jail for failure to pay traffic violations. Students knew however, that you had to amass close to $500 in tickets before the State would go through the hassle of towing your car.

They made the ten-minute drive over to the house party. Hamilton slowly rolled the Grand Cherokee onto the white gravel and weed driveway. The driveway was situated on the south side of the old two-story white house on Grove Street. The house screamed of character and undoubtedly held many memories and secrets. There were already four cars parked in the driveway, only one spot remained. He was thankful that he wasn't likely to be blocked in. This was the rare instance when it paid to be a little late.

"I must thank you for being late my dear," he chirped.

"You can thank me later," Eileen quipped and she raised her eyebrows in a playful manner.

Hamilton placed the burgundy envelope containing Mike's birthday present into his back pocket and walked around to open Eileen's door.

Hamilton couldn't wait to see Mike's reaction when he gave him season tickets for the men's MSU basketball season. Hamilton was giving him seats located in the IZZONE section, the zaniest and loudest section in the Breslin Center. A lucky three thousand students ruled the IZZONE. Much to the chagrin of the older alumni seated in the rows behind them, the section stood the entire game. The IZZONE was frenetic and often blocked the view of the patrons seated in the expensive booster seats behind them. Because of this, the University had issued letters to the presidents of student groups and fraternities requesting them to encourage their members to only stand up and cheer at critical moments. Such letters only encouraged more robust behavior.

The students weren't concerned about the University's proposal of moving the student section further from the floor. The entire lower bowl was comprised entirely of bleacher seats, and the older alumni preferred the comfort of the back supported seating in the upper level. Because of the bleacher situation, the students knew that the administration's threats of moving the student section carried little weight. The basketball team didn't want the students ousted from the lower bowl either. These rabid students supplied them with one of the best home court advantages in the country. The MSU Board of Trustees finally came up with the solution of removing some of the backed seats so that the students could stand without blocking anyone's view. As a definitive solution, the Trustees voted to remove the back three rows of the IZZONE and the front three rows of the alumni section. This reduced the Breslin Center's total seating capacity, but satisfied both parties' concerns. Newspaper columnists questioned why this wasn't done when it was originally built.

The basketball players were happy to see the IZZONE remain intact, since rambunctious students near the court gave the Spartans a distinct home court advantage in the Big Ten Conference. Some of the other tougher arenas to play in the Big Ten conference were Minnesota's Williams Arena and Iowa's Carver Hawkeye Arena. In an attempt to gain a psychological advantage, Iowa went so far as to paint the opposing team's locker room bright pink. William's arena was difficult to play in due to the boisterous crowd and also the unusualness of the floor being raised four feet from the ground. Opposing players found it difficult to adjust to the possibility of falling off the court diving for a loose ball. Players on the bench had the unique eye-level view of seeing sneakers for forty minutes.

Hamilton was thinking how he had really outdone himself this time by scoring such remarkable seats. He was so entrenched in thought that he was completely unaware of the four watchful eyes across the street; eyes that were affixed to his every move.

"That's it. That little bastard's got the burgundy envelope

in his back pocket. This will be easier than I thought, but that girl with him might be a problem," said an irritated Garcia as he watched Eileen and Hamilton walk up to the house party.

"Don't worry, we'll take care of her, in fact we'll have some fun with her," said Sanchez.

"But boss said to make sure it was a clean job," questioned Garcia.

"Oh it'll be clean. Boss didn't say we couldn't have our fun, did he?" said Sanchez, a sinister grin crossing his smoke stained teeth. "All work and no play makes for a very long and weary day. If the girl so happens to get in the way, well that's her fault isn't it?"

The party was in full swing as Hamilton and Eileen entered the front door. They were instantly greeted with the pungent scent of cheap domestic beer. It was drastically warmer inside than outdoors. Radiant body heat was creating this greenhouse effect as flesh pressed against flesh in a vain attempt to get chalices filled with the frothy golden beverage. To an outsider, it looked like a soup kitchen lined with homeless persons who hadn't eaten in days.

Eileen spotted her little brother, Mike, slouched against the wall in the corner. His friends were still trying to force the twelfth shot of alcohol down his throat, a brutal shot of Bacardi 151. Despite recent alcohol related birthday deaths at Michigan State, students still continued the tradition of force feeding themselves with as much liquor as possible on birthdays.

"I think he's had enough for tonight boys," said Eileen. Mike's friends booed in disapproval, but since most of them had secret crushes on her, they didn't argue.

"Are you all right Mikey?" asked a concerned Eileen.

"Yeah, need bed," was the best Mike could muster before he decorated his sandals with a chunky liquid lunch. The boys let out a big simultaneous "ohhhhhmaaannn!" Before starting to laugh hysterically.

Eileen quickly cleaned up the mess. She joined Mike in the bathroom as he prayed at the porcelain altar. "Chris, why don't you

## CRISIS

go downstairs and have a good time. I can take care of Mike," said Eileen.

"Are you sure," asked Hamilton, thinking how great a mother Eileen would be one day.

"Yeah, I'll be fine. I'll meet you down there in a couple of minutes," insisted Eileen.

"Okay, Happy birthday Stud, I'll give you your present tomorrow, when you can see straight and appreciate it and also not lose it," said Hamilton as he messed up Mike's hair actually making it look better in the process. The only reply he received from Mike was a loud and sustained belch. The smell of alcohol and cheese popcorn quickly filled the air. Hamilton held his breath and quickly headed down the narrow stairs.

He remembered the times he'd been like that on his birthdays at MSU, especially his twenty-first. He couldn't remember if he made it to twenty-one shots that night. He didn't think he had, because he was a lightweight when it came to drinking. He could only recollect up to shot number seventeen, which happened to be a "Cement Mixer." He still cringed at the sensation; a shot of brandy and limejuice then shaking his head violently back and forth to mix the liquids. This "mixing" and the resulting liquors curdling and become solid didn't gel well with his stomach.

The house party was really kicking now, as "YMCA" by the Village People blared out over the stereo. College students loved hearing cheesy songs like this after they were toasted. Beer was being spilled all over the place as people tried to form a C with their arms when they spelled out Y-M-C-A in sync with the music. The hosts of the party didn't mind the spilled beer. The floor's finish had been striped long ago and was now reduced to weathered gray and yellow wood. The beer could be easily removed in the morning with Murphy's Oil Soap & water. This clean-up effort was a small price to pay, considering the amount of revenue the party would generate at $3 a head. The hosts had already covered the cost of the kegs and were now working on pure profit. The roommates estimated that they would probably clear $200, or $40 each.

One of Hamilton's friends, and also a host of the party, handed him a cold twelve ounce plastic cup of Busch Light. Hamilton tried to give him three dollars, but his friend would have nothing of it. Hamilton's popularity made it difficult for him to ever pay for a beer, no matter how hard he tried. He joined the beat of the music, which was now "Blue Dog" by Kidd Rock. He really hadn't kicked back in a long time. He justified this little respite as a reward for acing his Management 409 exam earlier that morning.

"Guess who," said the high-pitched voice about a foot from Hamilton's left ear. The mystery girl's sensual hands were held firmly over his warm brown eyes.

"Mom, is that you?" jokingly asked Hamilton.

"No, it's me sill," said the perky girl as she violently spun him around and gave him a big bear hug.

The girl's face was attractive, but definitely not stunning. She still had freckles around the bridge of her nose, which were actually quite cute. Her body, however, was stunning. The girl knew she had a good body and showcased its perfection by wearing a skintight white tube-shirt and cheek hugging "Daisy Duke" denim shorts. Her tight shirt stopped short of her waistline revealing a small portion of her lean stomach and belly button ring. Onlookers were tantalized and teased by this exposed epidermis. The tube-shirt looked like it was spray-painted onto her bodacious body. It was also apparent that she didn't want to be restricted by a bra this evening. Her firm breasts didn't miss the support as they seemingly defied gravity.

The girl currently clinging to Hamilton was Amy Klein, his ex-girlfriend. She was probably the last person in the world that he wanted to bump into right now. He felt uncomfortable around her, for he'd broken up with her after they'd been dating for six months. He felt terrible about the break-up, but he thought it was the best thing. She was a little too wild for his conservative style. Hamilton's buddies thought he was crazy to break up with her. She had an incredible body and was always up for a good time.

To Hamilton, Amy was nice to look at, but that was about

it. His opinion of her appearance was shared by most of the male population. Currently, all the drunk and horny males at the party were starring in her direction. Onlookers weren't disappointed; every movement she made resulted in her curves jiggling.

"Where have you been hiding, I haven't seen you in ages. Are you still seeing Eileen?" Amy asked without taking a breath.

"Yes I am. Actually, this party is for her little brother's nineteenth birthday. She's upstairs taking care of him in the bathroom," said Hamilton.

"Oh good, I'd like to talk to her. She's really quite a lucky girl," said Amy as she squeezed Hamilton's right hand.

Although Hamilton was right handed he always held his drink in the left hand. It freed up his right hand to greet people.

"Eileen should be down any minute, and I'll tell her you're here, Amy," said Hamilton, thinking how agitated Eileen would be. Eileen detested Amy, and called her "Psycho;" she felt Amy still hadn't gotten over Hamilton. Hamilton thought this notion was ludicrous, but everyone else knew Eileen was quite keen; Amy was indeed still infatuated with him. Hamilton used the excuse of refilling his beer to escape the clutches of his current predicament, and headed toward the bar.

He slid over to the keg and found temporary shelter behind the makeshift wood-paneled bar. He continued to throwback the cold drafts of Busch Light as he joked around with his friends. After ninety minutes he had forgotten all about Amy and hence didn't notice her heading his way until it was too late. He was trapped behind the bar and the only exit led in the direction of the rapidly approaching Amy. He observed that her walk was a little tipsy and that her eyes were more glazed than a Honey Roasted Ham.

She was now only a couple of feet away. Hamilton turned to his closest friend and purposely yelled for her benefit, "I better go upstairs and check on Eileen and Mike." He quickly squeezed his way through the mass of compressed bodies, which included Amy. She intentionally rubbed her rigid ta-ta's up against his chest; this didn't exactly go unnoticed.

"You're so sweet. Don't be too long, I'll be waiting down here for you," said Amy.

Hamilton struggled up the creaky wooden staircase. A rather large person was coming down the stairs and it was difficult for both of them to squeeze by on the narrow staircase. He found Eileen and Mike in the bathroom in the same position he'd left them two hours earlier.

"How's MSU's finest feeling?" asked Hamilton as he entered the bathroom.

"Oh, what do you care! I'm surprised you left the side of Psycho for a few precious seconds," said a pissed-off Eileen.

Hamilton was caught off guard by her reaction. He assumed she was upstairs the whole time, and he couldn't have talked to Amy for more than five minutes. Even if he did talk to her, what was the big deal? Eileen should know that he only had feelings for her and if she didn't, their relationship wasn't as strong as he thought. He also didn't feel like arguing, he never liked arguing, so he quickly tried to change the subject. "How's Mr. Nineteen year old doing?" asked Hamilton.

"He'll be alright, no thanks to you. You looked real concerned about him when you were chugging beers with your buddies," yelled Eileen.

"I'm not going to apologize for having a good time at the party. Besides, you told me to have a good time. Look, let's not argue about this. It was really nice of you to look after Mike, and I'm sure he appreciates it. Since Mike seems to be all right now, let's put him to bed and go downstairs and have one or two more drinks before we head out. You'll have to drive us home; I've had a few more drinks than I planned. You don't mind driving do you?" asked Hamilton stammering to gain his balance in the doorway.

"Why don't you get a ride from Psycho? You seem to be hitting it off so well with her. I've got to protect Mike from those animals he calls friends. I won't be going home tonight.

"Oh come on they're harmless. The worst that they'll do to

Mike is draw funny things all over him with magic markers. He'll be all right," said Hamilton.

"Yeah, that's easy for you to say. How do you think my parents are going to like it if they show up tomorrow to take us out to brunch and Mike has: "Big Hairy Balls" scribed in permanent red marker across his forehead?" asked Eileen. They both knew the answer to the question; her parents would not be amused.

"Fine, if it makes you feel better, stay with him all night, it's no skin off my nose. I'll wait downstairs for a little while longer if you decide to change your mind. If not, I'll walk home by myself. The walk will help me wear off my buzz before I go to bed, so my hangover won't be as bad. If you want me to walk over in the morning and drive you home give me a call, I should be up around nine o'clock," said Hamilton as he headed back downstairs. Even though he was certain to have a nasty hangover, his schedule was too busy for him to sleep in. Hamilton noticed his hangovers becoming progressively worse with each passing year.

Hamilton didn't mind walking home; he knew Eileen's mood wasn't worth tampering with. She always got ridiculously upset when one of his ex-girlfriends was around. She especially disliked Amy, probably because she was the most physically attractive of the old flames.

After talking with some chums for a few minutes he made his way through the maze of people to the front door. Nelly's lyrics echoed in his ears as he stepped out into the cool autumn night. The incredibly refreshing air was like water to a fish. Amy saw his silhouette in the doorframe and quickly headed in his direction.

"There he is," said Garcia to Sanchez.

"Yeah, but where's the damn girl?" asked Sanchez.

"I don't know. It won't be as much fun without the girl, but it's probably better. It'll be clean and easy like boss wants," replied Garcia.

"You mean boring," said a disgruntled Sanchez.

"Keep a sharp eye out for her, we don't need any unexpected complications," said Garcia.

Sanchez and Garcia quietly exited their car.

Hamilton walked hurriedly down Charles Street. The fresh air was nice, but cool. Hamilton quickened his pace to keep warm against the frigid night air.

Sanchez and Garcia increased their strides to a brisk walk and continued to gain on Hamilton.

Amy ran on the opposite side of the street, making sure to remain hidden from Hamilton's view. She giggled to herself mischievously.

Sanchez and Garcia were now ten feet from Hamilton, and were closing fast.

Hamilton was about a half of a mile from the house party, when he abruptly stopped, "Damn it," he cursed under his breath. He'd just remembered he'd blocked in those four other cars in the driveway. He felt the car keys in his pocket, and thought how stupid it was not to have given them to Eileen. However, he was happy that he'd at least remembered this before going to bed. Otherwise, his Cherokee would've been forcefully moved by drunkards, or at the very least, soaped and keyed extensively.

He planted his heel and did an about face. Sanchez and Garcia immediately confronted him. Both men were dressed in black, and Sanchez firmly grabbed Hamilton's right arm. Meanwhile, Garcia grabbed his left arm and stuck the jagged edge of a twelve-inch hunting knife sharply under his rib cage.

"Don't be stupid, and you won't get hurt," stated Sanchez.

"Who, what the...." protested Hamilton.

"Shut the fuck up, we'll do all the talking Mr. Hamilton, " said Sanchez forcibly under his breath.

Hamilton wondered who the hell these guys were, and what did they want? How did they know his name? He hoped it was some sort of fraternity prank, but he doubted it, these guys looked pretty serious.

"You better hope this isn't opened pretty boy," said Garcia, as he pulled the scarlet envelope from out of Hamilton's pocket.

Garcia now held the envelope with Mike's birthday card and

accompanying tickets, and a puzzled look came across his face. The envelope was still sealed, but looked a little bigger than the one Garcia had seen earlier that day. He thought his mind might be playing tricks on him, as it often did when he was deprived of sleep.

Garcia flipped it over and read MIKE in bold letters; he knew it was a different envelope. To make sure, Garcia quickly opened the envelope and discovered the basketball tickets. Out of frustration, he immediately tore the season pass to shreds.

"What the fuck is this!? This is the wrong envelope; strike one for Mr. Hamilton. "Where's the fucking letter? The one you got this morning," demanded Garcia.

"What letter? I don't have a clue what you're talking about. Why the hell are you tearing up those basketball tickets!" said Hamilton.

"Don't play fucking games with us! I told you be smart and you wouldn't get hurt. You're not being very smart, now think," said Sanchez.

"I honestly don't know what you're talking about. Who are you guys?" Hamilton struggled to say, for he was scared to death.

Sanchez hammered Hamilton in the stomach with a swift left knee. Hamilton groaned and doubled over in pain. If not for Garcia's forceful grip, Hamilton would be on the pavement. Amy was too drunk, and too busy skirting behind the bushes to notice this confrontation.

"We'll ask the questions. Where's the envelope? It looks a lot like this one. The one you got it in the mail this morning. We know you have it. I saw it with that mailman of yours. We checked your mailbox this morning and it wasn't there, so don't play dumb with us you little faggot," said Sanchez.

Sanchez was becoming impatient with Hamilton's lack of knowledge, and pressed the knife harder into Hamilton's side, while clinching down his grip on his arm.

Amy could hardly contain herself as she watched Hamilton and his two companions inch their way closer to her hiding spot. She was disappointed that Hamilton had company, but they'd probably leave if she asked Hamilton to walk her home. Her chaperon request wasn't unreasonable. It wasn't ever safe, even in a nice area like this, for a female to walk home alone at night. Being an extremely attractive and sloshed female walking home alone only made it that much more precarious. Perhaps the extra company wasn't so bad after all, with three people she should get a much louder reaction to her antics. They were now only a couple of feet away. Amy crouched on her toes and sprang out from her hiding place in the shrubs.

"Surprise!!!" Amy shrieked in the still night air.

Garcia instinctively jumped back. In the process he accidentally inserted the blade of the sharp serrated knife about six inches into Hamilton's soft abdomen. Hamilton buckled over and fell to the ground like a sack of potatoes.

Amy screamed when she saw Garcia pull the knife out of Hamilton's stomach. Her terror was short lived, as Sanchez hit her over the head with the butt of his revolver. Sanchez, acting quickly, removed the cream colored Duke Lacrosse hat from Hamilton's head and placed it on his own.

After putting on Hamilton's blood-soaked fleece pullover jacket, Sanchez fumbled around until he found the keys to the Jeep in the front zipper pouch. He sprinted back to the party.

Garcia dragged the two limp bodies into the shadows of some nearby bushes. The only noise was the wind whistling through the leaves and Hamilton's faint breathing, which was becoming fainter by the minute.

As Sanchez approached the party he stopped running and walked briskly to the Grand Cherokee. There was a young couple standing underneath the light on the front porch.

"Oh, there you are Ham my man! Are you moving your car? Cause, we need to get out," asked the young man on the porch. Sanchez nodded to the young man, making sure they couldn't see his face. It was difficult for the couple on the porch to see anything, for the cars were in dark shadows of the trees and night. Plus, the couple had enjoyed more than their share of cocktails that evening.

# CRISIS

He turned his back to the couple and slipped into the Grand Cherokee.

Hamilton and Amy were in the same spot where Sanchez had left them. They were by the bushes, just off the sidewalk. The bodies were now completely out of sight of the street traffic. Hamilton was wheezing softly at this point and coughing up large globs of blood. Amy was still unconscious. Garcia quickly grew tired of Hamilton's wheezing and knocked him unconscious with a swift kick to the head. He placed both bodies in the front seat of the car. When he'd completed this tiring task, he quickly wiped up the blood from the sidewalk with a towel and placed that along with Hamilton's cap back on the unconscious body.

Garcia stiffened at the sound of two young men approaching. Both appeared to be in jovial spirits, as they were playfully swaying back and forth with their arms around one another's shoulders. As the two students approached, he calmly closed the passenger side door. The two guys passed as he slid into the back seat. The shorter of the two guys made a loud scream, "Get some!! Now those two in the front, they know how to party like rock stars. I gotta respect that!" yelled the shorter of the two.

"Yes sir, know how to party hard oh great one," replied the taller student, doing his best Ed McMahon impersonation, an impersonation which needed a lot of work and was outdated. Sanchez watched in the rear view mirror as the two men continued their journey merrily down Elizabeth Street.

It was now well past two in the morning, and aside from the two stumbling drunks, the streets were deserted.

Sanchez found a city park off Burcham Street and parked the Grand Cherokee. Amy began to wake up and tried to acclimate to her unfamiliar surroundings. She tried to remember what had happened, did she have that much to drink? Did she pass out on the way home? Was she in Hamilton's car? What the hell was going on? Questions with no answers filled her foggy head.

"Well, well, well, it looks like sleeping beauty is finally coming to life. I guess we'll have some fun after all," drooled Garcia.

Garcia and Sanchez liked this new girl a lot better than that prissy girlfriend of his, Eileen. They thought Eileen was prettier in the face, but wasn't quite as sexy. Amy's body reminded Garcia of the dancers at the Flamingo Hotel in Las Vegas, except she wasn't as tall as the professional dancers. She screamed at the sight of Hamilton's blood. The blood was clearly evident on the graphite colored upholstery. Garcia brutally silenced her scream with his cupped left hand and forcefully pulled her from the sport utility vehicle.

He pulled her in a tight clamp across the wet grass of the park. Her resistance was no match for his brute strength, and his large paw muffled her screaming. He threw her down onto the hard dirt of the softball field. They were positioned five feet from home plate, down the third base line. He proceeded to take off his left sock and tightly secured it around her head as an effective gag.

"That ought to shut you up for a while," said Garcia.

Amy writhed on the ground in a futile attempt to escape. The small sharp stones of the baseball diamond started to grind into her flesh with every wiggle, but they went unnoticed because her mind and body were gripped with terror. Garcia was positioned directly above her and had her arms forcefully pinned down with his muscular arms. She tried to kick her legs, but his weight was too much to overcome. He reached for his belt, letting go of her left hand. When he glanced down to undo his belt, she violently swung her left hand upward toward his face. Her long nails raked across the side of his left cheek. Chunks of his flesh now were embedded beneath her nails.

"Aargghh, you fucking bitch!!!!" yelled Garcia as he forcefully backhand slapped Amy across the face with his right hand clenched in a tight fist. Blood trickled from the corner of her left lip as a result of this tremendous blow.

"Oh we want to play rough do we? Well I like to play rough," said Garcia between gritted teeth. He powerfully turned Amy's body face down onto home plate, and tied her hands painfully tight with his black leather and brass buckled belt.

CRISIS

Satisfied that her hands were secured, he turned her over to face him in all his glory. Tears streaked down her face and an uncontrollable tremble and nausea consumed her body.

"Oh, there's no need to cry. This will all be over soon, and you'll actually enjoy me. Besides, it could be a lot worse. We could get that big sweaty partner of mine to join us, or perhaps you'd enjoy a little ménage a trois? I really enjoy these magnificent breasts. Young breasts with no sag, just how I like them honey." Garcia aggressively groped her naked breasts.

Amy hopelessly tried to keep her legs together, but was no match for Garcia's strength. He pulled down her shorts just below her knees and sliced her lime-colored underwear with the same knife that he'd used on Hamilton. In fact, not all of the blood had dried, and a drop dripped down onto her pelvis. Amy's mouth was dry from shock and she wanted to throw-up when she felt the beastly man violently overpower her.

Twenty minutes later, with her clothes torn to rags, Amy was thrust back into the passenger seat with Garcia's hand firmly placed behind her head. She was no longer trembling. She was in deep shock from the horrific last twenty minutes; she truly didn't care if she lived anymore. She got her wish sooner than expected. With tremendous force, Garcia smashed her forehead against the dashboard. She passed into the next, hopefully more pleasant, life.

Hamilton was now positioned in the driver's seat of the car. The Grand Cherokee was placed on top of the hill, looking down on the road that came to an end at East Lansing Elementary School.

Sanchez arrived with the other car and Garcia went around to the trunk to fetch the fifth of Grey Goose Vodka. He hated to waste good Vodka, but Sanchez insisted he do it. He opened both Amy's and Hamilton's mouths and poured the remaining liquor down their throats. He then smashed the bottle against the steering column. He picked the largest piece of glass off the floor, making sure his latex gloves covered his fingerprints, and inserted it into Hamilton's knife wound. For good measure Garcia made the wound larger with the glass. Hamilton, although still alive, couldn't feel the glass going into his body; he was numb from pain.

Garcia and Sanchez got into the Lincoln Town Car. The Lincoln then pushed the Grand Cherokee, using its front bumper against the Cherokee's rear bumper. The Grand Cherokee quickly gathered speed on the sloped avenue and the speedometer on the Lincoln reached fifty-mph. The Lincoln slowed at the turn, released contact with the Grand Cherokee, and abruptly turned left onto a side street. The Lincoln was around the corner and on its way. Garcia and Sanchez heard the crushing sound of the Grand Cherokee hitting the brick elementary school. Despite not having the requested envelope, they still felt it was a good and enjoyable days work.

# CHAPTER 8

# RICHMOND, VIRGINIA

Lisa Appleton once again looked over the old *Washington Post* article. She first looked at the small article on Barbara Fernandez's death. She was positive it wasn't the result of a robbery as indicated. Someone was behind this, and she suspected Ricardo Valez had a hand in it one way or another.

The second batch of articles was a little more difficult for Lisa to deal with. These articles all related to her twin brother's unfortunate death, two years ago. Her brother, George, a sophomore at Georgetown University at the time, was found dead in his room at the Chi Theta fraternity house. The coroner on the scene attributed George's death to an overdose of heroine.

Lisa knew George had experimented with marijuana in high school and found he didn't like it. She was certain that he wouldn't experiment with hard-core drugs like heroin. She distinctly remembers a conversation she'd had with him a week prior to his death. They were discussing an article he was writing for his fraternity chapter's newsletter, and he was extremely excited about it. He thought he might have unearthed information that would propel his article into the national spotlight, but he still needed to confirm its authenticity. At the time, she didn't think much of it, for he was a dreamer and often tended to exaggerate. But, she vividly remembered that the bulk of the article was on Ricardo Valez. She tried in vain to find the thumb drive or a hard copy of the article after his death, but his room was in disarray and no remnants of the article were to be found. She explained her story to the authorities, but they said that she was just in denial and would eventually realize that her brother, like millions his age, should have just said NO to drugs. She didn't accept this explanation and was determined to resolve her brother's death.

Following her brother's funeral she began to vigorously investigate the matter. Not wanting to cause concern, she didn't tell her parents about her endeavors. The only person who knew what she was doing was her fiancé, Eddie. At first, Eddie was supportive; he determined that she probably just needed to get it out of her system. After a couple of weeks Eddie figured she'd give it up. Well, he was wrong. The more dead ends she ran into, the more determined she became. Her brother's death became all consuming.

Eddie was used to receiving a tremendous amount of attention from Lisa, and she was now devoting almost all of her attention to the investigation of her brother's death. Eddie, who was supportive of Lisa at first, told her she would be better off dropping it altogether. He believed it wasn't healthy, especially for him. If the authorities said her brother died of a drug overdose, who could argue? She thought that Eddie might be right and besides, if Eddie didn't believe in her, who would? Despite these rational thoughts, she knew in her heart that her brother would never willingly overdose on drugs. He was too smart to do something that overtly stupid. With the prodding of Eddie, Lisa abandoned her research of her brother's death. That was until a few days ago.

A recent article regarding an alleged drunk driving death involving a Chi Theta named Chris Hamilton at Michigan State inspired her renewed interest in the death of her brother. The paper clipping currently in her hand discussed the death of Chi Theta's National Secretary, Barbara Fernandez. Lisa had a hunch that these two recent deaths were somehow connected and that they could provide insight into her brother's mysterious death. This time around she wasn't going to stand idly by, no matter how difficult things became. She also wouldn't listen to what Eddie said, in fact she wasn't going to tell him what she was doing. Whoever was responsible for these two recent fatalities was also probably involved in the death of her brother and she wasn't going to leave anything to chance.

Lisa glanced in the mirror one last time. Her makeover was complete and she was satisfied with the results. It was crucial that she get this job. Her preparation had been thorough to ensure that her attire was convincing.

She made herself look plain and boring. This was no simple task as her striking features were extremely difficult to hide.

Much of her flowing brown hair had been sacrificed, however it still went past her shoulders. Her hair was now parted in the middle and lying straight on either side. Although lacking style, it still produced a radiant glow. She thought about pulling it into a tight bun, but this would have accentuated her statuesque features even more.

Her laughing walnut eyes were still prominent behind the thick black-rimmed glasses, which were purposely too large for her rounded, diminutive face.

Earrings were absent from Lisa's earlobes, however this wasn't unusual. She had only gotten her ears pierced two years ago, and she didn't wear earrings except for on special occasions. Her oversized mushroom-colored sweater hung on her as unflatteringly as possible. The sweater cost only five-dollars at the local Army/Navy store, and did an excellent job of concealing her flawless body.

While at Lexington High School in Virginia she excelled at basketball, volleyball and softball. At 5'9" and 122 pounds, she continued her volleyball career at the University of North Carolina. Male attendance at the women's volleyball matches immediately increased upon her arrival to campus. The tight spandex shorts and tight long sleeved volleyball uniforms usually looked horrendous on most of the gangly and poorly proportioned female players. However, on her, these uniforms captured every young man's imagination. She had a solid four-year career and was elected team co-captain by her teammates her senior year. As co-captain, she was able to lead the Tar Heels to their first NCAA Title game in many years. For her efforts, she was selected second team All-American.

Lisa was still in perfect playing shape, although she'd graduated in May and was starting her first year of Law School at the University of Virginia in Charlottesville. Lisa remained active by playing volleyball with the boys at the Slaughter Intramural Facility (SIF), located in the heart of Virginia's picturesque campus.

Polyester black slacks and ridiculous looking black clogs were currently concealing her healthy body. The disguise had the effect of making Lisa appear four years older than her actual twenty-two years.

Just as important as the clothes to the disguise, was the way Lisa conducted herself during the interview. She had to portray a poor woman who was dependent on others for strength. Her plan was to appear plain and act timid. She hoped that the acting course she took in undergraduate school would finally payoff.

She was accustomed to projecting a strong presence, yet internally it was a different story. A difficult life had made everything a mess on the inside. Her grandmother had passed away from cancer when she was thirteen. This devastated her previously loving and good-humored father, as he became increasingly bitter over the years. Lisa was usually the target of his tirades. However, as her younger brother became braver and stronger, he often unselfishly took the brunt of these verbal blows. They watched their parents' marriage quickly unravel before their eyes. Mrs. Appleton couldn't stand being around her husband's negativity any more than the kids could. Their father died soon after Lisa's younger brother's unexpected death.

She originally became involved with sports to get out of the house and take her mind off the troubles at home. She spent countless hours after practice doing drill after drill to improve her skills and, more importantly, prolong her time away from the haunted house called home. Ironically, she would find herself in a worse nightmare several years later when her boyfriend, Eddie, began beating her. A once perfect relationship with Eddie had soured as the pressures for Eddy of living up to his father's unrealistic expectations became too much for him. As a result, Eddie began to take out his frustrations on Lisa through verbal and often physical abuse. Questions about vicious bruises from Eddie were easily brushed off as the result of diving on the hard gym floor to make returns in volleyball.

Lisa adjusted the blouse on her disguise, making sure to cover up the brown bruise on her neck. Sports were no longer a viable excuse for these bruises, so she did her best to hide them, along with her pain. This bruise was courtesy of Eddie, now her fiancé.

Accounting for average rush hour traffic, it took a good forty-five minutes to reach the University of Maryland's campus. Playing four matches and a Christmas tournament in Maryland's Cole Field House had made her somewhat familiar with the campus. Some of her best volleyball had been played at Cole Field House and it held a special place in her heart. During her junior season she'd won the tournament's Most Outstanding Player Award.

She was fairly certain of where the Pocomoke building was located, but gave herself an additional fifteen minutes just in case. The Pocomoke building was formerly the Old College Park Fire Department and was located behind the Sigma Beta Tau fraternity house, one of the tips of the Fraternity Row Horseshoe.

The Chi Theta National Headquarters were located in the middle of the horseshoe of fraternities and sororities appropriately named "Fraternity Row." It was quite a spectacular site having uniformly built houses beautiful running parallel to each other. On most college campuses, the fraternity and sorority houses were highly dispersed and unique in appearance. But, here on Fraternity Row, all of the houses were built exactly the same and stood side by side. Fourteen of the campus' twenty-one Greek houses had their address on Fraternity Road. Each house in this horseshoe was composed of the same red brick pervasive throughout campus. The houses were rectangular in design while white pillars adorned the front of each chapter. Several basketball and sand volleyball courts were situated in Fraternity Row. It was a campus oasis. Students were constantly surrounded by the opposite sex, had plenty of competition for any sporting event, and didn't have to walk far for parties or to class. The walk to class was particularly short, especially if one opted not to attend.

Lisa repeatedly practiced pushing her glasses up the bridge of her nose and shyly glancing at the floor. She was banking on the assumption that Valez would be looking for a secretary whom he could intimidate. She also suspected that he would want to hire someone of pedestrian appearance, so as not to arouse suspicion amongst the co-workers. If her assumption about Barbara Fernandez's death was correct, that Valez was somehow connected to Barbara's murder, than he would be hiring a new secretary for window dressing and nothing more. With these factors in mind, she had transformed herself into the meek alias of Holly Cane for the interview.

# CHAPTER 9

Tip stared down into the empty beer mug. His reflection was a blur on its annular bottom. He thought his life paralleled an empty beer mug. However, there was no magical tap to refill an empty soul. His elbows rested atop the bar with his arms sprawled out on the black Formica. The rest of his body was hunched over the bar and was being supported by his chin. The Formica bar at Rick's American Café wasn't comforting. Rick's was a popular watering hole just North of Michigan State's campus, and Tip frequented it often because of its proximity to the fraternity house. This was the first time he'd had a drink in here since meeting Hamilton a few years ago.

With the exception of Tip, the bartender, and a bored waitress, Rick's American Cafe was deserted. The bartender and waitress were both new employees and hence were scheduled to work the worst shifts. These bad shifts were the day shifts, the dead periods. It was a beautiful midwestern fall afternoon, and Tip would probably be Rick's only customer before nine o'clock that evening. Then the bar would begin packing people in like sardines, students arriving in droves to capitalize on Rick's dollar pitchers of Natural Light beer. This special usually caused a line to wrap around the building. However, at four in the afternoon the place was not much more than a ghost town.

Questions painfully bounced around inside Tip's head: Hamilton would never drink and drive, it went against everything he believed in and preached. Was Hamilton human like everyone else and had he simply snapped from all the pressure and strain he encountered on a day-to-day basis? What the hell was Amy Klein doing in the car? Hamilton didn't have it in him to hurt a flea, let alone rape and kill someone. Besides, he was hopelessly in love with Eileen. Hamilton didn't even care that much for Amy when he was dating her, let alone now that they weren't dating at all. The fifth of vodka found in the car was also very odd. Hamilton hated Vodka, and Tip recalled that Amy was allergic to potatoes, thus she'd be allergic to Vodka. The only reason Tip remembered this odd fact about her was because she'd ordered a combination meal at McDonald's and didn't get the fries; not the wisest economical choice.

Tip tried to speak with Eileen this morning, but it was a lost cause. She was a wreck and all he could get from her was hysterical screams of "Why? Why?" It was a very good question, and he hoped to find the answer. Although it appeared to everyone else that it was just another unfortunate mistake of youth, he wasn't buying it. The pieces of the puzzle were not quite meshing for him.

Tip had talked with Mr. and Mrs. Hamilton briefly at the funeral a few days ago. They looked in almost worse shape than their son's pale corpse. It was a very trying time for them. Not only did they lose their only son, but also their son's good name was tarnished by the pending accusations of rape and drunk driving. These accusations were on every publication, radio station and television channel.

Mr. Hamilton's business practice would likely be adversely affected. The majority of his female clientele could possible take their valuable accounts with them, due to the reports of possible rape. To make matters worse, the Klein's had filed suit against the Fraternity and also against the Hamilton's. Mr. and Mrs. Klein wanted someone to be held accountable for their daughter's death. If the Hamilton's lost the lawsuit, they'd also lose the money in Allison's trust fund. They had officially gained control of the trust a few months prior when they became Allison's legal guardians.

The funeral service was tastefully done. Tip did a good job of fighting back the tears during his reading of the eulogy. The burning fire of anger inside of him helped evaporate his reservoir of tears. Blocking out the flashbacks and painful memories of his parent's funeral proved difficult. Their eulogy was still freshly engrained in his brain. He had broken down during that reading and cried uncontrollably for several minutes. This time around the anger inside him held the tears at bay.

The funeral procession was enormous, halting traffic for a minimum of five minutes at each intersection. The procession was comprised mainly of students, including all one hundred and twenty members of Chi Theta. None of the University administrators that Hamilton had worked with attended the funeral. It would be politically incorrect for them to attend, given the circumstances surrounding the incident. Professors didn't want angry parents accusing them of condoning rape and drunk driving by their presence at the funeral. They wouldn't be able to attend any Hamilton related function until his name was cleared of the allegations. Their decision, or lack there of, was made easier when the Dean issued a formal statement advising that it would be in their best interest to distance themselves from the situation. The lone dissenter was Hamilton's humanity teacher, Dr. Tily. His presence meant the world to the Hamiltons.

"Would you care for another one?" the female bartender asked, momentarily breaking Tip's recollection of the funeral from earlier that morning.

"Please," replied Tip automatically.

His head felt like it was going to explode as the images of his parent's funeral and Hamilton's funeral ran together in his mind over and over.

Tip was still alive, and at times it seemed like he was the only survivor. He pondered if he should join his loved ones in the world beyond. However tempting this solution, he had some responsibilities to face; Allison, the Hamilton's, Chi Theta and his best friend's honor. Whoever was responsible for the death of Chris Hamilton was going to pay in spades. Tip didn't have time to grieve this death (there would be no Chris Hamilton to help him this time). He only had time for revenge.

He gulped down the frothing beer the bartender slid before him and hastily ordered another. The sudsy liquid was refreshing to his dry mouth and was also soothing to his soul.

# CHAPTER 10

Lisa thought the interview went well. She believed that she'd be offered the secretarial job at Chi Theta's National Headquarters. She was surprised to be interviewed by someone other than Chi Theta's Director, Ricardo Valez. Holly (Lisa) was informed that the new secretary wouldn't be handling the same duties as the deceased Barbara Fernandez, which only strengthened her suspicions about Valez playing dirty pool. She would interview with John Jay before conversing with Valez.

John Jay, was the Alumni Relations Coordinator and he couldn't say enough good things about Valez. Mr. Jay cited that contributions and donations to the fraternity had quadrupled since Valez arrived four years ago. Valez was a persuasive speaker, and the alumni loved him, showing their love by opening their checkbooks. The undergrads revered him for his practice of generously funding renovations of dilapidated chapter houses.

After listening to John Jay for thirty minutes, Lisa began to question her hunch. Maybe her brother's, Barbara's and Chris Hamilton's deaths were just coincidence. Even if they weren't coincidence, maybe Valez wasn't responsible.

Following her interview with Valez, she skipped across Baltimore Avenue. She was ecstatic. The interview had gone better than she could have possibly dreamed. Majoring in psychology had apparently paid off; Valez behaved exactly as she had predicted.

A timid secretary that would stay out of his way and not ask too many questions was exactly what he was looking for. Lisa's Holly Cane character was so impressive that he offered her the job immediately following their half-hour conversation. It was obvious to her that he was merely going through the motions of the interview.

It was probably for the benefit of the rest of the office. No matter how intentionally vapid Lisa made her responses, he simply nodded and said good, very good.

Lisa and two other girls made it past the screening process of John Jay. Lisa was fortunate to be the first person interviewed by Valez. He had limited patience to play this charade, and after talking to her, he didn't want to waste any more time on the matter. Holly Cane would be his new secretary.

During the interview Lisa was able to stay in character and her performance was close to flawless. She would recommend the acting class to future North Carolina students. However, it was difficult for her to stay in character. Valez had an eerie affect on her, sending chills up and down her spine. It was a sensation she had never experienced, and one she didn't want to experience again.

Holly Cane was hired to handle the day-to-day correspondence of the National Headquarters. Specifically, she was to oversee the 208 Chi Theta Chapters nationwide. Her primary job entailed answering students' questions, concerns and complaints. This alleviated Valez from such trivial matters allowing him to concentrate on more pressing concerns. He explained that this secretarial job was important and thus demanded an overqualified person. If the job were performed correctly then it would free up his time to make public appearances, attend conventions, and fundraise. Most of the General Directors for fraternities in America were giant figureheads like Valez.

It was difficult for Lisa to sit and take his baloney, but she had to admit that he was slick. She could see how he was capable of pulling the wool over the eyes of everyone else in the office. To her, the thing that betrayed him the most was his lack of remorse whenever Barbara's name was mentioned. He had worked with Barbara for such a long time. To not show any outward signs of affection was suspicious.

Several people worked in the National Headquarters building. Three others were retained as field consultants and traveled across the country to the various chapters. Lisa also would be responsible for documenting the reports and expenses of these consultants.

Valez explained to her that he'd only be in the office about twice a week and that she would work from 8 till 5 each day. She was glad he would be doing so much traveling, since his absence would give her plenty of time to snoop around.

# CHAPTER 11

Tip's back was starting to ache from sitting on the barstool the past four hours. He slammed the remainder of his last brewsky. He was enjoying each successive brew more and more. However, they still weren't as tasty as the real thing. This non-alcoholic Sharps beer, made by Miller, did the best job it could, which would have to do. The main drawback to drinking these Sharps was the cost. Sharps were expensive in East Lansing. College bars didn't stock very many near beers, since the students drank beer for the buzz rather than taste.

Tip wiped the beer away from his lip with his forearm before whispering one of his father's favorite sayings, "For one to properly fix a wound, one must have been wounded previously."

"Excuse me sir, did you say something?" asked the bartender.

"Yeah, pray for justice and vindication," replied Tip. He proceeded upstairs and into the afternoon sun.

# CHAPTER 12

Tip's first stop was the scene of the accident. The yellow police tape still marked the area at the damaged elementary school. The sight of the blood stained grass was nauseating. After an hour of thoroughly investigating the school grounds, Tip decided he wasn't getting anywhere. He headed down to 453 Elm Street, home of Dan Knapp. According to the Lansing State Journal, Dan Knapp was the first person on the scene of the accident.

Tip knocked on the front door of the gray two-story Colonial. After waiting a minute, he knocked a second time. Again, there was no answer, and he turned to go. To his surprise, the door swung halfway ajar. In the doorframe stood a 21-one-year old student who'd obviously been disrupted from a sound sleep by the incessant pounding. His scraggly long hair was matted on the right side of his head, covering up some of the graphics on his black Blink 182 T-shirt. The matted hair gave away the fact that he preferred to sleep on his right side in bed, or in this case, couch.

"What's the deal?" asked the student in an irritated morning-voice.

"My name's Paul Tipton, and I'm looking for a Dan Knapp," said Tip.

"What do you want him for?" asked the student rudely.

"I just wanted to ask him a few questions, that's all," replied Tip.

"I thought Dan told all you scum bags from the press to beat it. He's not talking to anyone anymore," exclaimed the student as he began to shut the door.

"Maybe so, but I'm not with the press or the police, I'm Chris

Hamilton's roommate, and I'd appreciate a little more respect," said Tip.

"How do I know that's true," said the student, "Some reporter-tool was trying to pass himself off on me as Hamilton's brother. He didn't even have a brother."

Tip handed him a recent picture of Chris and himself, a picture that was well worn. The picture hadn't left his possession since the fatal accident. The edges of the photo were dog-eared from him constantly fiddling with it while he lost himself in thought.

"Okay, come on in," said the student, eyeing up Tip.

Tip walked into the house. The student extended his right hand to him, "Paul, Dan Knapp, nice to meet you."

―――――-

"Boss was really upset huh," Garcia asked.

"Yes, for the twentieth time, he's pissed as hell. Boss didn't like us creating such a commotion, killing an innocent girl and all. He's also extremely perturbed that we killed that Hamilton kid, since he's the only person who knows where that damned envelope is located. An envelope, which by the way, if we don't find we don't get paid," snapped Sanchez.

"Why the hell didn't boss tell us the kid was so important?" said Sanchez.

"Let's just drop it. And let me do all the talking in there," said Sanchez as both entered the Eli Broad College of Business building and trotted downstairs to the counseling office. This building was opened in the fall of 1993. The building bore the name of the philanthropist who donated over $10,000,000 to the effort. Before the building was constructed, the old business building was too small to house all of the University's business classes. It was now much more convenient for business students to only have to go to one centrally located building. This greatly helped the MBA program move up in the all-important *Business Week* rankings.

Sanchez and Garcia got in line behind an extremely irate student. The student was noticeably agitated, and it was apparent that he was tired of getting the run around by the University administration. Currently, he was taking his anger out on the unsympathetic and under qualified secretary. After completing his five-minute tirade, the student threw his papers into the air and left in a huff. The student brushed by Garcia's shoulder and shook his beet-colored face from side to side in disbelief at the idiocy of bureaucracy.

"The nerve of some people," said Sanchez s empathetically to the secretary.

"I'm used to it," said the secretary as she stuffed her face with another oozing, half-melted double fudge Bon Bon. "How can I help you gentlemen?"

"I was hoping to get a copy of Paul Tipton's schedule," said Sanchez.

"If he's a student, I'm afraid I can't do that, I don't have the authorization to give out anyone's schedule without their written permission," said the secretary popping the last of the Bon Bon's into her mouth, getting smeared chocolate all over her lips and fingers in the process.

"Oh I was fearful that this might happen. You see, I'm his uncle, and I just happened to be swinging by East Lansing on business and found myself with some free time and wanted to surprise him. We stopped off at his house, but Paul wasn't home. I understand your policy, for you obviously don't want to give it to any lunatic off the street. I appreciate your time, and I hope you have a nice day. I guess that I'll just wait till Christmas to see him and give him his present. Although I don't believe this chocolate Halloween candy will keep until then, would you like it?" asked Sanchez and he extended the marvelous treats within smelling range of the chocoholic.

"Come on, give this loser a break. His nephew is one of the few members of his family that still can stand to talk to him," hammed up Garcia.

"I guess I can bend the rules a little just this once, but you can't tell anyone," said the secretary, and she grabbed a piece of Halloween candy as reward.

"Oh, thank you. You're a sweetheart. I promise that I won't

divulge our little secret to anyone. I'm not even from this area anymore due to business. But, from the looks of you, I wish that I still lived around these parts," said Sanchez.

The secretary blushed and went to another room for a minute before coming back a few minutes later with a print out of Tip's schedule. There were some smudges on the corners of the snowy paper, courtesy of the secretary's chocolate fingers.

"Thank you so much. I know Paul will appreciate it tremendously. Have a nice day," said Sanchez with Garcia as they waltzed out the yellow double doors.

# CHAPTER 13

I'm sorry about being a dick at the door, but the press and police have been all over my ass. I actually knew Chris Hamilton: he lived a floor above me when I was a freshman. He was really a cool cat. We had some good times together. It really pissed me off to see the pigs and papers drag his name and reputation through the mud. And then, that girl's parents filing the lawsuit really pissed me off. You know, everyone's just out to make a buck off of anything these days. Speaking of suits, there have been lawyers popping by here all the fucking time, trying to get a testimonial from me. Yeah, I'll give them a testical-monia. I told them all to go to hell, I mean don't they have any respect or understanding of the delicacy of the situation? Lives were lost for crying out loud! I hate those goddamned blood-sucking lawyers. I'm sorry, I haven't gotten much sleep lately because of this and lack of Z's makes me irritable. To make a long story short, I have to thoroughly screen everyone that comes to the door-so don't feel like I'm just fucking with you."

"Don't sweat it," said Tip.

"Now, what can I do you for?" asked Dan.

"If you don't mind, I'd like you to tell me everything that happened that night. I'm sure you're tired of talking about it, but it's important. And, if it's any comfort, I'm not looking forward to it much either," said Tip.

"All right, if that's what you want. I kind of figured that's what you were going to ask me anyway. I'll start from the beginning. It was Monday, and I got home from studying at the Engineering Library and tried studying on that couch over there by the window," Dan pointed to a raggedy old couch tightly tucked away in the corner below a large old window. The window had globules of white paint all over it, the results of a half-hearted paint job. This type of shoddy workmanship was ubiquitous on student housing in the area.

The couch in the corner was in worse shape than the paint-splattered window. The springs looked like they'd been trampled by a herd of elephants. The thoroughly stained and outdated fabric made one wonder if this couch came straight out of the trash.

"You know how studying on the couch goes...doesn't happen. My ass was out like a light after about two minutes. It must have been about two in the morning or something. Now comes the weird part. I wasn't awakened by the sound of the crash, but rather I swear it was the sound of squealing tires of another car, moments before the big ass crash. The screeching sounded as if the car was also coming from the schoolyard area. The crash was loud as hell, and I immediately ran down the street to the school. The car was completely totaled, and so I needed to check to see if the dudes were all right. I approached the driver's side first and found Hamilton hunched over the steering column. Man, he was in bad shape. I pulled his body off of the car horn, which wasn't easy to do since the stupid air bag was in the friggin' way. Once I got him clear of the steering column is when I noticed the nasty ass gash across his stomach and there was blood everywhere. He looked like hell. I've never seen a dead body in person before, well besides at funerals and all. I double-checked his pulse, and though very faint, he was still barely alive. Upon letting go of his wrist, he muttered something to me that was pretty hard to understand, but maybe it has meaning to you.

"What did he say," asked Tip.

"Well, as I mentioned it was very faint so I'm not quite sure I heard exactly what he said, but it sounded like he said the word crisis. Does that term mean anything to you?" Dan asked.

"Crisis? No. I can't say that it does. That's all Hamilton said was crisis?" asked Tip.

"Yes, well that's all that I could make out. I think he tried to say something else, but I couldn't quite make it out before he passed away. I'm sorry I know this must be hard on you," said Dan.

Even though this was about the thirteenth time he had told the story it was still difficult. He could only imagine what Hamilton's best friend was feeling, hearing the story for the first time. Dan was somewhat amazed at how well Tip was taking it – he just had a steely and intent look on his face.

"No, it's no problem, feel free to continue," encouraged Tip.

"After determining that Hamilton was now dead, I walked around to the passenger side of the car, and there discovered the dead Klein girl. Her head was indented and crushed almost like an empty can. It was one of the weirdest and most disgusting things I'd ever seen," Dan's face turned a little green as the grotesque image flickered in his mind. "Her eyes were wide open with fright, and she was also half naked, which was fucked up. I read in the papers that autopsy reports said she might have possibly been raped. Like I said before, I can't believe that the Chris Hamilton I knew would ever do anything like that. Well, anyway, I then checked the backseat, and thankfully found nothing else. Mr. Harvin, who lives in the yellow house on the corner, then arrived on the scene. I shouted for that no good old fart to call 911. The EMS and police arrived on the scene about ten minutes later, and I'm sure you know the rest. As I said, probably not too much more than you already knew," apologized Dan.

"No, no, it's helped out a tremendous amount. You mentioned that squealing tires caused you to wake up. Do you think these tires were from Hamilton's car or another one?

"It's difficult for me to know for sure since I was half asleep. But, if I had to say, I'm pretty damn sure the squealing tires came from another car. The cops said there was no indication that Hamilton attempted to slow down, he was at maximum speed when he hammered the school. An I'm no CSI agent, but I would say this also indicates that the squealing probably came from another car," responded Dan confidently. "And, I don't know this for sure, but I saw the cops thoroughly inspecting the pavement on the street that Hamilton's car sped down. I thought I overheard them say there were some fresh tire marks from another vehicle. So, I started thinking that maybe those were produced by the car that woke me up. It's probably irrelevant anyway. That's all I have dude."

"Thanks for your help man," said Tip as he got up and nonchalantly touched fists with Dan.

"No problem. It you need anything else give me a buzz. The number's in the campus directory under my roommate's name, R-I-N-G-H-O-L-D, " said Dan.

Tip walked out of the house more confused than ever. Hamilton was reaching out to someone for help or to give someone a clue to help solve the mystery, but the revelation of the word crisis didn't help at all. On the other hand, Tip thought maybe Hamilton was just delirious during his final moments of life, or maybe he was trying to say something else and Dan just misunderstood what he'd said. Maybe he was asking for a Chris, God knows he knew enough of them. Or, perhaps he was telling Dan his name was Chris, who knows?

Tip lowered the brim of his faded maroon South Carolina Gamecocks hat. The hat had originally read COCKS in ebony lettering across the top, but wear and tear had eliminated the stitching of the O and S so it now read C_CK_. The maroon color was badly faded, and resembled an indescribable color, but was closest to a reddish-gray.

Rain dripped off the front of the hat. The sky quickly darkened and the drizzle became heavier by the minute. Students at MSU swear East Lansing is the rain capital of the world. Every student had a great weather war story. These stories ranged from snowball fights to bike wipeouts to being splashed with muddy water by a bus on the way to class.

Most undergraduate students walked, biked, or in-line skated to class. MSU was one of the few remaining non-driving campuses in the country, and student parking was only available on the perimeter of campus. This lack of student parking was inconvenient for students, especially during the cold winter months, but it helped preserve one of the nation's most beautiful campuses. Also, since it wasn't a commuter campus, MSU enjoyed having the largest on-campus student population and housing facilities in the country. The interaction and bonding resulting from these close living quarters produced a family-like student body and alumni that was the envy of other universities.

Tip turned left off Elizabeth Street onto Abbott Road. Out of habit he almost walked straight ahead to the front door of the Chi Theta house. He wasn't going home just yet. He still had to visit the police station.

The East Lansing police station was located about a block away from Chi Theta on the opposite side of the street. Although most would think that having the police station so close to the fraternity would be a nightmare for the fraternity members; it was actually a blessing. They had developed a relationship with the East Lansing Police. They made a practice of informing the police and surrounding neighbors of every upcoming event or party. A couple of Chi Theta brothers majoring in criminal justice usually clerked at the police station during the school year. Chi Theta also sponsored a co-ed flag football tournament and donated the proceeds to the families of East Lansing policemen who had been injured or killed in the line of duty.

Of course, Chi Theta still had their share of run-ins with the police. Tip couldn't help but laugh remembering the sight of two Chi Thetas hitting golf balls off the fraternity house roof at the police station during the wee hours of morning. He could laugh now, because the three golf balls that were hit had fortunately not hit anyone or anything. The white spheres just bounded harmlessly down the road and perplexed looks crossed the faces of pedestrians standing on the street. Many of these pedestrians decided they'd had enough to drink after seeing this bewildering sight.

Tip opened the glass door and walked down a corridor that featured a putrid brown carpet. He walked briskly past the general information desk; he knew exactly where he needed to go in the station.

Tip, unfortunately, knew his way around the East Lansing Police Station. He'd spent many a night in the "drunk tank" after late-night run-ins with East Lansing's finest. It had been a couple of years since his last stay, but he still had unpleasant memories of waking-up in the foreign, yet all too familiar room. Sometimes he'd get lucky and have the single mattress to himself. Other times he'd awaken to another intoxicated student retching in the stainless steel toilet in the corner of this otherwise non-descript room. He knew that a night in the "detox hotel" had the going rate of fifty-dollar bail in the morning.

He proceeded down a flight of stairs and through a set of double doors reading "Evidence and Materials."

A middle-aged woman was attending the "Personal Belongings" cage and Tip casually approached her.

"Good morning sir. How can I help you?" asked the attendant with a big smile creating laugh lines around her eyes and revealing an impressive array of gold caps.

"Good morning, I'm Paul Tipton, Chris Hamilton's roommate. I called a little earlier on the phone, I'm here to pick up his stuff."

"Oh yes, I remember talking with you. One moment please, dear," said the woman. She disappeared into the back room, slowly shuffling her feet. Tip was amazed that one could be so slow.

She returned several minutes later with a cardboard box in her hands. On the side was written C. Hamilton with the date of the accident below it. Tip thought it quite sad that Hamilton's life was simply another cardboard box to the local authorities.

"There you are sir. Now if you would please sign by his name here," said the lady as she extended a clipboard with a form attached to it. "I will also need to see some identification please."

"Just out of curiosity, are there any other belongings that the police may have retained to possibly use as evidence?" asked Tip.

"Well, ordinarily that's classified information, but since no formal investigation occurred regarding the accident, no materials would probably be kept, but you didn't hear that from me. I'm terribly sorry about your friend dear. Is there anything else I can do to help?" asked the sympathetic lady. At least this lady thought that perhaps Hamilton was more than bric-a-brac in a box.

# CRISIS

"No, that should do it. Thank you very much," said Tip as he picked up the awkwardly weighted box and headed for home.

To his delight, the rain had ceased and the sun had parted the clouds. A rainbow sparkled on the distant horizon. If ever he needed to find a pot of gold at the end of a rainbow, it was today.

Unbeknownst to him, at the end of the street waited Garcia and Sanchez, stalking his every move. Not exactly the pot of gold he was hoping for.

Garcia took a swig out of his pint of Smirnoff Vodka, "What the hell does he have in his hand," asked Garcia.

"It's probably just Hamilton's shit that he picked up at the police station," replied Sanchez.

"Do you think the envelope might be in there?" asked Garcia.

"No way. The only items in there are from the night of the accident. And we searched him thoroughly. And from the looks of it, you seemed to have thoroughly checked out that Klein girl," grinned Sanchez.

"You didn't leave any evidence in his jacket did you?" asked Garcia.

"No. I'm not a fucking dumb ass. I'm a professional. What do you think I am, an idiot?" asked Sanchez.

"I just don't want anymore screw-ups," said Garcia.

Once in the confines of his room, Tip spread the articles of the box onto the octagon white marble table that was in the center of the room. He picked up Hamilton's broken wristwatch. Its glass face resembled a spider web, and the time matched the exact time of the accident. He painstakingly checked Hamilton's pants, finding Hamilton's wallet in the left back pocket of the Levi's jeans. Inside the wallet were various pieces of identification: student ID, driver's license, Blockbuster Video card, Panchero's frequent eater card, blood donor card, insurance card, American Express card and a Master card. There was also $70.

So, if Hamilton was indeed murdered, robbery wasn't the motive. The only other object Tip found was a movie ticket-stub in the coin pocket of the jeans. He then turned his attention to the

Patagonia jacket, but only fished out Hamilton's Swiss army knife and broken Ray Ban sunglasses. He was extremely discouraged and began twirling Hamilton's favorite hat in his hand while letting his mind fall into deep reflection...

How can I help you Hamilton when I don't have the faintest clue of what the hell happened? Maybe you did just get wildly drunk and kill yourself like the papers said. Maybe you just snapped for a few hours. It had happened to upstanding people before. Neighbors of ax murderers always seemed to say, "he was the nicest guy" and "I just don't know how this could have happened." Despite these doubts, Tip was still convinced that Hamilton was wronged.

He was staring at the hat when he happened to turn it over. He suddenly stopped twirling the hat and peered closely down into it. What caught his attention was a strand of thick black hair inside the hat, a hair that definitely didn't belong to Hamilton. This was extremely odd, because, while Hamilton was very generous, the one thing he never let anyone borrow was his hat. Eileen wasn't even allowed to wear it; not that she wanted to.

It was possible that one of the people handling it down at the police station had inadvertently allowed one of their hairs to fall into it thought Tip. This hypothesis was quickly destroyed, as he found two more similar strands deeply embedded into the hat. Someone other than Hamilton had worn this hat the night of the accident. Tip felt gratification, then anger, upon his discovery that there was more to Hamilton's death.

# CHAPTER 14

Lisa turned the handle to Valez's office, but once again it was locked. It was worth a try, she thought, just on the off chance he had forgotten to lock it. It was her third day on the job, and Valez had been out of the office for a portion of all three days.

She paid close attention to the layout of his office whenever she could sneak a peak, primarily when he entered or left. She had a difficult time accomplishing this without looking suspicious. To make matters worse, the office was extremely dark. She had attempted once to bother him by knocking on the door to ask him a simple question. He sternly told her it wasn't necessary for her to bother him with such trivial matters. He made certain that Holly understood she wasn't to bother him unless it was an extreme emergency, and in that case she was to contact him over the intercom speaker to his telephone and resolve the issue without coming into the office.

Lisa was thankful for the tongue lashing because it allowed her to get a decent scope of the office. The thick glasses worn by the Holly Cane character helped obscure her eyes and the shy mannerism of glancing down and away helped her scan the room for details.

In the center of the room was a large desk, but Lisa couldn't determine whether the drawers had locks on them. She assumed that the drawers were locked. It would be out of his character if they were not impenetrable.

On top of his desk were two phones, each with a separate line. A large wooden box of Cuban cigars and a large black porcelain ashtray rested on the front edge of the desk. Flanking the south wall were three file cabinets of varying heights. The modern cabinets stood in stark contrast to the rest of the room. Lisa assumed these were probably Barbara's cabinets, because they looked liked they matched the size of the carpet indentations by her desk in the hallway. It hadn't dawned on her before, but now she found it odd that she didn't have access to any of Barbara Fernandez's files.

There was an ornate nineteenth century Italian vase along the opposite wall and an assortment of early eighteenth century French paintings decorated the room as well.

Besides trying to figure out a way to get into Valez's office, she had been handling the day-to-day paperwork and correspondence necessary to run the fraternity's headquarters. She was surprised to discover that she actually enjoyed the work and that the pay was pretty good. Little did she know that her salary was only a fifth of what Barbara Fernandez made.

She especially enjoyed taking calls from the undergraduates at different chapters across the country. A lot of the undergraduate concerns were the same, but there were some very complex legal questions. She jotted down the legal questions for the attorney, Jim Sutter, to mull over.

A lion's share of her workload was devoted to filing alumni donations. Time for this duty was increased by the fact that she inconspicuously made photocopies of all incoming donations for her own records. In these records, she also made sure to include the return address on the envelope. She was happy to have found some spare time to conduct more research on Valez's background. Unfortunately, he checked out clean as a whistle.

Valez had been a Chi Theta at a small private college in New Jersey called St. Cecilia. He rushed Chi Theta as a sophomore and was elected social chairman as a junior. He also helped pay for his tuition by selling advertising space for the school newspaper, *The Seed*. He graduated with honors and a 3.6 GPA in Building Construction Management. He was the son of immigrant parents from Columbia, and was the first one in the Valez family to go to college.

Upon graduation, he went on to work for a small construction company located in East Rutherford, New Jersey, called Merchel Construction. Merchel, a small upstart company at the onset, quickly quadrupled in size and eventually expanded out of New Jersey and handled work all along the eastern seaboard.

He worked as a hired hand on the construction sites for four years, before being transferred to the sales department. His career took off and he quickly climbed the corporate ladder, ascending to Director of Sales. He held this position for less than a year before accepting the job as director of the fraternity.

She was surprised to find his past record of involvement with the fraternity was far from spectacular. He hadn't made a single donation until two years before his appointment as General Director. He also had never attended a homecoming function at his alma mater. Something must have gotten into his blood, for the two years before his appointment he was involved with everything the fraternity was doing. He started donating large sums of money to the National Headquarters, while at the same time, cutting deals for structural repairs on chapter houses through his connections in Merchel.

Lisa also wondered why he would quit a job where it appeared he was on the fast track to upper level management. He also took a pay cut of $100,000. Actually, $200,000 when you factored in lost stock options. Merchel had acquired Braxton Construction out of Chicago, giving them a national presence in the construction business. Valez was a year away from being fully vested when he quit.

Valez was quoted in numerous papers and publications as saying, "That he'd run into an old Chi Theta who did him a favor, and the brotherhood was magnetic. I'd been missing that type of personal connection since college, a bond that money can't buy. I told myself that I wanted to give something back to Chi Theta in return for what it had done for me. I wanted to ensure that Chi Theta would be around to touch the lives of others for years to come."

However, she didn't buy into his act, and was determined to get to the bottom of it.

# CHAPTER 15

Sanchez had a difficult time adjusting to Garcia's attire: a dark green sweatshirt with "Michigan State" embroidered in white block lettering. The letters on the sweatshirt were stretched wide, because the medium sized sweatshirt was too small for Garcia's extra-large chest.

It was Homecoming weekend at MSU, and that explained why the town's XL size sweatshirt supply was exhausted. Alumni making their annual voyage to the serene East Lansing campus had stocked up on green and white paraphernalia. Although undersized, Garcia's MSU alumnus disguise would be necessary in a few hours.

The green MSU Alumni baseball hat covering Garcia's head was completely out of place, for he hadn't even graduated from high school, let alone a Big Ten University. Sanchez was in the same undereducated boat.

It had been five days since the death of Chris Hamilton, and the elusive burgundy envelope had yet to be recovered. Sanchez and Garcia were getting desperate and they sensed that Valez's patience was also wearing thin.

Today would be their best opportunity to get into the Chi Theta house and look for the missing envelope. God had blessed the hundreds of thousands of fans with a picture perfect day for college football. There was hardly a cloud in the sky and the sun reflected off the dazzling colors of autumn.

The unobstructed sunlight caused the mercury to rise to an unseasonably warm 75 degrees with a gentle breeze blowing out of the West. MSU's campus was alive with activity. It was homecoming and it was the Spartans' first Big Ten game of the season. MSU had their work cut out for them. Their opponents were last year's

Rose Bowl Champions, the Ohio State Buckeyes. Both teams were undefeated in non-conference games. The game was being nationally televised on ABC. There was also an interesting subplot to the game, which the media ate up. Last November, the Spartans had destroyed Ohio State's chance of a perfect season and National Championship by upsetting them in the "Big Horseshoe" at Columbus.

The MSU fight song could be heard in the distance as the marching band made its traditional voyage from nearby Landon Field to the newly renovated Spartan Stadium.

Sanchez and Garcia stood in the shadows of a giant oak tree on a tiny side street named Park Lane. Sanchez acted as if he was taking pictures of Garcia, who was posing in front of his old college house. This mock photo shoot served two purposes: it didn't make them look suspicious and Sanchez could keep a watchful eye on the activities at Chi Theta with the zoom lens.

A crowd of around two hundred people milled about on the lawn in front of the Chi Theta house. The crowd was comprised mainly of active brothers, Alumni and their wives. Most of the active brothers were clustered around the food table and accompanying icy half-barrel of Killian's Red Lager.

A few brothers were attempting to cook hamburgers on the large house grill. The grillers were having a difficult go at it since they had to flip the burgers by hand. The tongs were lost a couple of days ago and the house manager hadn't had a chance to replace them. This group erupted with laughter when one flip attempt hastily sent a half-cooked burger flying into the grass.

A couple of sorority sisters from Alpha Chi Omega were also sprinkled among the convivial pre-game tailgaters. The brothers would occasionally glance over at the girls and every so often a brave sole would actually approach them. However, most of the Chi Thetas were either too entrenched in taking advantage of the Alumni purchased pleasures or too intimidated to talk to the girls. This wouldn't last long however, as the beer was going down rather easily. There wasn't anything quite like a little "liquid courage" to ease apprehensions.

# CRISIS

"There his is," said Sanchez upon spotting Tip. "What time's the game again?"

"Kickoff is at a little after 1 o'clock, so it should start in less than a half-hour. He should be leaving fairly soon, I'd estimate that it's about a fifteen-minute walk to the stadium from here. I figure that gives us a good two to three hours to find that damn envelope," said Garcia.

"Tipton's leaving right now, but there are still a lot of people on the lawn in front of the house. We'll need to wait it out a couple of minutes longer," said Sanchez.

Tip took a deep breath, it was good to get out and take a break. He hadn't been out since Hamilton's death. He was exhausted and demoralized by the results of his investigation to date. Besides the strand of hair in Hamilton's hat, he hadn't found any clues to the death of his friend. And even the hair clue hadn't led him anywhere. He had gone over the term "crisis" in his head until he almost popped a blood vessel, but he still couldn't make any sense out of it. Was crisis an acronym or code he was supposed to understand? What was Hamilton trying to tell him?

Tip was on the precipice of losing his sanity: he felt helpless. He truly believed that he was letting the Hamilton's down. The Klein's versus Chris Hamilton lawsuit was rapidly approaching, and Tip was running out of time. He hoped he'd be able to relieve some of his frustrations and accompanying pressures at the game. The game would be more therapeutic if the Spartans won. Tip and one of his better friends, Mike Peters, were cutting across Landon Field. They could make out the back of the marching band promenading past Sparty. Sparty was the world's largest freestanding ceramic statue and, more importantly, an historic icon that embodied the University's values and valor.

Sparty was an aesthetically pleasing ten-foot sculpture of a young Spartan warrior. The street to the north of Sparty was lined with Michigan State supporters. The two lanes of the bridge were cleared to allow the band to cross the bridge stretching over the Red Cedar River. In the background, and to the east, loomed Spartan

Stadium. It was enormous, with a seating capacity of 76,076. However, for today's celebrated contest close to eighty thousand would fill the stands. Tip could see that the upper tier of the stadium was already speckled with green and white. The beat of the drums reverberated off Tip's chest, reminding him how much he loved the excitement of the big game.

"Let's move. It's not gonna get better than this. We've got about two hours. Let's go," said Sanchez. Garcia headed north on Abbott Road, taking a left on Orchard Road, continuing past the Sigma Nu house and swerving left down Evergreen Alley, placing him squarely in the back lot of Chi Theta Fraternity.

After carefully watching the house for ten days, Garcia had determined that entry through the rear door would be the most viable route for his mission. The large metal black door looked extremely secure, however Garcia noticed that the hydraulic mechanism responsible for closing the door was old and didn't quite have enough pressure to close it. The members of the house didn't seem to mind. It was a pain using a key to unlock it, especially if they had their bikes with them.

All bikes were stored in the bike room in the basement. The bikes used to be stored in a rack in front of the house. However, with the skyrocketing prices of bicycles, it wasn't smart to have thousands of dollars worth of them vulnerably exposed to weather and criminals.

At one time, the house attempted to put a combination lock on the backdoor, however it constantly broke and everyone on campus seemed to know what the secret code was. The only way the current door would lock securely was if someone manually shut it with a hearty push. Garcia had only seen a couple of the guys do this, and was confident that the door would be unlocked.

If the backdoor happened to be locked, Garcia had a second option. He'd noticed that if a Chi Theta didn't have a key on them, they usually got in on the side of the house through the sliding glass door leading into the poolroom.

Garcia hoped the back door was open. He figured he'd be less likely to be seen heading up the backstairs than if he had to go through the main part of the house.

Sanchez's voice came across the miniature walkie-talkie, "There are still about five older guys on the front lawn, and one just entered the house and looks like he's heading toward the downstairs bathroom. Be careful. Don't panic. If you get in trouble I've got your backup. There are also several Alumni milling around and the members of the fraternity will think you're an alumnus they haven't met.

Sanchez had positioned himself in the bushes in front of St. Lutheran's church, which lay in the shadow of Chi Theta, directly across Abbott Road. He had binoculars fixed on the front of the house, particularly on the inside lower lever. It was difficult for him to see inside the windows of the upper levels because the reflection on the glass concealed what lay behind them. He had a small earphone plugged into his left ear listening to the Michigan State vs. Ohio State football game. The game remained close with Ohio State leading ten to six in the second quarter. If the game remained close it would give Sanchez and Garcia more time to operate, because few fans would leave early from a close contest.

Sanchez relayed to Garcia that the lower level of the house looked clear. Garcia entered through the unlocked backdoor. Garcia was breathing heavily by the time he'd climbed the four flights of stairs. There was no activity in the house. Everyone was either at the game, tailgating at Munn Field or watching the game at the bar.

Garcia headed down the long and cramped corridor. The sundeck was on his right and rooms were on his left. Most of the room doors were open, and the room's themselves were unusually tidy. The undergraduates made an extra effort to clean the house knowing that the Alumni and their families would tour the fraternity during this homecoming weekend. The pledges were responsible for the rest of the elbow grease.

Garcia took a right at the end of the hallway and proceeded past the bathroom on his right and rooms on his left, including the computer room. Straight-ahead was a flight of carpeted stairs going down. To the right of this was a narrow passage leading to a corner room.

Brass numbers indicating room 10 hung on the thick oak door. Garcia placed his right hand on the brass doorknob and slowly turned it, however the handle didn't budge. He was surprised to discover that the door to the room was locked. He had no idea that Tip always locked his room, especially during Homecoming Weekend when he didn't want curious, alcohol fueled alumni snooping around his stuff. Tip had heard horror stories about previous alumni who entered the rooms and started reminiscing about their college days and acting like it was their room again.

Garcia pulled out one of his fake credit cards; this particular one was a Visa gold card owned by a fictitious Mark Engels. He slid the credit card between the wood molding and the lock and pushed it directly down toward the bolt. The click of the locking mechanism was music to Garcia's ears and he was thankful that the fraternity hadn't replaced these antique locks with modern ones.

Room ten was by far the largest and nicest room in the house. The room was fairly clean except for a bunch of scribbles on a pad of paper located on the white marble table in the center of the room. On the eight and a half by eleven sheet of college ruled paper was the word "crisis" with a bunch of scribbled acronyms surrounding it. Following the list of acronyms were several question marks. Garcia snatched up the pad of paper and discarded it back on the table; it wasn't the document he was looking for.

"I'm in," Garcia whispered into his remote.

"You're all clear," replied Sanchez's voice.

Garcia determined Hamilton's bed was on his left, which was inside a very large walk-in closet, or pit. His attention was drawn to two large beige file cabinets. The cabinets were locked, so he reached into his jacket pocket and removed a device that looked like a miniature crowbar. With the device, he effortlessly broke into five of the six draws. He began feverishly sifting through folder after folder but didn't come across the burgundy envelope.

The sixth and last cabinet drawer wasn't cooperating, so he

# CRISIS

sat down on the floor and placed his foot on the drawer to get more leverage. The lock finally gave, but not without producing a loud cackle. Garcia didn't care about the noise at this point. He was profusely sweating inside the poorly lit and stuffy closet. Students weren't supposed to put their beds in these narrow closets since they were fire hazards. However, the students knew when the fire marshal would be coming for inspection and would move them out temporarily.

Beds placed in these pits were fire hazards because a student reacting to the scream of the fire alarm might smash his head on the close ceiling and knock himself out. Garcia had already bumped his head twice in the small confines. He eagerly peered into the last file and discovered about twelve of the burgundy national headquarters envelopes.

He scooped up the twelve envelopes, hastily scanning postmark dates in the upper right hand corner. All of the red envelopes were postmarked prior to the date he was searching for. He violently threw the envelopes on the floor and began ransacking the place, turning everything over with the hope of somehow discovering the envelope. He was emptying the desk and dresser drawers onto the floor and sifting through the contents with his feet. A big light blue Rubbermaid chest rested in the corner of the room. An imposing MasterLock rendered it inaccessible. He didn't attempt to break the combination lock. It would take too much time. He was making such a racket, that he didn't hear Sanchez over the radio the first two times.

"What's your status, over. What's your status? Over," repeated Sanchez.

"Garcia come in. What's your status, over!?" asked Sanchez.

"I haven't found anything yet, I'm going to search the rest of the house in a minute."

The football game had been better than Tip could have imagined. The teams were deadlocked at twenty entering the fourth and deciding quarter. The student section was a whirlwind of excitement and nervous anticipation, and young co-eds were being passed up the stands left and right. Stadium security generally frowned upon this practice of passing up bodies, but at the moment they were too enthralled with the game to be bothered by the rambunctious antics of the students.

Other parts of the stadium were sitting down pretending like they were on the crew team by using the person's shoulders in front of them as oars and rowing backward all the while chanting ROW! ROW! ROW!" The sight of thousands of fans doing this in harmony was quite spectacular. The fans in the northwest corner were attempting to start the wave, but the Buckeye fans in the northeast corner weren't cooperating. Many of the spectators seated in the eastern part of the stadium were quite sunburn from the midday sun. Some fans even looked like raccoons, since they'd made the mistake of leaving their sunglasses on all afternoon. The sun would soon duck behind the stadium and allow the cool night air to roll in.

Tip loved this atmosphere, and knew his good friend Hamilton would have appreciated it all the more. They had shared season tickets for football the past three seasons. Hamilton had been an MSU football fan since birth, and this would be the first home game that he had missed in eight years.

This last thought about Hamilton slowly drifted from Tip's mind as he glared into the clear blue sky. High above he could see the Goodyear blimp. The blimp was a surefire sign that it was a big game, or as student's liked to say, *A Blimp Game!* Tip's attention was drawn to the biplanes flying above with their advertised streamers trailing behind them. He was amazed that these planes never collided with one another, since their flight patterns were constantly crisscrossing.

One banner message read "Happy 21st Birthday Beatrice-Love Dan." The other two banners read: "Tripper's Bar supports MSU football" while the other one read "Try six toppings for $6 at Papa John's Pizzeria." Tip reread the last message out loud; his heart momentarily stood still, "Trysix, trysix...crysix, crysix, crisis."

Of course, how could he have been so stupid? Tip thought

to himself. What Hamilton was trying to tell him was so simple that he should have seen it all along. He instantly forgot about the game and all the excitement around it, and jumped down off the aluminum bleachers and headed toward the exit.

"Where are you going, Tip?" asked one of his fraternity brothers that came to the game with him.

"I just saw my aunt across the way. I've got to go talk to her. I'll meet you guys back at the house after the game," said Tip.

"Hopefully we'll see you there, but we might just go to P.T.'s for some victory brews. If we win there will be a good three-hour line if we aren't there early, and there will be so many hotties there tonight-not that you'll talk to them," his friend jibbed.

"Yea, but it's better than looking at your ugly mug all night," said the third friend. Both were drunkenly laughing and didn't notice that Tip was already gone.

Tip's fraternity brothers thought he was crazy for going to talk to his aunt during the game of the century, but he had been taking Hamilton's death extremely hard and had been acting strange lately so they didn't question him. Little did they know that he didn't have any aunts or uncles.

He had a difficult time getting out of the stadium. The student section was so crowded that they'd spilled out onto the tiny concrete exit stairs in front of section eleven. Students were starring at him as if he was crazy for leaving. But, they sympathized and made room for him when he explained he needed to use the facilities. A couple of students were physiologically affected by his declaration and come to think of it, yes; they too needed to use the latrine.

Tip was so excited about his Hamilton revelation that he sprinted all the way home, a distance just short of a mile.

Sanchez listened to the radio as Michigan State scored the go ahead touchdown on an interception return with thirteen minutes left to play. Their plan was working out perfectly; no one in their right mind would be leaving the game early. In fact the former hustle and bustle of the street had taken on an eerie calm as everyone was either at the game or watching the game on TV.

"You're all clear on the lower level. As far as I can tell no one's currently in the house," said Sanchez over the two-way radio.

Garcia went over to the mail slots and began sifting through each of the eighty individual slots. Maybe he was careless the first time he was here, or maybe the mailman put the envelope in the wrong slot. Going through every individual slot was an exhausting task, especially since a lot of slots hadn't been emptied in a week. He finally reached the last slot, Todd Wisely. When the missing envelope wasn't there he became extremely frustrated and annoyed. He was about to rip a framed poster off the wall to release some tension when he heard Sanchez's voice over the walkie-talkie.

"Garcia, get out of there immediately. Someone is rapidly approaching. Head down the backstairs right now," said Sanchez calmly but with purpose.

What the fuck is he doing? Sanchez thought to himself as he watched Tip jogging, no, almost sprinting, directly toward the house. Tip quickly entered the front of the house with his key.

Garcia was on the back stairwell as Tip entered through the front door. Out of habit, Tip slammed the giant red front door shut and headed around the corner where the mail slots were located.

He stared straight ahead at the huge framed poster that he usually paid little or no attention to.

Before him loomed the often overlooked picture, a picture that he certainly wasn't overlooking now. The picture, or more accurately poster, was framed in a lightwood and glass frame. It was a color pastel of a non-descript MSU running back. The running back had his hands held high in celebration in the end zone of Spartan Stadium. The caption above the inspirational player read CRY FOR SIX!

One person who did occasionally pay attention to the poster was Chris Hamilton. Hamilton received piles of mail at a time, so he usually didn't have time to look through all of it at once. Instead of cluttering the room with stacks of mail, he'd discovered a neat hiding place for it. The wooden frame that surrounded the CRY FOR SIX poster was unusually heavy. Hamilton found that he could lift the poster from the wall and place his mail on the lip of the frame on the back lower left corner. Tip was the only one in the house that knew of Hamilton's secret hiding place for his mail. Hamilton wasn't saying "crisis" when he was dying he was giving Tip a clue to look behind the "Cry for Six" poster.

Tip grabbed the left corner of the frame and began to pull it off the wall. He quickly put it back against the wall when he heard the sound of someone slowly coming up the back stairs.

# CHAPTER 16

For the past few hours, Lisa had been compiling a list of all the people who had donated money to Chi Theta over the two weeks she'd been working at the headquarters. She'd received eleven donations all in check form. She cross-matched the names of the donors to an alphabetized master list of all activated Chi Thetas. The list contained the person's birth date, college, current address and initiation date. The process of crosschecking was time-consuming and tiring on the eyes, especially since she needed to perform this surreptitiously and kept an eye out for anyone approaching. The laborious process had already chewed up the majority of her lunch hour and she was relieved to see that only two names remained.

The first nine crosschecks she performed all matched a current alumnus on the list. Surprisingly, all the addresses on file were accurate. She concluded that they must be regular contributors to Chi Theta due to their accurate addresses and small amounts of the checks.

Lisa read the name on the tenth check: Chris King. She flipped through several pages till she reached the beginning of the K's. She scanned the list until she got to King. There were fourteen Kings listed. There was a Craig King from California-Berkeley and a Charlie King from the University of Alabama Birmingham. But there was no Chris King listed. She looked over the back page, which was the revision/correction sheet, but again Chris King's name was noticeably absent.

She viewed the photocopy of the check. She looked at the left corner where she had written the return address from the envelope from which the check was received. She had photocopied all the checks since she had to turn the originals to the bank for processing.

There was no address on the corner of Chris King's, rather scribed in Lisa's handwriting was PM Miami. Her memory was refreshed upon reading her own notation. She remembered that there was no return address on this particular envelope, but it was postmarked from Miami. This check for $10,000 was by far the biggest she had come across. Ten of the other twenty-one checks were also from Miami. She jotted down these numbers into her red spiral-bound notebook.

Lisa glanced at her watch. It was a quarter to one, which meant it was time to waltz down the hall of Chi Theta National Headquarters to Janice McDoogal's desk. She was a round, robust woman in her mid sixties. She'd emigrated from Ireland twenty years ago and still had a noticeable and lovable Irish accent. She worked all twenty years in the U.S. at Chi Theta. She watched over the undergraduate Chi Thetas like they were her own grandchildren, of which she had five. Most of the undergrads affectionately called her Maim, because they'd heard through the grapevine that this is what she preferred.

All the Chi Theta's went out of their way to please Mrs. McDoogal. Although grueling work, she always volunteered to go to the undergraduate conventions and seminars. Some Chi Thetas kept in touch with her years after they'd graduated. One gentleman had been corresponding with her for almost twenty years and she was proud to brag that he'd become a very successful neurosurgeon. People in the office kidded her about having a long running affair with the gentleman.

Lisa enjoyed Mrs. McDoogal's company, and made a practice of devoting fifteen minutes of her lunch hour to visit her. Not only did she enjoy Mrs. McDoogal's company, but she also learned a lot about Chi Theta listening to her and by constantly asking questions. Lisa was careful about the types of questions she asked, since she didn't want to arouse suspicion.

Mrs. McDoogal was wearing her usual content pursed-lip smile and was attempting to complete the challenging *Washington Post* crossword puzzle. Several crossword crib books were spread out

# CRISIS

in front of her. The rest of her desk had several knick-knacks that she'd collected over the years. Despite these souvenirs, the desk still exuded tidiness.

"Good afternoon Mrs. McDoogal, how's life treating you today?" asked Lisa.

"Hello Holly, jolly good. Thank you very much for asking. How are you doing?"

"Fine thank you, although I wish I could work outside today. It's so beautiful out there."

"Yes, I do love Indian summer myself, never had anything quite like it in Ireland. Sometimes I think Mr. Valez has his shades drawn so he isn't tempted by the outside pleasures," said Mrs. McDoogal. "I know that I eat my heart out every time I glance out that big picture frame window over there yonder."

"Yeah, on a day this tempting it would be a good idea to have the shades drawn. Although, daydreaming isn't all that bad every once in awhile. Enough about the weather though, that's what everyone always talks about when they have nothing to talk about. Anything new and exciting happening over here today?" asked Lisa.

"Nothing too exciting, unfortunately. Although, the parents of Jim Cruz dropped their lawsuit against us, which is great news. Remember he's the Sigma Chi from Purdue," said Mrs. McDoogal.

"I'm sorry, I know you told me before, but what was the reason behind the lawsuit?" asked Lisa.

"He was the kid that had his jaw broken in that Chi Theta sponsored softball tournament. Apparently our chapter president at Purdue was able to find the waiver the kid signed releasing all liability in case of injury. So that was good news, but unfortunately as soon as we dropped that lawsuit we just as soon picked up another one," said a chagrined Mrs. McDoogal.

"Oh really, that's too bad. If you don't mind me asking, what does this latest lawsuit entail?" asked Lisa.

"Oh no trouble at all my dear. Are you familiar with the automobile accident up at Michigan State?" asked Mrs. McDoogal.

"Yes vaguely," said Lisa in a searching tone. Lisa could probably recite all the articles related to that accident at the drop of a hat.

"Well remember that the Chi Theta, Chris Hamilton, had a girl in the car with him?" asked Mrs. McDoogal.

"Yes, I remember something like that, she passed away too I believe," said Lisa.

"Bless Chris's heart, he was just the nicest kid and had everything going for him. But you know what they always say…it happens to the best, for the Lord's ready for them in heaven. Anyway, as I was saying, the girl in the car was a Ms. Amy Klein. Amy's parents have slapped us with a rather large lawsuit. Apparently, the house party, which she and Chris attended, had more than ten Chi Theta's present, so it's technically an official Chi Theta function. The Klein's have us dead to rights the way the law is written, but hopefully they'll drop the case if it's drawn out long enough. A lot of these cases get dropped once the emotions of the survivors calm down and they have time to think it through.

It's just terrible that something like that had to happen to two young kids with bright futures. It's especially surprising that Chris Hamilton would drink and drive like that. He seemed so innocent and responsible. He's one kid that I distinctly remember meeting at the regional and national functions. You could tell that he was really going to be somebody someday, one of those natural born leaders you could say," said Mrs. McDoogal.

He probably was a leader thought Lisa. It just might have been made to look like an accident-just like her innocent younger brother.

"Yes you're right, it's a shame. Oh, I have something to ask you. I was sending out thank you letters to the people who have donated money to us recently, but one donor's name doesn't seem to be on our master list. Is it at all possible that someone other than a former Chi Theta would donate money to the National Headquarters?" asked Lisa.

"Yes, it would seem unlikely, but since Mr. Valez took over, some of our biggest donors are apparently not former Chi Thetas.

Don't ask me how I found this out, but I do remember hearing something to that effect. That's one of the reasons Mr. Valez has been one of the most, if not, *the* most, successful General Directors," said Mrs. McDoogal. "He just seems to be a master at raising money. Even though he gets all of these donations he doesn't spend it frivolously. A majority of this money he reinvests into the upkeep of the Chapter houses across the nation. The students love him for this, because in the past most of renovation expenses were paid by the local chapter."

"That is rather interesting. Do you happen to know where I might obtain addresses for the non-Chi Theta donators? I'd like to be able to send them thank you notes. I've already checked the envelopes and accompanying checks for addresses, but with a rare exception, the address is omitted. If I could somehow determine their addresses, that would be a big help," said Lisa.

"I'm not sure where the random address list is located now. I know Barbara-Mrs. McDoogal had to stop talking, for she was getting very choked up at the thought of her former friend and co-worker. I'm sorry, I still haven't gotten used to it. It was so sudden and brutal. Barbara used to keep them in a file cabinet, but they aren't there anymore. Most of her stuff had already been moved when I returned from her funeral. Ask Mr. Valez, he might know where they're kept. He probably knew Barbara the best...the eulogy he delivered at the funeral was very moving-he is really a warm man once you get to know him."

"Okay, I'll be sure to ask him about the file cabinets," said Lisa as she glanced at her watch. "Looks like it's time to get back to work, I'll talk to you later."

"Go man the fort, Holly," said Mrs. McDoogal as she saluted Lisa with her right hand, which was still a bit moist from wiping back the tears caused by her thoughts of Barbara.

# CHAPTER 17

The footsteps on the backstairs were getting closer and closer. The sounds quickly approached the first floor. The structure of the Chi Theta house was set up so that if you entered from the front you were on the first floor, however if you entered from the parking lot in the back, you were in the basement.

The footsteps stopped and the door to the stairs swung open. Standing in the doorway was Brian Green, last year's President of the fraternity. Green was now working in Atlanta as a tax consultant for Home Depot.

Tip had seen Green at Hamilton's funeral, but didn't have the opportunity to talk to him. Green was one of those people who seemed to get along well with all kinds of people and groups, which is one of the main reasons he was previously elected President of the fraternity. As it turned out, he was a great choice for President, because he kept everyone loose. This liaise faire attitude contributed to him being nicknamed "The Joker" by his peers.

"Tip, what's up? I'm so glad someone is here. My car broke down on the way up here, but I finally got it running again. I'm so disappointed I'm missing such a great game. Ohio State just tied it up with a ninety-seven yard kickoff return. How come you're not at the game?" asked Green.

"I was at the game, but then I started feeling sick. I think I ate too much of the homecoming food we had put out for the alumni. I probably got a hold of some mayonnaise that had been out in the sun too long," lied Tip.

Green didn't buy Tip's response, but he didn't pursue it. He had heard that Tip had been acting very strange since Hamilton's death. It was understandable to him why Tip would react this way. He always saw those two as being inseparable.

"Is there anyone else in the house?" asked Green.

"I just got back a minute ago, but I don't think anyone else is here," responded Tip.

"Do you know what bar everyone went to?" asked Green.

"I know the line was too long at P.T.'s, so I think everyone went to Harpers," answered Tip.

"Alright, I'm gonna try to catch the end of the game there. Do you want to come with me?" asked Green.

"No, I think I'd better go lie down and give my stomach a chance to calm down. I want to make sure that I'm in good shape to go out tonight. This town will be crazy if we win," said Tip.

"Okay, I hope you feel better. I'll catch you later," said Green as he headed out the door for Harper's. Harper's, including its sister bar, Sensations, located in the basement, was the largest bars on campus. Sensations was very popular with the freshmen and sophomores. 19-year-olds were admitted. Harper's was the sports bar that appealed more to graduate students and alumni. Although Green didn't frequent Harper's much during his college career, it was a great place to watch a football game.

Now that Green was gone, Tip's attention returned to the CRY FOR SIX poster. He glanced over both his shoulders to see if anyone else was around. Convinced of his solitude, he gripped the lower corner of the poster with his right-hand. He pulled it away from the wall, while at the same time feeling behind the poster with his left-hand.

There were small scratch marks on the beige wall from the friction of the frame over time. He felt around, but there was nothing. He proceeded to do the same technique on the left side. As he had hoped, his hand clasped around a bundle of envelops. A small smile of satisfaction spread across his determined face. He quickly tucked them under his arm, and jaunted upstairs.

Tip was surprised to see that his door was cracked open. He could have sworn he locked it before leaving the game. He reasoned that perhaps an alumnus who'd lived in the room before had picked the lock with a credit card and gained access. Most of the guys in the house had learned to pick the locks. At one time or another everyone had locked themselves out of their rooms.

Almost every brother had a war story about how they were about to hook up with a beautiful co-ed only to find their room locked. The stories varied as to how each brother was able to ingeniously overcome the hurdle of the locked door. Solutions varied from scaling the house to enter through the window, to burning the door down. It truly behooved Chi Theta occupants to learn how to pick a room's lock with a credit card.

Tip cautiously approached the door and peered through the small crack into his room. The part of the room he could see was a mess, and it definitely wasn't an alumnus who'd broken in. Alumni may litter or rearrange things, but not too this degree.

He waited by the door and listened carefully for a couple of minutes. After making certain that no one was in the room, he cautiously entered. He immediately scanned the room again to make certain the intruder was gone.

He cleared a space on his tattered brown couch and sat down, making an effort to face the door. He got up and walked over and locked the door and placed a chair under the handle so the he was certain no one would be able to barge in.

The football game was drawing to its conclusion. The television set was to Tip's right and was currently showing the exuberant Michigan State students appearing like popcorn in the stands. The student body accomplished this popcorn effect by jumping up and down sporadically. Tip didn't even notice that the television was on. He vigorously sifted through Hamilton's mail.

The pile of mail consisted of a couple of credit card bills. Tip tossed these onto the floor. A telephone bill and a coupon book from the Student Book Store also found their way to the floor. The only two envelopes of significance were one from Hamilton's Aunt and an envelope from the Chi Theta National Headquarters.

Tip started by opening the envelope from Hamilton's Aunt and he was disappointed to discover that it was a belated birthday card. Inside the card was an apologetic note from his aunt and a check for twenty-five dollars. It drearily reminded Tip that Hamilton would have no more birthdays to celebrate.

He got a queasy feeling in his stomach as he stared ahead at the burgundy envelope with the Chi Theta crest embossing. He broke the envelope open with his right pointer finger, and was bewildered at what he discovered inside. Inside was a money deposit slip with a buck-slip attached. The memo was handwritten with a blue felt tip pen on cream-colored stationary. In very neat handwriting was the following message: Corrigan-Things went smoothly in New York. Will proceed as planned per your direction. Amount enclosed is less than usual due to costs incurred on the New York job, Sincerely RV. Below the signage were three one line typed and indiscernible abbreviations.

The first line of these notes had been crossed out in black pen and was difficult to read. The following three lines read as follows: 1014SFCC, 1018EPCATT and 1021CHIB271239E. The entire message made absolutely no sense to Tip as he reread it three times. He moved onto the personnel check, and his heart skipped a beat. The amount on the bank slip was $500,000. The bank slip appeared to be from a Cayman bank, as he couldn't read any of the writing except for the American dollar amount and an English phrase at the bottom that read: It's been a pleasure serving you.

Corrigan for some reason or another sounded familiar to Tip, maybe he had a math teacher in high school by that name. On the bottom of the memo was the initials RV.

Hamilton did want him to discover this envelope. He wondered if Hamilton knew what was inside the envelope. Obviously he didn't, because he hadn't opened the envelope before putting it behind the poster.

Whoever had ransacked Tip's room hadn't found what they were looking for. Tip now knew that Hamilton probably wasn't supposed to receive the contents inside the envelope. He also knew that whoever was in his room earlier that day wouldn't hesitate to

# CRISIS

kill again in their quest to obtain the envelope. Tip wished Hamilton were here. He could probably make more sense out of this discovery than he could.

His heart fluttered as the silence of the Chi Theta house was violated by the sound of the large red front door swinging violently open. The audacious sound was immediately followed by a drunken rendition of the Michigan State fight song. A dog-pile of Tip's fraternity brothers had returned from watching the game at the bar. Tip quickly stuffed the envelope into the front pocket of his jeans. All this time, Tip had completely forgotten about the football game. Judging from the jubilation downstairs, the Spartans must have been victorious.

Tip heard the high and whinny voice of Johnny Arnold above the vociferous clatter. Arnold was just the man Tip wanted to talk to. Arnold was a James Madison major and was filled with trivia and world events. James Madison was a college located in the heart of MSU's West Campus, which emphasized liberal arts, social sciences and pre-law.

Arnold was always the first person approached when someone in the house had a question that needed to be answered immediately. Arnold was famous for being able to win a Trivial Pursuit game on just one turn.

Tip followed Arnold's voice, which eventually lead him to the poolroom. Arnold was playing pool with fellow fraternity brothers Mark Oldey, John Dirton, and Tom Whittle. A cardboard case of Busch Light beer buckled between Whittle's massive calf muscles. Whittle was very protective of his beer.

"Hey guys what's up" said Tip as he entered the poolroom.

"The Spartans baby," roared Oldey and all four of them simultaneously raised their beer cans high in the air.

"Was that not the best game it was awesome baby!" yelled a rapturous Dirton.

"You were at the game, weren't you Tip? It must have been crazy being there, it looked crazy on TV. What a great day too. I'm surprised you aren't beat red from the sun baby!" said Whittle.

"Yeah, it was great," said Tip.

"You got back here pretty damn fast-or were we just screwing around at the bar and 7-Eleven longer than we thought?" asked Dirton in more of a statement rather than a question. "We thought for sure that we'd be the first ones back to the Lodge."

"I can't believe the freshman kicker made that forty-seven yarder. Plus, that freshman made a fifty-yarder early in the first quarter. That boy is getting L-A-I-D tonight," emphatically gyrated Arnold.

"Hey Tip, did you run onto the field after the game?" asked Dirton as he sank the eleven-ball in the corner pocket via a difficult two-ball combination.

"No, I didn't quite make it out onto the turf. It was kind of a zoo. The cops also started to arrest students that were jumping down from the stands to save the grass from getting torn up. With the way the stadium is set-up the field is so much lower than the stands. It's a good seven-foot drop to the turf. I didn't feel that my knee would appreciate such a leap." Tip made the liars mistake of going into too much detail. However since his fraternity brothers were highly intoxicated they didn't notice. "Where did you guys watch the game?" asked Tip, dexterously changing the subject. He was dying to ask Arnold some questions, but it wasn't quite the appropriate time or place.

"We watched it at BW3's. There are still a bunch of Lodgers there right now. It was so packed and crazy, it was awesome. Everyone was singing the fight song, and some old band members, they must have been fifty, brought their instruments and were jamming. There was tons of hot snapper everywhere, and everyone was hugging each other after the game. God I love college!" said Oldey. "By the way, why again did we leave the bar?" rhetorically asked Oldey to his pool playing pals.

"Yeah, I can imagine the excitement. It was like that at the game. Where are you guys off to tonight?" Tip asked. He was attempting to seem interested. He would normally be interested, but not today, he had too much on his mind.

"I know a couple of Theta Kappas who live at thirty-five Grove Street. They're throwing a little sin-dig tonight. It's the big, white house on your right, right next to a gray duplex. Some Delt Sigs nicknamed it the BOG house for *Babes on Grove*. It should be a great party, Tip you should come with us," said Whittle trying to coax Tip into going out. Whittle knew Tip hadn't done a thing socially since Hamilton's death.

"Yeah, we saw a couple of the hosts of the party at BW3s and they were already drunk," iterated Dirton. "Those girls are pretty damn hot, too."

"Yeah, thanks, that sounds like fun. Maybe I'll swing by there, what time are you guys heading over," said Tip although he had no intention of going.

"We're going to head over there in about an hour when Trey and Steak get home from Crunchy's," said Whittle as he headed into the guest washroom to release some of the beer he'd guzzled down at the bar.

Crunchy's is one of the older bars on MSU's campus and a favorite of the students and alumni. Crunchy's is renowned for serving buckets of beer. Each bucket is the equivalent of a case of draft beer. Presentation takes a backseat there, as the beer is dropped into a common plastic bucket. The buckets are similar to those typically used for washing cars or painting. To purchase a Crunchy Bucket, the table needs to have at least six people. Fraternities and some sororities had their own personal buckets with members names scripted on them, and they received a three-dollar discount when they took them down from the wall and filled them up. Some of these white plastic buckets had a distinct brownish tint from years of use.

Crunchy's was probably the craziest bar on campus. Promoting an atmosphere of lunacy made it difficult to get thrown out by the bouncers. The only sure-fire way to receive an early exit was to get naked or throw-up singing on the Karaoke Machine. Unfortunately, or fortunately, some people had been kicked out in the past.

"Oh, Arnold ...I had a question for you. Have you ever heard of anyone by the name of Corrigan?" asked Tip.

"Corrigan, like David J. Corrigan the Governor of Florida?" asked Arnold.

"Yes, I guess so," said Tip.

"Actually, I just wrote a ten-page paper about him for my political science class. God I hate that class. The teacher is such a joke. Why do you ask about Corrigan?" said Arnold.

"He was assigned to me in my Communications class. I have to do a five-minute speech about him on Tuesday," lied Tip. He didn't even have a Communications class.

"Bummer about the speech. I hate getting up in public. Thankfully, I'm not alone; the number one fear among the population is public speaking. But, I digress. I can't believe I used the word digress when I'm hammered-what kind of a loser am I? If you want to borrow that paper feel free, it's up on my desk in the orange folder by the phone. I have to warn you, the paper is shoddy at best. I wrote it in about an hour at Pete's Laundromat," said Arnold.

Arnold was extremely humble. A "shoddy" paper by his standards still meant it was a phenomenal piece of work compared to the average student.

"Yeah, if you don't mind. It'll help me out tremendously," said Tip.

"Don't mention it, my room should be unlocked. If the room's locked just call down and I'll run up there," said Arnold.

"Thanks, maybe I'll see you tonight," said Tip as he headed for the back stairwell.

Tip went up one flight of stairs and turned right to head down the forest green carpeted hallway. At the end of the hallway was room twelve, Arnold's room. He shared the room with Whittle and John Dumucci. The room was extremely tidy, reflecting the fact that the three roommates were unusually organized for college students.

The orange folder, which Arnold had described to Tip, wasn't by the phone as he had indicated. After a few seconds of searching, he spotted the folder sitting by the fish tank in the right corner of the room. Two good size piranhas, nicknamed Dumb and Dumber, swam peacefully. The vibrant orange of the folder reflected off the immaculate glass of the fish tank. He grabbed the folder and headed to the pacific confines of his room.

---

"You couldn't find it? It's got to be in there somewhere. Are you sure that you checked the room thoroughly? Are you sure that you were in the right room?" questioned Sanchez.

"Yeah, it was his room, and I checked that thing from top to bottom. I'm telling you, that fucking envelope is not in that room. I mean I destroyed the place. I checked every Goddamn mail slot, and it wasn't in there either. I think that little piss-ant Hamilton gave the envelope to somebody," said Garcia.

"It's definitely not out of the question, but I don't think so. If the contents of that envelope are as important as we think they are, anyone in their right mind that saw it would have reported it to the police after Hamilton's death. Although it would be fucking nice if we knew what the hell was in the envelope, it might help us track the frickin' thing down. Has your East Lansing Police contact indicated any new developments to you regarding the investigation?" asked Sanchez.

"Nope. No word from him yet and he better start bringing some value to the table, because I'm sick of sacrificing some of our up-front earnings to that leach," said Garcia.

"It pisses me off as well, but we've got to have an informant at the station just in case there are any developments. I really don't think Hamilton gave the envelope to anyone. By the bewildered and scared look in his eyes the other night, I think Hamilton was telling the truth, I think he misplaced it somewhere and never even saw the contents of it. Hell, we haven't even seen what the hell's in there. We better be damned sure we find the envelope and its contents before someone else does," said Sanchez.

"Well we aren't going to get a better chance than what we had today to check the house. What the hell was that kid coming home from the game so early for? If you ask me, there's something fishy with that kid not only coming home early, but also sprinting to get home. I mean, what was he in such a hurry for? I was going to stay and check the kid out, but another snot-nosed punk came in the backdoor, so I had to leave. If you ask me, I think that we best checkout this Tipton punk. He sure has been acting a bit off," said Garcia.

"I'm thinking along the same lines. We're definitely going to have to keep a close eye on him," said Sanchez.

---

Tip opened the cover of the orange folder and immediately said "of course." Of course he'd heard of David J. Corrigan. Printed on Arnold's coversheet in bold lettering was Governor David J. Corrigan. He was the Democratic Governor form Florida who was the chief supporter of the President's ban on illegal Cuban entry into the United States. Since most television talk shows and radio call in shows couldn't book the President, they usually had Governor Corrigan on the air instead to discuss this controversial topic.

Tip flipped through Arnold's report, which as expected, was extremely thorough. The report explained that Corrigan had held the Florida seat in the Senate for the past five years, and was extremely popular with the Florida residents. His popularity was attributed to his strong position on stopping the illegal importation of drugs into the state. Arnold's report went on to explain that under Corrigan's "Beat the Street" policy, more than a thousand drug busts had been made over the past three years in Florida. This number of arrests was greater than the arrests for the past twenty years combined. These busts also confiscated over fifteen million dollars in drug money; money which was contributed to local community programs and parks.

As a result of the good public relations received from the "Beat the Street" program, Florida tourism, the state's greatest source of revenue, was booming at record levels. This increase in tourism resulted in approximately 7,000 more jobs for Florida residents and an additional $125,000,000 in state revenue.

There were a couple of photocopied pictures in the middle of Arnold's report. Corrigan was very handsome and in phenomenal shape for a guy in his early forties. There was also a picture of his wife and kids-the All-American family. His wife was strikingly attractive and three years younger than him. They had an eight-year-old son and six-year-old daughter. Arnold's report explained that Corrigan was the projected independent candidate for President, attempting to dethrone the popular Republican incumbent, John Marshall.

Tip went down to the basement copy room, an old unused closet that now had a small, but effective Cannon copier. The Chi Thetas had purchased the copier after they'd raised a tremendous amount of money hosting a sand volleyball tournament at the Lake Lansing Recreational Beach last spring. The copier was two years old and everyone wondered how they'd survived without one for so long. The nearest copy place was Kinko's Copies on Grand River, about a ten-minute walk from the house. Kinko's was also rather expensive on a college student's limited budget. Tip duplicated Arnold's report and returned it to its natural resting-place by the piranha tank.

Tip walked through the house looking for Tom Fozzy. He had almost given up looking for Fozzy, when he stumbled across him lying on the couch in room zero. Fozzy was busy (or not so busy) watching the highlights of that afternoon's MSU football game. He looked completely whipped from a long day of partying, cheering, and celebrating. He was attempting to keep the Sandman at bay when Tip entered the room.

"All right, just the man I was looking for," said Tip as he sat down in the burgundy recliner by the beat-up plaid couch.

"What can I do for you, or do you for," asked Fozzy.

Fozzy was a criminal justice major with plans of going to law school when he graduated in two years. His uncle was in the FBI and was killed in the line-of-duty two years ago. He was obsessed with becoming a FBI agent, and loved reading any material discussing the subject. He owned a nine-millimeter and went to the shooting range at least once a week. He had to keep the gun in a locker at the range however, for guns and knives weren't allowed in the fraternity house.

Fozzy loved telling his uncle's FBI stories to anyone who would listen. Though, most of the stories were very interesting, he did have a tendency to embellish the truth. The guys in the house teased him by calling him Dirty Harry. At a time when most college students were trying to figure out who they were and what they wanted to become, one thing was certain: Everyone knew that Fozzy would make a great FBI agent someday.

"Foz, I've got a question for you," said Tip.

"You can't borrow my car. I already lent it out," stated Fozzy.

"No, I don't want your car, I've got a question about the FBI," said Tip.

Fozzy's eyes widened and ears perked up at the sound of this, the Sandman would have to wait. "Go ahead shoot, no pun intended," grinned Fozzy.

"At least you harbor no ambitions of become a comedian my friend. If you had to report something to the FBI or police about a crime or discovery, and you were a regular citizen, is their a specific channel you're suppose to go through?" asked Tip.

"Yes, why, what's up?" asked an aroused Fozzy.

"Oh, it's really nothing to get excited about, it's just my little sister, she's kind of taken an interest in the FBI after watching the movie *The Fugitive*. She's a huge fan of Tommy Lee Jones. I told here I might be able to answer some of her questions and maybe get some information from you, if you don't mind," said Tip.

"Yeah sure, I'd love to help her. I'd be glad to give her some information," said an excited Fozzy. Fozzy got up and walked down the hall to his room, room three. Fozzy spent more time in room zero than in room three, since room zero had a huge comfortable couch and big entertainment center: thirty-two inch plasma TV and killer stereo. The occupants of room zero, brothers Fitzpatrick and Vanilla were rarely there. Vanilla played on the basketball team, while Fitzpatrick had a serious girlfriend. Most girlfriends liked the gentlemen of Chi Theta. But, at the same time, girls didn't enjoy spending an exorbitant amount of time in the Lodge. After all, the Lodge housed seventy guys; guys being testicular idiots most of the time.

Tip could hear Fozzy rustling in the file cabinet before he returned to room zero with a pamphlet in hand.

"The number for the FBI Midwest area contact is on this sheet. There's also some additional information you may find helpful as well. If she wants to call this number they will be more than happy to answer all of her questions and send her some updated material," said Fozzy.

"Oh this is great, she'll love this. Do you need it back?" asked Tip.

"No, no go ahead and give it to her. I have a subscription. They send me that stuff all of the time. I use most of it for scratch paper anyway. For the most part it's just general info that I already know," said Fozzy.

"Great, thanks a lot. Oh, by the way, are you going out tonight?" asked Tip.

"Yeah, I think I might go to that Pledge party at Sigma Chi, but I've got to take a nap before I think about doing anything," said Fozzy. Fozzy laid his six-foot-three and brawny body back down onto the cushy couch.

"Maybe I'll see you at Sigma Chi," said Tip as he exited the room. He was pleased with the amazingly good luck he was experiencing today and hoped it continued.

Tip didn't enjoy having to lie to his friends, but he thought it was the best thing to do given the situation. He didn't want to create a huge stir and cause chaos to erupt in the fraternity by suggesting that Hamilton may have been murdered. Rumors would start flying and pretty soon the press would swarm like a bunch of hyenas to a fresh kill. No, he couldn't tell anyone, for he currently had the advantage. Whoever the enemy was didn't know that he had a hunch that there was more to the story then a simple drunk driving accident. He knew that if word got to the press, he'd have no chance of ever catching the killers. If the story became public it would also jeopardize his safety and that of those around him.

He scaled the ladder that was carved out of the wooden wall and hopped onto his bed. All of his stuff was still in order up here. The intruder obviously didn't realize that a person slept up here. The loft he was resting on was difficult to notice. It was just above the door and about twelve feet up from the floor. His bed could not be seen from the floor, and he enjoyed this seclusion. It was worth the pain of climbing the uncomfortable square rungs of the inset ladder.

It was still debatable whether it was worth suffering through the unbearable heat of September. Tip's loft bed was at the uppermost corner of the house and it was ridiculously hot for the first few weeks of the semester, but it was very pleasant thereafter.

Tip leaned forward and grabbed his phone. He skimmed the top page of the pamphlet Fozzy had given him, until he found the number he was looking for. He punched in the numbers for the general information line and waited for the long distance call to go through.

"Hello, you've reached The Federal Bureau of Investigation. If you have a touch-tone phone please press one now," said the computer generated female voice. Tip proceeded to press one.

"Thank you. If you're calling regarding tour hours or our location; press one; if you're calling regarding group tours, press two. If your call is regarding information pamphlets about the FBI, press three. If your call is to inquire about joining the FBI, press four please. If your call is relating to any other matter please stay on the line and an operator will assist you momentarily," said the computer voice.

Tip waited on the line for about two minutes before a sweet, southern, female operator answered the phone.

"Federal Bureau of Investigation, this is Virginia speaking how may I help you?"

"Yes, I believe I've stumbled upon some evidence that may be pertinent to an investigation," said Tip.

"Have you reported it to the local police, sir?"

"No, I haven't reported it to the local police."

"Is there a reason you haven't reported it to the police sir?" asked the operator.

"I feel it's probably beyond their capability. But the main reason is, I don't want this leaked to the local press. I believe that whoever is behind the wrongdoing is still in the area, and I don't want to alert them. What I believe to be relevant evidence, may not be evidence at all. But, I'm hoping that someone there can try and help make sense of it. As I previously mentioned, I think that another party is very interested in the information I currently possess," said Tip.

"Well sir, we always suggest that pertinent information be reported to the local authorities, but we occasionally make an exception. If you don't mind, I'll need to ask you a few more questions. Why do you feel someone else would like to obtain the information you have?"

"Well, take for instance today. Just a couple of hours ago, someone broke into my room in the Chi Theta fraternity at Michigan State University and ransacked my belongings as well as my roommate's. My roommate was killed in a car accident last week, but I don't think it was an accident. I feel that the document I found today is incriminating to some third party and that they were here today looking to find it."

"Is anything missing from the break-in?" asked Virginia in her smooth southern accent.

"Everything seems to be here, as best as I can tell. I just got home a couple of minutes ago and haven't had the chance to take a thorough inventory," said Tip.

"Have you reported this break in to anyone?"

"No, I haven't, due to the reasons I stated earlier,"

"Do you feel you're in any danger now?"

"No, not right now. There are about seventy other fraternity brothers in the house. However, I feel that if this other party determines I have the information they want, I may be in grave danger.

"This will be difficult, but the best thing to do is to act naturally and continue with your typical daily routine. I'm now going to transfer you to the investigation department, please hold while I transfer you," said the operator.

Tip waited on the line for about a minute before hearing the phone start to ring, it was picked up on the second ring.

"Investigations, this is Karen. How can I direct your call?"

"Yes, I believe that I have some information that someone in your department may find relevant, or help assist me in its meaning," said Tip.

"This information sir, do you know what it pertains to. If you could be as specific as possible it will make our process a lot simpler," said Karen kindly.

"I believe, it might in some way, involve Florida Governor David Corrigan," said Tip.

After some further preliminary questions from Karen, Tip finally got the answer he was looking for:

"Thank you sir. I'm going to transfer you to Agent Nick Potts, he handles all correspondence related to Governor Corrigan. He probably won't be able to take your call today, but he is in. He's going to eventually need a written statement from you with the information you've obtained. I'm going to give you his mailing address. It's Mr. Nicholas Potts, Investigation Department, Federal Bureau of Investigation, Floor #5, Office #34, Washington D.C. 48309," said the operator.

"I'm sorry did you say office number forty-four?"

"No, office thirty-four sir. I'm transferring you to Agent Potts now, please hold," said the operator.

It wasn't unusual for agents to work on the weekends. Many often took two weekdays off instead. It was unusual for Karen to transfer Tip to him, however. But Potts instructed Karen; along with the other receptionists that morning to immediately transfer to him any calls relating to David Corrigan.

Tip once again went through the same procedure, only this time his wait was around five minutes.

# CRISIS

"Hello Mr. Tipton, this is Agent Nick Potts speaking. Karen informs me that you may have some information related to Governor Corrigan. I apologize for all the questioning you had to go through, but we receive an average of fifty calls a month associated with Governor Corrigan and only about three of those are legitimate. And, with the election coming up, things have been even more hectic. Most of these calls are bogus, so the operators must screen all the calls. I hope you understand."

"Not a problem at all sir. I'm actually pleasantly surprised to be talking to an agent," Tip said sincerely.

"We're always thankful for legitimate individuals who make the effort to contact us, and Karen believes you're legitimate. I know you just told this info to Karen, but please tell me what you have. If you don't mind, be specific as possible but also try to be brief, I've had an extremely busy afternoon," said Agent Potts.

Tip was puzzled by the contradictory requests, but preceded to tell Agent Potts the quick version of Hamilton's death. Tip then told of his eventual discovery of the letter that was intended for someone else. He even read the note to Potts.

Agent Potts listened intently and waited patiently until Tip ended his story before saying a word. "Do you have any idea what the contents of the letter mean?" asked Agent Potts.

"No, not really, I'm not even sure if it involves the Governor. It could very likely be someone else with the same name. I just assumed that the letter had to involve someone of importance for someone to want to kill for it. I'm going to try and decipher the contents, but I felt I had to alert the authorities about it in the meantime. I was hoping you could do some of the investigation for me, because I'm by no means an expert, rather a novice, in fact," said Tip.

"Have you told or shown anyone else this information?" asked Potts.

"No, I haven't yet. I didn't want to excite anyone if it turned out to be nothing. As I explained to the first operator, someone ransacked my room this afternoon, and I feel they were looking for this letter. I didn't want whoever was in my room this afternoon to know that I was privy to this information, you can imagine the ramifications," said Tip.

"You did the right thing by coming to us first Mr. Tipton. You're right, it would be best for all involved if you didn't mention this to anyone else, at least not until we have more clarification on the matter. There are a lot of Corrigan's in the world son. It's probably unconnected to the Governor, but it's worth having us check it out.

I'm going to need you to Federal Express me the original letter and envelope, preferably as soon as possible. Our workload is fairly light right now, so if you could get it to me, preferably tonight, I might stand a chance of checking into it. Is there a place convenient to you to overnight a package Mr. Tipton?" asked Potts.

"Yeah, I can do it at the Union's Fed Ex Drop Box which is just two blocks down the street," said Tip.

"Great, I'd really appreciate it. Send the package to me at home, because I won't be in the office tomorrow." Potts proceeded to give Tip the address. "Hopefully I will have time to look over the matter this week, and give you a call. However, if I'm too busy, I'll definitely get in touch with you next week. I'll need your phone number and address in case I need to reach you." Tip supplied Potts with the necessary information. "Also, on the Fed Ex package, check the box that says bill the recipient, and you'll be glad to know that if your information is relevant to any of our investigations, you will be eligible for a two thousand dollar cash reward," said Potts.

"You can keep your money, Mr. Potts," said Tip.

"Well, I'll keep an eye out for that package, and you're doing the right thing by keeping this matter confidential between us. Once again, I thank you for your assistance and will be speaking with you soon. If you need anything else in the meantime, don't hesitate to call," said Potts.

"Thank you, I'll keep that in mind," said Tip and with that he hung up.

Tip slid a waffled heather-gray long-sleeve shirt over his head. FBI Agent Potts immediately placed another phone call.

# CHAPTER 18

With the exception of the check and accompanying envelope of the deceased Chi Theta donator, Lisa hadn't found anything significant during her investigation. She was still attempting to do a background check on this gentleman's estate. She thought it might have been in his will to donate a certain amount to the fraternity for a certain length of time. Further information on this man was extremely difficult to track down because his address was so nebulous. This was understandable since he died in 1997. She didn't even know if he had any surviving relatives; she was constantly running into dead ends.

A fax transmission was currently printing out across from her desk. She slid out of her low-backed swivel chair and crossed the room to get it. It was a construction quote from Merchel for proposed restructuring work on the chapter house at Arizona State University. She had seen three other quotes from Merchel like this one. The previous work quotes she'd perused were for the chapter houses at the Indiana University, Syracuse University and the University of North Carolina.

Lisa had already done some exploratory research on how other fraternities handled renovations and repairs on their chapters across the nation. She discovered that Chi Theta was the only fraternity that contracted every job to the same builder, no matter what was necessary or where the chapter was located. All other fraternity chapter houses hired out local labor, usually private contractors for maintenance and renovation. Moreover, National Headquarters only reimbursed them if the renovations were approved in advance, and not all requests were approved. Chi Theta chapters submitting requests to the National Headquarters for renovations or maintenance were rarely, if ever, turned down.

Mrs. McDoogal explained to Lisa that Chi Theta had an agreement with Merchel to handle all of their contract work. This enabled Chi Theta to get supplies from a large vendor at a superincumbent rate and also allowed a majority of the chapter houses to have universal fixtures and furniture. In essence they were able to achieve economies of scope and scale. Mrs. McDoogal also explained that Mr. Valez was extremely popular with the students because he approved every rebuilding/renovation request that was "reasonable." Valez could afford to do this by virtue of the generous amount of charitable donations the National Fraternity steadily received. He also had the philosophy that this policy of goodwill would reap benefits in the future. Valez hypothesized that students who became successful in the business world would remember these renovations and donate money back into the system.

Lisa took the fax transmission over to her desk, sat back down and pulled a file from the lower left drawer. She found the reference sheet she was looking for inside the file. To avoid the hassle of being consulted on every construction quotation, Mr. Valez had produced a sheet with specific numbers on what each construction job should cost. Every job on the sheet had a ceiling price, and if the quotation was over that price, she was required to get Mr. Valez's signature. If the quote was under the ceiling price, then she was able to rubber stamp Valez's approval.

The three previous quotations Lisa had reviewed were all well under the ceiling price. The repair quote she currently held in her hand was for the replacement of an old brick walkway leading up to the chapter house at Arizona State University. This quote fell under the category of porch and sidewalk repair. The quotation for the job was about $10,000, which was below the $12,000 ceiling price on Valez's matrix. Lisa quickly stamped Mr. Valez's approval and made a copy of it for her files. She then placed the approved form in the overnight envelope.

# CRISIS

Tip headed out the front door of the fraternity and cut right across the lawn and dirt driveway of the neighboring Alpha Omicron Sorority house. The grass had long since been worn away on this route since members used it as a shortcut instead of using the right-angled sidewalks. The Chi Thetas knew their geometry; the hypotenuse is always shorter than the sides of a triangle. Tip usually made a point of trying to save the lawn by using the sidewalk. But today, he was too focused on his mission to attempt preserving the pulchritude of the lawn.

He headed for the Student Union at the end of Abbott. Walking at an extremely brisk pace, he crossed over at the Abbott and Albert Street intersection. Beggar's Banquet and Rick's American Cafe whizzed by on his left. He didn't realize the significance of the name *Rick's American Café* until he'd studied "Casablanca" in his film class. Rick's American Café was the name of the bar in the movie.

A line had already formed at the back of P.T. O'Malley's. P.T.'s had capacity for two hundred patrons. Once capacity was reached, the Fire Marshall forced the owners to work on a one in, one out basis. P.T.'s had ingeniously roped off the alley directly behind its backdoor entrance, making this contained space an adjunct to the bar. This was of legal importance, because P.T.'s could now serve patrons waiting in their tedious line. This incremental business supplied a hefty profit, since students would wait in line for two to three hours. It also appeased the students, who in the past had grown surly and angry when their buzzes evaporated while waiting in line.

Most of those waiting in line didn't seem to mind the overpriced beer today (four dollars for a can of Bud Light). At a wholesale price of $14 a case, discounting overhead, the bar would make a nice margin. Many of those waiting in line were recent alumni with high paying jobs and no dependents. The bar waitresses loved Homecoming, as the alumni were munificent tippers, the opposite of the usual monetarily challenged student clientele. Some of the older bartenders and waitresses thought it ironic that the affluent alumni there today were the budget riddled students of yesterday. These alumni had not forgotten those days, which is a main reason why they often foisted ridiculous gratuities at the staff. The hefty tips were also the result of the twenty-year-old waitresses effervescent demeanors.

Tip passed by the Land Shark Bar and Grille and headed across Grand River Avenue. He had to break into a jog to make it across the street before the flashing Don't Walk sign became solid red.

Tip took the concrete stairs leading into the Student Union two at a time, requiring only three strides to reach the front door. The Michigan State Student Union is an impressive building. Although fairly modern, built in 1967, it was designed to match the architecture of the older buildings on North campus. Ivy was prevalent over its beautiful brown stonework, culminating at a point approximately five stories above the giant oak cathedral-style doors. He entered the Union and climbed the ten stairs two at a time and headed through a set of double doors, placing him on the main floor. He felt a rush of warm, humid air come over him.

This temperature fluctuation was the result of heat generated by the five hundred people gathering at the Union's large screen television. The crowd was comprised mostly of students who were intently watching the post-game celebration in Spartan Stadium.

The television was located in the lounge area, which was a huge open space with comfortable chairs, couches, and tables. Most students used this area to take a break from studying or to conduct meetings with their respective study groups. Those huddled around the television were the truly unfortunate ones on campus. These "huddlers" either had to work at the Union or had vainly attempted to study on a football Saturday.

Normally, Tip would have been joined them. But today he whisked by the crowd and climbed the side stairway to the copy center located on the second floor. He grabbed the #5 rectangular plastic copy counter. He made sure he inserted the correct end of it in the upright position (the orange arrow pointing up helped), and proceeded to photocopy the letter.

Upon completion, he walked over to the counter to pay for the copy. There was no attendant in sight, so he left a dime along

# CRISIS

with the tabulating cartridge on the counter. The attendant wasn't there because she was entrenched in the outcome of the dramatic football game. Most of the Union's stores were also deserted since the irresistible force of the football game had drawn customers and employees to the big screen.

Tip headed back downstairs, and was again hit by the massive heat wave as he proceeded past the lounge and toward the post office. Tip performed the seemingly arduous task of completing the required Fed Ex paperwork. The Fed Ex drop-off station was close to full and he had a difficult time jamming his letter into the shoot. He was startled by the cacophony of sound that erupted from the lounge. Students were diving over the furniture to hug one another after watching the replay of Michigan State's game-winning forty-seven yard field goal as the clock expired. Everyone already knew that State was victorious, but many were seeing how they won the game for first time. Other students, who had already seen the play, still couldn't believe it and their overabundance of exuberance proved it.

Tip was in his best mood since Hamilton's death. He'd found a vital piece of evidence concerning his friend's mysterious death, and the home team had won in dramatic fashion. It was difficult not to get swept up in the euphoria of the moment.

The post-game show drew to its conclusion and Tip was washed out the door by the he rd of students intent on expressing to the outside world their ecstatic feelings about the victory. Others pouring out of bars, dorms, and surrounding apartments joined these students. By this time, students who attended the game had made their way back to the campus hub at the intersection of Grand River and Abbott. Traffic ceased to flow as students celebrated in the streets.

---

Sanchez and Garcia didn't spot Tip coming out of the Union, even if they had, there was no way to get to him. A wall of jovial human flesh surrounded them. All traffic on Grand River was at a standstill; the students had taken control of the streets. Students in the westbound lane were chanting Go Green! While the Eastbound lane retorted Go White! Some drivers were becoming frustrated, but most had just come from their post-game tailgates and were happy to wait and relish the big Spartan victory. A couple of passengers actually got out of their cars to join this impromptu block party. Smart drivers understood that it would be unwise to confront the emotional crowd.

Amazingly, nobody was getting violently out of control to the point of causing injury or damage to personal property. The only troubling event occurred when two excited students climbed atop the roof of the bus shelter and then leapt on top of a Metro bus. The students were enjoying the moment by dancing on the bus to the delight of the crowd. However, when the bus was eventually able to move through the traffic light, the now "bus surfing" students were even more excited. With arms raised in the air in triumph, one of the students barely missed being clocked in the head by an approaching stoplight.

Tip went with the flow of the crowd, which was taking him toward his house anyway. He encountered numerous friends on the way home and was hugging and high fivin' everyone. One of the television stations wanted to interview him. They wanted him to describe the scene, because they didn't want to risk going into the rambunctious crowd. It was now dark and everyone would be going crazy to get in front of the camera if they turned on its powerful light in the sea of bodies.

Tip entered the house and veered straight for his bed. He realized that he was probably the only student on campus that wasn't going to party tonight, however his heart was partying at the thought of vindicating Hamilton's death.

---

Sanchez answered the phone on the second ring. He recognized the deep breathing on the other line and immediately wished he hadn't answered the call.

"What's our status?" asked Valez.

"Not good, we haven't been able to locate the envelope," said Sanchez.

"I know you haven't. Another kid has it. A kid named Paul Tipton," said Valez.

"He does. How do you know?" asked Sanchez.

"I said he has it, and that's all you need to know," said Valez.

"We've been following Tipton the past couple of days, because he was the other kid's roommate. He was acting rather strange today," said Sanchez.

"He's mailing the envelope to the FBI sometime today. Before he does, make sure you take him out and get the envelope. I don't have to remind you to make it clean this time. Ice his body where it'll be difficult to find. The authorities are going to be very suspicious when he's missing," said Valez.

Sanchez gulped and debated whether to tell Valez what had probably already happened. He decided it was better to take his medicine now, "Boss, we've been following Tipton most of the day and have temporarily lost him. We had him until he went into the Student Union building. I checked, and there's both a post office and Fed-Ex drop-box in there. It's difficult to follow him because this place is crazy with football fans. He certainly had a chance to mail something."

"You'd better find him immediately and any copies of that letter," said Valez. The phone went dead.

## CHAPTER 19

Tip made no further progress on the mystery Sunday or Monday morning. He was exhausted and decided to lie down for a quick nap.

After ten minutes of peace, he was awakened by a short series of raps on the door. It wasn't obnoxious by any means, but it was still annoying to be awakened by someone knocking on a door. His response was typical of someone being abruptly awakened from a sound sleep-a surreal point when everything seems five times as loud.

He debated whether to answer the knock at the door, but figured it was time to get up from his nap anyway. He began his descent down the ladder; he'd never get used to the uncomfortably hard wooden rungs on his bare feet. He once considered strapping some form of cushioning over the rungs, but he didn't want to cover up the natural wood with something tacky like shag carpeting. He skipped the last two rungs by jumping down to the old floor making a huge thud as he landed-he was happy to not feel anything in his knee. His landing sounded like a clap of thunder to the residents directly below in Room 3.

Tip unlocked the door and pulled it toward him.

"Oh, my bad. Were you sleeping? I didn't mean to wake you up, sorry about that," said Jason Burke.

Burke was almost a spitting image of Tip. The only noticeable difference was Burke was about an inch shorter and weighed about nine pounds less. Their likeness was amazing, and people on campus constantly mixed them up. The worst part of the mix-up was the onslaught of apologies Tip and Burke had to endure when a stranger realized their mistake. Now, side-by-side they looked very different. However for strangers, the mistake was easily understood.

Tip really enjoyed Burke's company. He'd even given Burke, who hadn't yet turned twenty-one, his old drivers license. Although they couldn't enter the same bar together, they could meet there. The bouncers had to card so many people over the course of an evening that they usually wouldn't remember a particular name. In fact, most bouncers rarely looked at the name if the face matched the picture and the birth date equated to twenty-one. That being said, a bouncer at the Land Shark did give Burke a hard time once. The Land Shark bouncer apparently knew Tip from high school. In that particular instance, Burke just calmly snatched the ID away from the bouncer and strode home to the shouts of the bouncer fading in the distance. Fortunately for Burke, that bouncer graduated last spring. Also, Tip only went to the bar a handful of times a year anyway.

"What are you up to?" asked Tip.

"Just stopped by here after class to grab some grub," said Burke.

"What is for lunch today?"

"Submarine sandwiches, minestrone soup and potato salad. The potato salad is awesome. You better hurry down to the kitchen before it's all gone; there wasn't much left when I was down there."

Most fraternities were notorious for having horrendous food but Chi Theta had been fortunate to hire a great cook two years ago. Mrs. McManus was like a mother to the guys in the house. And in return, the guys treated her with the same respect and love they would give their own mother. In some cases, guys treated her even better than their own mothers.

Her presence also caused the meals to be more civilized. Before her arrival, it wasn't unusual for a food fight to occur at least once a week. These food fights were also the result of the food being more suitable for throwing than eating. The only problem with her cooking was that a majority of the out-of-house brothers came over to eat meals on a regular basis. A brother's out of house dues entitled them to only three meals a week at the house. For an extra $100 they were entitled to unlimited meals for the term. Due to this unorthodox system, random numbers of brothers showed up everyday. This made it difficult to plan, so Mrs. McManus always cooked for eighty people. A brother was pretty much guaranteed a wholesome lunch if they made it to the kitchen before one o'clock, but anytime after that was risky. Tip glanced at the battery powered wall clock. The old black plastic hands were bent but still clearly said twelve-forty. It was definitely time for him to motor his ass down to enjoy Mrs. McManus's latest creation.

"Yeah, you're right, I better go grab something right now, I'll swing back up here in a couple of minutes," said Tip.

"Okay, I'll hang out here, I don't have anymore classes today," said Burke as he plopped down on the sofa and grabbed the stereo remote control.

Tip returned five minutes later holding a white porcelain plate with two submarine sandwiches and a huge helping of potato salad. Clenched between his teeth was a miniature bag of Rold Gold pretzels.

"The stupid juice machine is broken again," mumbled Tip with the bag of pretzels still in his mouth.

"Yeah, apparently it went out this morning. Do you know who we should call to get it fixed?" asked Burke.

"Unfortunately I don't."

Tip knew that Hamilton would've had the situation corrected by now. Besides missing Hamilton as a friend, Chi Theta missed Hamilton as its chief administrator. Hamilton knew the ins and outs of the house, and aside from a little help from the house President, ran the house by himself. Hamilton had been elected Brother of the Year as a junior. It was the first time in the award's fifty-one year history that a junior classman had been bestowed with the honor.

"Tip, I need to ask you a huge favor. Remember that job I took last week working at Melting Moments Ice Cream Parlor?" asked Burke.

"Yeah, you showed me that hot pink uniform you had to wear. You were damn sexy," laughed Tip.

"Well…I think you'll look like the man in pink baby. I have a ten-page paper due in my War and Morality class tomorrow at eight o'clock. I had the thing done last night, but when I was proof reading it, I accidentally erased it on the computer and I hadn't yet printed out a hard copy. Anyway, my first day of work is tonight from five to ten, and they really don't know what I look like. I just dropped off the application and didn't need to go through a formal interview process. Since you look like me, I was hoping you could take my shift tonight. That way, I can keep my job and they won't be too suspicious when I work the next shift. I'm banking on different people working the next shift.

There will only be one other person working there, and the manager shouldn't be there either. The manager apparently has a Karate class on Mondays. You'll get paid seven bucks an hour and if you want I'll give you an extra twenty, I'm desperate. I really need to get a good grade on this paper, but at the same time I also need to keep that job to pay for my books."

"I'd love to help you, but I have a class tonight at eight o'clock, and I'd skip it, but attendance counts as part of your grade. Unless….. you went to class for me, otherwise I don't know how I could help you," responded Tip.

"That might be an idea, how long is the class?"

"Less than an hour. It's supposed to go from eight to nine-twenty, but the professor always lets us out at eight-fifty or before."

"Yeah if you don't mind working for me, I can definitely go to your class. Where is it?" asked Burke.

"It's in Erickson Hall, and I think the room number is number one-twenty. It's the first room on your left if you came in from the wing closest to the river, you know the one facing Wells Hall," said Tip.

"I know exactly where you're talking about. This will work out great because I'll be at the computer center working on my paper, so I can just pop right over there. It might even be a nice break for me.

# CRISIS

I'll be able to give you the notes from the class tomorrow at lunch," Burke said excitedly.

"Yeah, and if I'm not here just throw the notes on my bed. Burke, you should pay attention, because the professor sometimes gives us a quiz at the end of his lecture. Don't worry, if you're even remotely listening during the hour you can ace it with ease. You still have my ID right? The professor will ask for it if he gives you a quiz. He's really paranoid about cheating. A tall blonde guy might sit next to you his name is Steve. You may want to arrive just as class starts or a little late and try to sit by yourself. Otherwise, Steve will talk your ear off and he will definitely recognize that you are not me. Do you have the Melting Moments uniform with you?" asked Tip.

"Yeah, it's right here in my backpack," Burke pulled it out, "wow it got kind of wrinkly, sorry about that," said Burke.

"Imagine that, a shirt got wrinkly after being stuffed in a backpack all day, what's the world coming to?" It was the first time Tip had used his sarcastic wit since Hamilton's death. "What kind of duties am I going to have to perform while I'm pretty in pink?"

"It's simple. You're basically going to scoop ice cream for most of the night. I'm sure the person that's working with you will teach you how to ring up the sales on the register and explain your other duties. The next time I work they're going to think I'm an idiot when I don't know anything that they're going to teach you tonight."

"Don't worry, Burke, everybody already thinks you're an idiot," interrupted Tip.

"I'll leave your uniform on my bed, and you can pick it up when you drop off my notes tomorrow. You don't have to pay me twenty extra. It'll actually be nice to get my mind off of things. Before I forget, here's my student ID," said Tip handing Burke his MSU student identification card. The Professor accepts driver's licenses, but prefers the Student ID.

"Great, I owe you big time. I'd offer to buy you some brews, but since you don't drink anymore I'll grab you some grub or something at the next football game. I hope you have fun tonight. I gotta go get started on my paper," said Burke as he headed out the door.

"Good luck on your paper Burke," stated Tip sincerely. He knew what a pain in the ass term papers could be. He hypothesized that nine out of ten students would prefer taking an exam rather than writing a paper. The only thing worse than writing a paper was giving a speech. An unfinished paper was like a black cloud hovering over one's head. The cloud formed the day the paper was assigned and didn't blow away until the day it was handed in. Even in the rare instance when one actually finished a paper with time to spare, the cloud was still there until it was handed in. There was always the fear of losing the hardcopy of the paper, or having it erased from the computer. The latter is what Burke was suffering through.

Tip realized he hadn't given Burke his notebook, but then decided it was probably best anyway. He figured he'd remember the material better for the final exam if he recopied Burke's notes into his notebook.

He washed the rest of the potato salad down with his remaining skim milk. It was time for him to head to Jenison Field House to lift weights, swim and run on the indoor track. Jenison was about a fifteen-minute walk from the fraternity house. The sandwich and potato salad would be digested by the time he got there and he would be ready to workout.

Tip exercised everyday after lunch, from about one till four o'clock. This was the only time that Skip Connor, his student trainer, could accommodate him. Skip was also the student trainer for the women's ski team; the ski team was currently training indoors at Jenison. Tip didn't like having to share the equipment with the women's ski team, but it could be worse. The team usually came in at about two o'clock to do some legwork on the Nautilus machines. So, he really only interacted with them for about a half hour during his workout.

The women's ski team however, loved Tip's presence. By the time the women usually got into the weight room he would've already been working out for an hour. By that time, his muscles were fully pumped up with blood. The old building was always rather humid, and Tip's gray T-shirt usually clung to his ripped muscles. He didn't need to have his shirt tucked in to decipher that his back formed a sharp V. His chiseled six-pack stomach would make Budweiser jealous.

The girls rarely talked to him in the gym, even though they wanted to. The ski team had strict orders from their coach that if flirting became a problem Tip's workout privileges would be revoked. The girls kept their end of the bargain because none of them wanted that. What the ski team coach didn't realize was that Tip's presence actually made many of the girls work harder in a futile attempt to impress him.

Every so often, a girl would try to shoot Tip a flirtatious stare. He never saw these attempts because he was never looking in the girls' direction.

Tip was happy to see Skip, but he was even happier to hear Skip tell him the girls wouldn't be coming in today. The girls were given the day off to abide by NCAA practice regulations. Under NCAA Division I rule, teams weren't allowed to practice more than twenty hours a week. Teams also had to have one day off per week. Most teams were able to skirt the twenty-hour rule by not factoring in film sessions, training table, etc. However, coaches rarely chanced pressing the "day-off" rule.

Tip completed his workout twenty minutes earlier than normal. Having Skip's undivided attention and the absence of the ski team provided not only a quicker workout, but also a better one.

Tip jogged home, cutting between the Yakley and Campbell dormitories. Yakely-Gillcrest was the only all-female dorm remaining at Michigan State. Because of this dubious distinction, it was affectionately referred to as the Virgin Vault. A more accurate designation would be the Labyrinth; the old dorm was a maze of hallways with many entrance and exit ramps. There were many frustrating dead ends and no visible road signs to guide visitors.

Yakely's confusing design was probably intentional. Any gentlemen wanting to call on one of its female occupants had a difficult time finding his desired destination. Yakely was now behind him as he cut sharply on his right knee to avoid a speeding biker. He realized, after-the-fact, that there was no knee pain associated with the adroit maneuver. This was the first time in a while that an athletic movement involving his knee wasn't met with corresponding pain.

Tip was in the best cardiovascular shape of his life, even better than his high school playing days, and he was also much stronger. Trainer Skip had helped pace him to his best mile time an hour earlier, breaking the tape in 4:42. Tip had been working out that much harder since Hamilton's death. It became his only release for all the anger and anguish.

Tip headed up the backstairs of the house. In an effort to prolong the workout he didn't skip any steps. He entered his room and placed his pointer and middle fingers to his lips, and then touched them to a picture of Hamilton and himself on the wall. Since Hamilton's death, he'd performed this ritual every time he entered the room.

The picture was of them each holding a twenty-one inch Walleye. The picture was taken two summers ago during a fishing trip at Lake Malikatoba, Canada. Tip chuckled inside every time he looked at that picture. He remembered that right after it was taken Hamilton had leaned forward, lost his balance, and fell out of the boat. In the process both fish were lost. If not for the photo evidence, it would've been another "fish that got away story." Tip found the picture more meaningful since Chris' death.

The nearby quacking of the duck phone rudely interrupted his thoughts. Tip fumbled for the phone and grabbed the cumbersome Mallard handset just before the third "quack."

"Hello. Is Mr. Tipton in, please," said the suave voice.

"Speaking."

"Oh, hello Mr. Tipton, this is Agent Potts from the FBI, we spoke yesterday." Yes of course. "I just wanted to let you know, Mr. Tipton, that we received your package. Thank you, and we should be able to look at it sometime soon. Our caseload has been relieved a bit."

'Well that's great news," replied Tip.

"I need you to do something for me, Mr. Tipton. I've only taken a quick glance at the item you shipped me, but I'd say it's definitely worth us checking into. You indicated that this document is probably of grave importance to someone and I wouldn't argue with you. That's why it's imperative, for the sake of your personal safety, that you do not have any copies of this document.

Since the original documents are safely in our hands, it would be unnecessary and also dangerous for anyone else to have a copy, especially you. Out of concern for your safety, I just wanted to confirm that you don't have any copies of this document," explained Agent Potts.

"No, I did just as you instructed yesterday. I just sent you the original copy. To my knowledge, that is the only copy. I'm glad to hear you received it," replied Tip.

"Well great then. Thank you again and I'll let you know if we find anything," said Potts as he concluded the call.

Tip quickly changed out of his damp workout clothes and threw a towel around his waist. Tip effortlessly slid on his well-worn flip-flop shower sandals. Everyone in the fraternity wore sandals into the bathroom shower. No brother wanted to risk finding out what kind of fungi grew there. Tip's flip-flop model of choice featured snake-like rubber straps that barely fit between his big and second toe. He had opted for these models because they were cheap, only $4 a pair at Target. Students affectionately referred to the discount store as "Zar-Shay," since the French flair made it seem more chic. They did the same thing to Goebel (pronounced Go-Bull), an inexpensive domestic beer...Zhh-o-bell, the champagne of beers.

Tip took a long cool shower. If he took a hot shower immediately after a tough workout he'd still be sweating. He and his buddies described the shower as "not taking" if the aforementioned sweating phenomenon occurred.

After finishing his cheese ravioli dinner with garlic bread, he slid on the hot pink Melting Moments work shirt. The shirt was a little tight on Tip, especially the black elastic trim on the sleeves. The strained sleeves accentuated Tip's well-defined biceps.

"Melting Moments" was written in red cursive on the upper left side of the shirt. Tip was one of the few people who could look good in this uniform. The hot pink did a good job of showing off his dark complexion, and the black trim matched his jet-black hair.

Tip tucked the shirt into his denim Levi 544's, and threw on his charcoal Patagonia pullover jacket. For good measure, he had saved a red mackintosh apple from lunch. He put the apple into his coat pocket as a precaution against hunger. Tip didn't want to indulge on any of the ice cream during his shift. Eating fatty ice cream would be counter-productive to his intense training for the hockey season.

The doctors, however, had warned Tip that he probably would never be able to play hockey again. One thing was for sure, if Tip were able to play, it wouldn't be until next year. Tip was running out of "next years" and wanted to make the hockey team and contribute this year. He had talked to the MSU head coach during the summer. The coach indicated that he'd grant him the opportunity to try out this season, but that there were no guarantees that he'd make the team. He would be vying for one of only two available walk-on positions and they usually preferred to save those slots for younger players they could develop.

Tip went out the front door of the house and flipped up his hood to combat the evening's light drizzle. Tip checked his underwater sports-watch; the illuminated hands read quarter to six. Tip reached the doors of Melting Moments at five to six. Melting Moments' giant pink awning was a town landmark, and although difficult to miss, it wasn't too obnoxious.

Tip figured he probably wouldn't be bombarded with customers tonight. The dreadful weather wasn't conducive to ice cream consumption. He entered through the front glass door that had the Melting Moments logo etched in it. There was a couple sitting to his right eating mint chocolate chip ice cream. They were sharing a large sized paper cup that was placed in the center of their small table. It was obvious to Tip that it was the beginning of a budding relationship. The couple wasn't talking much; rather they were just sneaking peaks at one another. Eating the ice cream was just passing the time; it was an excuse for them to go out without many strings attached. It would be wise for these lovebirds to switch over to fat free yogurt; they each unknowingly were downing large quantities of ice cream. Hell, they probably wouldn't notice the difference if Tip switched out the ice cream with Wheat Germ.

The only other person in the parlor was the boy working behind the counter. He was about average height but extremely thin and pale. The shirt of the boy's uniform was faded and was unflattering on his frail body. His numerous pimples indicated that he was probably a freshman, or at most, a sophomore. He also probably spent too much of his adolescence flipping greasy hamburgers.

Stiff smudge marks were everywhere on his stiff shirt, a sure sign that the uniform had been absent a wash for sometime.

"Oh great. You're here. You must be the new guy. My name's Jonathan, welcome aboard the good ship lollipop," said the boy in a nasally tone.

"Thanks, I'm Jason Burke. It's a pleasure to meet you," said Tip almost drawing a blank on Burke's first name. No one referred to Burke as Jason in the fraternity. It was always just Burke. Most young men called each other by their last name. This was especially true in a fraternity house, where a majority of the members were only known by their nicknames such as Rockhead, Train, Cruiser, Buck, and Chocco.

"Sorry, Jason, but I've got to run, Sam's in the back and will be out in a minute. Have fun, "laughed Jonathan, a laugh that was closer to a disagreeable snort.

Jonathan grabbed his shinny blue Detroit Pistons jacket and headed out the door. Tip wasn't disappointed to see Jonathan disappear, and hoped that Sam wasn't as big of a dork as Jonathan seemed to be. It would make for a very long evening if he had to be trained by a toolbox like Jonathan.

Tip removed his coat, hanging it on the same hook Jonathan's coat was just on. The other coat on the hook was a lady's coat, and since the two other patrons were wearing their coats, Sam must be short for Samantha. Upon removing his coat Tip discovered instantly that it was extremely cold in the store. Goose bumps immediately formed on his sculpted forearms. The goose bump sensation was rather pleasant and refreshing to Tip-it had been awhile.

Fortunately, Sam was indeed short for Samantha. She entered in grand fashion from the back room. Her dark hair, brown eyes, and striking features indicated that she was probably of Latino descent. Her shirt was tucked firmly into her black denim jeans. Her tightly drawn shirt announced a well-endowed chest, one that wasn't constrained by a frivolous bra. Since she wasn't wearing a bra, it was easily discernable that she was colder than Tip. Her standing nipples came to a point and easily pushed out the thin cotton of her Melting Moments polo shirt. Tip would have to be blind not to notice this.

"You must be Jason. I'm Samantha, but you can call me Sam," she said pointing to her nametag, which was located on the precipice of one of those pencil-eraser nipples "we've got to get you a nametag before we do anything," said Sam. She turned around and opened the white cupboard door behind her and bent over to grab something. Her tight black pants revealed the trace of her skimpy thong panty line creeping up her tight butt. She rummaged around in the cupboard for about a minute. All during the search, her hips rotated from left to right in hypnotic rhythm.

She eventually turned around with a new name tag in her right hand. Her long hot pink nails matched the color of her shirt and also her thong underwear. Over the past year, she had developed a fetish for matching her underwear with her nails; a few men on campus were lucky enough to experience this newfound hobby of hers. Her face was slightly flushed from bending over for such a long period of time. She grabbed the label-maker and quickly punched Jason's name. She struggled attempting to peel the backing on the label, but soon she conquered this challenge and produced the finished product.

"Here you are, this elegant nametag makes you official, you

must be so proud," Sam said sarcastically. "It probably won't be very busy tonight, which will be good for training purposes. I can teach you how to do everything and I mean *everything*, without the customers' constant interruption. The manager, Karen, has a cardiovascular boxing class tonight, so it'll just be you and me. Don't worry, I'll make sure that we have a good time," said Sam in a flirtatious voice. Tip didn't catch the flirtatious inference.

"The best part about this job is that you can eat as much ice cream as you like, the only rule is you can't eat it in front of the customers. Would you like to try anything?" asked Sam.

"No thanks," said Tip.

"I thought maybe you wouldn't. It doesn't look like you eat too much fat," said Sam. Sam approached Tip, for he was still fumbling with the nametag. The design of the safety pin on the back of the nametag was asinine, and was it was nearly impossible for him to get it on by himself.

"Let me help you with that, they're kind of tricky. I always put mine on before putting on my shirt," said Sam.

Sam reached up and started fiddling with the nametag. Although she could have completed the job in seconds, she purposely took her time inching her body closer to his, until they were finally touching. Sam's firm nickel-sized areolas rubbed gently across his washboard stomach.

"There you go," said Sam, her long nails lingering a split second on Tip's rock-solid left pectoral muscle.

"Well, I'm going to have a scoop of cookie dough ice cream, two hundred fat grams and all," Sam said while picking the ice cream scooper out of a water filled stainless steel cylinder. Facing Tip, Sam leaned over to obtain the scoop of cookie dough ice cream. Not one of the three buttons on her shirt was in use, thus, her beautifully sculpted breasts dangled dangerously in the air. The piedmonts of her nipples were darker than the rest of her skin, and the summits were extremely long and frosty at the moment. The "snow caps" were probably a result of their proximity to the frigid dairy below.

---

The cool rain felt good on Burke's face, especially after being cooped up in the hot and stuffy computer lab for the majority of the day. Going to this class would be a good break thought Burke, besides he was almost done with his paper. The fifty-minute break would also give him a fresh perspective to proofread his work. He did not look forward to editing his paper. It was the most tedious aspect of writing. He hoped it didn't rain any harder because he hadn't brought an umbrella and he was still recovering from a nasty head cold. He was also aware of the fact that Michigan State's classrooms were known to be cold and clammy in the fall. Having damp clothes in the classroom would inevitably bring back his cold.

Burke had no problem finding Tip's classroom in Erickson Hall. Burke promptly sat in the second row by the window as Tip had instructed. Burke had purposely arrived seconds before class was to commence so there would be less of an opportunity for anyone to talk to him. It was a relatively small class by Michigan State University standards, being comprised of only about sixty students.

The professor started lecturing right on time, and Burke actually became interested in the material he was covering. The lecture was summarizing some of Sigmund Freud's theories relating to war and the id. The professor lectured for forty-five minutes, and Burke was actually disappointed that they weren't going to have a pop quiz at the end of class. Burke was confident that he'd ace the quiz since he was attentive throughout the class period. Burke wrote the name of the professor on his notebook with the intention of signing up for the class next semester.

Burke exited Erickson Hall the same way he'd entered, in back. To his dismay, the autumn air was now much darker and wetter. But, the weather couldn't dampen his good spirits. He was going to be done with his paper and actually get a good night's rest, something he hadn't enjoyed in weeks. This lack of sleep was probably the cause of his head cold.

Burke headed down the dimly lit asphalt path leading toward a bridge crossing the Red Cedar River. The bridge was the fastest way to get back to the computer center. He stared at the raindrops splashing into the water below. He could only see the water in places where the tall floodlights illuminated. The floodlights were positioned along the pathway on the northern bank. His thoughts drifted to the upcoming formal date-party. It was going to be a barn dance, and he calibrated what his potential date options were. Should he lock-up a sure thing right away? Or should he gamble and ask the tall blonde with the great legs that always sat by him in his American Thoughts & Literature class? He was pretty certain he was going to roll the dice. If it came to it, he could always call one of his old standbys. However, the "day before call" was embarrassing for both parties. The reason it was embarrassing was that the "standby girl" could deduce that obviously she wasn't his first choice being called the day of and all. However, the standby always said yes despite this because date-parties were generally a blast.

This term's date-party would be particularly good. The extravaganza entailed a four-day weekend in Toronto with tickets to see the Phantom of the Opera. The fraternity typically traveled by bus down to Detroit's Greek Town and ate at Fishbones restaurant for the date party. However things were different this year since the house was currently banned from Fishbones. The ban resulted from the actions of "The Cruiser." At last year's date party, Brother Cruiser attempted to climb the world's largest indoor waterfall located in multi-storied Fishbones. Cruiser was lucky not to have slipped on the water-covered marble of the waterfall and split his head open. However, the massive hangover he suffered through the next morning had the same effect.

Burke was so entrenched in thought concerning the date party that he didn't notice the footsteps approaching rapidly from behind him. Even if he had heard the approaching footsteps, he wouldn't have thought anything of them. He would have figured that they were the footsteps of other students hurrying to get out of the rain as quickly as possible.

Sanchez and Garcia weren't thrilled about having spent the last hour in the rain waiting for Burke to come out of the classroom. The large oak trees they were hiding behind supplied some cover, but not enough. Sanchez and Garcia waited patiently for that hour, although they could have made a killing by mugging all the individuals who walked alone in front of them in the dark night.

The foresight to obtain Tip's schedule was a stroke of genius, and it was now paying dividends. The stalkers were only inches behind their unsuspecting prey. They were mistaking Burke for Tip, for he had come from Tip's class and he looked almost exactly like him in the dim lighting.

Garcia stretched out the ductile metal strand in his gloved hands until it became taut.

Burke felt a strong force clasp around his neck that jerked him forcefully back. The powerful thrust almost lifted him off the ground. He immediately attempted to fight his invisible attacker. However, the more he resisted, the tighter the object clamped around his neck. His head was bent back toward the night sky and he couldn't tell what was going on. A helpless feeling descended over Burke and it was causing him to panic.

A whisper came from in front of Burke, "how do you feel now, you nosy little faggot? Couldn't leave well enough alone could you? You had to be a hero," said Garcia dragging Burke off the sidewalk and into the shadows of the tall oaks by the river.

"If you play along with us nice, we'll play nice with you. Or you can play games like your friend Mr. Hamilton. If you want to play games, that's fine with us, we'd love to let you join his dead ass. Now where's the fucking burgundy envelope and its contents Mr. Tipton," asked Sanchez.

Garcia loosened the wire around Burke's neck so he could only produce a whisper. "You've got the wrong man...I'm Jason Burke, not Paul Tipton," wheezed Burke.

"Oh, so you do want to play fucking games. You're either deaf or dumb. I just said your friend played games with us, you're about two seconds away from a reunion with him," said Sanchez, Garcia tightened the wire around Burke's neck.

"We'll see who the hell you are," said Sanchez, who began rummaging through Burke's pockets. Sanchez pulled a roll of Life

Savers out of Burke's left pocket and chuckled, "You're going to need more than this to save your sorry little ass," Sanchez found what he was looking for in Burke's back right pocket. Sanchez removed Tip's I.D. from Burke's pocket.

"Let's see what we have here. According to your ID, you're one Paul Blair Tipton, a.k.a. piece of shit," said Sanchez. Burke shook his head no, but was restrained by Garcia.

"We don't have much time, now for the last time did you make any copies of the content of the envelope, and if so where are they," Sanchez said between gritted teeth an inch away from Burke's face.

A good sized class was now being let out of Wells Hall about two hundred yards from where Burke, Sanchez, and Garcia now stood. The immense number of students indicated that this was probably a class being released from lecture hall B108. Wells B108 was the second largest room on campus with a capacity of three hundred and fifty students, the only room larger than it was the lecture hall located in the Vet Clinic on the Eastern part of campus.

The approaching students were going to make the remaining discussion rather laconic.

"Time's up for you motherfucker," said Sanchez in a slightly louder voice this time.

Burke still didn't know what was going on, but he did know enough to realize he needed to act soon.

Burke lifted his right arm and hammered his elbow between Garcia's third and fourth left ribs. The wire around Burke's neck released momentarily allowing him to slide his hands between the wire and his neck. He then violently tucked his body causing Garcia's massive body to flip over him and onto the base of a hardened tree stump. Garcia aspirated a puff of air before he went unconscious. Burke quickly jumped to his feet and tried to get his bearings.

No sooner had he acclimated himself, when Sanchez attempted to smash the butt of his nine-millimeter across Burke's face. He was fortunate to see the approaching weapon and, at the last instance, ducked away. The revolver only grazed his face, opening up a slight gash just above the right eyebrow. He attempted to yell for help but at that precise moment, Sanchez's strong hands clasped around his mouth and forced him into the mud by the edge of the river. He tried to resist the force but was helpless as his head was pushed down into the murky waters of the Red Cedar.

The bustle of students hadn't yet reached the area where the skirmish was occurring. It was nearly impossible to see anything under the shadows of the trees at night. Burke could sense that Sanchez was on his right and mustered all of his strength to wrap his right arm around Sanchez's neck and with a dying will thrust Sanchez's head down into the water. Sanchez's grip on Burke's neck lessened for a second in response to Burke's latest tactic. Burke seized the opportunity and struggled to get his head above the water. Burke now had the upper hand. Burke's upper hand didn't last long as Sanchez swiftly turned his body so that he was now facing Burke. Sanchez used his superior upper body strength to viciously throw Burke over him into the Red Cedar. Burke held onto Sanchez's arms tightly and the inertia helped drag Sanchez into the water with him.

Now, both men were immersed in the dark waters of the river and were being swept away by the strong current. Both men grappled with each other and the Red Cedar. The splash of river water onto Garcia's face caused him to awaken from his stupor. He looked up and saw the struggle in the water.

Garcia hurriedly walked along the sidewalk, attempting to keep pace with the skirmish. He did not want to break into a run, as this would only rouse suspicion. It was extremely difficult for him to see the bodies, let alone tell who was winning the battle. He could only catch periodic glimpses of the battle. These glimpses occurred when the tussle hit a patch in the river that was slightly illuminated.

Sanchez had a firm grip on Burke's throat and was desperately groping for the knife he had tucked deep into his left sock. Burke struggled to keep his head above water and, although he was well built, he was not very athletic. He was a terrible swimmer and only his sheer will to live had kept him alive this long.

# CRISIS

Burke caught a glimpse of the library bridge as they were swiftly swept under it. The bridge signaled to him that a three-foot drop in the river was rapidly approaching. He reserved his strength for the move that he was planning when they hit the small waterfall.

Once past the library, the tree cover became sparse and the river was illuminated. Garcia maneuvered closer to the river's edge and now had a clear view of both bodies. By now, all of the students had cleared out of the area. There were no witnesses around. He removed the revolver from his arm holster and deftly attached a long silencer onto its muzzle. He didn't raise the gun at this time because it was still too difficult to get a clean shot at Burke without risking harm to Sanchez.

Garcia noticed some white water ahead and just beyond it, a dip in the water level. There appeared to be about a three-foot waterfall in this area. He could see that the river bottom in this area was a steel trough.

Sanchez still had a firm grip around Burke's throat and pressed it underwater, while he fumbled for his knife with his other hand. Burke was conserving all of his strength for one final rapid burst of rage and thus held his breath underwater for as long as possible. Sanchez's fingers tightened around the handle of the switchblade and he removed it from his sock. Burke heard the approaching sound of the small rapids indicating the drop off was near. His body went limp.

Sanchez was pleased that the kid finally had drowned, but was still going to cut him up for good measure. He raised the knife to within inches of Burkes throat when he noticed that they were on the crag of a sharp drop in the river.

Burke, who had been playing dead all along, suddenly came to life and violently turned Sanchez over. Now Burke was on top. As they cascaded over the waterfall, Burke tightly clasped his hands around Sanchez's ears and braced himself for the fall and landing. Sanchez's head cushioned Burke's landing as his head hit squarely on the steel/cement bottom of the River. Sanchez was knocked unconscious. Burke navigated his way through a small series of shallow rapids and used Sanchez's body as a floatation device. Once clear of the rapids, Burke released Sanchez's body and took several breaths of air before wading through the calmer waters toward the southern bank of the river.

Garcia watched Burke wade toward him and patiently waited behind one of the few remaining trees. Burke finally reached shore with barely enough strength to pull his waterlogged body onto the bank. He lay silently, exhausted, with half of his body on the bank and the other half still in the Red Cedar.

Garcia placed the cold steel silencer of the gun squarely on Burke's left temple and pumped the trigger twice. Garcia quickly and quietly slid the body onto the mud and into the murky water of the Red Cedar, tossing Tip's ID card upstream. He then moved down the walkway straining to locate his partner's unconscious body.

He exited from the woods and merged onto the smaller of two cement pathways. Even though he hadn't seen anyone for a while, he remained cautious and intentionally stayed in the protective shadows of the trees. A bike winged by on his left, brushing his arm. The rider turned around in his seat, "Jesus Christ man. Pull your head out of your ass and get off the bike path, dumbass!" shouted the rider. If only the bike rider knew whom he was yelling at, thought Garcia.

---

Tip was actually happy to be mopping the floor at Melting Moments. It was the only activity he'd done that warmed his body sufficiently to combat the chill of the twenty-five flavors. Sam had put on a Melting Moments sweatshirt when Manager Karen made a surprise visit. Her cardio-boxing class had been canceled because the instructor came down with the flu. Karen was in her late thirty's and was Sam's aunt.

Sam loved her aunt, but was disappointed when she showed up tonight. She wanted to be alone with Tip all evening. They would have been virtually alone all night, too. Only about ten people had come into the store all night. And of these ten, only seven actually ordered anything. They'd sold four chipwiches, two mint chocolate cups and one pistachio cone. On a warm evening, there would be a thirty-minute wait to get through the door and another twenty-minute wait to reach the counter. Sam liked both the busy and slow nights. Tonight she was glad it wasn't busy since Tip was there. The time was going fast and she didn't need customer interaction to keep her occupied.

"Thanks Jason, that'll be all for tonight. That's the best the floor has looked in months, good job. I'll see you next week. Although, I sure could use you to work the cart at the basketball game this Saturday," said Karen.

"Oh thanks, I'll have to check my schedule tonight and give you a call tomorrow. If I'm available, I'd love to work the game," said Tip. Karen disappeared into the back room.

Tip grabbed his coat off the rack. Sam grabbed his hand firmly.

Tip was a bit surprised by this aggressive gesture, but handled it in stride, "It was a pleasure meeting you Sam. Thanks for teaching me everything. I hope I wasn't too inept. I guess I'll see you next week, or possibly at the game, if you're working," said Tip pulling his hand away.

Tip glanced at the Eskimo Pie shaped clock above the door as he exited. It was quarter after ten.

Sam stared at his firm buttocks until he was no longer visible and sighed contently.

---

Sanchez and Garcia awoke the next morning, and weren't bothered at all by the fact that they'd cut short three promising young lives the last two weeks. To them, these boys' lives were like giant dollar signs. Sanchez and Garcia actually took pride in accomplishing their required duties. Just as a lifeguard took pride in saving life, Garcia and Sanchez took equal pride in taking a life.

Sanchez had a difficult time getting the large van up the narrow ramp leading to Chi Theta's parking lot. He finally managed to do it with some hand directions from a Chi Theta who was patiently waiting to leave for class in his car. He pulled the van straight ahead within inches of the house, not in a designated spot, but out of everyone else's way. He and Garcia had observed several different services: catering, plumber, etc. park in this spot over the past two weeks.

Sanchez and Garcia jumped out of the van and both adjusted their light gray polyester uniforms.

Sanchez's sewn on patch had the name Ted in block letters, while Garcia's read Joe. On the back of the shirts, stitched in black, was a picture of Ben Franklin flying a kite with the caption *Electricity is the Key* directly above it. The backdoor of the fraternity was wide open and it smelled like burnt toast. Sanchez was still recovering from his bout with Burke in the water the night before and thus his sense of smell and hearing were still a little out of whack. Despite this, they both could hear people eating in the basement.

They heard footsteps coming down the stairs as they continued nonchalantly up them. The ascending and descending parties met on the second floor landing and exchanged pleasantries. The young, but stocky student was carrying a mop-bucket full of dirty hot water. The student turned his body sideways to allow Sanchez and Garcia to pass by. The oval shaped pin with the Greek letter X (Chi) on the young man's chest indicated he was a pledge. The bucket of mop water in his right hand confirmed it.

Sanchez and Garcia reached the third floor and proceeded down the narrow corridor. To their right, on the sun deck, was a fairly tall and skinny Chi Theta. This young man was wearing gray gym shorts, a black tank top, and three-quarter hoop shoes. He was shouting down to someone in the parking lot below, "Hey dude, wait up, I'll be down in a second, I just need to grab some Gatorade from my room." Upon receiving nonverbal acceptance of his plea, the skinny Chi Theta sprinted back into the room nearest to the stairwell; room sixteen.

A few doors down, Tip stretched across his twin-sized mattress, perched high atop the loft that overlooked room ten. He furiously

# CRISIS

sifted through his plastic crates of clothes for his weight lifting gloves. The search was beginning to cause some slight perspiration. Wearing a heavy sweatshirt was not lessening his perspiration or agitation. If he didn't find the gloves in the next minute he was going to cut his losses and head to the gym without them.

Gloves or no gloves, Tip was looking forward to his workout today. In particular, he was looking forward to trying out his new pair of Reebok running shoes. These shoes were a gift from his friend on the basketball team. The basketball team received the most gear, and rightfully so. They had been consistently ranked in the Top Ten nationally the past few years and also had a history of greatness: 1979 and 2000 National Championships, Big Ten champs 1957, 1959, 1967, 1978, 1979, 1990, 1998 1999, 2000, and 2001. Michigan State's former basketball players included Magic Johnson, Steve Smith, Scott Skiles, Eric Snow, Mateen Cleaves, Morris Peterson, Jason Richardson, Zach Randolph, and Alan Anderson.

Sanchez and Garcia were fortunate that there weren't many people in the house. Although most fraternities are portrayed in the movies as emporiums for belching and beer drinking animals, Chi Theta fell into this stereotype only on the weekends. During the week the members of the house were diligent with their studies and jobs. Work hard, play hard was the fraternity's adopted motto.

The members of this particular chapter were extremely ambitious young men. Even though there were over fifty members living in the house, it wasn't unusual during the middle of the day for no one to be around. Most were away at class, studying, working, meeting with a class group, or doing some recreational activity, such as pick-up basketball, jogging, or football.

Aside from meal times, most of the members of the house rolled in after eleven o'clock at night. The late evening was a time to relax and hang out in each other's rooms to talk about class, girls and sports. But, the conversation usually revolved around sports, especially recently. The Spartan football team was having such a successful season that everyone in town was talking about it.

Sports were the lifeblood of the fraternity. While not all the members were great athletes they all loved to play or to watch sports. As a result of this shared affection, inseparable bonds were created over the sweat and tears on the playing field. These kids would be successful far beyond their college years by the fundamental teamwork and dedication they learned from each other.

Many Chi Thetas would learn a lot from Brother Matt Sanders, a Rhodes Scholar. While Sanders, in turn, would learn the true meaning of the word courage from Brother Joe Henson. Henson was a sophomore confined to a wheel chair due to a brutal snowmobile accident. The young men that lived within the walls of the Lodge weren't spoiled rich brats. They were bright and ambitious students seeking to squeeze all they could from life and the friendships that developed over their tenure at the University.

Sanchez and Garcia were happy to see that Tip's door was wide open. It would be difficult to avoid looking suspicious if they'd been required to pick the door lock. They entered the room, crossing over the two rhombus shaped patches of sunlight that streamed through the windows. Relieved that no one was in the room, they slowly closed the door behind them and locked it.

Neither of them spoke. Sanchez began picking through Tip's belongings searching for the missing letter. Meanwhile, Garcia was busy placing a "bug" on the phone that rested on top of the old wooden cabinet. They were planning to monitor Tip's incoming messages the next two days just to be sure no one else knew about the letter. They figured that Tip's body wouldn't be found for at least five days. Valez had requested they search Tip's room again to ensure there was no incriminating evidence and also to set up the monitoring devices just as a precaution. When the authorities learned of the second death there would be more suspicions and investigation.

Tip lay motionless on his bed taking in everything that was happening below him. He'd been able to crouch down, undetected, in the northwest corner of the loft. He was positioned where he could see more than half of the room. Persons below the loft couldn't see him, unless they were sitting on the windowsill. Tip determined the two intruders were unaware of the loft's existence. The loft stairs were so well integrated into the wood of the wall, that only about one in ten would notice them the first couple of times in the room. Tip had no idea that these two intruders had mistakenly killed his good friend Burke the night before in a case of mistaken identity.

Tip's adrenaline was pumping, and he could hear his heart pounding. He was nervous while at the same time enraged. If these two intruders were in anyway responsible for Hamilton's death, he wanted to kill them with his bare hands right now. If he knew that his friend Burke was also murdered by these parasites last night, it would probably be too much to contain. As strong as this rage was, he knew he had to contain it, now was not the appropriate time for revenge. He still needed more answers and more proof.

It took Garcia less than five minutes to have the phone tapped, and upon completion motioned to Sanchez to head out. Sanchez reluctantly turned toward the door.

A high-pitched ring filled the still air of the room. The offender was Tip's radio alarm clock three feet from where he was now. Tip had forgotten that he'd hit his snooze button fifteen minutes ago after awakening from his nap. He now wished he'd turned the alarm off instead of hitting the ever-popular snooze.

Sanchez and Garcia each drew their pistols. Garcia quickly positioned himself by the corner of the couch nearest to windows and could see a couple of shelves with various pictures on them. He couldn't believe he'd missed them. Sanchez intrepidly scaled the wall ladder.

Tip whipped his large radio alarm clock down at Sanchez on the ladder. His aim was a little off and it didn't hit Sanchez on the head, but rather on the right knuckle of his ring finger. Despite being askew, it did slow Sanchez's ascent.

Tip forcefully kicked the dry wall of the sloped ceiling. Three strong and swift kicks created a hole large enough for him to slide through. He felt the cool, damp air of the storage room rush through the hole he'd just created. He closed his eyes and entered the narrow hole, scrapping his sides on the edges of the broken drywall.

The hole in the wall connecting to the ceiling of the storage room was easily created because Tip purposely kicked a previously spackled area of the dry wall. Two guys wrestling around after a night at the bar had created the original hole more than a year ago. The occupant of the room had done a haphazard job of spackling it. He figured why do a good job? No one ever saw this part of the room anyway. His poor handiwork had just saved Tip's life.

As more of his body entered through the narrow hole, gravity pulled Tip down feet first and he tightened his body in preparation for the worst. He fell about eight feet, but it felt like a bottomless pit when you couldn't see the ground. He violently crashed into a large object, his tailbone taking most of the impact. A sharp pain shot through his right arm and he felt a warm sensation of blood trickle over his right hand. His arm had scraped up against an old metal door screen during his descent. He could now tell the object he'd landed on was a giant old vinyl covered chair.

Tip was in the storage room, which was only accessible by way of the third-story sun deck. Since different students moved in each year, any unused furniture was stored here, along with extra screens, mattresses, and other miscellaneous items. Tip was wishing he'd landed on one of the mattresses.

Sanchez cautiously poked his head into the recently created hole. He could feel the cold air and also the stench of mildew. He could hear movement but couldn't see anything. Although he had a silencer on his pistol, he couldn't fire randomly into the dark. Besides, killing a third person wouldn't make Valez happy.

Tip fumbled around in the dark with his right hand, finally finding the wall, which he used as a guide to the door. He had a difficult time gaining his balance. He was walking over various chairs, tables, and couches. A coil from a bunk bed spring sliced across his ankle and he winced in pain. He lost contact with the wall as his left foot found nothing but air. He dropped two feet to the ground and a shivering pain shot up through his bum knee.

Sanchez lit his Bic lighter and slowly peered through the recently made port in the wall. He couldn't see much, but he could tell it was a good drop, and he deduced the only escape was through a door down below. He quickly scrambled down the ladder, placing his revolver out of sight as he headed out the door. Garcia followed close behind.

Sanchez and Garcia abruptly turned the corner of the hallway. They were trying not to look anxious or conspicuous, just in case someone was up on the third floor watching them.

Tip's hands gripped his left leg just below the kneecap as he gritted his teeth to keep from screaming. The pain slowly subsided, and he prayed that it was only a "stinger" and that his knee had held up. He slowly got up, being cognizant to put all of his weight on his right leg. He slowly lowered his left leg and gingerly placed it on the ground. He shifted his weight cautiously until it was evenly distributed on each leg. He knew his knee was going to be sore tomorrow, but determined that it was okay, and began shuffling toward the door.

His grueling rehabilitative workouts had just saved his knee. A year ago, his knee wouldn't have been able to take such a hard blow without severe damage. He extended his right hand for the door. Another two-foot drop had indicated to him that he was in the door well, and sure enough he felt the cold steel of the door. He pulled the door slightly ajar and peered through the crack. He shielded his eyes from the bright sunlight; it took his pupils a couple of seconds to dilate. Seeing that the coast was clear, he stepped out onto the sun deck and vowed to himself that he would someday clean out that ridiculously overcrowded storage room.

The sunlight and cool air felt good, the sun had just broken through after several minutes of rain. Tip noticed that he'd worked up quite a sweat during the events of the past minute. Determining that his knee was okay, Tip bent his knees to sprint for the door, which stood twenty feet away at the end of the sundeck. The door rudely swung open, shutting the chances of using that as an escape route.

In the doorway stood the imposing figures of Sanchez and Garcia. Sanchez and Garcia didn't get a clear look at Tip's face, so they still didn't know it was him. The only thing standing between Tip and the enemy was the corrugated rows of weathered wood. A myriad of objects had fallen between the cracks of wood over the years. The fraternity brothers joked with one another about how much bottle return money lay below the deck. The State of Michigan mandated that a ten-cent deposit be placed on every beverage can and bottle. A conservative estimate placed the value of the "deck cans" at sixty dollars. The value of the deck pile would grow in escrow as no one was going to clean the underneath of the deck for a long while. Objects on the deck included a lawn chair and fresh hair clippings from an impromptu haircut that morning.

Upon hearing the door open, Tip immediately spun to his left and peered over the steel railing of the sun deck. Fresh raindrops coruscated off the bright red paint of the rails. He glanced four stories below at the black asphalt of the house parking lot. To his dismay, not a sole was to be found in the parking lot to assist him in his escape. Sanchez and Garcia were blocking the only safe way down.

No external ladders existed on the house. Rather, the rooms were equipped with retractable aluminum ladders, which conveniently folded underneath a bed or couch. The members of the house hadn't performed a fire drill in years, so no one knew how stable these ladders really were. There was no use in Tip shouting for help. His pursuers had guns and no one in the house was allowed to posses a firearm. Also, there was no sense in putting other members of his house into jeopardy. This matter was between him and the men with the guns.

Tip sure wished there was a fire escape to the house now, because his predicament looked hopeless. Despite recent renovations, the house was still a virtual firetrap. The majority of the smoke detectors were obsolete, and those that weren't had been knocked off the ceiling long ago. Most smoke detectors fell prey to various ball sports not meant for indoors. Everyone screwing around with the fire extinguishers rapidly depleted their contents. The boiler in the basement was ancient and unsafe. Despite all these deficiencies, amazingly enough, the house had never experienced a severe fire since the brick portion of the house was added in 1950.

Tip didn't bother to look to his right. It was just a wall of white aluminum siding behind which was the upstairs bathroom. A few years ago, Tip could have glanced through two petite windows to check if someone was using the porcelain facilities. Although the windows had been replaced to combat both an extremely cold winter draft and a lack of privacy for the bathroom occupants.

The reconstruction of the bathroom wall had been free of charge. The Chapter had simply filled out a renovation request form and sent it to National Headquarters. National Headquarters, in turn, was generous in funding an expedient renovation. Their chapter had received many generous contributions from National Headquarters since Ricardo Valez became General Director. Tip and others couldn't say enough good things about the great job Valez was doing.

Tip thought about going back into the storage room, but there was no lock on the door to keep Sanchez and Garcia from following him. Besides, he'd be unable to reach the drywall hole leading into his room and would thus trap himself. Even if he could reach the hole, by the time he'd get through it, Sanchez or Garcia would be waiting in his room again.

Throughout Sanchez's and Garcia's pursuit, they couldn't get a good view of the Chi Theta's face. The large gray hood of the sweatshirt was drawn close around Tip's handsome facial features.

"Stop or we'll shoot!" shouted Sanchez.

Via peripheral vision, Tip witnessed Sanchez and Garcia inching ever closer to him. He was surprised that they hadn't shot him yet. If these guys didn't have a problem bumping off Chris Hamilton and Amy Klein in their quest, then surely they'd kill a person who'd actually seen what they were desperately searching for.

Tip knew he couldn't waste time asking himself questions. He quickly placed his right foot on top of the steel railing before him with no plan in mind other than instinctively to somehow get out of his current predicament. With his left hand, he grabbed the side of the sloping roof. The sloped part of the roof was just above the attic storage room and rose to a point, which formed the ceiling of his room.

Garcia stood watch by the sundeck door. Meanwhile, Sanchez lunged toward Tip in an attempt to grab his leg on the railing. "Come here, you little bastard."

Tip pushed off the railing and threw himself fearlessly onto the slanted roof, causing Sanchez to miss. "God damn it! Okay, so you DO want me to shoot you I guess, you stupid little prick."

A hollow thud resonated from Tip's forceful landing. He flattened his body against the roof, digging his nails into the charcoal shingles. His feet rested on the gutter and this was only thing between him and certain death in the parking lot four stories below.

The u-shaped gutter was formed from a solid metal composite as opposed to sheet aluminum. The house put these sturdy gutters in several years ago. The Treasurer before Hamilton was tired of having to replace the flimsy, albeit more attractive, aluminum gutters. These new gutters were also bolted firmly onto the house and were much easier to clean. It was possible to direct an extremely powerful blast of water, almost fire hose strength, through the gutters channels without doing any damage. Since these gutters were so wide they were also difficult to clog. Chi Theta's joked that only a beaver could produce enough "cholesterol" to clog their gutter system.

The toe of Tip's shoe was the only portion of his foot currently touching the gutter. Sanchez, with Garcia holding onto his belt, was standing on the second of the three-bar rails. Tip's face was pressed firmly against the decrepit roof shingles, facing westward and away from the intense stares of Garcia and Sanchez. His aversion to face his attackers was fortuitous. He wasn't aware that if they recognized him, he would be killed instantly. He had no way of knowing that Burke was dead, let alone that they believed they'd killed Paul Tipton last night.

All Sanchez and Garcia could see was the gray pointed head

## CRISIS

of Tip's sweatshirt. Tip moved his toe off the gutter and started churning his legs trying to get a toehold on the shingles. Once his feet "caught" onto the shingles he started to gradually inch up the steep roof. The only things touching now were the toes and palms of his hands. The shingles were extremely coarse and the friction was painful on his calloused hands. However, it was better than them being slick and smooth. The texture on the shingles gave him more traction.

Tip felt a sharp tug on his left leg, and his right leg almost gave out with it. Sanchez's strong right hand was clenching his left shoe. Tip pulled mightily with his left foot, and his leg finally shot up and nearly caused him to lose his balance. Sanchez hurtled back with Tip's untied shoe clenched tightly in his fist. It took all of Garcia's arm strength and the help of the gutter to prevent Sanchez from hurtling over the edge.

Tip had turned around to see his attacker when Sanchez grabbed his leg. Garcia recognized Tip instantly. Garcia thought his eyes were playing tricks on him-hadn't they killed this kid last night by the river?

"God damn, you are heavy, pull harder. He's getting away," Sanchez did just that and pulled harder on Garcia's arm allowing him to get back up on the sundeck.

"Dammit. I thought we killed that kid last night, in fact I know we did. Screw it, we don't have time to think about it now-we can't let him get away," said Garcia. He pulled out his gun, which was tucked into his black leather belt. The belt's oversized silver buckle made removal of the gun difficult.

Tip frantically shuffled his feet against the decrepit shingles, causing some of the more worn-out ones to fly off the roof. He started to gain better traction toward the top of the roof and could almost reach the peak of the house at this point. Sweat was flowing off his forehead like a washcloth being wrung out.

Garcia extended his right arm and squinted his left eye to get a better bead on his fleeting prey. He now had the small steel sight aimed squarely on the upper portion of Tip's broad back, right below the neck. Garcia wished he could paralyze Tip instead of kill him, that way he'd have to suffer more, but Garcia couldn't risk having him live a second longer. There was no way he could miss him now, being only eighteen feet away with a slowly moving target. Garcia steadied his aim and squeezed the trigger with his right pointer finger.

Tip felt relieved when he was almost able to reach the uppermost part of the sloped roof. Then he relaxed his body a moment. This slight rest caused his feet to slide out from under him. He lunged forward with his left hand grasping for the sharp angle of the top of the roof. His fingers wrapped firmly over the peak and he felt a pulling sensation on the left side of his body. His muscles were stretched to their limit, as his two hundred plus pounds tried to resist the unrelenting force of gravity pulling him downward. He felt the rush of a bullet whiz by his ear the instant he'd slipped. He realized this slip had just saved his life.

Without hesitation, he placed his other hand on the peak and swung his body over the top of the roof. He winced at what felt like a hot snakebite piercing into his upper right shoulder as Garcia's second shot found flesh.

Unfortunately for Tip, the other side of the roof was just as slanted as the West Side, only half as long. His momentum from his spontaneous action was uncontrollable, and he barrel rolled speedily down the sloped roof. He couldn't tell what was east or west, up or down, as his head spun like that of a bobble-doll in a tornado.

He was grasping wildly for something, anything, to stop his forceful tumble. He no longer felt the roof below him as he thrashed in the air for a brief moment before his left shoulder crashed into the wood railing on the front deck eight feet below. The sturdy, wood rail halted his momentum and he crumpled onto the tar of the old sundeck. He winced at the pain in his shoulder but was relieved that a quick self-check suggested no further bodily damage. No further damage, that is, except the bullet in his right shoulder, which was beginning to burn intensely.

He was standing on a portion of the old sundeck. At one time the sundeck had gone completely around the house. For reasons of safety and expansion, the deck on the front of the house had been closed long ago. The deck was officially closed that year as a result of a severe accident. Several partygoers on the roof decided it would be fun to play catch with a Nerf football. They were playing catch with others positioned below on the front lawn. Everything was fun and games until an errant toss from the roof sent one of the receivers on into Albert Street. The receiver's eyes were intently focused on the spiraling football, and the poor kid didn't even know he was in the street. It was too late when he saw the approaching car. The driver of the car also had no chance to brake. The roof was still structurally sound, but was now only open at the back of the house.

Garcia, with a helpful boost from Sanchez, made his way onto the roof. He was more cautious than Tip, and could afford to be, since no one had a gun pointed at his back. Garcia proceeded gingerly toward the apex of the roof.

Tip heard Garcia approaching and quickly looked for an escape route. He knew that he didn't have much time to figure it out because his pursuer would be able to peer over the top of the roof in less than a minute and would have a clear shot down at him.

Tip determined that the window to Room Eleven was too small for him to fit through, but began incessantly rapping on the window for someone to open it up. He could sense that Garcia had crossed the peak of the roof and was now inching his way cautiously on his butt, all the while getting closer and closer to where Tip now stood.

He looked to the elm tree on the south side of the house, but it would collapse under his two hundred pounds. He thought about scrambling back up to the slopped portion of the roof, but he knew that he'd have a bullet in him before he reached it. Garcia inched closer and closer to the top of the roof, but still couldn't see Tip, pressed against the window of room eleven. Garcia could now see the white wood railing of the front of the house and prepared to drop down onto the front part of the sundeck.

"I've got you now. Why don't you make it easy on everyone and come back up here?" taunted Garcia to Tip.

Tip never was one to take the easy route. Tip knew he had to make a move now. Tip ignored Garcia's taunts, took a deep breath and sprinted as hard as he could. On his last stride he leapt up and landed his foot on top of the railing. The railing acted as a springboard and launched him dauntlessly into the crisp autumn air.

Tip's arms frantically whirled in circles in a vain attempt to maintain his balance. His adrenaline and sheer athleticism had allowed him to launch himself a good fifteen feet from the house. Despite this effort, Tip still prayed he would make it. His airborne journey soon came to an end as his chest collided with the thirty-foot tall aluminum flagpole in front of the house. Tip gladly welcomed this pain. His legs intuitively clamped around the steel pole, and he felt the pole uproot slightly from the ground. For a disheartening second he thought the pole was going to crash violently into the street. The pain in his arm from the bullet was becoming unbearable and he was fighting not to pass out.

Fortunately, the pole solidified itself, and now it slightly resembled the Leaning Tower of Pisa. Confident of the pole's stability, Tip slid down the pole like a champion logger.

Garcia was caught off guard by Tip's bold move. This slight hesitation caused him to miss an easy target. This "target practice" was made more difficult for Garcia since he was still balancing himself on the sloped roof. The gun silencer made it less accurate, which also didn't help hit the moving target.

Tip felt one bullet whiz by his ear as he hurried down the pole and his feet landed firmly on the uprooted grass surrounding the flagpole. A bullet hit the pole just above his head creating a brilliant spark and a loud ping that was exceedingly painful to his eardrum.

Tip instinctively ducked his head and ran toward the house. The overhang of the house provided temporary protection from the gunfire high above.

Garcia pounced onto the flat part of the roof and quickly approached the rail, but was too late to get a clean shot. He watched helplessly as Tip streaked around the corner of the house.

# CRISIS

Garcia heard the soft whistle of Sanchez, and immediately pulled himself up on the nearest portion of the inclined roof, and scrambled awkwardly back the way he'd come. Garcia and Sanchez rumbled down the backstairs like water bursting from a dam, and were in the back parking lot in no time.

Tip made a beeline between the two student houses next to Chi Theta and raced across Oakhill Street and up Evergreen Alley behind the Sigma Nu House. He glanced over his shoulder to see Garcia and Sanchez pour out the backdoor and point in his direction. Tip made a sharp left behind the old, barn-shaped yellow house.

Garcia and Sanchez grabbed two rusty and unlocked mountain bikes from their resting-place against the backdoor. Sanchez and Garcia headed down the inclined driveway and veered in the direction of their prey. Garcia came to an abrupt stop, and threw the bike down in disgust. Garcia's bicycle chain dangled helplessly from the sprocket; it was obvious why this bike was unlocked. Sanchez pressed on with the chase. Garcia followed Sanchez, trying furiously to keep pace on foot.

Tip sprinted up the hilly backyard leading up to an enormous gray student house on the hill. This particular house overlooked Forrest Street. He allowed himself to glance over his shoulder again and saw Sanchez on the bike. Tip shouldn't have stopped. Sanchez spotted him. Sanchez slammed on his brakes, and turned toward Tip.

Tip was exhausted and his arm ached like hell, but somehow he dug deep within himself and continued to motivate his legs. He didn't even notice the pain of his shoeless bleeding foot that had been scratched up while on the roof. Fortunately for Tip, Sanchez was slowed by the tall grass and steep incline, but peddled feverishly nonetheless. Sanchez's quadriceps burned intensely, but he knew he couldn't let this kid slip through their fingers.

Tip sprinted across Forrest Street and ducked onto a small narrow asphalt driveway that ran between two large gray student houses. The road was badly worn, with tall tufts of grass sprouting randomly from the dark pavement. Tip didn't have time to worry about twisting an ankle or knee on this crumpled alleyway as he forged ahead. The road ran straight for about five hundred yards before joining with a hidden side street.

Sanchez cursed to himself as he jumped off the mountain bike because he wasn't able to maintain momentum up the steep hill. He pulled his firearm from the back of his black pants and continued up the hill.

Tip nervously glanced over his shoulder again and saw the top of Sanchez's head pop up from behind the hill. He noticed he was no longer on the bicycle, but was still charging fast. Tip reached Dorothy Street, which was quaint and serene. He was familiar with this area. Varying Chi Thetas had lived in 227 Dorothy over the past five years. This street was unknown to most students and locals. Whenever the residents of 227 threw a party half the guest couldn't find it.

Tip was in great shape, but no one was in good enough shape to continue sprinting much further on only one shoe and a bullet injury to the shoulder. He glanced over his right shoulder one last time. As he suspected, the houses favorably blocked him from Sanchez's line of sight. With this in mind, he headed over the curb and across the grass of the familiar lawn of house 227.

He cleared the four steps leading up to the front porch with a single prance and noticed the slight pain in his foot for the first time. It also left a small trace of blood on the top step. He grabbed the small metal handle on the wooden screen door. As usual, the door was unlocked. The door sprang quickly away from him, Tip grabbed the door with his hand just before it closed, preventing a loud slam.

Sanchez was not in sight when Tip entered. The screen enclosed the front porch of the house. Several old musty couches and chairs were strewn about randomly. These couches lay in wait for a sunny day, when their owners would pull them out onto the lawn. The city was currently attempting to pass an ordinance prohibiting students from bringing couches onto their front yards. If this ordinance passed, it would terminate one of the most enjoyable traditions at Michigan State University.

# CRISIS

Sanchez barreled around the corner, and Tip instantly hit the floor to keep out of sight. He slithered along the wood porch just like a marine passing under treacherous barbwire. He reached the cellar stairs and slinked down headfirst. This proved to be a fairly difficult task, and he had to rest most of his weight on his arms, and his right arm and shoulder ached like hell from the bullet wound.

Sanchez sprinted down Dorothy Street to the next avenue, Lilly. Sanchez's dark brown eyes darted east then west down the deserted street; Tip was nowhere in sight.

Tip dragged his sweat-drenched body under his friend's loft where he collapsed onto the mattress. Using every ounce of strength he had left, Tip took the elastic cord that his friend used to stretch and work out with and made a decent tourniquet for his wounded arm. Once this was complete, Tip's head crashed back and he closed his eyes. The game had begun.

Sanchez looked up and down Dorothy Street but Tip was nowhere to be found. He was about to turn and go when the "meow" of a cat caught his attention. What caught even more of his attention was the drop of blood that the cat was investigating. Sanchez barreled over the stairs scarring the skittish cat and then went cautiously into the house. The old wooden floorboards creaked underneath his weight. Sanchez saw that another drop of blood led in the direction of the basement. Sanchez quickly followed this trail and was now on the basement floor. About him was a small dank room with few amenities. There was one double bunk loft with two bed sheets hanging down giving the sleeping quarters some privacy. One of these sheets slightly moved. Pistol raised, Sanchez rapidly pulled the sheet back. To his dismay Sanchez looked at the large open ground floor window. There was blood on the sill, but Tip was nowhere in site.

# CHAPTER 20

Lisa brushed the back of her hand across her left cheek gently, and gave a slight wince. Her cheek was still sore and tender. The bruise was well concealed behind the layers of tan and rouge make-up. Lisa had become quite the cosmetic specialist the past year, and could probably show the folks in Hollywood a trick or two. Lisa could hide the bruise, but trying not to show the pain was a more difficult task.

Eddie's father, Eddie Braggert Jr., had just completed his third term as governor of the state of Virginia. He was the third Braggert to hold the title of Virginia Governor. The Braggerts had also continued making sound real estate investments and owned most of the land in their town of Oak Hill. Eddie's father, grandfather, and great grandfather all attended Yale, graduating near the top of their respective classes.

Eddie and Lisa had been dating since the ninth grade. Their courtship drew a tremendous amount of media coverage due to the Braggert's notoriety and the attractiveness of the young couple. Lisa was stunningly attractive and Eddie was her male counterpart, handsome and possessing a boyish charm.

Eddie wasn't blessed with the intellect of his forefathers and found school to be a struggle. With hard work and generous teachers, Eddie did fairly well in high school. But, Eddie performed miserably on the ACT and SAT college entrance exams. Because of his low scores, Eddie had a difficult time getting into a good college. With help from his father, however, he was admitted to The University of Virginia at Charlottesville. Without his father's influence there was little chance that this prestigious university would have admitted Eddie.

Eddie could feel the palpable pressure from his father. Eddie's less than spectacular board scores were a source of great embarrassment to the family. His father incorrectly attributed his poor scholastics to a lack of effort on Eddie's behalf. This wasn't the case. Eddie studied hard for the entrance exams, but knew all along that he'd be a great source of embarrassment. He'd been presenting the façade of a decent student to his father all along. Hard work coupled with an easy high school curriculum allowed Eddie to achieve good marks. These marks weren't up to the Braggert's usually high standards, but they were still very respectable.

Eddie wound up doing fairly well at UVA, but his success was attributable to the efforts of many others. Eddie didn't earn an honest mark during his four-year tenure at UVA. Ironic, since UVA is one of the nation's strictest universities when it came to academic fraud. Each UVA student is required to sign a cover sheet specifically stating that they have not cheated or assisted anyone in cheating on every exam they take. If anyone is ever caught performing an unethical act it goes to a review board.

The review board is comprised of sixty percent students, thirty percent faculty, and ten percent alumni. Certain cases eventually made it before the entire student body for a vote. Whether cheating students should be expelled is often placed in front of this committee, and almost always the students are expelled. Despite this strict policy, if someone has the means, they will find a way around the system. And, Eddie's father had the means. The saying, "rules are made to be broken," definitely applied in Eddie's case.

Eddie possessed a very likable and charismatic personality; people wanted to be around him. When Eddie wasn't in a torrid rage, he was the old Eddie. The Eddie Lisa loved. Around others, Eddie was always congenial and charismatic, so he didn't have too difficult of a time finding students that would assist him in cheating, especially when he flashed a couple of crisp Ben Franklin's their way. Even the best-intentioned students had to pay their surmounting stack of bills. A thousand greenbacks to write a simple paper wouldn't hurt society. Eddie actually wound up graduating

# CRISIS

with honors from The University of Virginia and, although it wasn't Yale, his parents weren't too embarrassed. But, the guilt caused by his constant deceiving and cheating needed to be released somehow. Unfortunately his shortcomings were brutally taken out on Lisa's beautiful, yet fragile skin and heart.

The abuse started about eight months ago, when Eddie realized the LSAT was rapidly approaching. With a decent score on the LSAT, Eddie would be able to get into Yale law school, largely due to his father's political clout. Eddie needed a score of 165 to have a legitimate chance of getting in. A Virginia student who achieved the grades Eddie had would have about a seventy percent chance of obtaining this score; Eddie knew he didn't have a prayer of achieving the score required. His grandfather had scored a 175 only to be topped by his father's perfect 180. The pressure had become too much for Eddie, and he was releasing his frustration on Lisa.

After the first beating, Lisa didn't speak to Eddie for two weeks. Eddie courted her like never before, sending her flowers everyday and promising her it would never happen again. Lisa was too ashamed to tell anyone at the time, and eventually trusted Eddie. She agreed that it was probably attributable to the pressure applied by his father and it really wasn't the real Eddie. He'd just snapped under the pressure and she was in the wrong place at the wrong time. Besides, he had never broken a promise to her before.

A month after getting back together with him, the drinking and beatings started again, only this time they were much worse. Lisa really had no one to confide in. Her father and her only brother had passed away, leaving only her mother. Mrs. Appleton wasn't a viable option though as the two unexpected deaths left her extremely traumatized. The situation was exasperated when the second death occurred eight months after the first. Her mother began dropping weight dramatically, to the point were she could no longer stand. Lisa's mom had been hospitalized for over a year now. Lisa had nowhere to turn, but knew that she needed to stop seeing Eddie. She needed to get as far away from this sadistic animal as possible. But, getting away was complicated by the fact that her mother was in the local hospital and wouldn't be able to move anytime soon.

Mrs. Appleton resided in the Shanty Creek Retirement home just off of Interstate 64, near Monticello. This home was usually reserved for people thirty years her elder. Lisa loved her mother dearly and visited her everyday at the home. The doctors were wary at first of letting her visit. They explained that Mrs. Appleton couldn't tolerate undue stress or anxiety in her fragile condition. The doctors went so far as to arrange a weeklong training seminar for Lisa. This precautionary seminar instructed her about what she should and shouldn't say during visitation hours. She knew she couldn't broach the subject of Eddie's beatings. Ms. Appleton loved Eddie and frequently told Lisa that what kept her alive was the vision of one day seeing their grandchildren.

So, Lisa pretended things were fine with him. She did have trouble making up excuses as to why Eddie wasn't there on Sundays. In the past, Eddie had always stopped by the retirement home after church on Sunday mornings. Lisa decided she would tell her mom that he was taking a preparatory class for the LSAT on Sunday mornings. This ploy would work for at least a little while. Lisa intended to continue this charade with the hope her mother would get better. Once her mom was better, Lisa would wait for an opportune time to gently tell the horrific story.

Lisa never had the opportunity to implement this plan, however. The older Eddie Braggert caught wind of the young couple's troubles and quickly put an end to it. Eddie Braggert Jr. would have no part of this nonsense; this was an election year for crying out loud. Braggert was already in a difficult race against a young homegrown Republican, Todd Brook. If the press got wind of Virginia's prized "romance novel" being on its last chapter, it would be disastrous. News of the couple breaking up could be enough to push Brook over the top. And, if the voters discovered the cause of the couple's break up, which would be inevitable, then he'd be soundly defeated.

While the American public was becoming incessantly tolerant of political scandals and immoral acts, such things didn't play at all well in the conservative South. This dilemma caused significant concern for the Senior Braggert. But, as was the case so many times before, he had an ace up his sleeve.

# CRISIS

Lisa's family was extremely poor, and when her father passed away it only made matters worse. She tried to manage the best she could. She started working long hours at the University of Virginia's Libraries for extra income. She sent all discretionary income home to her mom. But, there was no way she could cover the cost of the expensive nursing home.

Mr. Braggert, who never missed an opportunity for some good publicity, graciously stepped in to pay for Mrs. Appleton's stay at the retirement home. Mr. Braggert didn't visit the home often, but when he did, a reporter and photographer always happened to be on his coattails. Governor Braggert was deft at expressing surprise and disdain at the media's presence at the retirement home.

Mr. Braggert emphatically told Lisa that, if she didn't settle her differences with Eddie, then he'd have no other option than to cut off his monthly checks to Shanty Creek for one very sick patient. Mr. Braggert knew that money was power; he loved power.

Lisa's only alternative was to do what Braggert said, but she didn't have to be cooperative about it. Lisa avoided all non-essential contact with Eddie, only talking to him at public functions where the Governor required her presence. The past sixth months had been a living hell, and she felt like a prostitute. She kept telling herself that she had to do it for her mother's sake. The only saving grace was that Eddie said he felt terrible about the whole situation and was a perfect gentleman every time they came into contact. Eddie even began sending Lisa her favorite flowers, Daisies, every other day asking her forgiveness. Lisa almost fell for Eddie's ploys again. But, last night following the Governor's Ball, Eddie's reformation once again gave way to alcohol and violence.

Lisa winced again as she accidentally came into contact with her cheek while brushing her hair. A small trickle of a tear rolling down her cheek soothed the sting slightly. She looked in the mirror and was totally disheartened. The invisible cell that had become her life was becoming too difficult to face. No matter how difficult her life was, before all was said and done, she was determined to clear her brother's good name.

# CHAPTER 21

Tip quickly paid the driver of the Spartan Cab exact change for the fair. He'd barely scraped together enough money for the flight, and, as much as he'd like to give out a much-deserved gratuity to the cab driver he just couldn't afford it. He only had $200 remaining for food and lodging, and this money had to last him for the remainder of the trip. He'd definitely be asking for an extra bag of peanuts on the plane. He hoped he didn't get on of those flight attendants that hoarded snacks like they were little bags of gold. He didn't even know if airlines gave out peanuts anymore due to a tragic allergic reaction a few weeks ago.

Tip told his fraternity brothers that he was going home to visit his sister for a couple of days and not to worry about him. Tip told the Hamilton's that he'd be on an Outward Bound trip with a couple of friends in his study group for a project and that he'd be in the wilderness without much cellular phone coverage.

Tip entered Lansing's Capital Area airport and made his way toward the Northwest Airline's terminal.

Tip plopped down on a bedraggled gray vinyl seat and picked up an abandoned portion of a *USA Today* newspaper. The only section left behind by the unknown owner was the sports section, which was fine with Tip. He turned to the Hockey page and began scanning the box scores from the night before. He finally found the game he was looking for: New York Rangers 3 Colorado Avalanche 2. One of his high school teammates, Bob Reynolds, had bypassed college to play minor league hockey. Reynolds had excelled in the Avalanche's farm system, and had been brought up to the majors less than a month ago. Tip ascertained that Reynolds had played about two shifts but didn't have any notable statistics to speak of.

Tip smelled the distinct and disgusting smell of a cheap cigar filling the air and peered up from the newspaper to pinpoint its location. He glanced to his right, then to his left before finding the source of the air pollution. The offender was sitting across from him and about five chairs down. The man slowly turned toward Tip. As the man's face came into focus, a hard lump formed in Tip's throat.

Tip raised the Sports section up to conceal his face. He then loosened his baseball cap from his backpack's hanger loop with his free right hand. Tip kept the newspaper held high and calmly pulled the baseball lid tight to his head, resting it barely above the brow.

The hat wasn't much lower than he usually wore it, since this extremely low position was in style on campus. Tip cautiously glanced up again, and once again, he was starring right into the beady eyes of the man he'd run into yesterday afternoon; there was no mistaking those coal-like eyes. Tip slowly scanned the room, never losing sight of the cigar with his peripheral vision. He was looking for the thug 's buddy to make an appearance, but there was no sign of him. He checked the other gates around him, and noticed that his flight was the only one leaving for quite sometime, hence "coal-eyes" must be on the same flight. He thought they'd have a great conversation if seated next to one another.

Tip stiffened as he felt a light tap on his right shoulder-his arm was still throbbing from the wound from the grazed bullet. He slowly turned and saw a little 10-year old boy.

"Excuse me sir, can you please tell me what time it is?" asked the pretentious kid who was wearing a Mighty Morphine Power Rangers watch.

"Timmy, turn around and leave that nice man alone," shouted a frazzled mother who was busy dressing Timmy's little sister. Timmy's sister didn't appear to be cooperating and was producing a painful scream to express her displeasure. "Timmy, I told you we'll be on the plane in ten minutes, now sit down and behave yourself, you're embarrassing me."

Timmy did as his mother instructed, but not before sticking his tongue out at Tip. Tip blocked out the three-ringed circus

# CRISIS

around him and turned his attention back to the dark-eyed man. Tip stared at an empty seat in disbelief and in a panic lowered his newspaper to give him a clear view of the entire terminal. Tip didn't see him anywhere.

"Mom, I'm hungry," whined Timmy.

"You'll have to wait 'til we get on the plane, the nice people will feed you then," answered the mother quickly, obviously used to this tedious line of questioning.

Tip wanted to strangle the little brat who was now writhing in mock hunger pain next to him.

Tip checked out the immediate area again and stared at the line forming at the TCBY Yogurt station. There stood the man in the tan trench coat sucking the remaining life out of his cigar. His partner whom Tip had the pleasure of also meeting the previous afternoon now joined the dark-eyed, dark-haired man. The two gentlemen were a good distance from the check-in counter, so Tip seized his window of opportunity. Thankfully, there was no line at the check-in as Tip approached.

The stingy haired Northwest ticket agent limply took Tip's ticket from him.

"Sir, you're all set. You've already checked in," he said in a high-pitched voice with a slight lisp. The agent's uniform was perfectly ironed, and not one of his few hairs was out of place.

"Yes, I know. I was wondering if there were any seats available in the back," asked Tip.

"In the back?" the agent asked, obviously intrigued by such a strange request.

Tip glanced over to the yogurt line. Both Sanchez and Garcia were now ordering something from the burger stand adjacent to it.

"Yes, I'm afraid of flying and prefer to be near the restroom in case there is an emergency situation," said Tip.

"Oh, a big man like you shouldn't be afraid of anything, least of all flying. Here it is, a window seat in the very last row okay," asked the agent.

"Yes, that would be perfect. Thank you," said Tip as he took the ticket from the agent. He saw the Sanchez and Garcia making their way toward the jet way.

"Noooo, thank *you*," said the agent helplessly fawning over Tip.

Tip took six fluid strides toward the jet-way. People were funneling toward the jet-way in response to the first boarding call. Those privileged to board the plane first were the first class and preferred flyers.

Tip arrived in line at the same time as a bald and portly gentleman in his mid-thirties. Tip wanted to be as far ahead of Sanchez and Garcia as possible, but he didn't want to create a scene. He kindly let the gentleman go ahead of him. He took another glance at the queue behind him, and spotted Garcia and Sanchez about seven people back. Tip was comforted by the thought that if he did have another run-in with Garcia and Sanchez, they wouldn't have their firearms on the plane.

The flight attendant accepting tickets at the gateway was a spunky blonde in her late twenties. She had an overwhelming smile and was a little too perky. She'd also over-applied her hairspray. Tip kept his eyes forward and kept shuffling toward the jet-way, he would not chance looking back again.

"How are we doing today?" the flight attendant asked Tip.

"Fine, thank you," said Tip under his breath.

The flight attendant glanced down at Tip's ticket and crisply tore it along the perforation line, "You're in seat 37A, Mr. Tipton!"

# CHAPTER 22

Lisa rested her head in her right palm while glancing down at the numerous photocopies of donation checks that had poured into the Chi Theta headquarters since she'd been working there. Also spread out in front of her on the large oak tables at the University of Virginia's library where numerous vertical files and financial reports on the Merchel Construction Company. She once again starred at the five donations that didn't coincide with the Chi Theta alumni list.

Her investigation progress was dealt a slight blow earlier that afternoon. Mrs. McDoogal explained that the Chi Theta roster wasn't as accurate as it really should be, since the data was stored on paper in the earlier years instead of by computer, and there were bound to be a few pages lost in the shuffle. Mrs. McDoogal went on to explain that a tremendous amount of material was lost or misplaced when the National Headquarters was relocated from Duke University in 1988. This news didn't deter Lisa, however, because she had a strong hunch that it wasn't just coincidence that all these large and unusual checks were all being sent from the same city. It's true that a few may be attributed to outdated lists, but she didn't believe they all were.

Lisa picked up a small article from the *Wall Street Journal*:

*Newark, NJ: In a surprise move today, Ricardo Valez stepped down from his post as Managing Director of Merchel's Construction's Eastern Operations. CEO and close friend, Mark Hernandez, stated that no immediate predecessor had been announced and indicated that the company prefers not to lose good people like Ricardo Valez. Hernandez said the search would take awhile since Valez was so instrumental to the company's rapid success. Valez leaves Merchel after fourteen years and was one of the few original employees of the company. With Valez's departure, there are now only two remaining original employees, Spencer Tanke and Mike Wasco.*

---

Tip let out a paroxysm of coughing when the flight attendant started to say his name after reading his seat assignment. The coughing effectively drowned out her perkiness and prevented her words from carrying to Sanchez and Garcia.

"Stupid Michigan weather," Tip said for the benefit of the flight attendant.

"Please watch your head sir and good luck getting rid of that nasty cough," said the flight attendant with full red lips at the end of the jet-way.

Tip ducked his head and entered the Northwest 737. The cabin was filling rapidly and the bustling caused it to be somewhat balmy. The overhead air outlets had yet to be turned on. This contributed to the swamp-like atmosphere. These overhead outlets only worked when the plane was in motion, not the smartest design.

Tip kept his eyes focused on the bald spot in front of him. The portly gentleman came to an abrupt stop at the eighteenth row and was struggling to find room for his carry-on. Most of the overhead compartments were stuffed. The man's short stature wasn't helping matters, so Tip assisted him. Tip made sure he kept his head facing rearward as he helped the stranger store his bag. The stranger felt inadequate as a man having another guy help him. He needed Tip's assistance, and thanked him quietly, averting his eyes in a shameful manner.

Tip now had clear sailing to his seat, and calmly made his way to the back of the plane. When Tip arrived at his seat, he made sure to look at the floor allowing his baseball hat to conceal his face. Seat 37A was a window seat, and Tip had a difficult time cramming his large body into the second-class seat. Tip usually got to the airport early enough to reserve an aisle emergency row seat.

Tip removed the in-flight magazine from the seatback in front of him. This month's issue had a picture of Jessica Simpson on the cover. He acted like he was entrenched by the literary masterpiece. He was actually looking over the top of it in an effort to locate Sanchez and Garcia.

Both men were in dark blue suits and were currently waiting behind a red-haired woman in a purple and pink sweat suit. Garcia and Sanchez both had their ties loosened and collars unbuttoned to combat the heat in the plane. Tip noticed that the fingers on Sanchez's right hand were wrapped in medical tape. No doubt a result of his escapade on the roof yesterday afternoon. Tip found satisfaction discovering that he wasn't the only one hurting from yesterday's events. He was notably stiff and sore from yesterday's activities. Tip was used to this aching feeling from years of playing the rough and tumble sport of hockey. Today reminded him how much he relished this sensation during his playing days. Soreness was an indication that he had let it all hang out the on ice the night before. However, the lance on his shoulder from the bullet was a new kind of pain. It was a continual burning sensation. Fortunately, the bullet had only glanced his shoulder. Tip could imagine how painful a direct bullet hit would be; he didn't want to find out.

The lady in the purple sweat suit finally planted her ass in her seat, much to the chagrin of the college student seated next to her. Garcia and Sanchez were about fifteen rows from Tip, but didn't look like they were going to stop anytime soon. Tip frightfully looked at the two empty seats next to him. Sanchez and Garcia were now five rows from him. Sanchez glanced down at his ticket and finally stopped. Sanchez took off his jacket, revealing two large pit stains on his black shirt, and threw it in the overhead storage above seat thirty-three and Garcia proceeded to do the same. Tip breathed a sigh of relief.

The elderly couple next to Tip braced themselves as the plane touched down at Washington's National Airport. The fasten seat belt sign was extinguished and everyone popped out of their seats. They comically resembled bread popping out of the toaster when the plane's tone generator "binged." Everyone was in a frenzy to get their belongings out of the overhead compartments as quickly as possible, and thus the obligatory plane departure dance began in earnest. The passengers were in a frenzy to get their luggage only to have to stand and wait. Hurry up and wait. Clearly, no one was getting off the plane anytime soon, yet everyone was standing in the aisles clutching their baggage trying in vain to ascertain what the hold-up was.

Tip blocked out the commotion around him and kept a watchful eye on Garcia and Sanchez from his slumped position. The elderly couple was very deliberate in their plane departure procedures, which didn't bother Tip too much because it would be difficult to lose sight of Sanchez and Garcia who were also stuck in this human traffic jam.

The line of people finally began to shuffle toward the bulkhead. He was the last one on the plane to stand up and, although stiff, it sure felt good. Anything felt good after slumping for roughly two hours in a cramped seat with your eyes constantly searching the plane in front of you. Besides being physically fatigued, he was mentally exhausted by the rapid developments of the past twenty-four hours.

Tip extended his left knee a couple of times to clear the cobwebs and stiffness caused by the flight. Tip still had his hat tugged down tight, and was ready to look away if either Sanchez or Garcia decided to turn around.

The cool air of the jet-way was a pleasant relief from the flying oven. Tip scanned the mass of bobbing heads moving forward in front of him. Sanchez and Garcia were now about fifty yards in front of him and would definitely lengthen this lead once they reached the concourse. Tip was trapped in the slow moving traffic inside the jet-way.

It was now a little after four o'clock in the afternoon, and the airport was teaming with activity. Tip was thankful that the only main exit was to his left, as he'd lost sight of both Sanchez and Garcia. This was the only way the two goons could have taken. Tip began taking longer strides, and started to pass people left and right.

Tip accidentally brushed into a couple of people, but at this point he didn't care about being polite to strangers.

Tip could see over the tumultuous sea of hair, which undulated in the concourse, and was looking for the familiar jet-black hair of Sanchez and Garcia. Tip was approaching a fork in the airport terminal. The left fork went to the baggage claim and the right fork took travelers to ground transportation.

Tip recalled that Sanchez and Garcia each had a decent size carry-on bag and veered right in the direction of ground transportation. The sea of hair made its way toward the baggage claim and Tip sliced his way through the crowd whenever he saw an opening.

A huge sign with a picture of the capital building and Lincoln Memorial welcomed travelers to the Nation's Capital. Tip proceeded through the automatic glass revolving door glancing to his left and right. Damn, he spotted Garcia standing about thirty feet to his left taking a long draw off a hand rolled cigarette. Tip stayed in the revolving door and let it take him back toward the safe confines of the airport terminal.

The door revolved Tip around, but suddenly he was facing Sanchez who was twenty feet away and rapidly approaching. Tip exited the door with his head down avoiding eye contact with Sanchez and actually brushed Sanchez's shoulder, and he could only hope that Sanchez didn't notice him.

Tip slid over to a vestibule next to the valet parking cashier's desk and removed his charcoal Patagonia pullover coat as he was starting to sweat profusely. Tip was safe in his current location. The afternoon sunlight was hitting the building, and there was no way Sanchez and Garcia would be able to see him through the reflection on the large glass partition separating them. Garcia ground his cigarette butt into the sidewalk, and after a brief exchange of words with Sanchez, got on the payphone.

"Yeah, we took care of it. Boss wants to have dinner with us tomorrow to discuss the details? No problem. See you then," said Garcia, and he hung up the phone.

Sanchez hailed a red cab, and both men entered the backseat solemnly.

Tip raced out the door frantically looking for a cab. There were none immediately in sight. Sanchez and Garcia's cab hurried away and out of sight. By the time Tip was able to hail a cab, Sanchez and Garcia were long gone.

Tip exited the cab after his short journey and pulled his coat collar closer to his neck to protect himself from the rain. Tip looked ahead through the gray drizzle and saw the blue neon vacancy sign, which actually read V C NCY, since both A's no longer illuminated. Above the vacancy sign was a much bigger rectangular and unlit sign that stated that this was the Capitol Inn. The faded sign was difficult to read, especially in the rain, but Tip's 20/15 eyesight came in handy.

Tip had instructed the cab driver to deliver him to a cheap, yet clean hotel on or near the University of Maryland campus. The Capitol Inn definitely looked cheap. Hopefully it was clean.

## CHAPTER 23

Valez's ominous figure formed in Lisa's peripheral vision as she continued to type busily on the computer in front of her. Valez's back was to her as he exited his office and he habitually locked the door upon exiting.

"Who's that handsome man? Oh it's my nephew Ricardo," said a portly older woman dressed in a long gray wool skirt and red sweater.

Lisa recognized the woman as Ricardo's Aunt-Aunt Gloria. Aunt Gloria worked in the Student Services building. She was the Corporate Recruiting Director for the University of Maryland's Masters of Business Program. Aunt Gloria was responsible for bringing businesses to the campus to conduct seminars or to interview qualified student applicants for entry-level positions with their companies.

Whenever her day's activities brought her to Ricardo's side of campus, she stopped in for a visit. As one could imagine, Valez wasn't always around when she stopped by, so she'd usually have a long chat with Mrs. McDoogal. Lisa had spoken with Aunt Gloria on one other occasion and she was indeed a very pleasant lady, although she was rather long-winded.

"Oh what a GLORIA-ous surprise," responded Valez, a stock response he'd been using since he was eleven.

Aunt Gloria blushed and gave Valez a huge hug and a soft peck on the cheek. The scene before her caused Lisa to conjure up images of embracing hippos wearing tiny moo-moos.

"I hate to do this to you, Aunt Gloria, but I'm on my way out right now. Someone's coming to pick me up," said Valez.

"Oh, no trouble at all, I was just in the area. I'll walk with you on the way out," said Gloria and they both headed for the doorway with little room to spare on either side of the hallway.

A small metallic object on the wooden bookshelves caught Lisa's attention. It was less than six feet in front of her by Valez's office.

---

Lisa focused in on the metal object resting on the wooden bookcases. She couldn't believe her eyes- it was the key to Valez's office. Valez must have placed it there when he went to give Aunt Gloria a hug and had forgotten about it.

Lisa glanced in both directions to determine if anyone was watching, and headed for the bookcases. The bookcases shelved all of the past editions of the Chi Theta newsletter, *The Sakoa*. *The Sakoa* tree was the fraternity's sacred icon. *The Sakoa* symbolized the fact that the first chapter of Chi Theta was founded on Stanford University's campus in 1889. *The Sakoa* was in the same genre as other sorority and fraternity publications such as Theta Chi's *The Rattle*, Delta Sigma Phi's *The Carnation* and Chi Omega's *The Owl*. Lisa researched all other Fraternity and Sorority newsletters to see if there was anything unusual about *The Sakoa*. She discovered that *The Sakoa* didn't differ much from the others.

Lisa bent down next to the section of cases that stored the 1970's editions of *The Sakoa*. She placed her hand on the top of the shelf as if for balance and deftly palmed the medium sized brass key.

---

Tip woke up after a long and deep sleep and was still extremely sore from his escape activities two days earlier. The hard support bar in the center of this cheap bed didn't help matters, but that is what one can expect for the low-price of thirty-nine dollars a night in the Nation's Capital. The cabbie was right; although the room was sparse, it was clean. Tip did a hundred military-style push-ups to get his blood pumping. During check-in last night, he ascertained that the hotel was about a fifteen-minute walk from Fraternity Row. He tidied up his bed before leaving, because the hotel only changed the sheets every third day for extended guests. Tip assumed that he would be spending at least one more night in this room.

The desk clerk's directions were very accurate and Tip found Fraternity Row with no trouble at all. He was amazed at how new the buildings looked and that the exteriors were identical. He thought it would be great to be in a fraternity that was located in the midst of all the other Greek houses on campus. Yet, at the same time, he didn't like the idea of living in such a "cookie cutter" environment. While all of these houses were nicely decorated, they lacked personality, character, and charm. He enjoyed the walk from the Capitol Inn to Fraternity Row because it was a gorgeous fall day and it helped limber up some of his stiff and sore muscles.

Tip plopped himself down against a large oak tree. The bark supplied ample back support and Tip was facing in the direction of the Chi Theta National Headquarters. He laid his black Eddie Bauer backpack beside him and pulled out his Accounting 325 Book entitled *Corporate Tax*. *Corporate Tax* was merely a prop. He wouldn't read a word from it during his stakeout. Since he was perched high on the grassy hill, Tip had a great vantage point to view the Chi Theta National Headquarters and any associated activity.

The house looked the same as the pictures Tip had reviewed over the past couple of days. From the photographs, Tip had imagined the house being much larger than what stood before him. The grounds surrounding the house were taken care of with immaculate precision. A ground crew comprising two male students was performing routine maintenance on the lawn and shrubs. Any intricate jobs would require their manager's skill. The taller of the two students was painstakingly clipping the two shrubs in front of the Headquarters. One shrub was shaped like the Greek letter Chi (X), while the other was the Greek letter Theta (Θ). The other student was attentively raking the few shriveled leaves that had fallen on the lush lawn.

Tip watched two portly individuals exit from the side door of the house. One was a male and the other female. His review of Chi Theta photographs prior to the trip would soon help his cause. Tip recognized the Executive Director of Chi Theta, Ricardo Valez. Tip couldn't identify Valez's female companion.

A long, black Lincoln Towne Car pulled into the circular brick driveway and halted in front of Valez. Valez gave the women a hug and a kiss on the cheek and headed toward the backseat of the Lincoln. Garcia stepped out of the passenger seat and opened the rear door for Valez. Tip couldn't help but drop his book from in front of his face. Staring dumbfounded at Garcia, Tip forgot for the moment that he needed to be inconspicuous. Snapping out of his trance, Tip once again concealed his face behind the textbook. He was now more confused than ever, but knew that this was definitely a huge clue in this enormous puzzle. What piece of the puzzle it was he didn't know, but time would hopefully tell.

---

Lisa eyed the key in her small purse pouch. She told herself over and over again that it was indeed the key to Valez's office. She didn't dare test the key during working hours, not while the other Chi Theta employees buzzing about. She would have to wait and come back when the office was closed. She still had to deal with the problem of avoiding the security guard, Joe Laplanski. She knew Joe, because his shift started at five-thirty in the afternoon and continued until roughly eight-thirty in the morning. She generally ran into him first thing in the morning.

Joe was a very large individual, ranging to about six-foot-four and tipping the scales at about two hundred and seventy pounds. Lisa estimated him at about forty years old. Every morning Lisa (Holly Crane to Joe) came in early, Joe's empty box of a dozen Dunkin' Donuts was in the wastebasket. She routinely said "hi" to Joe every morning, but that was about the extent of their relationship. She had to remain true to her Holly Crane façade of being a meek little mouse. If the rumors were true, then Joe Laplanski spent a majority of his security hours fast asleep. Lisa believed there is some form of

# CRISIS

truth in every rumor, which, in this case, would be a tremendous help to her snooping plans.

---

Tip's lower back was really hurting from sitting beneath the tree. He'd only allowed himself two breaks from the tree trunk throughout the long day. One break was used to visit the restroom at a nearby restaurant and the other was for lunch. He would pack his lunch tomorrow. He didn't have the time or the energy this morning to visit the local grocery store to obtain the ingredients to make an adequate meal. Going the entire day without eating wasn't an option, so he had to improvise for lunch this afternoon. He selected a dorm nearby. He clandestinely merged his way into the lunch line at Worchester Hall.

"Oh, crud. I left my card at home, would it be cool if I swung through here? I can bring it back at dinner."

"Don't worry about it this time, but you should probably put it in your wallet dude," replied the student working the door to the lunchroom.

Tip had to admit that the food was much better at Roslin Hall than it was at Michigan State. That was saying a lot, because Tip thought MSU's food wasn't half bad.

Tip liked the fact that this Maryland cafeteria had a plethora of fresh fruit. Michigan State's dorm food was always good, but was loaded with starch and carbohydrates. Tip could have easily gorged himself with food for two hours, but allotted himself only thirty minutes. He knew that he had to get back to his stakeout position by the tree. That was another reason why Tip would need to pack his lunch tomorrow. He couldn't afford to miss any of the activity at Chi Theta.

Tip also liked the food at Worchester Hall for another reason: he didn't have to experience the traditional bowel movements that he was accustomed to after eating at the MSU dorms. Freshmen at MSU always had to fight for bathroom time ten minutes after they'd finished their meals. Either their bodies got accustomed to eating at the same time everyday, or the dorm food just went right through their system. Most of the bathrooms were shared amongst four persons and thus you didn't want to be batting clean up, literally. The seat would be nice and warm, but the air wouldn't be so nice.

Staking out was a long and arduous process, but it was worth it. Seeing Garcia associated with Valez this morning had already justified the trip and accompanying time commitment. It eliminated any remaining doubts. He was now truly convinced that Hamilton's death was no accident, and that the unusual letter was directly related to it. He needed to figure out what the underlying connection was, and what the unusual letter meant.

Tip watched Lisa exit from the Headquarters at exactly five-thirty. He took the opportunity to stretch out his cramped legs. It was the same girl that Tip had witnessed arriving at eight-thirty that morning. As she was exiting, a very large man in black polyester pants and a tight black security shirt entered the headquarters. Both parties exchanged pleasantries, although it was difficult for Tip to tell this, since the girl was constantly looking at the ground.

Even with the binoculars, Tip could barely make out the red semi-circular patch on the security guard's sleeve. Tip determined, after much adjusting and squinting that the bantam red patch read Bradley Security. Tip quickly jotted this information down into his spiral notebook. Tip had been keeping track of all the individuals and nuances he'd observed around the headquarters in this journal.

Most of the log was comprised of times and descriptions of individuals who came and went. According to Tip's notes, with the departure of Lisa, there were only two others that were still in the building. Tip would wait for these two to exit the building before he granted himself another break.

Tip turned his attention back to Lisa, who was now about two blocks from the headquarters. Tip noticed that the girl no longer had a sheepish walk. The girl now held her head high and her shoulders were aligned in proper posture. An air of confidence almost surrounded her, which wasn't the case just a minute ago. Tip thought this rather odd and noted it into his journal. Tip hypothesized that perhaps the girl was so weighted down by the demands of her job that she became a different person once the worries of the day were lifted. Tip would have to test this hypothesis, because he deemed this theory highly unlikely. Tip suspected that anything that seemed unusual at the Headquarters probably was indeed just that—unusual.

---

Sanchez was glad that he was driving. He could act like he was concentrating on the road and didn't have to meet Valez's stare. Garcia seated in the passenger seat wasn't so lucky.

"You know I don't have to waste my breath stating how extremely disappointed I am in you fellas," said Valez.

Sanchez nodded in agreement without turning his head. He knew that it wasn't wise to argue or make excuses with Valez.

"Please tell me if I have this correct. I send you two up to Michigan to get one lousy envelope, a bright red envelope at that. For this easy task you were to be paid an extremely generous sum of $10,000 each. I actually debated about calling you guys on this job, figuring that it would be a waste to use such great professionals on an easy job. But, I heard that the tables hadn't been too kind to you boys lately, so I thought I'd do you a favor. Hell, you guys have done good work for me over the years. However, instead of getting this envelope as I instructed, you bring me back three dead students. Mind you, I don't mind the deaths, but I do mind the suspicion and messiness it creates. I've already heard the details on the first set of deaths, and that's an unfortunate circumstance. Please fill me in on who and why this third individual was erased.

Sanchez tried to be as concise as possible in explaining the extenuating circumstances around the third death. Sanchez needed to be careful and put the correct twist on it so that Valez would agree that this third corpse was unavoidable.

Valez listened intently and waited for Sanchez to finish. "Do you agree with what Mr. Sanchez has said Mr. Garcia?" Valez asked in a measured voice.

"Yes, sir," said Garcia.

"Well, then I guess we'll chalk that one up as an unfortunate occurrence as well. As I mentioned, I told you guys to bring me the letter to me in order to get paid. Now, since you've both explained to me that no one can possibly have the letter or know about the letter, then the job is just as complete as if I actually held the letter in my hand. However, since I don't have the letter, I believe it's reasonably fair, almost generous on my part, to pay you boys half of the your contract fee. Are we in agreement?"

Both Sanchez and Garcia nodded their heads in unison.

"Good, I'm glad we all feel that way. Now, I hope for your sake, that the letter doesn't suddenly resurface. If it does happen to resurface, well, I'd be very unhappy," Valez said in a threatening tone.

Garcia and Sanchez knew what they were risking by accepting money from Valez for an uncompleted job, but they both desperately needed the money. This financial position was the driving force behind Garcia and Sanchez's agreement that morning to accept any money offered them. Another exponent that factored into their decision was their honest belief that the letter wouldn't turn up again. Both of them would have loved to ask Valez what was in the letter, but thought better of it.

# CHAPTER 24

Tip cautiously peered through the East Side window of the Chi Theta Headquarters. It was eleven o'clock at night. He was well concealed by the dark shadows of the building. The majority of the lights within the headquarters were off. He looked up and down the office doors. The interior, like the exterior, was familiar to him from the various manuals he had digested on his flight to D.C. Tip noticed that the carpet had been recently replaced. What was once gray was now a rich royal purple. The only office that Tip recognized was that of the Executive Director.

Several of the brochures that Tip had reviewed had photographs of Executive Directors standing outside of their office doors. However, all the doors in the Chi Theta Headquarters were identical. One of the more recent pictures was of an executive director sitting behind the desk inside his office. The view behind him was of Fraternity Road, which clued Tip in that the Executive Directors office had to be located at the West corner wing of the headquarters.

Tip stared across the length of the headquarters to the Executive Director's corner office suite. There were four desks placed evenly apart in the administrative area. The secretary's light outside of the Executive Director's office was on and was tilted toward a rolling chair. On this chair sat the corpulent security guard. The guard had the chair positioned so that his back was to Valez's door, and he was looking out on the open area and toward the front entrance.

The guard was reading *People Magazine* while he was eating the remaining array of flavored donut holes like a machine gun. Tip could almost hear the guard getting fatter as he stared in disbelief at the empty Dunkin' Donuts box at the man's feet. The side of the donut box indicated that, at one time, it had contained 60 donut holes.

Tip carefully inspected the window and adjoining window frame before him. He was pleased to see that the frame was quite old. A simple driver's license or credit card would allow anyone easy access. Also conducive for illegal entry was the low placement of the windows in relation to the ground. There would be no need for a more complicated and probably more conspicuous means of entry.

Tip returned his attention to the guard and thought it quite a peculiar location. It seemed to Tip that the security guard would be centrally located on the grounds to provide the most effective surveillance of the building. Instead, the guard was positioned to the corner furthest from the main entrance.

Tip scrutinized the guard, checking for any concealed weapons. The guard appeared to only be armed with a Billy club. A two-way radio was noticeably absent from the "rental cops" thick belt. The absence of a radio was peculiar since most large security agencies supplied their employees with them for obvious emergency reasons. Most "rental cops" also had heavy walkie-talkies or radios as a means of defense. The radios appeared harmless to most, but the heavy bottom could really pack a wallop if necessary. Security agencies generally didn't allow their personnel to carry guns since it, ironically, made the guards more susceptible to violent acts. Experience showed that criminals were less likely to kill or maim if they didn't feel threatened. It was also a liability issue for many security firms to bear the right to carry arms. Tip couldn't see a gun on this man, but that didn't mean that he didn't have one concealed somewhere nearby.

---

Lisa entered an old hardware store just outside of Arlington, Virginia. The glass door read Sandelston's in gold lettering. The gold lettering was shadow-lettered in black, which made it appear three-dimensional. The little brass bell attached to the top of the door made a jingle when she entered. The musty smell that she'd

# CRISIS

remembered as a little girl was still eminent. Lisa weaved her way through the store and found Bob Sandelston Jr. in the back talking to a customer about the virtues of wing nuts. Bob looked up, smiled at Lisa, and continued to assist the customer. The customer was finally satisfied and carried his ten wing nuts up to the cash register at the front of the store.

"Well, hello there Lisa. Long time no see. How's your mother doing?" asked Bob sincerely.

"She's doing a little better, thank you for asking. Her improvement will be slow for awhile, at least according to the doctor," replied Lisa.

"If I know your mom, she'll get through it, she's a strong woman and a fighter. Our prayers are with her and also with you," sincerely expressed Bob. The Sandelston's and Appleton's had known each other forever. Bob was ten years older than Lisa and babysat her when she was younger.

Bob Jr. was a tall, thin man with a boyishly round face. He was married to his high school sweetheart and they had two adorable daughters, Cindy and Samantha. He had assumed ownership of Sandelston's hardware store when his father passed away two years ago. He was the third generation to run the store. Lisa had only seen Bob about three times since she left for college. But like most small towns, people treated you as if you never left. The years had been kind to Bob. Aside from a few extra pounds around the middle and a few less hairs on the crown, he looked like Lisa remembered. Her brief reverie was interrupted by his query.

"What brings you by today?"

"Well, I was hoping you could do me a favor."

"Sure, anything, I'm sure that I owe ya one. What do you need."

"I need a key duplicated."

"Hell, that's no favor, that's part of my job," Lisa handed Bob the key. "Oh, I see...this is a tricky one, but let me see what I can do. I've got to warn you that this may take awhile," said Bob. Bob knew it was illegal to duplicate this type of key. He was also sure that Lisa already knew this. So, he didn't need to insult her by asking why she needed a duplicate made. He'd just help out as best he could and leave it at that. Bob sensed that Lisa was in trouble, but it wasn't his place to pry. If she needed more help he'd certainly do it, but she'd have to ask.

Metal flats for this type of key were only made by one company, BEST, and weren't distributed to local merchants. Thus, he wouldn't be able to make her a metal duplicate. Instead, he'd need to use a moldable plastic.

"I need to know how durable of a material to use for this type of duplication. How often are you planning on using this key?" Bob asked.

"I'll probably only use it one time," replied Lisa in a quiet tone so that a nearby customer wouldn't hear her. The customer was busying himself with checking out the lawn rakes on the nearby pegboard.

"Good, that makes things much easier. I'm going to generate the key-flat out of a hard plastic material. It should last about five times before the teeth become worn. Fives times sounds like it will satisfy your needs just fine. It'll take me about twenty minutes to duplicate and then I'll be back. If you don't mind helping out any customers while I'm gone I'd appreciate it," said Bob as he headed into the backroom. Lisa had helped around the store when her mom dropped her off as a child. She was pleasantly surprised to see that not much had changed. The town was still too small for Sandelstone's to worry about a Home Depot or Lowe's placing a store in the area and stealing all their business.

Bob returned about fifteen minutes later. "Here you go, this should do the trick. The plastic was giving me some malleability problems because it is a bit old, but it should work alright," Bob said reassuringly.

"I'm sure it'll be fine, you always do great work. I can't thank you enough, how much do I owe you?"

"This one's on me, just make sure you give your mother my

regards and please be careful, and do take care of yourself," said Bob and he held his gaze on Lisa emphasizing the word careful.

"Lisa leaned over and gave Bob a quick kiss on the cheek, "You're just too good to me, it was great seeing you again," she said as she exited by the side door which, unlike the front door, didn't have a brass bell attached to it.

―――――

Tip's feet were getting cold from the damp topsoil beneath them. He was also weary from the long day he'd spent observing the activities at the Chi Theta headquarters. Tip peered through the window one last time and saw that the guard still hadn't moved from his place in front of Valez's door. It was now about midnight. Tip had noticed that the guard never went on regular rounds to check the rest of the building. The only time the guard got up was to use the bathroom midway down the hall. Tip noted there were no windows in the bathroom, which might prove useful. Tip rose from his squat and started for the Capitol Inn.

# CHAPTER 25

The next day, Lisa came in at about eight o'clock, which was earlier than usual for her. Traffic in the nation's capital was very unpredictable. Traffic patterns fluctuated greatly in the Washington DC area, so commute times varied greatly. Lisa said her traditional good morning to the overweight security guard and began her routine of putting her coat away and logging onto her computer.

Lisa was thankful that Valez wasn't in the office yet, not that she expected he would be. Valez had never arrived before nine in the morning the whole time she'd worked there. She knew Valez hadn't arrived yet since his obnoxious cigar stench was noticeably absent from the air. Valez always had a cigar half-finished by the time he arrived in the morning. She watched the security guard stand and stretch his large frame. She paid close attention to the type of weapons and accessories he was carrying. She was trying to act naturally and avoid conveying her newfound apprehension to the security guard, but it was difficult not to squelch her nervousness. She knew the security guard was on a different team. The security guard didn't know Lisa was the enemy, and she intended to keep it that way.

Lisa had discovered through her investigation that Bradley Security didn't employ a Mr. John Laplanski. They had no record of ever supplying service to the Chi Theta Headquarters. Lisa knew that "John," if that was even his real name, had to be one of Valez's thugs. The only other time that Chi Theta required security was during the Million-Man March back in 1996. However, according to Mrs. McDoogal, there had been a security guard, like John Laplanski, since day one of Valez's appointment to Executive Director.

Mrs. McDoogal made her usual cheery morning entrance past Lisa's desk. She made a point to compliment Lisa on something everyday. Today, Mrs. McDoogal was telling Lisa how she loved arriving to work after her in the morning. The reason she loved it was because it meant that Lisa's perky face was the first thing that greeted her at the office.

Mrs. McDoogal's arrival was the guard's cue to leave. The guard could leave once two employees arrived after eight o'clock. With the guard out of the picture, Lisa reached into her purse to grab the original brass key in one hand, and a Kleenex in the other. She pretended to blow her nose and rubbed the Kleenex gently over the key to remove any incriminating fingerprints. She then proceeded, with Kleenex in hand, to the bookshelves and stooped down like she'd done before. Only this time she placed the key back where she'd originally found it.

Lisa stood up and glanced over to insure that Mrs. McDoogal was still preoccupied with brewing the office's morning Java, which she was. Since it was so much better than anyone else's, Mrs. McDoogal was the only one allowed to make coffee at the headquarters. Lisa had to admit, although not a big coffee fan, Mrs. McDoogal's brown gold was definitely the best she'd ever tasted. To Lisa's satisfaction, Mrs. McDoogal was still struggling to separate some of the Irish coffee filters that her family had sent from Dublin. Mrs. McDoogal's rosy face became more and more crimson the longer the filters contested her.

Lisa proceeded to unclip her Circular Polarizing Filter from her new Gateway computer monitor and shined the monitor with Windex and a soft cloth. With the Polarizing Filter and the help of the florescent lights shining above, the glare on Lisa's computer screen replicated a mirror. Lisa was now ready to do her covert monitoring of Valez. The thick glasses she wore for the character of Holly Cane also did a good job of obscuring her eyes. She stifled a smirk when she thought the glasses provided a benefit analogous to the sunglasses worn by meatheads on beaches in order to eyeball beautiful women.

# CRISIS

Tip sat against a different tree on the hill, about a hundred feet from yesterday's post. This oak tree was a little younger and hence a tad bit softer. Even though the tree was softer, it was still going to take its toll on his already tight back muscles.

Tip observed and documented the usual parade of characters that entered and exited the building in the morning. First, there was the shy, young woman dressed in frumpy clothes and unflattering spectacles. Tip once again noted that this girl's stride and demeanor significantly changed when she came within a block of the headquarters. Ten minutes later, a jolly older woman, wearing a flowered dress arrived. The guard left five minutes after the woman's arrival.

Tip had researched the Bradley Security Guard system and learned that the company was located on the eastern seaboard of Maryland and all of their clients were located in that region. This information, coupled with his observation of the guard's actions last night, lead him to believe that this guard was a personal hire of Valez's. At 9:23 am, Tip noted Valez's unescorted arrival.

Lisa could hear Valez's constricted breathing as he approached from the front entrance. She also caught a good whiff of his half-finished cigar as he stood in front of the door fumbling in his pocket for his key. Ostensibly working on a Microsoft Word document, Lisa was actually focused on the screen's reflection which had Valez's movements perfectly framed.

Valez rechecked all of his pockets, and then checked them again. Lisa could see Valez becoming thoroughly agitated. Finally, he noticed the brass key on the oak bookshelf next to him. Valez quickly picked it up with his puffy hand and cautiously scanned the area for onlookers. Valez looked in Lisa's direction, but with her back to him, he couldn't tell that she was staring right back at him via the glare on her computer monitor. Valez entered his office and closed the door. Lisa couldn't help but let out a sigh of relief.

Despite the shade from the tree, Tip had gotten quite brown in the face from his two-day stakeout in the autumn sun. The sun had a tiring affect on Tip and since Valez had left at around three o'clock, he didn't see much sense in watching the headquarters any longer, besides he had a big night ahead of him.

In his hotel room at the Capitol Inn, Tip pulled the black turtle neck down over his head to complete that evening's active wear. The black boots, black jeans and black belt wouldn't look that suspicious on a fall evening; rather it would appear trendy or metrosexual. Tip looked rather awesome with his jet-black hair and tight fitting black turtleneck over his granite-like physique. Tip thought once again about his good friend Hamilton. The uncontrollable rage and pain started to boil inside him. He knew he'd have to control it and take advantage of it when the time came. To release some of this energy, Tip dropped to the gray carpeting and proceeded to do eighty close-grip push-ups.

———

Lisa was becoming nauseated by the smell of the glue from the fake eyelashes she was punctiliously placing on her brown eyelashes. Lisa had made the mistake of putting on her fake nails before her eyelashes and their long points were constantly getting in the way. The last eyelash finally decided to stay on. Lisa put on the curly amber wig and winked her left arachnid-like eyelash at herself in the mirror.

Lisa was going for the look of a hooker, the antithesis of her Holly Crane secretarial character. Her complete metamorphosis was amazing, and she could now compete with the best girls on the corner. Her dirty eyeliner and bright blue eye shadow were perfect complements to the long eyelashes. She had even gone to the trouble of developing longer eyebrows by means of a black make-up pencil.

Lisa layered bright red lipstick over her sensual lips. It matched the shade of her obnoxiously long fake nails. The tight black tube skirt was more comfortable than she'd imagined, but she would have felt naked without the white stockings caressing her long, sexy legs. The three-inch pumps were unbelievably painful, but they definitely showcased the beauty of her lissome calves.

Lisa laughed at the sight of her overflowing breasts-compliments

# CRISIS

of the push-up bra. Although not lacking in the upstairs department, this Wonder Bra made her look like Dolly Parton. The majority of both her breasts were showing and even a slight trace of her right nipple, but she quickly pulled up the tight noire corset for modest coverage. There were limits to what Lisa would subject herself to in order to pull off the disguise. She had to draw the line at exposing her nipple.

The cheap, leather half-coat was tight and she'd have to be careful not to tear the fabric. The Salvation Army only had a size medium, and Lisa, with her broad shoulders, needed a large. The large fake diamond snowflake earrings felt like deep-diving Rapala fishing lures hanging from her ears. The crown jewel on her entire makeover was the large, fake, almond-brown mole she'd placed on the left side of her upper lip. The cheap perfume made her smell like cocoa butter. The aroma was thankfully overpowering the odious smell of the eyelash glue.

Lisa was beginning to enjoy these costumes and characters she was creating. Playing the part of someone else allowed her to forget the dreadful role she'd been assigned in real life. The make-up also helped to cover up the bruises from Eddie.

Lisa dropped the can of mace into her tacky black plastic shoulder purse. The mace was there as a precautionary measure, just in case her plan went awry. Lisa wore a long dinner coat over her half-coat so that she wouldn't arouse suspicion until she had arrived at her destination. Lisa double-checked her purse one last time to insure that the duplicate key to Valez's office was still secure. The key was there, as she knew it would be. But, just like when she had an important report to turn in for school, she always triple checked her backpack. Of course, what Lisa was about to do was much more important than any term paper she'd submitted over the course of her superb academic career.

---

Tip jumped out of the taxicab in front of *Santa Fe's*, a local college bar. It was about one in the morning. Although it was fall, it was still warm enough for the patrons to party on the outside portion of the bar. The place was jamming pretty hard for a Wednesday night. *Santa Fe's* always had good beer specials on Wednesday nights and this drew in the desiccated college students.

Tip thought about going into the bar to kill some time but noticed a long line to get in and a three-dollar cover charge for the band, Mud Puppies. He also knew better than to surround himself with alcohol-especially alone. A big frothy beer would really help to take the edge off, but he knew he wouldn't be able to stop at just one.

The cab ride to Chi Theta headquarters took half the time he'd expected. Ten minutes later, Tip crouched down by the same window from the previous night, and peered in. The guard was in the same slumped position at the desk that he was the night before. The guard was methodically dipping a powder-sugar donut into a Styrofoam cup of lukewarm coffee. The guard's eyes were focused on *The Adventures of Superman* Marvel Comic Book. The guard looked fairly alert for so early in the morning, but Tip knew he'd soon become groggy. Or, more likely, the guard would have to relieve himself of all the caffeine he was drinking. Whatever the case, Tip could afford to wait patiently for the opportune time to make his move.

The big-haired redhead who walked through the front door grabbed Tip's attention. Tip deftly slid his Platinum Master Card across the windowsill and opened it a wee crack to hear the conversation between the guard and the redhead. The woman appeared to be a lady of the night, but something about her just wasn't quite adding up. For some reason, the woman's gait seemed familiar. The redhead was rather tall and voluptuous. Annoyingly smacking her large wad of chewing gum, she didn't appear to be comfortable in the sky-high heels she had strapped around her supple ankles.

"Hello, Baby-Cakes. Do you mind if I use your restroom while I wait for a cab? I got stiffed, and I'm stranded here," said Lisa who surreptitiously removed the three sticks of Juicy Fruit gum from her mouth. The gum was making her nauseous and she discarded it into her purse. The purse was going to be thrown out after tonight, so she saw no harm in this frivolous action.

"Well, it's against policy, but I don't see any harm in it. Just make sure that you're quick about it. The latrine is right over there," indicated the guard with his sugar-powdered index finger.

"Thanks honey. I promise not to be long. If you don't mind me asking, what's a strapping man like yourself sitting in here on a perfectly good Friday night? You shouldn't be so selfish, let the ladies enjoy your looks," Lisa laid it on thick.

"That's a good question, but what's a beautiful woman like you getting stiffed on a Friday night? I mean it just ain't right and don't make no sense," replied the guard.

"Oh, aren't you just the sweetest. Excuse me for a second," Lisa said while pointing her finger and winking at the guard as she closed the restroom door behind her.

Tip's temperature was starting to rise as he tried to comprehend the curveball that had been thrown at his carefully laid plan. If the girl just left after the bathroom than everything would continue as planned, but what if she stayed? What would he do then? Maybe it would work out better if the guard had his hands full? Maybe this horny guard would leave with this soliciting slut, or perhaps he'd pay for sexual favors in the office. Tip was still tossing scenarios around in his head when he heard the knob on the ladies room door.

"Oh, I hate to trouble you officer," it was obvious that the guard enjoyed being called "officer," by the strikingly attractive lady, "but the hot water on the faucet appears to be stuck and I'm afraid I'm not strong enough to open it." This was laughable, because Lisa's father and brother always had to swallow their pride and let her open all of the tight jar lids in the house. There wasn't a jar or faucet that Lisa wasn't able to conquer. "It's a good thing we've got your muscle around," said Lisa as she licked her fire engine red lips.

"Sure, no trouble at all. I sometimes have problems with it myself. It's this damn old building and its rusty water," explained the guard. The guard was full of it, he'd never recalled having trouble with the faucet, but he figured it was probably because he *was* so strong. At any rate, this girl would be easy to impress.

The guard struggled to get his fat ass out of the swivel chair before plodding over to the bathroom. His butt had fallen asleep and it was sort of surreal to him to not have any feeling in the largest part of his body. He gave Lisa a crooked smile and a nod of the head, all the while holding his breath in a futile attempt at sucking in his jelly-donut belly.

Lisa let the guard enter the bathroom first and secretly removed a small rope with small lassoes on either end.

The guard turned the hot water tap with no trouble at all and was amazed at how strong he truly was.

"There you go. It's all fixed Miss."

Lisa had no intention of ever going into the bathroom however, and she slammed the bathroom door on the guard before he knew what had happened. She then quickly secured one end of the rope around the doorknob and the other around a contiguous door. She had measured the rope out perfectly from her calculations taken earlier in the week. Neither door would budge since the rope was taught between them.

The guard tried furiously to open up the door and then began pounding ceaselessly against the door and throwing all of his weight against it. The hinges gave a little under his enormous weight, but held fast. Working in Lisa's favor were the petite dimensions of the old bathroom that precluded a long, momentum gathering charge. Lisa ignored the guard's pleas and proceeded to get down to the business at hand.

Tip rubbed his eyes in dismay; he couldn't believe what he was seeing. What should he do now? This definitely wasn't one of the scenarios he'd envisioned. He told himself that the important thing at this point was to remain calm. The worst possible thing that he could do was to panic.

Lisa fetched the duplicate key for Valez's office out of her purse. Her heart stopped when she found the big wad of gum had become attached to the key. She was having a difficult time removing the gum from the key and she didn't want to rush things and cause the gum to be embedded into the grooves of the key. The impending guard's pounding made it difficult not to become frazzled.

She kept her wits about her and remembered an old Girl Scout trick. She pulled out the hairspray from her cheap black purse and saturated the gum until it became hardened. She was then able to easily remove the gum in one solid piece.

Tip watched this whole display and had to admit that he was impressed by the girl's ingenuity. It reminded him of the old television show "McGyver," where the star always saved the day by making gadgets like bombs and rockets out of ordinary substances and materials. Tip knew that this girl wasn't just a common hooker and tried to fathom where she fit in the scheme of things.

Lisa's heart was racing at top speed and she prayed for good luck before inserting the key into Valez's office door. Now that the key was in the lock she was having a difficult time turning it. She jiggled it back and forth gently in an effort to properly engage the tumblers in the lock mechanism. The guard's manic pounding came to a sudden halt. The silence made her even more nervous, and she looked to make sure the bathroom door was still secure. Her increased anxiety caused her to jiggle the key more feverishly, which wasn't helping matters. The key's teeth finally engaged on one of the jiggles. She breathed a sigh of relief as the doorknob rotated. She stealthy slid into Valez's office.

Tip decided he needed to get closer to the action, especially with the security guard temporarily removed from the picture. He slid the window up further. It was now just barely open enough for him to slide his muscularly sleek body through. He hardly made a sound as he slithered through the window.

Once inside, he positioned himself out of sight, but close enough to view the action in and around Valez's office. He noticed the guard had quit making such a racket. In fact, there was not a sound being produced from the bathroom.

Lisa uncrumpled the yellow Post-It note she had discovered stuck to the underside of her desk during her first week of work.

This Post-It note was the only piece of evidence Barbara Fernandez left behind. Everything else in the desk had been removed. The person who cleaned it out must have missed this note. The Post-It note was stuck underneath the desk drawer and she only discovered it when the adhesive gave way and gravity pulled it down to earth. Lisa was hoping the apparent computer username and password were still current. The blue ink had been smeared somewhat, but it was still legible.

The computer slowly purred as Lisa flipped the power strip with her toe. While the computer was warming up, she did a quick check of the large file cabinets that lined the wall. As expected, they were all locked. She then attempted to open the drawers of the enormous desk, but once again her effort was in vain.

Three successive beeps indicated the computer was warmed up and waiting for its next command. Lisa typed in "p" to be linked to Valez's private portable server. She had to reference the yellow Post-It for the User ID information and quickly typed in "Gvalez" and now nervously hesitated before typing in the password she hoped would work. She slowly entered the password MARSHALL PLAN. The type didn't appear on the monitor, rather a successive string of asterisks and she sure didn't want to make a typo now. Lisa down-stroked the enter key and let out a sigh of relief when the computer started to whirl.

Once in the system, it looked like any other Window's set-up. She went to the Excel spreadsheets and wasted several minutes opening and quickly closing many files dealing with Chi Theta's maintenance and upkeep records for the past several decades. Her fingertips froze on the keyboard when she thought she heard some movement outside of the door. Perspiration beaded on her forehead as a result of her excessive make-up and the fact that the entire office gave her the creeps. Evilness enveloped her the moment she'd stepped into the dark, odorous office. The residual cigar stench was so repulsive that she had to breath through her mouth.

Despite these discomforts she was making her way through the files with great alacrity. Fortunately there weren't too many to sift through. Finally, she hit pay dirt! She stumbled upon a complete listing of all donations for the past three years, with most of the larger donations being conveniently highlighted in orange. She quickly downloaded these onto her USB thumb drive. With this vital information securely copied, she closed the file and opened the last remaining file.

Tip, crouching behind the desk furthest from Valez's door, was startled to see that the security guard had somehow escaped the confines of the bathroom. Lisa and Tip weren't aware of the numerous trap doors and escape routes that the paranoid Valez had installed under the guise of building repairs. The guard was familiar with most of these secret passages, because one of the night builders had let it slip during one of their conversations. This particular laborer liked to imbibe in a little sauce while he worked and once drunk, he got loose lips. The guard took every opportunity during his long night shifts to snoop around for these secret passages the laborer had mentioned in passing.

The guard was furious he hadn't remembered the secret passage in the bathroom immediately. All he had to do was remove the oversized mirror from its hinges in the bathroom and slide through a hole that had a large framed piece of artwork on the opposite side. Fortunately for the obese guard, this passage was designed with Valez's lard ass in mind.

Tip's head filled with numerous scenarios and he meticulously started calculating what his next move might be.

The last electronic file finally opened for Lisa. It appeared to be a detailed log documenting a series of payments, most of which were for substantial dollar amounts. The log covered the past three years. Lisa was getting nervous about the amount of time she'd been in the office and rapidly downloaded the information to her disk without further review.

With the download complete, Lisa pulled out the thumb drive and dropped it into her cheap black purse. Lisa turned the computer off and fastidiously wiped down all the items in the office that she had touched.

Lisa turned off the lights and quietly shut the door. She locked it with the temporary key and noted that the key should only work three more times. Lisa let out a loud scream when she turned around and was greeted by the full girth of the loathsome night guard.

"Oh, sorry about that scream. You startled me," said Lisa attempting to rapidly regain her composure.

"Don't play stupid with me, lady. I may have fallen for your trickery once, but it'll take a lot more to dupe me twice," said the guard.

"Oh, don't be silly. I'd never try to do something like that to you honey. You know that," smiled Lisa.

"Well you can tell that to my boss, the one's who's office you was snooping around in," said the guard and he quickly grabbed Lisa's wrists and bound them tight with some heavy-duty duct tape which he seemingly produced out of nowhere. The normally lethargic guard now seemed full of vigor and determination.

The guard positioned Lisa in an old hardwood chair in front of his usual post. The guard sat in his chair with a slight smirk on his face staring at Lisa and picked up the phone receiver and began dialing.

WHAAMMMM! The phone flew violently out of the guard's hand as all of Tip's weight was thrown into the guard's enormous perimeter. Tip had arrived on the scene like a linebacker hitting a quarterback on a blind side blitz.

Tip pressed his right knee into the nape of the guard's chubby neck while grabbing the role of duct tape off the desk. Using his teeth, he tore off a length of tape and secured the guard's arms and legs before slapping a strip across his mouth.

With the guard a non-factor, Tip turned his attention to the girl, who'd already shaken herself free. She was hurriedly heading for the door. It was difficult for her run with her hands tied behind her back and the towering heels she was wearing weren't helping matters. Nevertheless, Tip was impressed by the headway she was making.

He quickly overtook her, grabbing her around the shoulders.

Lisa spun and sent a swift left knee toward Tip's groin. Anticipating the move, he easily avoided it and proceeded to wrestle her to the carpeted floor. There, he pinned both of her arms down.

"What do you want from me?!?" spat Lisa

"Who are you?" exhaled Tip.

"What's it to you?" piped Lisa.

"Why were you in Valez's office?" asked Tip.

"None of your Goddamn business. Now let me go! If you don't let me go, I swear I'm going to scream bloody murder," threatened Lisa.

"Well aren't we rather ungrateful to the guy who just saved you from the clutches of Mr. Friendly over there. Oh, how soon we forget," said Tip.

"I'm sure you're just as whacked-out as he is. What do you want from me? Why are you here, you obviously don't work for Valez. If you don't let me go…"

Lisa stopped talking, as both she and Tip were startled by the presence of someone standing over them. Clap, clap, clap…"Very good deduction my dear Ms. Watson," said Garcia. "Thank you for all of your handy work in leading us to a man we've had a tough time getting our hands on. Thank you also for making our job so easy in regards to you, Holly Cane, which I'm sure isn't your real name either. As far as screaming is concerned; I wouldn't waste your breath. You're going to need all the air you can get where you're going."

"Why such the flabbergasted face, you didn't think Ricardo Valez would triple check every two-bit loser he hires." This ironically came out of Sanchez's mouth, who had just arrived.

"Although we'd love to research your background in depth, we'll get to the bottom of things real quick tonight-because both of you are expendable-especially the little prissy hockey player over here. With you out of the picture, Paul Tipton, we can be certain that no one knows the information that was accidentally leaked," declared Garcia victoriously.

"How can you be so sure that I didn't send copies to several friends before I left?" Tipton retorted.

"Because I know how someone like you works. You think you've got to solve the problem yourself. It's you against the world. And that's your problem and the entire reason why you're in the predicament you are. You're stubborn, and internally contain all of life's problems, which only eat you up inside. You are like a little pressure cooker, ready to explode at anytime. Well, playing Mr. Hero has cost you and everyone else involved big time." Garcia leaned down close to Tip, who was still straddling Lisa. Placing the muzzle of his Smith & Wesson at the back of Tip's head, Garcia whispered into his ear, "I enjoyed killing your friends. Of course, you helped kill them, especially that last one."

Tip's fist instinctively reacted to such cruel words. Sanchez easily squelched Tip's reaction by delivering a Mark McGwire-like swing with a long baseball bat. The end of the bat landed squarely on Tip's abdomen and he collapsed sideways into a hunched position. From this position, Tip began coughing violently and spitting up blood.

"You aren't very bright are you boy?" laughed Sanchez.

"Hey, do you mind if I step to the plate," inquired the now untied guard.

"By all means be my guest," laughed Sanchez as he handed the black Louisville slugger to the Teutonic guard.

The guard casually caressed the black lumbar before swinging it over his head. In one swift stroke he brought the heavy bat thundering down onto Tip's exposed back. The blow landed directly across his broad back hunched over like an agitated cat. Tip writhed on the floor in sheer agony, biting his lip to control the trembling. Although Tip wanted to fight back, he knew it was best to remain in a fetal position to protect his vital organs from any more blows. The hits had done significant damage and Tip wasn't certain that he could stand-up even if he wanted to.

"Would you stop hitting a defenseless man, you cowards," blurted Lisa.

# CRISIS

"Well, well, well...got a little spunk in Ms. Holly Cane after all. Good, I like that," Garcia brushed his hand lightly across her check which Lisa repulsed and tried to block out the images of Eddie's beatings. "You're in no position to take sides with Wonder Boy over here. Wonder Boy truly is pathetic, causing all of his friends to die and doing nothing to fight back. Don't you think it would be wise to join the winning team instead of this wimp over here on the floor, I mean, just look at him. Who knows, if you're nice to us boys tonight, maybe we can tell Valez that you were never here," offered Garcia.

Tip's face was pressed tight against his abs and thus his flashing eyes, red with rage, weren't visible. He didn't care if he died doing it, but he was taking these vicious bastards down before this whole thing played itself out.

Sanchez and the guard thoroughly duct taped Lisa and Tip together. They positioned them back-to-back and bound them. They were taped at the wrists and also across their shoulders. Lisa and Tip were coarsely thrown into the enormous trunk of the black Lincoln Towne Car. The guard slammed the trunk shut with great bravado. Tip figured they were in for a long ride, thus he allowed his body and senses to relax. He would need the all the mental and physical strength he could muster when they reached their destination. Once again, Tip's world went black.

Lisa was trying not to get sick from the circumstances and the bumpy ride of the car. Tip was awakened thirty minutes later by a large bump in the road. He was less concerned with motion sickness as he was trying hard to suppress the pain of where he'd been struck with the vicious blows of the baseball bat. These areas on his back and stomach could feel every bump in the uneven road. Despite sleeping for half an hour, Tip was still attempting to gauge the direction and distance the car was taking them. He was also trying to suppress his claustrophobia by not thinking about how small and dark it was in the trunk.

Several cramps started to tenaciously tighten throughout Lisa's calves and neck. She could only imagine how the person tied to her back felt. She was fortunate to be facing up looking at the inside of the deck lid. Meanwhile, her counterpart, the stranger that intervened earlier, was face down with her weight on top of him. She also knew his body had just been pummeled.

Tip could tell that they had originally headed west upon leaving the fraternity headquarters. They had taken several large swerves before maintaining a westward direction. Tip passed out while they were still traveling west, and he made the assumption they were still pointed in that same direction.

Lisa and Tip had been in the car for roughly forty minutes and Tip estimated that they had been traveling between forty and fifty mph. Tip also noted that they were also on a little-traveled road. A deserted road didn't tell Tip too much, since it was late at night, every road was probably this way.

The car slowed and took a sharp right turn. No streetlights were seeping through the cracks in the trunk and the sound of the road changed dramatically. Tip guessed they were now on a country road. Lisa could sense this as well, and an uneasy feeling swept over her. Their journey continued as Lisa and Tip individually agonized. Lisa was enduring the excruciating pain from her leg cramps and she was numb everywhere else. Tip sweated profusely as the trapped body heat made the trunk cabin a miniature sauna.

Tip lifted his mouth an inch from the dirty-carpeted trunk floor. "Hey, I don't know who you are and I don't care to know. But the only way that we are going to get out of this predicament is if we work together," said Tip.

"How do I know I can trust you?" flashed an irritated Lisa.

"Because, for one, I saved your sorry ass from that perverted guard and, two, you really don't have a choice at this point, now do you?" said Tip. "If I thought I could do it myself, believe me, I would. But those guys will be watching me very closely, so I'm going to need to rely on you to catch them off guard."

"I can handle myself just fine. I don't need your help," said Lisa.

"Look, we don't have time to argue! If you want to get yourself killed, be my guest. If you want to get the hell out of here, then we've got to start working together. Now. These guys aren't going to drive us around all night," said Tip with convincing authority.

"All right. But, I still don't trust you." said Lisa

"Frankly I don't give a damn if you trust me or not. Just do what we need to do to get the hell out of here. We can worry about trust after that," exclaimed Tip

Ten minutes later, the large car finally rolled to a stop. Although Lisa and Tip had only been in the car for about fifty minutes, the pain, darkness, and uncertainty made it feel like an eternity.

Two car doors slammed almost simultaneously. Little could be heard outside of their captor's languid shuffling on gravel. Tip and Lisa heard whispering, but couldn't make out any of the conversation. The whispering concluded after five minutes and the trunk was popped open by Sanchez. Looking at Sanchez's smug grin peering down upon them wasn't a pleasant greeting for Tip and Lisa. However, they were grateful that the interminable car ride was over. A new sense of fear began to slowly enrapture Lisa's entire nervous system when she saw the Machiavellian stares of her captors. This confirmed her decision to team with her fellow captive. The perverted guard was nearly salivating.

Sanchez observed, "Oh, what a pretty picture. I didn't realize that a nice sweet couple like you would be so into bondage. Although, might I suggest that it would be more effective and enjoyable if you weren't back to back.

It truly is a shame that we don't have more time, because I would love to show you a good time." Sanchez moved some of Lisa's hair away from her face. "And for you big boy, or is it little boy? Well, my guard friend over there would've really found out tonight. You see the big fella is what they like to call a switch hitter. But, as I said, we don't have time, so we just gotta kill ya," Sanchez cackled.

The guard, Garcia, and Sanchez easily lifted Lisa and Tip out of the trunk. The duct tape dug painfully into Lisa and Tip's wrists. Lisa let out a slight whimper, but Tip wouldn't give these slugs the satisfaction.

The sadistic henchmen took pleasure in violently tossing Lisa and Tip onto the dirt road. Tip's face hit the ground first with Lisa's weight and head slamming down on him simultaneously. Tip's right eye actually hit first and he could tell that a large gash had been opened up as a red haze quickly clouded his eyesight. Despite the pain, he gritted his teeth and remained silent.

Lisa squirmed and struggled to move off Tip, but Tip motioned with some non-visible hand pressures that he was okay and she should not waste her energy. Besides, her struggling was only causing his face to be ground further into the dirt road.

Garcia tied a five-foot rope to the bundled captives, and he and the guard grabbed the rope, threw it over their shoulders, and began dragging Lisa and Tip across the stony road.

Lisa and Tip could feel every rock in the road painfully cut through their clothes and into their flesh. This spurned Tip's imagination and he began groping for any stone or rock he could find within his restricted reach. The first couple of stones he obtained were far too small and dull for his desired task. Tip was like a kid looking for the perfect skipping stone, a skipping stone that was very pointed on one end.

The loose gravel on the road was diminishing, which was good for his shoulders, back and legs. It was bad for the stone search. He could sense that time was running out. He finally obtained a stone that was suited for the task, although it was a bit smaller than he'd hoped. He palmed this stone in his right hand and felt for Lisa's hand. Tip cautiously passed the stone into her palm and gave her two successive hand pumps indicating she should get started. Lisa understood the hand gesture immediately and began working on the thick, resilient duct tape. Tip now began to search for the bigger brother of the rock he'd just given Lisa.

"If your friend there were a gentleman he'd let you ride on his back so that your beautiful dress and body wouldn't get all dirty," jibbed Sanchez. "Instead, he's letting both of y'all get dirty."

"He's not my friend," shot Lisa.

"Well, you now seem to be singing a different tune now.

You seemed to be pretty teamed up when we found you back at headquarters. It's your loss for picking such a loser. But don't you fret; you and I are going to make a great team before the night is over. It will be your best, and last, memory. I said we didn't have time for your friend and the guard over there. But, I'll make time for you," Sanchez stated matter of fact. Sanchez roughly moved his callused hand from Lisa's ankle up her beautiful thigh and through a recently made whole in her white stockings. His hand now rested just inside her thin white panty line by her hip.

This horrifying action sent shivers up and down Lisa's spine. It was all she could do to not vomit.

Tip clutched another sharp stone, still not as large as he'd have liked, but definitely larger than the first one. Tip strained all of his faculties to prevent the stone from slipping through his fingers as the three ogres gave a sudden and strong jerk to the rope.

Tip knew that their final destination couldn't be much further, and he began working feverishly on the rope. Tip hoped he'd be able to meet Lisa's sawing halfway. Lisa was having a tough go at it. Her hands were much smaller than Tip's and it was all she could do to hold onto the stone, let alone get enough leverage to slice through the tape. Tip's larger and sharper stone and his greater strength were making a much better go at it, however it still remained an arduous task.

"Don't worry kiddies, we're almost home. Once we get there, we can tuck you in for a long, long rest. Oh, you are going to truly enjoy this stretch of road," intoned Garcia.

Tip's disdain for these cravens was beyond measure and he used this hate to quicken his pace on the tape.

Lisa's head thumped on the unforgiving wood of a railroad tie. If the dirt road was painful, this took things to a whole new level. Tip strained his neck to glance ahead and could discern that the bridge was fairly long and also about sixty feet above a river.

With the successive thumping on the railroad ties, it was difficult to make anything but slow progress on the tape. Tip estimated that he was close to halfway through and hoped that

Lisa's rock would meet his sometime soon. He also was praying for a little luck, since they were more than likely not sawing on directly opposite ends of the tape.

The rope around both of their shoulders was another problem. Lisa and Tip would have to address this at some point, but getting their hands free was of greater importance at the moment.

Tip glanced at both sides of the river and noted that it was a steep and precarious drop on both sides. It also appeared that there wasn't easy access to the river further down.

Although they were making slow progress across the bridge, they were roughly two thirds of the way to the other side. Tip and Lisa were now both frantically hacking away at the tape because they knew their window of opportunity was narrowing every second. In order to pick up the pace, they needed to be less discreet about their actions, which increased their risk of being caught. At this point, it was a risk they'd have to take.

Tip clenched the rock in his hand and once again tried to pry his arms apart in an attempt to break the remaining strand of tape. Tips deltoids burned and his face became beat red, however, once again the rope remained strong. Tip took three more small hacks at the tape and gave hand motions to Lisa to try to pry the tape apart with him. Both released their energy into one last hurrah and, thankfully, the unwavering tape gave way, and not a moment too soon. The three kidnappers had almost reached the end of the bridge.

They now had more movement of their arms, but were still restrained by the strand of rope that was fastened tightly around their arms holding them together. They tried to pry free from it, but weren't having too much success. Tip repositioned himself and jammed his two feet deep into the tight space between railroad ties and braced himself.

The rope became taught as the three men strained to pull the two occupants the remaining seven feet off the bridge. They were tired of dragging over three hundred pounds and didn't appreciate this added nuisance.

"What the fuck is going on? You better not be fucking around back there," screamed Garcia as he dropped the rope and headed back toward Lisa and Tip.

The guard also loosened his grip on the rope, which Tip noted. Sanchez, to Tip's dismay, still held steadfast.

"Oh, you little prick I'm going to teach you your last lesson right now," said Garcia as he raised his chukka boot to bring a crushing blow down on Tip's knee.

"Roll now!" shouted Tip at the top of his lungs and Lisa obeyed the steadfast order as he violently shifted his weight to the left rolling Lisa over the top of him and they both fell free of the bridge and into the unknown darkness.

Garcia's leg came flying down on empty air and went straight through the space between the ties where Tip's knee had been. Garcia took the railroad tie straight in the sweet spot and his inertia carried him off the bridge and into the darkness below. A large and succinct splash was heard indicating that he'd landed in some shallow water.

The guard wasn't any luckier. The violent swing of the rope caught him square across the back of the shoulders and flung him headlong down the gully. The guard bounced off the sharp edges of the ravine and he landed headfirst in shallow water. The grotesque sound of his neck snapping echoed through the canyon. Sanchez tried to hold onto the rope attached to Lisa and Tip, but it was a lost cause as it burned fiercely through his hands.

Tip and Lisa instinctively held each other tight, anticipating the inevitable end to their flight. Time seemed to stand still as Tip and Lisa hurtled toward the dark and mysterious ravine below. Both were surprised at the eerie silence of the descent. Any noise to distract them from their fate would be welcome.

They felt like watermelon props on a David Lettermen special as they hit the water with tremendous velocity. Their ears rang with excruciating pain and their feet stung from the force of breaking the permeable surface of the water. Tip and Lisa were fortunate to hit feet first as their momentum carried them to the bottom of the ravine.

Tip opened his good eye but couldn't see more than an inch in front of his face in the murky water. His bad eye felt as big as a softball and like it would burst at the seams any second. He found Lisa's hand and gave it a good firm squeeze. He was hoping for a responding squeeze. There wasn't one. Her hand was limp. She sustained most of the impact since her body had twisted in flight and hit the water first, at a weird angle, with Tip on top of her. Tip gave the hand another pump and once again there was no response. Without sight, Tip gathered his faculties and gave a forceful push off the muddy river bottom. Given Lisa's added weight and the mucky bottom, Tip didn't get a good launch to the surface. Tip's feet simply dug deep into the soft mud and couldn't find the necessary resistance to push off.

The medium current was also pulling Tip and Lisa along the bottom. Tip could feel the restriction in his chest from lack of oxygen and was thankful that he was in such great cardiovascular shape. It was nearly impossible for him to generate any momentum since the rope that bound the two of them constricted him. He raised his arms with all his might to loosen the rope that they'd almost conquered on the bridge. The rope had loosened in the water and he was able to wiggle enough to have the rope slide its way up their bodies and gently float off them. This last effort exerted the remainder of his oxygen supply and he needed to get to the surface in a hurry. He shook his arms to get the blood flowing again.

Tip wrapped his left arm around Lisa's petite waist and began kicking with a flourish to get to the surface. He was having a difficult time of it. Lisa's deadweight was one problem and the water logged weight of both their clothes was another. Tip didn't have much energy left and needed to reach the surface now or never. Lisa was still unresponsive.

Tip's lungs were burning and about to burst as he mustered everything he had for one final push. He kicked with superhuman fervor, his legs churning just as they'd done during countless hours at the rehabilitation swimming pool.

# CRISIS

He attempted to navigate through the endless sea of darkness, just as he had navigated through the amorphous fog of his alcoholism. Images of his parents, Hamilton and Burke materialized in his head. No, Tip wasn't ready to join his loved one's just yet. He was going to defeat the evil this time. This time no one would be let down by Paul Tipton. The water was no longer murky; he could picture images of his loved ones standing on the edge of the river shouting words of encouragement.

He broke free of the river's death grip and into the clear fall air of Eastern Maryland. He had a difficult time not hyperventilating as his exhausted lungs clamored for the oxygen.

Tip kept his arm loosely around Lisa's neck and used sidestroke to cut diagonally toward the shore without fighting the current. Tip noticed that they had drifted far downstream, as the silhouette of the bridge was no longer in sight.

Tip spotted an inlet along the steep bank of the ravine and set his course toward it. Increasing his pace to augment the quickening current, he was mildly pleased with his progress. Within two minutes, he had reached what turned out to be a sandbar leading to a glade. He swayed on his weary legs as he rose to drag Lisa up onto the sandbar. He cupped his forearms underneath her armpits and clasped his hands together above her ample bosom. There was a dry area of the sandbar and Tip pinpointed that as his final destination.

Tip cautiously laid Lisa down on the sandbar and aligned her with her body perfectly straight, her arms at her side. This is the same position Mrs. Willshire had taught him in his eighth grade health class during CPR week. Fortunately for Lisa, Tip's years of alcohol abuse hadn't killed the precious brain cells that stored this CPR information.

Tip opened up her airway by slightly tipping her head back and placed his ear over her mouth to listen for any indication of life. As Tip had surmised, Lisa wasn't breathing and he could only guess how long she'd been without oxygen. With no time to waste, Tip took a large breath, pinched Lisa's nostrils together and gave Lisa two deep breaths of air.

# CHAPTER 26

# AUSTIN, TEXAS:

Corrigan Campaign Stop: The narrow downtown street, flanked on either side by piano bars, country saloons, pubs, and discos was once again packed to the gills. Although this was Austin's famed Sixth Street, it wasn't packed with the usual Saturday night partygoers. Rather, these people had come out in droves on this hot and muggy fall evening to listen to Presidential hopeful David Corrigan.

Austin, the capital of Texas, hadn't been a popular stop on presidential campaign tours in the past. Instead, presidential candidates focused their efforts on the larger Texas markets of Houston, Dallas and San Antonio. However, the town of Austin had experienced tremendous growth over the past several years. This growth was primarily attributed to the surge in high technological activity with the likes of Dell, Motorola, 3M, Texas Instruments and Trilogy setting up business operations. Austin was indeed the Silicon Valley of the Southwest. It was anticipated by yearend that Austin would overtake Boston and Seattle in terms of population. Austin is a true anomaly or oasis in Texas in that it is hilly, green and surrounded by water. It also didn't hurt that former President George W. Bush resided in the capitol as Governor prior to his successive terms.

The large podium that Corrigan was standing behind was on the southwest corner of Trinity and Sixth. The police had barricaded all traffic access south of Ninth Street and north of Third Street. Every pub on the street was taking advantage of this hot fall day by promoting their air conditioning to the max. They provided a place where weary onlookers could watch the speech on a live cable feed in air-conditioned comfort.

Maggie Mae's and Pete's Piano bar, which had been closed for security reasons, were foregoing large sums of cash. These bars were directly behind the podium, and Corrigan's security advisors had mandated that they be vacant for the twenty-four hour period prior to Corrigan's appearance.

"Thank you, Austin, for the wonderful turnout. It's great to be back in the Lone Star State," exclaimed Corrigan. Advisors of Corrigan had instructed him to mention Texas as much as possible in his speech. This advice was based on the fact that Texans had a tremendous amount of pride in their heritage. The jubilant crowd roared its approval. "This is what America represents, the foundation that was built by our forefathers, the ability to peacefully assemble. However, this inalienable right has been revoked by the catastrophic events of the past two weeks. Terrorists, through their cowardly and inhumane acts, have instilled a sense of fear among Americans and your fear is justified. However, living in fear is no way to live, and by God, it's no way for a Texan to have to live." The crowd roared even louder.

Corrigan continued once the crowd subsided, "The media thinks these events were unexpected and uncontrollable. Both of these statements are true. The media has also said that the nation is defenseless against such malicious behavior. Given our current policies, the state of Homeland Security, this statement is also true. Individuals are defenseless against the unforeseen coward who steals babies in the night. But, collectively, we are not defenseless, and I, as well as you, will not stand idly by and let this treacherous behavior run rampant over our Red, White and Blue soil. No, it's time that lady liberty faces the offenders to pay for their inexcusable acts in a swift and severe fashion. You will derive great pleasure in watching these cowardly terrorists beg on their hands and knees for mercy before this great nation. Don't mess with Texas, and don't mess with the good ol' US of A!" The partisan crowd was whipped into a frenzy, and state troopers readied themselves for an impending riot.

## CRISIS

Corrigan calmed the crowd down at the appropriate moment by gesturing with his hands, "And, if I, David Corrigan, may have the honor of representing this great country, these cowardly terrorists will learn what the drug dealers in Florida learned, there will be no MERCY!" The national camera crews swarmed in to get some quick shots of Corrigan, but had a difficult time wedging through the fervent crowd. The chant was deafening. The sound couldn't escape, and simply bounced from the southern building walls to the northern building walls. "Corrigan! Corrigan! Corrigan!"

# CHAPTER 27

Lisa's ankles were still in the water and her noire corset barely clung to her skin. Her beautifully tanned skin turned to a pinkish hue. Tip felt along her breastplate for her clavicle and placed his right hand over his left, quickly interlocked his fingers and pressed down firmly with four successive strokes. Breathing steadily in and out with each thrust was helping to calm him down while allowing him to keep the proper rhythm. With each compression, his tremendous triceps bulged beneath his soaking wet shirt. After the four thrusts, he quickly repositioned himself to give her four more breaths of air.

On the fourth breath, Tip pulled away as a gurgling sound emanated from Lisa and up came a combination of river water and bile. An uncontrollable cough gripped her and she writhed violently on the sandy bank.

Her coughing slowly came under control and she let out a low moan. Where was she? She was disoriented and felt like she had been physically beaten again. But how could that be? She hadn't seen Eddie in two weeks and he was miles away, wasn't he? Her blurred vision started to refocus on the majestic emerald eyes attached to the charming, but battered, face towering over her. Yes, now she remembered the national headquarters, subsequent car ride and attempted escape from the bridge. It appeared as if the escape was successful. However, one question remained. Who was this mystery man that saved her life?

"Wow, you really had me scared there for awhile. Are you all right? How's that wrist?" Inquired Tip as he saw the pronounced gouge the duct tape had caused around her right wrist.

"It hurts right now, but will be all right in time. I'd be more concerned about your eye, if I were you. That gash is rather severe and it's continuing to bleed profusely. Our first priority is to get that thing sewn up somehow," ordered Lisa.

"Needn't you worry about me, I'll be alright," Tip replied stubbornly. Tip knew she was right. He needed to stop the bleeding because he was feeling weaker by the minute. "Besides, we aren't going to be able to go anywhere tonight," said Tip. "It would be too treacherous in our weary state to attempt to navigate our way out of this ravine with only the moonlight to guide us."

"Suit yourself, I don't care if you bleed to death," scoffed Lisa.

Tip felt the blood continue to trickle out of the bulbous knot above his left eye and knew he did have to do something. Tip pulled his wet, black, long sleeved T-shirt over his head so that it was now inside out. Tip than effortlessly tore one of the thirty-five inch sleeves off. Tip's back muscles glistened in the dim light and his six-pack stomach was still prevalent even though he was hunched over to tear the shirt.

Tip wandered around until he found what he was looking for, some good old southern red clay. He bent down and scooped up a handful of the cool clay heading toward the side of the ravine. At the base of the steep slope was some tall grass, and he jerked several of these stalks from the ground with his right hand. He mixed the clay and grass together, just as he'd learned when he was Silver Fox of the Potowanimi Indian Guide troop as a child.

With his fingers, he dexterously molded the clay mixture into a triangular wedge and forcefully pushed the point of the wedge firmly into his wound. He gritted his impeccable teeth in response to the prickle of pain. The pain began to subside as the cool clay started to work its magic. With his left hand holding the poultice, he dipped the previously removed shirtsleeve into the caliginous water and tightly tied it around his head to secure the clay in place. The dirt and mud covering his brawny frame coupled with the black makeshift bandana conjured up pictures of Rambo. Only Tip was more lithe and handsome.

Lisa moved over to adjust his bandage. The soft fabric and even softer hands felt good to his aching head. "There you go; that should do the trick. Although, I'd suggest we leave as soon as we are able to see our way. That bandage will only hold up so long," suggested Lisa.

"We should leave at sunrise. And, so you know, my name is Paul Tipton, but you can just call me Tip."

"Nice to meet you, Tip. You did say Tip? I'm Lisa Appleton and you can call me Lisa. And thank you. Thank you for dragging me out of the water and giving me CPR," replied Lisa.

The moonlight was shedding a beacon of light on Lisa's face. The color had returned to her face and the river water had removed all of the gaudy "hooker" make-up. Her wig had been lost during the dragging episode and her hair now hung wet and straight down behind her shoulders. The wet black skirt clung to her perfect body, barely covering anything at all, but it was difficult to extrapolate this in the dim light. What he could discern for the first time was the natural beauty of this girl. He hadn't had the company of a woman in a long time, but he was able to recognize and appreciate pure beauty. He couldn't deny that this girl was a beautiful creation of nature.

"AAAHHHH!" Lisa's penetrating scream echoed through the cavernous ravine. Tip sprinted over to where she stood on the waterline. He put his arm on her shoulder. She turned toward him with a frozen mouth and saucer sized eyes. He saw the cause of her trauma. He could barely make it out over her right shoulder, but he knew it was gruesome.

Floating face up with eyes wide open was the malformed body of Garcia. Garcia's gray and slimy neck swiveled back and forth with the current; it was apparent that he had the misfortune of landing in shallow water.

Lisa buried her head into Tip's powerful shoulder and began to shake. Tip stood motionless staring down at the doughy face of Garcia. He felt no emotion; this man had killed his best friend. It was also a man that would have killed him and Lisa had it not been for the daring escape. No, Tip was callous to death. He'd seen so much death in recent years that it no longer affected him. He was now unafraid of death. The only thing left in the world that scared Paul Tipton, was Paul Tipton. Would Paul Tipton fail again, and let everyone down? Well, this was the first battle and he was the victor. He would not stop until he fully avenged the death of his friends.

Lisa's hands were now around Tip's neck, which broke him from his trance. She was still sobbing and trembling. Not knowing this girl, Tip was in an uncomfortable situation, but it felt strangely comfortable. Facing her, he put one arm around her slender waist and the other arm he placed on the back of her shoulders.

"You'll be alright. We're alright, let's be thankful for that," soothingly murmured Tip. Lisa pressed up tighter against Tip and he couldn't help notice her ample bosoms heave up and down against his bare chest. Tip calmly stroked her hair and started to remember how good it could feel to hold someone. Lisa's sobs were controlled and almost rhythmic. It was surreal how beautiful the sound was flowing from her moist lips.

Tip could feel Lisa's heartbeat slowly begin to subside. The rhythmic heartbeat was comforting to him. Lisa's sobs also diminished and she pulled away from him.

Tip suddenly became cooler as they released their embrace. Lisa stared into his opaline eyes. The eyes were very intense, yet revealed deep warmth within, subtly suggesting a pure heart. Perhaps he had been hurt in the past, she thought. A man of honor and virtue was somewhere lost in there. "I'm sorry," whispered Lisa. Tip proceeded to wipe the remaining tears away from her face.

"No need to be sorry. Your reaction is understandable. We've both been through a lot today and we need to get some rest." Tip pulled away from their embrace. "I found a dry and level area over by the tall grass that is sheltered from the breeze. You may want to wring out your clothes while I tend to that guy over here. Maybe there's something on him that could be of use to us."

Once Lisa was out of sight, Tip began the dreadful task of removing Garcia's waterlogged body from the water. This was not going to be easy. As he bent over, Garcia's left-hand shot-up toward

Tip's throat...then flopped right back down from whence it had come. Tip had heard about such nervous twitches in cadavers, but he still wasn't prepared for something like that. Tip took a second to compose himself.

Pilfering Garcia's pockets produced a pocketknife, a cigarette lighter that still worked and thirty-seven dollars in cash. The only other significant thing in his pockets was a phone number on the back of a losing lottery ticket. The lottery ticket was dated a few days ago.

Walking over to the glade near the clay bank, Tip saw that Lisa had already fallen asleep beneath a large oak tree. Her head rested on the triangle of her bent arm and her legs were curled up beneath her. The remaining portion of his shirt was drying on the great oak's branches. Satisfied that his shirt was reasonably dry, he took it from the tree and gently laid it over Lisa's shoulders and upper body for added warmth. She was too exhausted to feel anything.

Shuffling back to the tree, Tip plopped down against the massive trunk. With Garcia's knife he began whittling away on a stick he'd fished from the river. This action was just a means to keep his hands working while his mind churned away at numerous questions and scenarios. He was hopeful that the mystery girl could shed some light into the black labyrinth he was currently meandering through.

What was she looking for and how did she fit into the entire puzzle? Tip estimated the time to be around one in the morning and knew that the sun wouldn't rise until about seven. Tip doubted he would sleep a wink, although his body was demanding a goodnights rest. He didn't have the luxury of sleeping, since he didn't know where the other attackers had gone. Surely the security guard and the other goon were out looking for him and the girl. He also had to stay awake since he still didn't completely trust the girl. Tip's mind kept him awake, stirring with many unanswered questions.

# CHAPTER 28

# SAN FRANCISCO, CALIFORNIA:

It was a typically beautiful fall afternoon in San Francisco, around seventy degrees and sunny. A mild breeze gusted off the bay making a delightful day even more pleasant. Resident's and businesspersons scurried back and forth accomplishing their various errands before heading back to the drudgery of their jobs. Tourists tried to avoid getting in the way, but couldn't help it. So they continued to take group picture after group picture overlooking the Bay. Several patrons were enjoying the sensational weather at outdoor restaurants and cafes. The wait staffs of these establishments were bronzed from the exhausting hours of work in the sun.

Zar Kumbadi casually took this in as he calmly glided back and forth across the bottom of California Street. The skateboard was at the command of his feet as its four wheels hummed in unison. Clad in a pair of taupe canvas Air Walks with white rubber outer soles, his feet were one with the board. The rest of his disguise entailed baggy jeans and a white T-shirt accented by tightly bound blue sleeve bands and matching v-neck collar. Several leather strap necklaces with colorful beads adorned his brown neck. Prodigious sideburns ensconced his face, coming to a crowning crescendo at the end of a mop of bushy brown hair. Slick silvermist shades concealed his surveying eyes. A small, black backpack was slung loosely around his shoulders.

Cable car number Fifty-Six had slowed to a stop about two hundred yards ahead. The cable car was in the process of unloading tired sightseers and picking-up a substantially larger set of new riders. Zar was delighted to see that old number Fifty-Six was almost at full capacity. Old number Fifty-Six began its steep ascent of California Street.

A fourth grade class on a field trip from the Oakland area occupied a large portion of the cable car seating capacity. The kids were beaming with excitement and were told more than once by the conductor to make sure that they didn't stand on the seats or lean over the railings.

The smiling 32-year-old schoolteacher, Mrs. Hu, kept a keen eye on all of her students. She didn't want to be embarrassed by any disobedient behavior. She was in for a grueling day, but that was part of the job, a job she loved. It was a job that involved education, patience and interpersonal skills. She had to deal with more bosses than any other profession: her principal, administration, parents, and sometimes even the kids. Most people would have trouble keeping thirty children occupied and under control for an hour, let alone teaching them anything.

Mrs. Hu, like a lot of the nation's teachers, received little compensation for her Herculean efforts. However, she wasn't in this profession for the money. Her hard work would soon payoff. Recognizing a future shortage of teachers, President Marshall was attempting to pass a bill that would increase teachers' salaries, making the education field more lucrative. It was a plan that Marshall boasted was to compensate for what he liked to call the nation's silent heroes.

Grueling days like this one for Mrs. Hu helped stoke the flames of the argument that schoolteachers were grossly underpaid. It was anticipated that the public school system would be thoroughly strained in the next few years, the direct result of the "echo effect." The echo effect was the large number of baby boomers who conceived children during their late thirties. The birthrate a few years ago was the highest since the mid-sixties. The school systems were already starting to feel this strain. Marshall's plan was being well received by both political parties and it was expected to pass in the coming weeks.

# CRISIS

To Zar, the sun was a nuisance today. It made the heavy black wig adorning his crown uncomfortably warm. The wig's heat, combined with the laborious pushing required to keep the skateboard's momentum up the steep incline would have caused beads of sweat on almost anyone. However, his face didn't have an ounce of perspiration, only a look of concentration.

Approaching the cable car from the back, Zar slowed to a stop. Three short dings from the cable car indicated it was ready to continue its steady climb up California Street. Two solid pushes with his right leg and Zar reached out with his left hand, grabbing the rear railing of Old Number Fifty-Six. Zar had the timing down pat, the result of surveying the speed and activity of the cable car over the past couple of days.

"Hey, Mister! Mister! That's a chill skateboard," said one of the school kids who was looking at Zar. Zar ignored the child. "Hey, mister, I said that's a chill skateboard!" The child shouted it as if he wasn't used to being ignored. The child's abrasive tone was a reflection of his home environment. Both his parents were attending graduate school at the University of Southern California, which was better known to the locals as the University of Spoiled Children. The child was an unforeseen accident and often didn't receive the attention deserved. That attention went to studying and interviewing for jobs. The only way the child could get attention around the house was to demand it.

Making eye contact with the child, Zar pointed his finger toward his own ear and gave the child some sign language. The child in return gave him an okay sign and then surprised Zar by signing a coherent response back. The child, Jimmy Jones, had a deaf older cousin. Jimmy Jones loved conversing in sign because it gave him a chance to show off his unusual talent in front of his classmates. Jimmy especially wanted to impress the fair-haired and brown-eyed Shelly Cairollia. Cairollia was Jimmy's crush since early in the fourth grade and perhaps she'd finally notice him if he continued to sign with the man on the cool skateboard.

Despite being surprised by the child's skilled response, Zar calmly signed back. Sign was one of the nine languages he had mastered. On top of that, he also had a conversational understanding of five more.

Zar signaled to Jimmy that he couldn't talk right now since he only had one free hand. Zar explained that he needed to concentrate on the road and told the child to look ahead and enjoy the breathtaking view.

Zar couldn't wait to see that kid blown to bits, but he had to wait for the exact time. Zar noticed for the first time that two teenage girls on RollerBlades were now having the cable car tow them on the opposite side. They both nodded at Zar, who gave them an unerring stare back.

Zar would make sure these girls relinquished their joy ride soon. The designated drop-off point was quickly approaching, and he hadn't yet secured the bomb. The bomb was concealed inside of his fanny-pack and he needed to place it onto the undercarriage.

Intervention wasn't needed on these girls, as they let go and scuttled their way across the street to the local Ben & Jerry's ice cream parlor. These girls had the right idea; it was the perfect occasion to leisurely enjoy some Cherry Garcia or Chunky Monkey in the rare lazy San Franciscan midday sun.

There was little time to waste in getting the bomb into position. The cable car passengers and street patrons paid little attention to Zar's activities. The pedestrian traffic was a little lighter on this portion of the street and it would be difficult for anyone to detect what was going on.

The fanny-pack had been adeptly readjusted so that the pouch was now in front of Zar's stomach. He unzipped the pouch and grabbed the small, but dense, plastic explosive. The explosive was skillfully placed in the small pocket near the chassis. Close scrutiny of the engineering blueprints in the City Library revealed this as the cable car's vulnerable point.

"Mister, Mister! What's that thing you put under there?" shouted the child. Zar couldn't hear over the noisy sounds emanating from the cable track and was completely caught off-guard by Jimmy who had made his way to the back. Jimmy had climbed over the railing and was within inches of Zar. Zar was so surprised that he made the mistake of looking up to the direction of the child's voice. "Hey, you're not deaf. What are you doing, what did you put underneath the cable car?" Zar recognized that it was his curious friend again. Jimmy was disobeying the teacher's orders, but this wasn't anything new. Curiosity always overruled orders in Jimmy's logic.

"Yes, I'm not deaf, but I had to sign with you because it was too loud to hear you. What's this? It's an extra turbo booster that will make the cable car go faster, just a little something special for your class. It was supposed to be a surprise, so don't tell anyone about it, it'll just be our little secret. Just like our sign language. Now, I've got to get out of here before any of your classmates see me and spoil the surprise. You won't spoil the surprise will you?"

Jimmy emphatically shook his head no.

"Good, I knew that I could count on you. Bye-bye." Said Zar as he let go and skateboarded to a nearby alley.

An aerodynamic tuck position enabled Zar to zip into the intended alley. He was now out of sight of the little boy. Zar headed for the appropriate dumpster, the one with the graffiti *Gays are people too* spray-painted on it. Someone had recently modified the line with incongruous red paint and it now read *Gays are 00's.*

Zar noticed there were no vagrants in the alley and swiveled his head around twice in an attempt to detect any other would-be-onlookers. There was no one there; he was somewhat disappointed that he wouldn't have to kill anyone face-to-face. He knew that an observant street person who would later serve as a witness in court often destroyed many a criminal's best-laid plans. He had selfish reasons to notice the ordinarily overlooked bums.

Zar had placed a lock on this particular dumpster earlier that morning. He had outfitted its interior to meet his required needs and didn't want anyone meddling with it. Zar worked the combination and removed the dial lock on his first attempt and opened the heavy plastic door of the dumpster. He placed both of his hands on its upper lip and gracefully lifted himself up and then down into the dumpster in one fluid motion. Such fluid movements had enabled Zar to win the Junior National Gymnastic Competition in his homeland as a youth.

Zar closed the top of the dumpster and it became pitch black inside. The magnet light in his hand instantly illuminated the small confines. The magnet light was placed on the steel wall and he readily got to work. Crouching down further, he opened his bag of tricks. In less than two minutes, the bag of tricks had transformed his attire and his persona.

He was now adorned in tight spandex shorts and a bright turquoise half-shirt. His hair was a long, scraggily blond with a complementing goatee. Long white tube socks tucked into a pair of black basketball high tops completed the ensemble.

Zar doused his previous disguise with a special chemical, placed it into the small incinerator and dropped a lit match into the appropriate hole. It was quite an ingenious contraption. Requiring little oxygen, it was able to burn materials without producing much smoke.

Zar exited the dumpster as quickly as he'd entered and headed toward a pink Huffy mountain bike that was chained to a street post. The bike had been purchased from a teenager at a suburban garage sale earlier in the week. Zar had attended the garage sale as an elderly and frail woman in a wheel chair. As the old lady, he had told the kid that he was buying it for her grandson. He left nothing to chance. Zar headed out of the alley, took a sharp left, and began his descent toward the Bay.

Following his brief interlude with the strange man on the skateboard, Jimmy Jones scurried back to his seat on the cable car before the teacher or his fellow classmates knew he was missing. But, the capricious boy couldn't contain his excitement and quickly stood up on his chair and blurted, "I know about the surprise you have planned for us Ms. Hu, I know about the surprise!" shouted Jimmy, clapping his hands. The well-mannered Shelly Cairollia shot Jimmy a disapproving look.

## CRISIS

"Jimmy, please sit down this instant! Quit making such a racket," said a fatigued Ms. Hu. She'd already had enough of his antics today. In fact, she'd had enough of him after the first week of school.

"But Ms. Hu, all I'm saying is that I know about the surprise," pleaded Jimmy with a long face.

"Good heavens, what is it this time?" asked an irritated Ms. Hu. She made her way to the back of the cable car toward Jimmy. In unison, the kids let out an all-knowing "ooohhhhh" in response to the tone of Mrs. Hu's voice. At the same time, they were beginning to get excited about the possible surprise. Mrs. Hu knew she had to nip this fallacy in the bud before the kids began feeding off of each other's energy.

"Jimmy, what is this nonsense you're babbling about? You better explain yourself right now and it better be good, because you've created quite a ruckus," said Mrs. Hu in a warmer, but still authoritative tone.

Jimmy leaned over and proudly whispered into Mrs. Hu's ear, "I know about the turbo-booster you had that man put on the back of the trolley."

"Jimmy, what on earth are you talking about? What man? What turbo-booster? Is this another one of your games? If it is, we are going to have to sit down and talk with your parents again," voiced Ms. Hu sternly. She didn't need to deal with the Jones's again. Their behavior was more childish than their son's behavior. It was apparent from these meetings to Ms. Hu that Jimmy's parents often used the child as a bartering piece during their domestic squabbles.

"No, no game. The man told me about your surprise, but don't worry I won't tell anyone," stated Jimmy.

Her irritation was now turning to concern. She remembered that this fieldtrip was almost cancelled due to the school children being killed in the New York bombings last month. The only reason it was still approved, was that the school had already paid to have substitute teachers for students that couldn't afford the fieldtrip.

"Jimmy, listen to me carefully, where's the man you're talking about and where's the turbo-buster?"

"Oh, he was the nice man on the skateboard with the weird black hair, but he's not here anymore," Jimmy said, happy to have his teacher's undivided attention.

"What did this man say?" hurriedly asked Ms. Hu.

"When I asked him what he put underneath the cable car in the back he said it was the turbo-booster you'd asked for. He was really nice Ms. Hu, I can see why he's your friend," said Jimmy, intentionally leaving off the part about the stranger instructing him not to tell anyone, that it was a secret. Jimmy didn't want to get in trouble for disobeying Ms. Hu's friend, especially since Ms. Hu was staring at him so intently.

"Ms. Hu, what's wrong with your eyes? They're scaring me," said Jimmy softly.

"Conductor!" screamed Ms. Hu.

Zar coasted his bike to a stop and hopped off. He calmly placed the bike along the railing of the wharf. He inserted two quarters into the panoramic viewing machine designed to provide close-up views of Alcatraz and the Bay Bridge. He glanced at his Ironman triathlon watch and looked through the tourist viewer. He wasn't interested in Alcatraz or the bridge. He was interested in what was about to happen on the top of California Street. Accordingly, he swiveled the silver apparatus in that direction.

Zar could see the schoolteacher frantically moving toward the front of the cable car and toward the conductor. Something unusual was definitely going on. Zar glanced down again at his watch and coolly noted that chaos would ensue in less than ten seconds. Even if the school teacher's hurried actions indicated she was aware of what was about to happen to her, there was nothing she could do at this point to prevent it.

The ground rocked like an earthquake as the cable car exploded into a blaze of glory. The force of the explosion caused all the windows within a one-block radius to break. The flying debris struck down pedestrians without warning. Flesh projectiles spewed from the cable car. The children's bodies were no match for Zar's death bomb and they hurled helplessly through the air. Their corpses lay grotesquely strewn about on a blood stained California Street.

The mass chaos he had anticipated and created filled Zar's viewfinder. The horrific and hysterical screams from the injured and dying filled the air. He smiled to himself; the sound of agony was much better than Bach or Tchaikovsky.

Old number Fifty-Six was a blazing fireball and black smoke billowed into the brilliant azure afternoon sky. Sirens could be heard as police cars, ambulances, and fire trucks laboriously climbed up the steep slope of California Street. Local shop owners and patrons descended upon the confusing scene in a desperate attempt to save any remaining cable car occupants, especially the school children. Their efforts were made in vain, as one lifeless body after another was pulled from the death caldron.

A small child could be heard coughing and whispering about twenty yards from the wreckage. A local restaurant owner heard these sounds and rushed over to the child. However, when the robust Italian knelt down next to the child, the child just whispered, "It was supposed to be a surprise, a surprise...," and the disfigured child closed his eyes forever.

***The San Francisco Chronicle:***
***"Terrorist Tremors Felt Across the Nation"***

*The nation has now been rocked on both coasts by terrorist acts. Exactly one month after the horrific bombing of the eNetwork building in New York, the nation is once again stunned by violence. The President is searching for the answers to these unprecedented acts and the American public is asking when it will end? The Bay felt a mild tremor yesterday, but a tremor that caused more deaths than any earthquake of recent memory. Sixty-five Americans, including thirty elementary school children, were pronounced dead yesterday afternoon, victims of a bomb explosion on the cable car they were riding. The children were on a field trip from nearby University Hills Elementary. Most of the children were eight or nine years of age. The children's teacher and chaperon, Ms. Tiffany Hu, age 32, died from severe burns.*

*No Terrorists organizations have taken credit for the bombing. The same uncertainty holds true for the bombing in New York. Authorities have no leads at this point and are continuing their investigation today. The Office of Homeland Security has yet to issue a statement as well. Surviving eyewitnesses said the car exploded into an enormous fireball. There were no surviving passengers from the cable car. The blast and ensuing debris killed thirteen pedestrians and wounded several more. Unlike the terrible events of September 11, 2001, there is no evil martyr like Ben Laden for the nation to point their frustration toward. These are also the first terrorist attacks on American soil since 9/11. The only connection authorities can make at this point between the two recent bombings is that both resulted in many children's deaths.*

**"President Cancels Campaign as a Result of Terrorist Action"**

*The President's scheduled campaign visit to Richmond, Va. was cancelled in order to accommodate a flight to San Francisco for a three o'clock press conference today. The President can ill-afford cancellations on his already light campaign tour. The President's once strong approval rating has slipped 20% over the last month (based on a Gallup political poll). A once insurmountable lead for the incumbent has now turned into a heated presidential race. Upstart Independent and David Corrigan, has gobbled up the majority of Marshall's lost votes. Corrigan's affable nature but strong actions have endeared him to a growing contingent of swing voters.*

*The President's campaign committee won't comment on whether there are plans for an increase in campaign efforts. The original campaign was designed to stay the course since the President's popularity rating was the highest of any President in history, substantially above Ronald Reagan's. This recent slip in the polls can be directly attributed to the egregious acts of terrorism that have recently occurred within the country's borders. The rattled public is concerned about their personal safety and security, a platform the incumbent was already weak on.*

*Conversely, surging David Corrigan's campaign is based on security and the abolishment of crime. His platform is strongly supported by the dramatic results he's achieved while serving as the Governor of Florida. The drug war in Florida has almost been won due to Corrigan's revolutionary work in the Sunshine State. Corrigan's campaign schedule has him attending Game Two of the American League Baseball Series between the Nashville Bombers and Boston Red Sox. The game is scheduled to begin at 7:30 on NBC from Fenway Park, Boston. The American public may even question if America's Pastime, baseball, is safe anymore.*

# CHAPTER 29

Tip and Lisa exchanged their related stories about why they were at the Chi Theta National Headquarters. Both found it ironic that Chris Hamilton's death had started their separate journeys toward the same goal. Tip listened intently as she described her brother's unusual death and how she took the secretarial job after reading about the deaths of Barbara and Hamilton. The story seemed believable to him. He knew that she wasn't on the same side as Valez, as evidenced by last night. Moreover, she told the story with such emotion and conviction, that Tip believed she was traversing through a desolate region of life similar to his own.

The roughshod last twenty-five hours had taken a toll on Lisa and Tip, both mentally and physically. Despite this, they were in the best spirits they'd been in weeks. The attempted termination by Valez's men proved they were on the right track and their murder hypotheses weren't that crazy after all. They both felt better having released some of their bottled-up mental demons. They also now had someone to confide in, someone that understood.

The afternoon was spent comparing notes, findings, and stories. Although the puzzle was far from complete, newfound synergy was helping to create a puzzle box cover that would serve as a map for the next steps of action. Now the trick was finding the puzzle pieces.

Lisa explained to Tip how she'd performed background checks on the donation checks that had been rolling into National Headquarters. It became obvious that many deceased alumni that had managed to stay on the Chi Theta mailing records were also responsible for the majority of the big monetary donations. The Chi Theta alumni list was only updated every two years. Large shares of these "bogus" checks were being mailed without return addresses. Suspiciously all had been mailed from Miami.

She than went in-depth about how Valez previously worked for Merchel Corporation, which was based in Chicago. Also, all of the Chi Theta's maintenance work on various chapter houses across the nation was performed or contracted through Merchel, at no cost to the local chapter. The Chi Theta brotherhood was ecstatic about Valez's construction and renovation policy, a policy he'd introduced when he first became National Director. In most cases, the local chapters wouldn't be able to afford such elaborate and expensive renovation projects and, thus, in their eyes, Valez was a god. Extensive research on other Fraternity and Sorority renovation and payment policies revealed that this policy of free repairs and renovations was, indeed, unique.

In the press, Valez boasted that he'd cut a tremendous deal from Merchel in return for such an exclusive arrangement. The "deal" however, wasn't great at all. Lisa's numbers indicated that Chi Theta National Fraternity, on average, paid Merchel fifty percent more than the industry average for similar work.

Tip allowed everything that Lisa was telling him to sink in. "It appears that Valez is allowing someone to use the Chi Theta Fraternity system to launder money in a very complicated and brilliant procedure. Or perhaps he is using it for his own means," said Tip.

"Yes, I thought that was the case as well. However, where is the money coming from? And, whom is he laundering it for? Do you think he's doing it for himself?" asked Lisa.

"Those are the questions that we'll need to answer, and unfortunately I don't think we have much time. Valez is on to both of us. And, if the operation is as big as you indicate, he's not going to pull the plug just because of us. Which means, he's got his hounds out for our trail right now. So, not only will we be on the run, it's now going to be more difficult to gather evidence than it was before. Everything is going to be air tight at that operation," said Tip.

"Do you think he'd shut down the operation if we were able

to get more power behind us in the form of the authorities," asked Lisa.

"That's a good thought, but I think you already know the answer. We don't have enough concrete evidence to support our loose story right now. I also have a suspicion Valez has people in high places, so we must watch ourselves. I already almost got myself killed trying to do what you suggested. Remember that lottery ticket I fished out of Garcia's pocket? Well, the number written on the back of it is the number of the FBI agent that I contacted. If we bring in the authorities we must have absolute confidence that we can trust our contact person."

"What were you trying to obtain from Valez's computer last night, and were you successful?" asked Tip.

"Well, I'd done just about all the research and fact finding that I could from my secretarial desk and it was helpful, but somewhat limited. I've never really understood the motivation or the beneficiary of such a money-laundering scheme. I was hoping that Barbara Fernandez, his deceased secretary, had transferred some of Valez's files from his file cabinets to his computer before she deceased.

When I logged onto Valez's computer system, I noticed that the total amount of the bogus checks from dead Alumni was far greater than the total amount paid to Merchel. Most of this variation is explained by Chi Theta's reserve pool of funds for litigation and contingencies, their form of a slush fund. However, I noticed that this fund had been tapped twice for large withdrawals during the past month.

Specifically, these withdrawals were made on October 7 and October 13 respectively. The amount of withdrawals coincided with two deposits credited to the same bank account number in Grand Caymans of three and four million dollars. A third amount of five million dollars was identified for potential future withdrawal from the reserve pool of funds. The five million had a note next to it indicating that it would be held in escrow. This money was placed in a pending column. I hypothesized that this money was earmarked for the Chris Hamilton vs. Amy Klein case in which Chi Theta was the defendant. However, I really don't think that's the case. It's my opinion that this five million will be making its way to the same Caymans bank account in the near future," said Lisa.

Lisa's deductions and ingenuity in obtaining this information impressed Tip. She was not only beautiful, but also resourceful, bright, and brave.

"I've also looked into the ten largest fraternity systems and sorority systems in the United States. Although these fraternities and sororities are private, with the help of my contacts, I was able to put together some rough estimates. I'm confident that Chi Theta's cash flows are almost five times that of the next largest fraternity, despite only being the eleventh largest fraternity in terms of lifetime members. Also, why is Chi Theta paying way above the going rate to Merchel when they have an exclusive contract with them? Is it because they have more money than they know what to do with in the form of donation? It's a chicken and the egg scenario and all I smell is rotten eggs. I mean, almost all contracts, in any form of business, result in more favorable pricing. But, in this instance, the opposite is true. Chi Theta is being overcharged for their exclusive agreement with Merchel.

I've conjured up several hypotheses and this is the easiest… Valez is being overly generous to his former employer. The reason for this could be any of the following or a combination of them: Valez is receiving kickbacks, still privately owns part of the company, or is being promised a lucrative job in the future. There is no evidence indicating that any of these are likely. Also, none of these scenarios explain the inordinate amount of donations the fraternity receives, especially the "bogus" checks coming in from Miami. You're right, now that you've said it, all the pieces do add up to a money-laundering scheme being run out of the headquarters," riantly gleamed Lisa.

"Whatever the answers, or whatever the reason, there is a lot of money involved. A tremendous amount of planning must have gone into developing such a complex plan. The challenge that we face is to find the answers before Valez and his gang catch up with us. At this point, I don't think it would behoove us to report our escapade to the police, since we were trespassing on National Headquarters property to begin with, and you were doing it under false pretense. Nice hooker costume by the way. I think you'd also agree that although we've learned a tremendous amount by swapping information, we still don't have enough yet to risk forcing the operation completely underground by bringing in the big boys," suggested Tip.

"Yes, I agree with that assessment," replied Lisa.

"At this time, I think that Valez is arrogant enough to continue whatever plans and operations he has in the works. Valez probably considers us a mere nuisance, and a growing nuisance at that, but nothing formidable enough to stop his large money laundering machine," pontificated Lisa.

"Because of his arrogance, He'll realize too late that we are going to foil his plans," prophesized Tip.

## CHAPTER 30
### New York Times

*I*ndependent candidate David Corrigan's recent Southwest campaign swing has him knocking on President Marshall's door as he once again gained in the voter polls. Inside experts contend that he also has an excellent chance of locking-up all the electoral votes in The Lonestar State of Texas. No candidate has ever won the Presidency without carrying Texas.

Conversely, Marshall had to cancel much of his already light campaign schedule to visit San Francisco in the aftermath of the bombing there. Marshall's home state is California, where he served as the state's Senator prior to obtaining the oval office. California possesses the most electoral votes. Marshall's stronghold on the Golden State has slipped substantially since the cable car bombing on California Street. Worse still for Marshall is the fact that Corrigan is cannibalizing most of these votes. Only a small percentage of these "lost" votes are going to Democratic candidate Peter Parkhill.

Corrigan's anti-crime and terrorism platform is starting to resonate with the public. His numbers are reaching new highs in the public perception polls on questions relating to crime and terrorism. He has supplanted Peter Parkhill this week and now has firm control on second place in the presidential race. More importantly, he is eroding Marshall's once insurmountable lead.

An Independent hasn't played such an important role in a presidential election since Ross Perot in 1992. However, Corrigan is a much larger player than Perot and has the genuine potential to pull off the largest upset in United States political history. Corrigan should be thankful that the Democratic hopeful, Peter Parkhill, is unusually weak. Analogous to a previous Republican Candidate, Bob Dole, Parkhill is much past his prime and out of touch with the issues important to the Baby Boomer and Generation X and Y majority. Americans are hungry to keep the economy booming and desire a young, energetic President. It seems that the voters are *starting to believe that a young upstart named David Corrigan possesses such qualities.*

*The only thing potentially holding Corrigan back is the uncertainty surrounding whom his potential running mate will be. Corrigan would become the second Florida Governor elected president in the nation's history.*

Corrigan finished reading the article and chuckled to himself. He laughed about how stupid Americans are, especially the media. Things were going better than he had hoped. "After my clandestine little mishap occurs in Chicago, this race will be over and the presidency will be mine," Corrigan confided in his brandy snifter.

Corrigan knew the article was astute in pointing out that he could not afford to wait much longer in announcing his running mate. The second position on the ticket would be critical in the upcoming election. Many experts believed that President Marshall's lead would have evaporated even further had it not been for the popularity of Vice President Duke.

Vice President Charlene Duke was the first female Vice President of the United States. "Charlie Duke," as she was popularly known across the country, possessed beauty, intelligence, and unparalleled charm. Charlie attended the University of Texas at Austin before going on to receive a law degree from Harvard.

After serving as Governor of Texas for four years, she was selected to run on the Republican ticket with Marshall. Marshall and Duke were both youthful and attractive, and it reminded many of the Kennedy years. Because of her unique qualities, Duke was able to help their ticket receive eighty percent of the female population's vote in the last election. The female population still strongly supported the Republican ticket, but they were becoming increasingly concerned about the recent growth in terrorism and crime. Many Marshall and Duke detractors pointed out that since the Vice President is a woman, she couldn't take a strong stand against crime and terrorism.

Corrigan rose from his chair after reading the last line in an article that speculated that a woman's presence in the oval office would signal to terrorists that America was weak. Despite these negative and sexist comments, many Washington experts were certain that Corrigan would select a qualified female running mate. Corrigan smirked at these supposed experts' opinions. Little did these experts know, that it would be a cold day in hell before he would let any inferior women, or non-white male for that matter, have the privilege of being associated with him on a ticket. He was going to take extreme delight in showing the world how weak "Charlie Duke" was. He was sick of the public fawning over her.

# CHAPTER 31

# CLEMMONS LIBRARY, THE UNIVERSITY OF VIRGINIA:

Tip was impressed at how well Lisa knew her way around the enormous library. He was even more impressed when a few of the librarians knew her on a first name basis. It was true that she had spent a good deal of time among the famous stacks here. What he didn't know was that she was fairly well recognized everywhere in the state of Virginia.

Both were still very sore from their adventurous evening. The long hitchhike ride from Maryland also didn't help matters.

He was surprised that neither librarian inquired about her purplish bumps and bruises, but he was glad they didn't. The lower the profile they, or more importantly he, could keep, the better.

With Lisa's help, Tip selected a couple of boxes of microfilm, which contained past editions of the *Miami Herald*. He thought that backtracking five years would provide a thorough search. This span of time would cover Corrigan's entire term as Governor of Florida. Unfortunately the *Miami Herald* only stored the past year's articles on their website.

Tip and Lisa both suspected that Corrigan was somehow connected in the whole puzzle from the note Tip had found in Hamilton's mail.

Tip didn't expect to discover anything significant, but at this point he was reaching for anything. Things got off to a bad start when the first pool of film was miss fed into the projector. It took over twenty minutes of delicate surgery from the librarian to fix the jam and properly rethread the film.

Lisa's equally arduous task was continuing her investigation of the Merchel Construction Corporation. While performing this research, she was paying particular attention to anything concerning Ricardo Valez. She headed off to the computer room to dig through volumes of material.

After four tedious hours, Tip was blurry eyed and tired. Fatigue almost caused him to pass over an article detailing the murder of a Drug Enforcement Agent last December. He was curious as to why this wasn't online. Perhaps he just missed it.

Tip reread the article and despite his current financial situation, decided to incur the thirty-cent charge to print the article in its entirety. This article may prove to be nothing, but it was more than he had expected to find. He decided to end his research on this upbeat note.

The computer lab had lost power and hence, Tip found Lisa surrounded by stacks of binders such as: *Standard & Poor's reports, Moody's Almanac,* and *Hoover's Handbook of Businesses.* Lisa had pulled her long, beach-brown hair into a ponytail. A black elastic "scrunchie" was holding it in place. A pair of rimless-wire reading glasses perched on her nose and a yellow pencil nestled behind her left ear.

The majority of the scratches and bruises were on the left side of her face. As a result, she rested her right cheek in the palm of her right-hand as she scanned through numerous articles and documents.

Tip hesitated before interrupting her. At the moment, he realized how truly beautiful she was. What made her even more majestic was the courage she had shown the other night.

Lisa was engrossed in her research, but was cognizant of his presence. She could focus on the task at hand, while being a keen observer of subtle movements around her. This acute sense was refined on the nights she lay awake waiting for the intoxicated return of Eddie from a local establishment. She lay awake praying that she wouldn't be the victim of another unjustified beating. Her acute peripheral vision may also be attributed to her years of playing team sports.

The man that stood before her in the library was a mystery, which was far better than any man currently in her life. Tip broke the silence with a low whisper as he sat down in the chair across from her.

"Any luck?"

"I'm afraid not, how about you," replied Lisa.

Tip slid the printout of the *Miami Herald* article between the stack of books and binders to her.

"It may turn out to be nothing, but I think it's worth checking into," said Tip.

She scanned the article. The journalistic writing was a refreshing change from the dry and factual business publications. Business analysts weren't known for their spellbinding prose.

**Miami Herald:**

*Drug Enforcement Agent Randall Hill was discovered dead in the front seat of his car early this morning. The apparent cause of death is reported to be two gunshots to the head. At this point, there are no reported eyewitnesses to this brutal suburban murder. Hill's body was discovered at 6:27 yesterday morning by his wife of six years, Josephine.*

*Carlos Alphonso's body was also found in Miami's forty-third precinct. Hill arrested Alphonso yesterday afternoon on charges of drug trafficking. Officials haven't confirmed whether the two murders are related.*

*Hill, a native of Jacksonville, has been working for the DEA for the past seven years. Hill leaves his wife and a three-year-old son.*

*Mrs. Hill told officials that her husband called at around midnight to tell her that he'd be later than normal; he'd be going to John Rathman's house if she needed to reach him. Mrs. Hill is a nurse at local Greggory Hospital and was working the graveyard shift. John Rathman, also a drug enforcement agent, has been Hill's partner for the past four years. Rathman confirmed that Hill had a break-through on a specific case. Rathman explained that Hill didn't want to discuss the details over the phone, and he met Rathman at his house a half an hour later.*

*Hill is the first officer to be killed in the line of duty since Governor Corrigan mandated his aggressive War on Drugs Policy three years ago. A viewing will take place from five to eight this Thursday at Derby Funeral Parlor in Broward County. The funeral service will be held this Friday at noon at St. Luke's Church. The funeral procession and reading of the eulogy will be open to the public.*

Lisa finished reading the article and slowly glanced up. Tip was astounded at how quickly she'd read the document. He was a fairly fast reader, but knew he would be no match for her. "What's your take on this?" asked Lisa.

"Well, I searched for articles that contained John Rathman and found an interesting little fact. Apparently, Rathman retired from the Federal Drug Enforcement Agency a week after Hill was murdered."

"Do you think he was shaken or scared into retirement? Or do you think he was somehow involved in a plot to murder Alphonso? Maybe he was working for Corrigan and needed to cap Alphonso because he knew too much?" inquired Lisa.

"It's tough to say, but I don't believe he was scared into retiring. In fact, a reporter asked Rathman just that very question. Rathman's answer was that he was retiring because he wasn't satisfied with the way Hill's murder investigation was handled internally," stated Tip.

"So, what now? I mean that article was interesting and arouses suspicion around Corrigan, but how does it help us? We're still at ground zero, aren't we?" asked Lisa.

"Not necessarily. I was able to pull Rathman's address and phone number off the Web. I suggest we contact him and see if he's willing to talk with us. It's a shot in the dark, but he may have some nuggets of useful information and insight," replied Tip.

---

Tip and Lisa strolled lazily down the dogwood-lined streets of campus. Passing the Rotunda and beautiful lawn it was difficult not to be impressed by the beauty of Thomas Jefferson's architectural genius.

Lisa and Tip had developed a strong bond over the past couple of days. This development wasn't that unusual, they reasoned. Human bonds often sprout from, or become, stronger during times of adversity. This phenomenon can be seen by the increase in the amount of spectators that sing the national anthem during times of war or other tribulations. Such shared experiences also create trust, as well. However this bond seemed to go a little beyond friendship, there were also some other feelings being stirred up. These feelings were becoming stronger by the minute.

# CHAPTER 32

It was a crisp autumn night and the stars in the Virginia sky were spectacular. Although she wasn't physically touching Tip, Lisa could feel a special warmth and vibrant energy radiating from him. She definitely wasn't ready for a relationship at this point in time. She questioned if she'd ever be able to expose herself to the possibility of another nightmare.

She knew that the mental scars of domestic violence usually remained long after the physical ones had healed. She wasn't ready to let herself fall in love with anyone. However, this didn't stop her from appreciating that Tip possessed a unique charisma. She felt safe for the first time in a very long while. A peaceful sigh was her recognition of the beautiful night surrounding her. Tip glanced over and gave a genial smile of agreement. Lisa's dazzling blue eyes smiled back.

Tip felt warmth stirring inside his heart; a low burning fire that hadn't been kindled in a long time. However, there were still several callous layers to penetrate before it could melt his icy defense shield. The fact that Lisa was able to slightly penetrate this carapace was more than could be said for any of her contemporaries. Her charm and intelligence were breaking down the barriers he had erected following his parents' deaths and subsequent betrayal by Stephanie and her so-called friends.

Rugby Street was filled with a mix of jovial University of Virginia students and Charlottesville residents. The confluent crowd was taking advantage of Mother Nature's nocturnal gift. Most of the passerby's couldn't help but sneak a glance to admire such a beautiful young couple. Tip and Lisa smiled at others on the street and occasionally glanced sheepishly at one another. Rugby Street was jumping, but it was tame in comparison to the midsummer and midwinter annual bashes that were thrown here. This street was conducive to partying because most of the Greek houses and off-campus students were situated here.

Lisa stopped in front of a small, white, colonial house. A little, finely trimmed lawn and sidewalk accompanied the quaint home. The narrow sidewalk led directly to the front door. The light hanging in front of the arched doorway was illuminated. Aside from this light, the house was shrouded in darkness.

A white Audi A4 was parked on the west side of the house, in its proper place on the two-tracked stone driveway. The small white automobile could benefit from a car wash, especially its mud-caked undercarriage.

"Well, here we are," said Lisa. "This is my old teammate and roommate, Jena's house. It doesn't look like anyone's home, but her car is here and, of course, it is dirty. I guess by the looks of the car, some things never change. Jena said we could crash here if necessary. I can stay in her room and she's got a pullout couch, which may be a bit small for you. But, it should work if you just angle your body diagonally."

"I'm sure it'll be fine. This is a nice house. If you don't mind, I'm going to head to the computer lab in Adelman library before it closes. The librarian said it's on McCormick Street. That's right around here if I'm not mistaken?" asked Tip.

"Yea, it's just two blocks up that way. It's on the same street as Clemmons Library," pointed Lisa, "What are you hoping to find?"

"Oh, I'm just trying to dig up some more info on Rathman. I'm also going to figure out the best travel plans to get us to Florida in order to talk to him," said Tip.

"Well, good luck. I'm going to swing in here, because Jena is expecting me right about now. You can meet her when you get back," said Lisa.

"Great, it shouldn't take me more than an hour round trip," said Tip. He broke into a slight jog, as he needed to get in the doors before the computer lab closed in twenty minutes. He hoped that his research didn't take long. He wanted to have time to grab a sandwich on the way home. Tip had heard some students talking about a great twenty-four hour deli called Little John's, which was located in the heart of campus. The thought of rye bread stacked high with roast beef, turkey, mustard, lettuce and tomato made his stomach rumble.

Lisa watched Tip gracefully fade into the night. She deduced that he had to be, or had at one time been, a great athlete. His body was too sleek and his movements too fluid for him not to be. He was also too masculine to be a dancer or a gymnast. Above all, Tip possessed that ubiquitous gait inherent to all natural athletes. However, if he was a great athlete, she was surprised that he hadn't brought it into conversation in a boastful manner. Every other male athlete she'd ever known always defined themselves by their playing prowess. What would make this guy any different? Maybe she was wrong; perhaps he wasn't an athlete at all. But who was he?

Lisa rapped the brass doorknocker against the arched door a second time. Again, there was no answer. She checked the door and it was unlocked. She had stayed at Jena's several times over the past year. Jena's place was her hideaway from Eddie's abusive nighttime behavior. Jena was more than likely sitting on the back porch listening to some Bach or Beethoven. Jena loved classical music, especially the brilliant B's. She loved them even more once she learned that research indicated that listeners of this music had increased levels of intelligence and creative thinking in the left side of their brains. Jena wondered if that's why she always seemed to excel in quantitative subjects like mathematics, accounting, and finance.

Lisa cautiously entered through the front door, all the while rapping her knuckles swiftly against the wood. She noticed that Jena had fixed the squeak in the door hinge. Funny as it seemed, she found herself missing that familiar squeak. It seemed out of place for that comfortable squeak to be absent.

"Jena? Jena are you home?"

The dark house answered with a foreboding silence. Jena should be able to hear her, even if she was on the back porch. Jena rarely had the volume of her classical music above conversation level. Lisa took a couple of baby steps into the foyer and closed the door behind her. She peered through the family room and noticed that the back porch light wasn't on and she didn't hear music playing.

She strained her ears to determine if perhaps Jena was in the shower; again silence. Why would the front door be open? Jena and her roommates always locked the door. Heck, they usually locked the door whenever they were inside of the house. Perhaps she'd left it open knowing that I was coming, thought Lisa. This would make sense, but she knew that Jena would also leave some kind of note if this were the case.

An eerie feeling swept over Lisa and she felt her way in the dark across the foyer's wood floor to the perimeter of the kitchen. She knew that there was a light switch there, and she turned it on.

"AAAHHHH!" Lisa let out a loud scream. She couldn't believe the horrific scene before her.

Jena's legs were sprawled out past the island counter on the mauve and crème tiled kitchen floor. Lisa rushed around the counter and the sight of Jena's severely beaten body knocked her to the floor.

Jena was a pint-sized, spunky girl from Italy. Jena was UVA's volleyball co-captain, alongside Lisa, and was also the team's best setter. A large portion of Jena's ebony hair was stiffly matted against the dried blood on her face. Lisa brushed the hair back and felt for a pulse on her neck. Jena's neck was still warm which was a good sign. After several anxious seconds, Lisa was able to detect a weak pulse.

Lisa sprang up from her crouched position and grabbed the telephone on the counter. The ivory-colored phone had dark blood smeared on the receiver. Even more blood streaked the Formica countertop. It was obvious that Jena had struggled to call the police. Lisa was going to do what her bantam friend had attempted to do.

"I'd put that down if I were you."

Lisa froze in mid-dial. Out of the shadows of the living room stepped her burly and malicious ex-boyfriend, Eddie.

# CRISIS

"Long time, no see Sweetheart," drawled Eddie. Gripped between his pointer and middle fingers was an almost empty half-gallon of Rebel Yell Tennessee Bourbon. The bottle casually thumped against the side of his well-worn and now bloody denim jeans. His left arm wasn't as slovenly. Instead, it fiercely held an old English fire-poker. Lisa's reaction was one of disbelief and shock. These feelings quickly transformed themselves into percolating anger.

"You cowardly pig! How could you possible do this to Jena! You're twice the size of her...you bastard! What did she ever do to you to deserve this!?" Lisa had to control her anger. She wanted to erase his little smirk with a swift kick to the face. However, she knew that now wasn't the time. She needed the element of surprise. Lisa also knew that Eddie, surprisingly, kept most of his faculties when intoxicated. However, Eddie did slow down after awhile. She could tell he wasn't at that point yet. The booze was definitely affecting him, but it hadn't yet started to scramble his motor skills.

"You're right. Jena did nothing to deserve this. The only one to blame for this unfortunate incident is you, Lisa. You caused it, you and you alone. You should be less concerned about Jena's health and more concerned with your own," demonically stated Eddie. He was extremely intoxicated, yet his words were concise and clear. His words bit through the air just as they always did when he was in one of his moods.

"What are you doing here, Eddie? What do you want?" asked Lisa in a strained voice.

"For starters, I want you to put the fucking phone down!" She didn't have a chance to, however, as he adroitly sliced the sharp edge of the poker through the wall unit. Eddie had a surprisingly long reach with the poker, and Lisa no longer felt comfortable with the limited distance between her and her intoxicated ex.

"Eddie, you're right, whatever has brought you here today has to do with me. It has nothing to do with Jena. We need to get her some help. She's terribly hurt for God's sake," pleaded Lisa.

"What, do you think I'm a fuckin' idiot. Well join the club, because everyone else already knows it," mocked Eddie.

"No one thinks you're an idiot Eddie."

"Obviously you're in the minority of people who didn't see it the paper last week. I flat flunked the stupid fuckin' bar exam again!," bitched Eddie.

"Eddie, you know you're not stupid. And you know I don't believe that either-I never have. Has your father been filling your head up with crazy thoughts again?" asked Lisa. Lisa didn't think Eddie was stupid, but she did think he needed professional help for his drinking problem.

"Shut the hell up, you filthy whore. We're not talking about me tonight. You're the one to blame here, not me. I wasted all of my time caring about you, instead of what I should have been doing which was studying. And how do you repay my loyalty? You repay it by abandoning me the second we hit a tough road. When I need you the most, you abandon me! I should have listened to my father when he said I shouldn't be dating such white trash. But the public never knew what trash you are. Virginians all love Lisa. Everybody loves Lisa. They love Lisa because of the image we created for you and nothing more. The people never got to know the real Lisa like I did. They don't know the deceitful, unforgiving, whoring Lisa that I know!"

Eddie's pupils were now just tiny beads of black. Lisa positioned the island counter between Eddie and herself. She frantically glanced around for anything that could serve as a weapon of defense. There was a block of knives near the sink, but that would put her dangerously close to Eddie. A meat tenderizer lay on the counter, but that wouldn't do much good. On the stove was a large saucepan on an electric burner set on high heat. Obviously Jena was about to prepare dinner when she was attacked.

She determined that her best chance was to try and calm Eddie by pacifying him for as long as was necessary. However, if the time came she would need to make a wildly deft move if she hoped for any chance of escape.

---

Tip stopped his jogging abruptly and cursed himself for being so stupid. In order to log on to the university computers, he would be required to punch in a student personal identification number or PIN. He had gotten on the computers earlier by having Lisa type in her PIN number. But, even if he had watched Lisa type, there was no way he was going to remember the eleven digit code. He turned and started sprinting back toward Jena's house. If he sprinted both to her house and also back to the library, he may be able to make it before it closed. Besides, he reasoned, it would serve as a good workout, and he hadn't had one of those since he'd left Michigan.

---

"And how do you repay that devotion? By not being around when I need you most-well that's just fucking selfish!" Eddie always repeated himself when he was drunk, especially when he began to tire. "So, tell me Lisa, where the fuck have you been the past week? I'm warning you, don't give me any of your bullshit! Where the fuck have you been!?" yelled Eddie.

"I was visiting my mother, and..."

"Bullshit! I visited that loon at the farm and she hasn't seen ya, nor has anyone else for that matter. Why do you always have to lie to me? I wanted to play nice and now you won't let me play nice. Why won't you let me play nice Lisa?

I knew you'd come here eventually. Jena could have saved herself a lot of pain if she would have just cooperated. Unfortunately, I've already given you too many opportunities to cooperate, thus you won't be extended the same offer. Rather, it's time for you to pay for the countless pain you've caused me," stated Eddie as he made his way closer toward Lisa. "Why are you so concerned about Jena's pain and so oblivious to the pain that you've caused me to suffer through?"

She knew that the only voice Eddie wanted to hear at this point was his own, and she wisely remained silent.

She was trapped in the corner of the kitchen and Eddie was methodically inching closer with every breath. "How about a little kiss for old time's sake Lisa?" gritted Eddie through his teeth. His grimy right hand placed the half-gallon of Rebel Yell on the counter and proceeded to reach out for Lisa's angelic face.

Lisa bit down hard on the flesh located between Eddie's thumb and forefinger and then quickly ducked down beneath his arms. It was fortunate that she was so agile. She barely avoided the swift swing of the poker, which clanged loudly against the oven. She immediately reached up and gripped the rubber handle of the frying pan. Lisa swung the frying pan around her head and toward Eddie. Eddie saw the pan approaching at the last moment and took the necessary action to make the pan brush harmlessly off his left cheek. The intense heat of the pan caused his cheek to blister slightly.

If Eddie was angry before, he was incensed with rage now. Lisa moved around to the other side of the island counter and jumped up onto the Formica by the sink in hopes of then jumping into the sunroom and heading for the screen door to the back porch.

As Lisa sprang from the counter, the fireplace poker caught the top of her left foot throwing her off her equilibrium. She flew head over heels into the sunroom and onto the beige carpet. Before she knew it, Eddie was on top of her.

"You want to act like a whore, by using me for everything I have and then leaving? Well then, I'm going to treat you like a whore," spat Eddie. Using the phone line wire, he tied her hands together and then to the base of the sunroom's heavy glass table. Her legs were pulled wide apart by the other cords. Eddie was now standing directly over her.

"See, it doesn't feel so good to feel helpless, now, does it? Well now you know how I've felt for the past couple of years," slurred Eddie. "I felt helpless having to put on a charade for my father and family all these years. Heaven forbid they ever found out that you, a product of white trash, were actually smarter. They were already ashamed of me enough, but you had to keep overachieving in everything you did. You were able to achieve, because you didn't waste any time trying to make our relationship work. Meanwhile I wasted all those years giving and giving to you and our relationship with nothing left to show for it in the end. Humiliation is the only thing I ever got. Well, now you're going to experience everything I've endured over the past few years. Only you're on the accelerated course tonight, after all, you're used to being at the top of your class."

"Listen, Eddie-"

"No, you fucking listen!" screamed Eddie, "this is Eddie's night and it's fine time you started enjoying it." Eddie casually stoked the fire with the poker and let the tip settle in the amber coals.

Removing the poker from the fire, he placed the sharp end just below Lisa's chin on her elegant neck. She could feel the heat radiating from the tip. Eddie proceeded to gradually undo her white silk blouse, button by button, with the hot poker. He then pulled each side of the blouse back exposing her white lace bra and blooming breasts. Try as she may, Lisa couldn't help but scream every time the hot poker touched her bare skin. The poker was in the process of burning through the front clasp of her white lace bra.

Tip was bounding up the tulip-lined sidewalk when he heard a scream. He barged through the front door and raced toward the scream. He discovered Lisa spread-eagle on the floor. He expediently attempted to scan the room, but it was too late. Eddie was up and charging fast toward the front door. Eddie unleashed an untamed swing with the poker that caught Tip squarely in the left shoulder, knocking him to the ground. Tip landed face down next to Lisa. He instinctively and immediately rolled to his right, narrowly missing being struck by the down-swinging poker.

"So, you're the reason this slut has been missing," growled Eddie. Eddie closed in on Tip, funneling him toward the kitchen in an attempt to corner him. Tip was at a severe disadvantage since he wasn't familiar with the layout of the house and the man before him had a weapon. It appeared that the man wasn't afraid to use the weapon either.

Tip nearly tripped over Jena and was startled momentarily by her presence. The slight hesitation cost Tip a slash across his lower abdomen courtesy of Eddie and the poker. Tip winced in pain, but was fortunate that the cut wasn't too deep or too long. The heat of the poker let it cut through flesh like a stick through a warm marshmallow.

"Yeah, pretty boy, I'm gonna cut ya up real good," declared Eddie.

"I'm not too concerned about some spineless coward who has to beat up on unarmed women for self-gratification. It's a good thing that you have a weapon and I don't, because otherwise it wouldn't be challenging enough for me to kick the tar out of you. You're a pathetic excuse for a man," Tip replied coolly.

That touched a nerve with Eddie and he reared back mightily with the intention of delivering a mind-erasing blow. Tip anticipated Eddie's reaction and sprang forward at the precise moment, driving his shoulder into Eddie's abdomen. Tip was like a professional boxer spotting an opening. He drove Eddie back against the counter. The sudden impact caused Eddie to lose his grip on the poker. Without the poker, Eddie was no match for Tip's raw strength and tenacity.

Tip grabbed the back of Eddie's head and slammed it down onto the orange glowing burner. Eddie shrieked in agony. At the same time he was scorching Eddie's face, Tip brought back Eddie's left arm and broke it like a chicken wing. The sight of the two victimized girls ignited Tip's rage and he wanted to return the favor to Eddie.

Eddie reached around with his left hand and attempted to grab and rip Tip's ear off. However, Eddie didn't get a solid grip on the ear, but his nails did do some damage digging into and ripping the skin on Tip's neck. Thoroughly incensed, Tip hoisted Eddie off the stove and body-slammed him headfirst onto the glass coffee table in the living room. An unnatural sound of flesh and bone echoed through the room. Eddie would be fortunate to live, but he would never walk again.

Tip returned to the kitchen to check Jena. Her pulse was faint, but still there. Tip called 911 and went to help Lisa. Before doing anything, he covered up Lisa's breasts with her blouse. He averted his eyes as politely as possible during the covering. Untying her wasn't difficult. Eddie had used nautical knots; knots designed for their intended purpose, but were easy to untie if you had the faculties of both hands. Tip deduced that Eddie must have done some sailing in his day. He was correct, Eddie's spoiled upbringing included weekends at the yacht club.

Tip noticed that his shoulder was already beginning to stiffen from the hard blow of the poker.

Lisa looked down upon Eddie's limp body and turned toward Tip, "Thank you," she said through moist eyes.

"You're welcome."

# CHAPTER 33

Tip and Lisa watched the paramedics carefully slide Jena, attached to a stretcher, into the ambulance. Minutes before, Eddie had been carted off in another ambulance. The paramedics deemed Eddie's injuries more severe and they required immediate medical attention. Jena's eyes were open now and although she'd have some permanent facial scars, the paramedics guessed that any permanent physical damage would be minor. Jena gave Tip and Lisa the thumbs-up sign when the ambulance doors began to close.

As the screeching ambulance faded into the night, Lisa and Tip's eyes locked. Their bodies gravitated toward each other like lost magnets. This embrace had much more meaning than the previous one on the riverbank. Back then, she needed a shoulder to cry on, any shoulder would suffice. At the time, he just happened to be that shoulder. At the riverbank there was still an invisible barrier between the emotional portions of their collective soul. This was not the case now. Feelings permeated back and forth between their bodies, producing comfortable warmth.

At the same moment they both released their holds and gazed into each other's eyes. Both sets had taken on a cosmic gleam that neither had ever experienced. Tip cupped Lisa's tender cheek into his welcoming hand and kissed her soft lips. Both reopened their eyes at the same mesmerizing instant. Lisa, still looking into his eyes, grabbed his hand and led him back into the house.

In the morning, Tip glanced over at Lisa's angelic face. A slight smile spread across her sleeping face. She looked lovely in the morning sunlight that streamed through the bedroom window. He gently stroked her silky hair while his eyes didn't waver from her face. As pleasant as this was, he knew it was time to go. He leaned over and kissed her on the temple before silently disappearing into the dusk of morning.

# CHAPTER 34

Sanchez sifted through the pages of printouts and accompanying photographs. The development of the Internet made his job of investigating a subject much easier. Sanchez was sure Tip and Lisa had died in the fall off the bridge and wouldn't be bothering their operation anymore. But, Valez vehemently told Sanchez that he didn't want to take any chances; too much was at stake.

Sanchez didn't mind this request. After all, it meant that he'd be paid for another week's worth of work, and easy work at that.

The fact that the authorities found the bodies of both Garcia and the guard, but not Tip and Lisa did concern Sanchez. However, Lisa and Tip fell in the same general area as the other two that night in the gorge, surely they didn't survive the fall. They were even tied together. Even if they happened to survive the fall, they wouldn't be able to swim tied up as they were. Sanchez assured himself that it was unlikely that his antagonists escaped the clutches of the Grim Reaper.

However, if Tip and Lisa did survive and decided to pursue their operation again, Sanchez would have the ultimate contingency plan waiting for them. Sanchez eyed the cheerful picture of Tip's little sister, Allison. A recent photo of Lisa's mom came up next on the monitor. He jotted down a few notes about both and smiled sadistically.

# CHAPTER 35

Tip stared down at the runway of West Palm Beach Airport. As hard as he tried, he couldn't stop thinking about Lisa. He knew he did the right thing by heading to Florida by himself, didn't he? There was no sense in both of them exposing themselves to the dangers that lay ahead was there?

He was fortunate to be able to walk, as his back was excruciatingly stiff. The flight was pure hell on his back. Fortunately he still had some Naproxen and anti-inflammatory medication leftover from his knee surgery.

Tip knew it was best if he worked alone, that way he'd be assured of absolute trust and the only person that could get hurt would be him. Despite all of these logical and rational reasons to work alone, he still felt guilty about leaving Lisa behind in Virginia. These types of feelings were ones he hadn't experienced in a long while and it concerned him that he was letting himself become emotional. Now was not the time for emotion-now was the time for revenge.

He wanted to get his mind off Lisa and cordially accepted the latest edition of the *USA Today* that the business commuter next to him offered up.

In the lower left corner, contained in the USA Snapshot, was a bar graph breaking out the top ten financial contributors to Corrigan's election campaign. Tip fumbled the pages uncontrollably when the graphic showed Merchel Construction Inc. as the largest contributor. He was disappointed that his research efforts hadn't unearthed this key piece of information. However, Tip knew there was no need to flog himself over this. The important thing was that he *did* discover it.

After obtaining the businessman's permission, Tip tore off the corner of the paper and leafed back to the political section. The presidential race was really heating up and this was evident by the amount of editorial space devoted to it.

The first article Tip devoured was about the "Charlie Duke" factor. It discussed Duke's contribution to the Republican ticket's stronghold on the Southwest region. The article explained that southwestern voters loved having an intelligent southern belle in office and they wanted to keep it that way. It went on to indicate that despite earlier reports of Corrigan's successful campaign trail through these important states, it looked like the Duke factor was going to keep the majority of the South locked on Republican, including the all important state of Texas.

Tip read a couple of other columns discussing Parkhill and the Democratic ticket. The articles conceded that he was essentially out of the running; it was now a two-man race between Corrigan and Marshall.

Tip turned his attention to the article detailing Corrigan's rise to prominence. The first half of the article dealt with Corrigan's background. The second half showcased the extraordinary events that had contributed to Corrigan's rapid rise in the polls. Most of the section analyzed the effect of the two catastrophic terrorist attacks in New York and San Francisco. The article indicated that the polls shifted considerably in favor of Corrigan following these cataclysms. This wasn't surprising, after all, Corrigan had built-up a strong anti-drug and terrorism platform while reigning as the Governor of Florida. All of a sudden it clicked in Tip's mind that the coded letter that had reached Hamilton matched up with the dates of the terrorist activity.

"Please remain seated until we come to a complete stop at the gate," announced the flight attendant over the airplane intercom.

Tip ignored the flight attendant's orders and jumped up to retrieve his backpack from the overhead storage. He reached into the upper section of his black Eddie Bauer backpack and unfolded the correspondence that was sent to Chris Hamilton from Chi Theta

National Headquarters. The businessman seated next to him was a little irked by these sudden movements, but he wasn't about to say something to someone of Tip's robust stature.

Tip laid down the crumpled mysterious piece of paper next to the charts detailing the chronologies of the terrorist attacks. Sure enough, the numbers were starting to make sense to him. The first codes began with four numbers. These numbers were now obviously the dates that were then followed by NYNET and SFTROL. These letters, with the help of the chart in the newspaper, were now clairvoyant. He now understood that NY was code for New York and that NET stood for the eNetwork Building. This first code was crossed off, and for good reason. This particular hit had already taken place when this list was accidentally shipped to Hamilton in Michigan. The San Francisco cable car hit hadn't taken place when this note was accidentally sent to Hamilton, and thus was unmarked. That line still read 1013SFTROL. Tip concluded that the TROL must stand for trolley, even though it was technically a cable car.

Tip glanced at the two remaining lines on the piece of paper, one of which sent a chill down his spine. The date on the next string of code indicated that the next attack would happen tomorrow.

## CHAPTER 36

## STUART, FLORIDA:

Tip thanked the retiree for the free ride and watched the white Buick Park Avenue slowly roll into the bright Florida mid-afternoon sun. He had gotten lucky and was dropped off closer to his destination than he thought would be possible by hitchhiking. He found himself standing at the corner of Monterey and A1A, roughly two miles from Tom Rathman's house. Rathman's house was located inside the Stuart Yacht & Country Club gated community.

It was necessary for Tip to hitchhike since his travel funds were nearly depleted. He still didn't know how he'd pay for his next destination, wherever that may happen to be.

Tip glanced at his watch and was glad to see that he was slightly ahead of schedule. Making the forty-five mile excursion from West Palm Airport to Stuart was quicker than he anticipated.

Rathman had agreed to meet with him after he explained that he wasn't a reporter or affiliated with the police. The warm Florida air felt great and Tip was outside Rathman's salmon colored ranch house on Clubhouse Place Drive in less than twenty minutes. Rathman was also curious to see what type of person was interested in reopening a case that had been closed for so long.

Rathman was a young looking fifty with only a slight touch of gray cropping up in his sideburns. The moderate sideburns were the only flash of style in his short and efficient haircut. Mrs. Rathman closely resembled her husband Tom. Both had short stocky builds complemented by infectious smiles. Tip accepted a glass of lemonade before adjourning to the den with Rathman.

Military awards and certificates adorned the walls of the spacious den. Most of these awards were from action in Vietnam. There wasn't the comfortable clutter of dusty paper and books found in many retirees' dens. Rather, everything was meticulously positioned in its proper place and an impressive laptop computer rested on the desk.

It wasn't Rathman's style to bother with much small talk and he cut straight to the chase. Tip was beginning to warm to him already. "So, you've trekked a great distance to discuss the Randall Hill incident with me, so I know it's important to you. Sorry I had to frisk you at the door, but you can never be too careful, especially when someone comes out of the blue to discuss a chapter in a sordid book. If you would, please tell me what has brought you here today and how do you think I can help. I am assuming that's why you're here, looking for my help," Rathman raised his right eyebrow as he finished his statement.

Tip nodded his head in agreement and launched into a detailed retelling of his harried travels and tribulations since Hamilton's death. He omitted Lisa and also his recent deciphering of the mystery note on the plane. He had a good feeling about Rathman, but decided it would be best, at least for the time being, to not disclose too much information.

Rathman was riveted during Tip's entire discourse, which lasted close to thirty minutes. Rathman knew you should never interrupt an interrogation. This restraint was drilled into him at the Bellstire Police Academy. Research had shown that most witnesses didn't disclose as much useful information if they were constantly being interrupted. Information was often disclosed in an attempt to fill a silence, similar to how poor public speakers use ums and ahs as crutches.

"Now, you mentioned calling FBI Agent Nathan Potts when you first found the letter to Hamilton. Yet, you haven't contacted him since, why is that?" asked Rathman.

Tip thought about withholding his hunch that the FBI agent

was crooked, but decided that there was no reason not to disclose this tidbit.

"To be frank, I was suspicious when Agent Potts was so eager to talk to me. I became even more suspicious when he was vehement that I ship the note to him overnight to his home address. My suspicions were confirmed when two of his henchmen killed one of my good friends whom they mistakenly thought was me." Tip gritted his teeth and tried to control the boiling pot of rage festering inside at the thought of Burke's unnecessary death. "These same henchmen paid me a personal visit soon after."

"Your hunch may have been right, the FBI agent's behavior does seem rather odd. Well, sounds to me like you are in a bit of a quandary. I pride myself on being a good judge of character and you pass with me, son. The one thing that I am struggling with, and please help me here...where do I fit in and how can I help?" inquired Rathman.

Tip was thinking it had been a good idea to leave Lisa in Virginia, just in case something happened to him. He would forward any new information to her when the time was appropriate. It was nice knowing that someone would be able to carry the torch if he were to fail in his mission. However, failure was still not an acceptable option.

"Well, Tip said, it's a long shot, but I was hoping that you could fill in some missing pieces of the puzzle for me. In particular, as I previously mentioned, there were several large donations to the Chi Theta fraternity postmarked from Miami, yet they were all absent of return addresses. And, persons donating the money must have somehow written the checks posthumously.

I also wanted to talk to you about Corrigan, since Merchel Construction is the largest donor. I have suspicions of illegal collaboration between Merchel and Ricardo Valez, the director of Chi Theta National Headquarters." Tip still wasn't ready to tell him about the specifics of the note.

"So, you're unaware of the fact that FBI Agent Potts was

assigned to the Alphonso case the day my partner was murdered?" queried Rathman.

Tip's astonished look gave the answer Rathman needed. Tip tried not to get too excited, but how could he not? He took this trip to Florida on a hunch, but it was beginning to look like this trip could help him put all the pieces together.

"Yea, Agent Potts was pushed on us via Corrigan. Despite our protests, we had to turn the Alphonso case over to him and assist him in anyway possible. We naturally were pissed as hell. As you may have read, Alphonso was under close surveillance by us. We had determined that he was one of Chaz Rodirquez's top men. We were convinced that if we could get to Alphonso, than we could get to Rodriquez.

To make a long story short, we never liked the FBI meddling in our affairs. Potts, we particularly disliked.

We knew Potts when he was in the DEA. He was one of Corrigan's boys and was therefore placed on the fast track. See there was a small subculture in the Florida law enforcement community. It was your typical good old boys network...Corrigan looked out for those who looked out for him. I was never a part of this group since I couldn't deal with all the political bullshit. Besides, I never really cared much for Corrigan, I always thought he had a secret agenda for all of his actions. In his case, my judgment indicated he wasn't a good egg.

As you can imagine, Randall and I weren't too pleased about being taken off the case. Randall was even more pissed than I was, since he believed he was close to cracking it wide open. Due to security leaks, we needed to suppress the fact that we'd apprehended Alphonso and that he was willing to cooperate. Corrigan, Potts, Randall, and I were the only ones privy to this information. Randall made the physical arrest and placed Alphonso in the tank downtown. The tank is a separate cell area away from the rest of the prisoners. It's also an area that only a select few know about and have access to.

My partner called me late that night and was excited and a bit nervous about information that Alphonso spouted off during his detainment. My partner said he couldn't talk about it over the phone because he was afraid the phones might be bugged. As you know, my partner never made it over to my house that night," Rathman said starring out his window that overlooked the third green-a slight mist forming over his eyes as he reflected on his former partner. A foursome of gray haired men badly in need of a fashion consultant currently occupied the immaculate putting green.

Rathman broke from his trance, "would you look at these clowns out on the green here, I mean everybody that turns seventy all of a sudden thinks they look good in polyester." Tip rationalized that this odd break in the story was Rathman's way of dealing with the loss of a friend and to avoid breaking down. It showed on Rathman's face that it still pained him to this day, and probably would stay with him till the grave. Rathman still had a difficult time shaking the image of Randall Hill's dead body lying still on the cell of the jail.

"Anyhow, where was I? Oh yeah, so Corrigan tells the media and law enforcement officials that he'll personally launch the largest investigation in the state's history to determine those responsible for the unacceptable deaths of Alphonso and Randall. This turned out to be all smoke and mirrors. The half-hearted investigation turned up nothing.

I did some investigating of my own and determined that Randall was correct, my phone was indeed tapped. I also went through Randall's house, but it was too late. Whoever was responsible for his death had already paid a visit and removed any noteworthy information and evidence. Randall had a habit of taking copious notes in a black book whenever he had a thought. There was a page missing from this book when it was found beside Randall in his car. It was obvious that whoever knocked him off knew exactly what they were doing and what they needed to look for.

As I mentioned, I did my own investigating, but kept running into one stonewall after another. I was getting little or no cooperation from anyone, especially agent Potts, that slimly little bastard," said Rathman under his breath. Anyhow, I didn't turn up anything, but I was pretty sure it was an inside job, and that somehow Agent Potts was involved. I also don't think it was mere coincidence that those two thugs came after you so soon after you talked with that spineless toad," said Potts.

"As you know, I retired when I determined my investigation was hopeless without the proper assistance. I have enough money to live comfortably and I couldn't stand to work another day in a culture that I felt, or better yet, knew, was corrupt. That's most of my story. I believe I've told you everything or probably more than you wanted to know in some cases. I hope it's what you're looking for and helps you solve your problem. If you have any questions I'd be glad to try and answer them for you. The only stipulation is that I've got a dinner date with another couple at the club in forty-five minutes."

Tip allowed Rathman's words sink in for a moment. At first glance, he thought the article he'd discovered in the library with Lisa would prove itself to be nothing. As it turned out, it was getting Tip close to solving the amorphous riddle that had plagued him since Hamilton's death.

"Thank you, but I've already taken up more than enough of your time. You've been more help than I could have imagined and I greatly appreciate it. If you could do me one more favor. A girl may call you asking for me, my whereabouts, or may ask you some of the same questions. Please do me a favor and tell her we never met and don't answer her questions. I'll give her all the information she needs in due time. Just trust me that it's in her best interest not to know the burden I carry at this time.

# CHAPTER 37

Tip gazed up into the stars as he lay on the beach at the Indian River Resort. The information blackboard outside the Spoonbill Condominiums had "water temperature 75°" lazily scrawled on it. The tepid water felt refreshing, as every third wave was daring enough to lap against Tip's outstretched feet. The air temperature was about eighty degrees and it was already eleven at night. It wouldn't get much below seventy degrees tonight-perfect sleeping weather. He needed to sleep on the beach to conserve money necessary for the final trip. Tom Rathman was kind enough to let Tip garner some information off the Internet before bidding farewell. He also graciously offered Tip his guest bedroom, but Tip humbly declined, feeling he couldn't impose anymore than he already had. He knew that Rathman had more than likely supplied the missing piece to the puzzle.

His eyelids only needed to rest for a split second before dreamland descended upon him…It was a warm sunny day in his dream. His beautiful mom and stern faced dad were waiting in line for cotton candy in the amusement park. Hamilton was there also, but it was a younger version of him. He was helping Tip's little sister, Allison, up from a fall that had skinned her knee. Tip was holding a woman's hand and when she turned, it was Lisa. She had a frolicsome look on her face. She looked as beautiful as an angel, and he knew he had to kiss her. The felling was so irresistible that he couldn't avoid it, no matter how hard he tried to restrain himself. The kiss was worth it, sending chills throughout the resting body.

All of a sudden, they all were waiting to ride the amusement park's grandest roller coaster. The sun was beginning to set and the park was deserted. They were the only ones waiting to ride the roller coaster. A mysterious fog descended onto the amusement park and almost all the seats on the roller coaster had "out of order" signs on them. Hence, there wasn't enough room for Tip, so he graciously waited for the next ride. Tip waved goodbye to his parents, Lisa, Hamilton and Burke, who had arrived on the coaster from the previous ride and was seated in the back. Tip wondered where Allison had disappeared.

As the roller coaster began to climb steeply into the sunset, Tip noticed that something was terribly wrong. The rollercoaster was under repair and the tracks were completely missing on the descent.

Tip's family and friends were oblivious to their brutal fate. He was the only one that could see what was happening.

"Stop the ride!" Tip shouted across the tracks in vain to the rail operator. But, the operator slowly turned around with an insidious smile; the operator was none other than Ricardo Valez. Tip looked to the security guard for help, but he too had the same evil smile. The security guard was Sanchez. The girl playing the records in the DJ booth was laughing hysterically. The laugh was familiar to Tip but it took a second to place. There was no denying it-it was the laugh of his high school girlfriend, Stephanie.

He went to leap across the tracks to take the reigns of control on the other side. However, the harder he ran the more stuck his shoes became to the platform. His shoes had mysteriously transformed into suction cups. The shoes eventually returned to their normal state and he made for another attempt to cross the chasm. He was moving like a bat out of hell in preparation for the precarious jump. This time he would make it to the other side. Seconds before the leap, he came to a screeching halt and couldn't jump an inch. Once again, suction cups anchored his feet to the platform.

A cacophony of mocking laughter came from the other side. But, the laughter was now being drowned out by the helpless screams from the roller coaster. Tip's loved ones all cried out for help, but they were beyond anyone's help. Tip tried mightily to jump again as they began to roll toward the deadly break in the track...

# CRISIS

Tip awoke to an early morning sun shining down on the beach at Indian River Plantation. He was sweating profusely from the sun's blaze and horrific roller coaster nightmare. Splashing saltwater on his face helped wash away the bad images. He removed yesterday's edition of the *Stuart News* off his chest and scanned the Atlantic Ocean.

Rathman said he'd do what he could with the overwhelming amount of information given him. But Rathman also said his connections within the FBI weren't nearly as strong as they used to be due to the passage of time. Even if they were strong, the FBI was still a slow-moving bureaucracy. Scandals of this scale weren't generally accepted with open arms at the Agency. Rathman tried to persuade Tip not to leave but knew that was futile. This was the one chance Tip had to avenge the murders of both Hamilton and Burke, as well as to chase away the ghosts of his parents' deaths. Rathman wanted more time, but Tip didn't have it. He wasn't going to stand there and watch the rollercoaster take its fatal plunge-not this time.

# CHAPTER 38

# ORLANDO, FLORIDA:

Zar Kumbadi arched his neck to peer up at the enormous structure before him. Zar had paid the $60 entrance fee to join the masses at the world's largest amusement park, Walt Disney World.

Despite it being considered off-season, EPCOT was still jammed. Zar was patiently waiting in a thirty-minute line in the shadow of AT&T's Spaceship Earth exhibit. Meanwhile, Mickey Mouse had ventured over from the Magic Kingdom and was attempting to entertain some of the bored kids in line. Mickey always provided a nice respite for weary parents; he was like a five-minute babysitter.

The AT&T geosphere was held aloft by six titanic legs that were sunk one hundred feet into the Florida topsoil. The geosphere itself weighed sixteen million pounds and measured one hundred sixty-five feet in diameter and reached one hundred and eighty feet into the sky.

The mid-day Florida sun shimmered off the surface of the enormous sphere. This covering was comprised of a quarter-inch-thick compilation of two anodized aluminum faces and polyethylene core. Nine hundred and fifty-four triangles of varying shapes and sizes contributed to the magnificent beauty of this one-of-a-kind structure. Zar knew all of these dimensions by heart.

He also knew that this enormous ball wasn't a perfect sphere despite its appearance. Steelworkers required the dimensions to be slightly uneven.

The Hispanic family of four in front of Zar was starting to

make quite a commotion. The two adolescent children were in a large shouting match over who was responsible for breaking the Snow White pencil. The mother was compounding the commotion by screeching over the children's already high-pitched, high-speed arguing. She had transformed into one of those dreaded "Disney" parents. A parent that had grew tiresome of a long week of long rides and screaming children. Just the slightest irritation at the end of the week would set her off into hysterics. Making the argument seem louder was the fact that the entire confrontation was conducted in colorful Spanish.

Zar understood every word of the argument, because Spanish was one of nine languages in which he was fluent. His gaze was transfixed on the youngest child's shoes, which periodically blinked flashes of green and red from the inserted lights in the soles.

Zar didn't know if he could wait to see this family die; he wanted to kill the annoying little bastards right now. What a worthless drag on society this family was, meaningless lives really. They were so inferior to him in every way and deserved to die for the benefit of the human race.

Zar peered up the long serpentine line and couldn't pick out one worthwhile human among the myriad of white trash, Euro-trash, yuppies, wetbacks and hillbillies. He would derive more pleasure killing each one of these spongers barehanded as a gift to Allah. But these frivolous thoughts were not part of a practical plan.

Zar nodded at two extremely cute blonde Norwegian girls that were admiring him from afar. He wasn't wearing a facial disguise today, why should he, Disney security was a joke and it was simple to blend in here. To commingle appropriately, he had selected a pair of white gym shoes with athletics socks, standard issue khaki shorts, and a Winnie the Pooh T-shirt. He liked when he didn't have to hide his precious face. Zar looked more Italian than Arabic.

The two girls giggled to each other. They were making their way back to work at the Norwegian pavilion and were adorned in traditional Scandinavian attire. It would be difficult to pick a pair that exemplified the famous Norwegian beauty better than these two. Dazzling smiles, brilliant eyes and rosy cheeks.

The staffing for the country exhibits at EPCOT was comprised mostly of college students from the respective countries. The majority of these youngsters were over for six-month periods, or a semester off from school. The students learned a lot about American culture and other cultures in the pavilion as well. The job was almost better than going around the world since so many diverse tourists visited EPCOT each year. On top of that, the pay was pretty good. Zar thought it a shame that he wouldn't be able to afford himself the luxury of visiting the Norway pavilion to examine these exquisite gems more closely.

The Looney Tunes backpack Zar had strapped to his back weighed close to forty pounds. He had carefully packed its contents to ensure the weight was evenly distributed for comfort. The weight was perfectly distributed, and he could hardly notice the two small hydrogen tanks and accompanying plastic explosives stuffed in the backpack. As a result, the backpack gave the appearance that it contained a light lunch and a change of clothes.

Zar was satisfied with the seat he had selected. The cars in Spaceship Earth each accommodated four persons, two in front and two in back. He was seated in back, alone. The Mexican mother and father that were near him in line were seated in the front. It was exceptionally dark throughout the ride and the music was ridiculously loud. The music almost drowned out the narration emanating from the speakers in the headrests of the car seats. This type of noisy and dark environment was conducive for Zar's dirty work. For aesthetic reasons Disney concealed all the large equipment necessary to run the ride underneath black draperies. It was a terrorist's paradise to have so many possible hiding places.

Zar was in his element. He wasn't going to charge his hiring party for this one, whoever his hiring party happened to be. He never met or knew his employers or their real names. He only required that their requests be handwritten in a grocery list format.

Professionals always worked through a middleman and never knew their direct client and they, in turn, didn't know them. The only thing Zar cared about was that his American terrorist missions continued to be funded by the silent third party, although he would happily do them for free if he had the means.

He placed one of the plastic explosives at the base of the exhibit depicting Michelangelo's painting in the Sistine Chapel. The next bomb placement was tossed among the burning ruins of ancient Rome. The Ride finally made it to its zenith and the spectacular hologram of the planet Earth rotating among the constellations of the Milky Way. This display filled the entire upper portion of the geosphere. Here, Zar strategically placed the tanks of highly condensed hydrogen discretely out of sight and slowly opened their valves.

# CHAPTER 39

Corrigan snickered as he read the *New York Times*. Experts agreed his selection of General John Patterson as a running mate was a sound decision. With the mystery of this important selection removed, popular opinion was that Corrigan would close the gap even more on Marshall. Corrigan crumpled the paper and tossed it into the corner when he read about the Charlie Duke factor being too strong to overcome. The article went on to hint that Corrigan might have been better off selecting a charismatic female running mate. Highlighted in the article was the fact that the Republican Party still had sixty percent of the female vote.

"No fucking woman will ever be associated with me!" shouted Corrigan at the top of his lungs, hoping that somehow the author of the article heard him. "Equal rights and Affirmative Action have made this country weak and I'm the only one with balls big enough to bail Uncle Sam out." He needed to release some frustration and hence shouted in the safe confines of his secretive and isolated basement of his Florida home. He glanced over fondly at his Ku Klux Klan Grand Wizard Hat. He knew those days were over due to the increased media attention. Still, he hadn't been able to bring himself to throw it out. He knew he'd have to destroy it and any of those memories soon. But when he rose to power, he would secretly work to foment its resurrection as an underground movement across the country.

Corrigan's mind shifted back to Charlie Duke. "Now about this problem called Ms. Charlie Perfect; well, we will all watch your tragic demise and I will have a front row seat for it," said Corrigan as he picked up the phone and punched up Valez's number.

# CHAPTER 40

The more the pieces of the puzzle fit together the more astounded Tip became. He also grew madder by the minute over the needless deaths and suffering caused by this whole affair. It had taken him a long time to figure out the convoluted plan, which was made even more difficult to decipher by the presence of two distinct, yet interrelated, operations. He retraced the entire puzzle in his mind, piece by piece, one more time, searching for holes.

When Corrigan was elected Governor of Florida, drug activity and crime were at an all-time high in the Sunshine State. His main platform was to lessen and eventually eliminate all drug trafficking in the state. After a year in office, crime, especially drug-related crime, had increased in Florida. Obviously, Corrigan was under intense scrutiny and pressure. Due to this, he decided to cut a deal with the top drug dealer in the Caribbean inner circle, Chaz Rodriquez.

Corrigan agreed to look the other way for most of these deals. In return, Rodriquez would send him some pawns and pigeons to bust every so often. These busts made for good newspaper headlines and helped increase his approval rating. These headlines alone weren't enough however, so he also shared Rodriquez's profits. He used this money to increase the police force and also inject some into the community for public relations purposes. All the new officers he hired were religiously devoted to him, and the inner circle began to take shape. He was able to open numerous soup kitchens and parks, and voters took notice. The remaining money, which was a significant sum, was stored in his secret Cayman bank account in preparation for his eventual presidential campaign. Drug related shootings in

Florida decreased, since fewer weapons were required because they knew the DEA wouldn't intervene. Similarly, infighting between drug lords lessened since illegal drugs were now simply another commodity in Florida.

The street price of drugs decreased since it wasn't as risky of a business for dealers and buyers. With the decrease in price and ease of accessibility, first time usage rates increased dramatically, especially among teenagers. The public wasn't made aware of this, all they saw were headlines proclaiming another drug bust, reduction in drug related crimes or the opening of a public park. Usage was only tracked on a federal level and was never broken apart by state.

This entire scheme was almost uncovered when DEA Agent Randall Hill apprehended Carlos Alphonso; one of Rodriquez's top men. Alphonso wasn't one of the pigeons that Rodriguez set-up, rather Hill, working on his own, kept a close eye on Alphonso and apprehended him when he slipped up. Alphonso was one of a select few of Rodriguez's men who knew about the arrangement made with Corrigan. Hill learned of the dirty dealings when Alphonso unwittingly released the valuable information while suffering through a bad acid trip and eventual emotional outpouring during his arrest.

Hill wanted to confide in his partner, Rathman, this very delicate information. Hill never got the chance. While seated in his car on that fateful night, FBI Agent Potts murdered him. Agent Potts then murdered Alphonso in cold blood in a little known cell in the basement of police headquarters. Potts removed the bugs from Hill's house that same evening while his wife was away at the hospital. He was also familiar with Hill's black book and was smart enough to remove any incriminating pages.

With all of this illegal drug money pouring in from Chaz Rodriquez's operations, Corrigan had to somehow make it "clean" so that he could use it in his Presidential election. In essence, he needed to somehow launder the money. If the money weren't cleaned, there would be plenty of questions without appropriate answers. That's where the Chi Theta Fraternity connection came into play.

Rodriquez, using deceased alumni names supplied by Valez, sent in checks as Alumni donations to Chi Theta. This explains why the majority of bogus donations Lisa discovered were postmarked from Miami. She was also correct in her hypothesis that Merchel Construction was overcharging Chi Theta for their building and repair services. In turn, they were using the majority of these profits to support Corrigan's Presidential Campaign. Nothing appeared suspicious, since it wasn't unusual for a Fortune 500 company like Merchel to back a particular candidate with corporate contributions. What is suspicious is a large company making millions of dollars off a fraternity.

A fraternity was an ingenious conduit for this money-laundering scheme. Chi Theta was a non-profit organization and because of this, it would be more difficult for auditors to scrutinize the accuracy of their book keeping since they weren't made public. However, Barbara Fernandez slipped up once too often, and the price she paid was her life. Valez knew Barbara had accidentally mailed Hamilton some incriminating information and he immediately sent his men to retrieve it. The odds of Hamilton figuring out the whole operation from the note were slim, but it wasn't a risk that Valez was willing to take. Too much was at stake.

When Hamilton couldn't present the letter, Valez's goons impatiently killed him. Amy Klein must have just been in the wrong place at the wrong time. Tip's head ached from the combination of rage and pain he felt over the loss of Hamilton. He rubbed his temples before continuing his retracing.

The letter Hamilton never opened revealed information and proof that Valez and Corrigan were working together. The note was a cheat-sheet or order form for Corrigan's sadistic terrorism plan, in grocery list fashion. Corrigan was astute enough to realize that the incumbent Marshall was one of the nation's most popular Presidents. America also had an ongoing love affair with Vice President Charlie Duke. It was an outpouring of American affection that hadn't been seen since the days of Jackie Kennedy.

The Republican ticket was a shoe-in for re-election and baring a major catastrophe, Charlie Duke was certain to become America's first female President in four years. Corrigan knew that he needed to attack the Republican ticket's Achilles' heel. Unfortunately for Corrigan, the Republicans didn't really have any chinks in their armor. Thus, he needed to create an Achilles' heel for them; one that would command headlines and create confusion and doubt amongst the voting public. What better way to accomplish this than to create a seemingly uncontrollable and sustained outbreak of terrorism on home soil?

Tip reviewed the infamous note to Hamilton, in his mind. A hard copy was no longer necessary as it was tattooed on his brain forever. The bombing of the eNetwork Building in New York and the San Francisco Cable Car explosion were obviously the first two terrorist attacks. The third incident was supposed to occur today. In fact, Tip realized it may have already happened and he was just oblivious to it. 1018EPCATT didn't give much help or indication of where this attack may occur. Turning the note over to some deciphering experts would be wonderful, but after the last FBI incident with Agent Potts, he just didn't know whom to trust anymore. It was frustrating knowing that something terrible was going to occur, and not being able to do anything about it.

# CHAPTER 41

Zar Kumbadi proudly looked up from the paper detailing the recent terrorist attacks. He confidently gazed at the cute Asian flight attendant making her way down the aisle with his first class dinner. He badly wanted to shout out that he was the man responsible for the EPCOT destruction. Didn't they know they were sitting among greatness? They should all be thanking him for not blowing up the plane they were currently on.

Two aisles behind Zar sat Lisa in the coach bulkhead seat. She stretched out her slender, long legs in the faded jeans. There was a plethora of space in the bulkhead row and she always tried to get to the airport early enough to put a request in for it. A bulkhead seat gave her extra legroom and also precluded the possibility of the person in front obnoxiously reclining into her lap. The headphones went on the instant the flight attendant announced that electronic equipment could be used. The headphones would help her avoid the meaningless and tedious conversations the hapless, single businessmen surrounding her would strike up. These sexually deprived middle-aged men had hit on her way too many times.

Besides, music allowed her to escape. It was the only remaining vice in her world. Today's musical selection was Alan Jackson' Greatest Hits. Jackson was one of the few country singers that she enjoyed. Lisa hoped it would take her mind off her visit with her mother earlier that day.

Her mother was getting worse every day and the entire ugly story about her and Eddie coming to the fore eliminated any progress she had made over the years. Lisa also knew that Eddie's father would no longer be paying to keep her mom in the home now that the story was public knowledge.

Lisa's mind flashed back to the troubled scene with Eddie a few nights ago. Jena, fortunately would recover. Eddie, on the other hand, would be confined to a wheel chair for the rest of his life due to the harsh landing he took on the glass coffee table. What would have happened if Tip hadn't shown up when he did? She shivered at the thought that she probably wouldn't be around today to ponder such questions.

Lisa was still upset about Tip's abrupt departure. Couldn't he have at least said goodbye or left a number where he could be reached? She wondered if she'd ever see him again...and wondered why she cared so much. She knew the answer to that as well. Although they'd only spent a few days together there was a special magic between them. He also seemed to be her natural security blanket, a beautifully sculpted and charismatic security blanket.

Had Tip been able to solve the Chi Theta mystery by himself? Rathman told her over the phone that he'd never heard of Tip. Rathman also said he couldn't discuss anything with her as he was about to head out the door on vacation. If Tip didn't visit Rathman, then where the hell was he? Even though she was mad at him, she hoped that he was all right. She thought for a second that, perhaps, he may have given up on the whole thing, but that was a slim possibility at best.

Zar reclined in his seatback similar to the way Lisa was situated. Zar and Lisa had no clue how interconnected their lives really were.

# CHAPTER 42

"Yes, the necessary steps have been taken. I assure you that our final execution will be flawless," stated Valez.

"Good, good. I've been very impressed so far. It would be a shame for us to get careless with the last and most important one," said Corrigan.

"Sanchez and I will be there, personally, to make sure there are no mishaps," said Valez.

"As will I. As will I," said Corrigan as he hung up the phone.

# CHAPTER 43

## USA Today:

*O*rlando Florida: *For the third time in less than a month, terror rang across this great land. At exactly five in the afternoon yesterday, an astronomic explosion illuminated the Florida sky. Initial reports indicate that two plastic explosive devices were setoff simultaneously inside the giant geosphere that overlooks EPCOT Center inside Walt Disney World. The bombs did a tremendous amount of damage by themselves, however, the brilliant explosion was caused by ignited hydrogen gas inside the upper portion of the AT&T Spaceship Earth geosphere. There are no leads as to how this hydrogen gas was released inside or who is behind the bombing.*

*Engineering experts said the tragedy would have been much worse if the pillars supporting the sphere had collapsed. Extra supports had been added to the structure in the months following the terrorist attacks on September 11, 2001. Engineers indicated these supports were the reason the EPCOT icon didn't collapse. A blazing giant eighteen-story ball could then have been rolling through EPCOT destroying everything and everyone in its path. "I was waiting in line for the Thunder Mountain roller coaster when I saw a tremendous flash in the sky," said one eyewitness who was a good two miles from the explosion. The explosion and accompanying smoke could be sighted from as far away as twenty miles.*

*The unofficial death count tallies 277. Disney and AT&T officials were unavailable for comment. Governor Corrigan is scheduled to cancel his campaign plans in Denver, Colorado and fly directly to Orlando. Corrigan promised to find the guilty party and bring them quickly to justice.*

Tip placed the paper down and an overwhelming sense of guilt consumed him. He felt like getting sick. The event at EPCOT Center matched up with the infamous note. On the grocery list,

EPC and ATT were assumed to be abbreviations for cities and transportation equipment like the previous hits in New York and San Francisco. However, hindsight showed that it was a location like the others. Tip was now extremely confident that the next, and hopefully last, terrorist attempt would be in two days in Chicago. Even if this hunch was correct, he knew that he still didn't know where in Chicago. This code, unlike the others, ended with a flurry of incoherent numbers, 1021CHIB71239E. Chicago was enormous and although he was familiar with the city, it would be nearly impossible for him to narrow it down.

The rhythmic click-it-tee-clack of the train was soothing and helped Tip think. The 1950's-style Chessie Box car wasn't too uncomfortable, although it did get a bit nippy last night. But, one couldn't complain, as the price was right. The good news in Tip's mind from last night's activity was that it proved his knee had to be close to one hundred percent. To be able to catch the accelerating train, grab on and swing aboard put as much strain on the knee as any activity imaginable. And, it was in the dark, to boot. Yet, the knee felt perfectly fine this morning.

Looking out the open door of the boxcar, Tip took in the passing blue grass of Kentucky. It was beautiful and eventually became a blur as his mind again began to wander into dreamland... he could vividly see his parents smiling at his fifth Christmas after they gave him his first pair of ice skates and a Lionel train set. Mr. Tipton's expression of disappointment wasn't concealed when Tip showed more interest in the hockey skates than the electric train. Model railroading was one of Mr. Tipton's few enjoyments outside of medicine and the family. Ironically, it was his dad's explanation of how railroads worked that enabled Tip to catch the Northbound Florida East Coast freight train two nights ago in Stuart.

Thanks to his Dad's train layout in the basement which had one portion dedicated to replicating this portion of US track, Tip knew this particular freight was going to Jacksonville where its cars would be switched onto other trains heading in various directions. Armed with this railroad knowledge and a Jacksonville freight schedule, he easily located the correct train. It was a CSX fast-freight to Chicago via Atlanta, Lexington and Cincinnati. The old Chessie boxcar he'd ridden from Stuart to Jacksonville was switched onto this Chicago-bound train. This was very fortunate because it was rare to find an open boxcar door on today's modern trains. But, based on what his dad had taught him, Tip thought it was worth a try. He didn't really have any alternative. It worked, because the Chessie system was one of several successor railroads consolidated to form the CSX railroad. Tip's Dad's face began to fade as Tip realized that his dad was helping him, even now.

The next image was of his parents' coffins entering the ground and Allison bravely holding back her tears. Next, Hamilton's smile floated through his mind. It was always an infectious smile and there Hamilton was, with that sly smile, looking at Tip as they shared a moment in the library. These moments usually occurred after pulling a prank on one of their friends. The next scene that flashed in his mind was one of him handing over a driver's license to Jason Burke, only it was dripping with Burke's blood.

Tip shuddered at this last image and tried to shake it off with pleasant thoughts-pleasant images. Lisa's beautiful eyes were transfixed on his face as her long sandy brown hair lay loosely over her left cheek. She wasn't speaking at the moment, but her eyes told everything anyone needed to know-everything was going to be alright for the first time in a long time...click-it-tee-clack, click-it-tee-clack, the train rolled on as Tip slept.

## CHAPTER 44

## East Lansing, Michigan

*The State News:*
*The prosecution will present their case today in the Klein versus Hamilton hearing. Amy Klein, a Junior Communications Major at Michigan State University, was killed in an automobile accident earlier this semester. The driver of the car, Chris Hamilton, was allegedly drunk at the time. Hamilton, a senior at MSU, was also killed in the crash. Amy's parents, Barbara and Jacob Klein, are suing the Hamiltons for punitive damages in the excess of $20,000,000. The prosecution is expected to call several MSU students to the stand to confirm they witnessed Hamilton drinking at a house party the night of the fatal crash.*

*This story has drawn national attention and as a precautionary measure, Judge Edith Lancaster closed the courtroom to the public.*

## CHAPTER 45

"CBS News Radio, it's twenty minutes passed the hour, time to check today's headlines. True to his word, Presidential candidate and Florida Governor John Corrigan has apprehended the individual behind the EPCOT Center bombing," the CBS anchorman intoned.

"These sadistic crimes have no place in a civilized state. Florida *is* such a state; hence there is no place for vile scum of the likes of Igor Trnichov. If our authorities are correct in their assessment of an overwhelming amount of evidence, then I will do everything in my power to make certain that our fine judicial system renders a decision by week's end. I will not tolerate this type of behavior, nor should you, the people."

"Governor Corrigan, do you feel this attack is related to the bombings that have occurred in New York and San Francisco?" inquired a CNN reporter.

"I doubt that the persons responsible for those other sadistic attacks are behind the one that occurred at Walt Disney World. Do I think they are related? They are somewhat related in the sense that I strongly believe that because no one has been punished for the crimes on the people of New York, San Francisco, and for that matter this Nation, others feel they can get away with it as well. However, as Mr. Igor Trnichov will soon realize, if you want to play in my backyard, you're going to pay. And pay dearly at that." Trnichov has been associated with the growing EL TREKE terrorist ring on the border of Afghanistan and Russia. "We will prosecute this scum to the fullest extent of the law-the death penalty-and expeditiously," concluded Corrigan.

"What you have just heard was a sound bite previously

recorded at Florida Governor and Presidential hopeful, David Corrigan's, morning press conference. Preliminary reports indicate that Corrigan's approval numbers have risen on news of this strong stand. However, experts still contend that Corrigan needs a strong showing in this weekend's presidential debate in Chicago to stand a legitimate chance at victory.

Corrigan's ratings are still suffering from the vice-presidential debate earlier this week. Corrigan's running mate, John Patterson, was thoroughly whipped by the popular Vice President, Charlene Duke. Patterson stumbled and seemed unsure of himself in the shadow of the poised and dynamic Duke.

---

Midway Airport, Chicago: Lisa walked stride for stride in the long shadow cast by Zar Kumbadi, oblivious to the irony. The Southwest Airlines flight had arrived on time as they generally did. A black-leather carry-on was all that was needed for this trip and she breezed past the luggage claim. She was headed toward the arrival pick-up area, where her friend, Matty, would be waiting. The ebullient Matty welcomed her with a warm hug. Matty's naturally curly, copper hair was cropped tighter than normal. The new look made her look younger and showcased her pretty face.

"It's great to see you. How long has it been, two-three years already?" exclaimed Matty.

"You look great, Matty. You haven't changed a bit, except, of course, I love what you've done with your hair. Listen, I really appreciate this, especially on such short notice. I hope it isn't too much trouble," sincerely stated Lisa.

"Please, don't mention it. It's the least I can do," replied Matty as they walked next to the line of yellow cabs in order to get to her white Plymouth Sundance. Lisa was relieved that Matty didn't hear about the incident with Eddie, but it wasn't a national news story so she didn't know why she was so paranoid about it. The paranoia was probably because the last thing she wanted to do was complicate her friends' lives.

# CRISIS

Lisa had contemplated staying in a hotel, but the cost of a room in Chicago was too steep. She needed to conserve money, especially now that Eddie's father would no longer pay to support her Mother. Lisa didn't know what to do about her poor old mother, but hopefully she would think of something. Lisa had enough in her savings to keep her mom in her current home for another two months. Lisa hoped that something would happen in those two months to render a satisfactory solution.

Even if Lisa wanted a hotel room, they were all sold out due to the vast number of people in town for the World Series. The World Series also jacked up the already ridiculous hotel rates. The Drake along Michigan Avenue was going for over five hundred dollars a night for a single bed.

"What are you up for doing tonight? Do you want to go grab some dinner at Stanley's or how about some pizza at Ranali's? Or, if you're full we can head to the Waterloo, Gin Mill or the Cubbie Bear for a quick drink. The Cubbie Bear should be especially hopping' with the World Series and all tomorrow," emphatically rattled off Matty.

"Well, I'm glad to see your attitude hasn't changed since college, Ms. Julie McCoy," laughed Lisa. Lisa affectionately called Matty Julie McCoy after the social director character on the very old television show *The Love Boat*. They both laughed together like old times, a time when it was a lot easier to laugh.

"I hate to be a big fat loser, because all of the places you mentioned sound great, but I've got a big day tomorrow and would really like to get some rest. But I should be raring' to go tomorrow night if you're still up for it?" said Lisa.

"Yeah, of course. I'll be up for it," said Matty. "I'm up for anything, I mean heck it's not like you're in town everyday. And, it's not like the Cubs play in the World Series everyday. I still can't believe it! We'll just save up for a big night out tomorrow. I can only really handle one crazy night a week anyhow-my body doesn't enjoy the hangover so much," said Matty with her infectious smile.

---

The panoramic view of the Lake Michigan waterfront was a view that was truly breathtaking at night. The North Beach Lifeguard stand Tip was sitting in was surprisingly comfortable or so it seemed after bouncing around in the freight car for the past three days. Off in the distance the giant Ferris wheel of Navy Pier stood in stark contrast to the night sky. The city was alive with energy tonight, as it was a resplendent fall night in Chicago and the World Series had everyone a buzz.

It was the perfect environment for Corrigan and Valez to perform their biggest ruse. Tip was still beating himself up over how long it took him to make the connection with Chicago and the World Series, but once he did, deciphering the code was fairly simple. The Chicago Cubs were hosting game seven of the World Series tomorrow afternoon at storied Wrigley Field.

He was almost a hundred percent sure that this is where the final terrorist attack would occur. However, one thing still troubled him. The note was sent a couple of weeks ago to Hamilton, before anyone knew that the Cubs would be in the World Series, let alone if there'd be a seventh game in Chicago. Granted, the Cubs were the odds on favorites to win the Series heading into the playoffs. The Cubs had a wonderful season and had eclipsed the 1998 New York Yankees record of most wins in a season.

Despite the Cubs' favored status, it seemed unusual to have this date predetermined in advance. However, there had been an asterisk next to the code: 1021CHIB271239E. Tip checked out all other major events in the area scheduled that weekend and only three came up: the presidential debate, an exhibition by the Gold Medalist Women's Gymnastic team and an arts 'n crafts show in Barrington, a Chicago suburb. The only thing Tip could surmise was that something spectacular would occur in Chicago around the presidential debate, if Corrigan's ratings weren't where they needed to be.

Corrigan had gained considerable ground on Marshall, much of this was the result of the terrorist attacks troubling the nation. However, Corrigan was still well shy of the necessary votes to win

# CRISIS

the election. This asterisked numerical code on the terrorism grocery list that was accidentally sent to Hamilton had to be a contingency plan, and it was Tip's best hunch that it would be implemented during the game.

The Cubs were playing the legendary New York Yankees. The Cubs were still considered America's Team, especially after a year in which they not only broke the record for the most regular season wins, but also shattered the attendance and television audience ratings records. Couple that with their long-time post-season futility and their opponent being the New York Yankees, and it helps to explain why this game was expected to generate a Nielsen Media Rating above that of the Super Bowl.

This high of a TV rating for baseball had never been seen before, and aficionados were proud to proclaim that the glorious game of baseball was back to stay. Some observers believed that baseball's resurgence was partially due to the fact that people wanted to take their minds off the tremendous terrorist activity that was occurring in the United States. Media experts hypothesized that baseball helped remind Americans of a simpler time gone by. Another helpful reason why America was once again enamored with baseball was the fact that there hadn't been a labor dispute since the near strike in 2002. Also, the steroid scandal of 2005 was now forgotten and the game was considered clean.

Tomorrow's game would serve as the platform for Corrigan and Valez' final dramatic act. Tip was hopeful that his interpretation of the 1021CHIB71239E code was correct. His belief was that CHI was short for Chicago and that 1021 stood for the date, just like all the previous codes. Bottom of the seventh inning was indicated by B7. Section one-twenty-three (123) and seat nine E (9E) completed the rest of the grocery list. He wasn't one hundred percent confident in the meaning of the last string of digits, but he thought what else could they be? If the deciphering was correct, then, the twenty thousand-dollar question was who would be seated in 9C? It could be anyone; the park was going to be filled with celebrities from around the world.

The moonlight was providing barely enough reading light as Tip finished writing the notes describing Corrigan's entire ingenious and diabolical plan. Five copies of this document needed to be made tonight. Tip had seen a Kinkos on Fullerton Street by DePaul University in his previous wanderings. Kinko's would allow him to make the copies and overnight them to Rathman, The Director of the FBI, President Marshall, Mr. & Mrs. Hamilton and Lisa. It was a contingency plan in the event that things went awry. Tip wanted to make sure the information he possessed would be transferred on if something were to happen to him.

# CHAPTER 46

Click-it-tee-clack, Click-it-tee-clack. The El train meandered its way through scenic Lincoln Park. The train had just departed the Fullerton station and was heading toward Wrigleyville at a methodical pace.

The budding morning sun glistened on the trees situated amongst Chicago's picturesque brownstone apartments. The streets were calm, which was typical for a Saturday morning in Lincoln Park. Aside from an occasional morning jogger, the majority of the youthful residents were still combating their wild Friday night with much needed sleep. Lincoln Park was comprised primarily of recent Big Ten graduates who were still trying to live the college lifestyle despite dissenting opinions from their wallets and bodies. Their plight was made worse by the fact that a majority of the local drinking holes stayed open until four in the morning, till five on Saturdays.

The train population was rather gaunt as well. In addition to Tip, the only other paying passengers in the El Car were a couple of young dudes who looked like they'd just made last call at Gamekeepers. Gamekeepers is one of the more famous late night establishments in the neighborhood, a virtual meat market from two o'clock until close. There was also a slender, black man trying to sell the latest edition of *Streetwise*; a newspaper produced and sold by the homeless in Chicago with the proceeds going toward assuaging their plight. Despite being low on funds, Tip gave the polite homeless gentleman his last dollar in exchange for a copy of the daily.

The sleeping city would soon be awake; millions of nubile bodies would flock to North Avenue Beach to take advantage of the serendipitous warm weather. Jogging, biking, rollerblading, beach volleyball, swimming, sailing, and people watching were activities available at the beaches along Lake Shore Drive. The El would no doubt be jammed beyond capacity later in the day as everyone tried to make his or her way to the World Series hoopla. For regular season Cubs games it was frightening to fight through the crowd, especially at traditional bottleneck areas, such as escalators. One could only imagine how bad the crowds would be for the seventh game of the World Series. Click-it-tee-clack, Click-it-tee-clack....

Wrigley Field was not new to Tip. While growing up in Michigan, once he and his pals were old enough to drive, they made at least one summer trip every year to the hallowed vine walls. The majestic stadium held a warm place in his heart. The resonance he felt toward it was analogous to a bowl of his mother's hot tomato soup following a cold day of hockey.

Murphy's Bleachers, the bar kitty-corner from the Wrigley bleachers opened early on this special day. Tip sat down at an outside corner table and received a complimentary virgin Bloody Mary, sans celery. He never really cared much for the taste of celery. He felt celery was useless anyway, since it was the only food that took more calories to eat than it contained. Free Bloody Marys were the norm as Murphy was smart to recuperate peoples' hangovers so that they would, in turn, start ordering the higher margin food products, beers, and liquors.

Tip's body started to tingle just as it did before big hockey games in high school. The nerves heightened and his senses became hyper-focused on the task at hand. The body was instinctively programmed to eliminate anything attempting to stop its mission.

Across the street from Murphy's, Sanchez casually stepped out from the backseat of the black Lexus sedan.

# CHAPTER 47

Corrigan reviewed his notes for the final Presidential debate for the sixth and final time. He then turned his attention to a couple of quotes he could use at the World Series in case some of the press wanted to interview him there. He didn't want to be shown-up by Charlene Duke, who it was well known, was quite fond of the game of baseball and was a fanatic Cubs follower.

Corrigan didn't much care for sports. Always being the last kid picked on the playground as a youth had left a bitter taste in his mouth surrounding all athletic activity. On this day however, he could ill afford to let Charlie Duke one-up him in athletic analysis the night before his debate with Marshall. This was particularly important if the game achieved the expected Super Bowl-like ratings.

Corrigan's attention was distracted by the television as his face on CNN mesmerized him. How can anyone deny that he was the smartest and most charismatic man alive? He thought why don't they have me on all the time? He felt that his comments had to be better than any of the other garbage on the boob tube. Well, he'd be on every television channel soon enough, once he pulled off the greatest upset in U.S. presidential election history. When he became President he would create another cable channel: The Presidential Channel. The Presidential Channel would be twenty-four hour coverage of the greatest man alive, him. It would chronicle what he had for breakfast, how he exercised, what his agenda was for the week, it would have it all. The countries youth would all emulate him and the nation would be stronger decided Corrigan.

# CHAPTER 48

Tip's eyes were trying to burn a hole in Sanchez's dark skinned temple. Tip knew Sanchez had to sense his presence because he was jittery, and justifiably so. It was Sanchez's day of reckoning and Tip was the inexorable arbitrator.

Tip's attention left Sanchez for the moment and focused on the approaching Indian Trails charter bus. It would be his ticket inside the ivy-covered walls of Wrigley Field. Earlier in the morning, Tip had garnered the appropriate attire for the evening. This attire was expensive, but Tip had every intention of returning the clothes to the store for a refund tomorrow. Tip straightened his necktie and slid on a sleek sport coat. A gold New York Yankee emblem on the left lapel accented the coat nicely. Tip had swiped this Yankee emblem from a local street vendor's stand and Tip planned to return it following the game.

A large black gym bag was slung over this left shoulder as well. A pair of Ray-Ban sunglasses obscured his eyes and a bulky pair of music headphones further disguised him.

Tip cautiously timed his approach to the bus, making sure that half of the Yankee players and support staff were already heading toward the stadium. He needed to reach the bus at the peak of the disembarking activity. He casually strolled up and blended in with the Yankee players, managers, coaches and other personnel. Halfway to the gate, Tip stopped to sign a few bogus autographs. He made certain that these autographs were illegible and intentionally omitted any jersey number.

The majority of the autograph seekers were younger kids who didn't know any better, they just thought it was cool to get an autograph. A select few of the kids were actually getting paid by collectors to get autographs on special merchandise and baseball cards. Major league baseball was trying to curtail this type of activity, but it was difficult to police.

It certainly felt like old times again for Tip. It reminded him of when he played for the State High School Hockey Championships. He never liked the attention back then, but it's funny, now that it was taken from him, he found that he actually missed it. The adage, "Be careful what you wish for, you just might get it," is one that Tip knew well.

Tip approached the moment of truth, the entrance gate. He blended in perfectly with the Yankee cavalcade. He was slightly taller than most of the players, although most of the pitchers were taller than his six-two.

The pious older security guards with their blue blazers looked importantly at their clipboards with computer printed lists. They were caught up in the moment. The keenest of the bunch looked up at Tip as he approached. Tip cockily returned his look and kept his sauntering gait. The last thing the guards wanted to do was stop a legitimate player and create a scene. They prided themselves on being an integral part of Major League Baseball. They didn't want to embarrass themselves in front of the large gathering of fans that lined the entryway.

The security guard glanced at his clipboard importantly and peered up into Tip's face as he was passing by. The guard put his hand out abruptly and stopped Tip's advancement.

"Look out for Wood's curveball. It's wicked," he said in a jolly manner.

"That's my pitch my man, the wickeder the better," Tip said and smiled. He was cognizant not to talk too loud and attract the attention of a legitimate player nearby. Tip was now inside the stadium.

# CHAPTER 49

Tip continued with the flow of the Yankee team as everyone headed toward the locker room. Two more blue blazers flanked the locker room door along with two armed policemen.

"I just keep heading down this corridor to get to the press box elevator, correct?" Tip asked one of the guards politely.

"That's correct sir, it'll be on your right after you pass the first concession stand," said the taller man with the mustache.

He continued striding confidently down the long, dimly lit corridor. Once out of sight, he ducked through the nearest doorway. Behind the door was a dark and cramped room that warehoused a couple of old vending carts. Most of these carts looked as if they were damaged in some way, and by the looks of the dust, had been here a long time.

Tip changed out of the coat and tie and slipped into a pair of running shoes, black nylon running pants and a heather-gray, mock turtleneck. He looked at the indiglo hands of his Lum Nox Navy Seal watch; six hours till the first pitch.

He cautiously opened the door, but could only see in one direction. No one was coming from that way. The door blocked the view the other way, but it didn't sound like anyone else was approaching from that direction. However, it was difficult to hear since the technicians were currently testing the public address system.

Tip stepped backward out of the door and forcefully bumped into someone. "Excuse me...." Tip couldn't complete the remark as he starred into the dark hollow eyes of Sanchez. Sanchez reached for the gun tucked behind his belt, but was a hesitation too late. Every muscle in Tip's body instantly became taut and his tunnel vision focused on the task at hand.

One of his famous hockey body checks sent Sanchez reeling until he crashed against the cement wall of the corridor. Tip had learned to use his body weight and momentum to cause severe damage to an opponent while he felt absolutely nothing. His right elbow struck Sanchez in the face as his body hit the wall. The mighty hit snapped his head back against the unforgiving cement. Despite the fact that Sanchez outweighed him by a good thirty pounds, Tip had no trouble swiftly picking him up off the floor and throwing him over his shoulder. Tip took pleasure in tossing him vigorously onto the floor of the cramped room that he'd exited.

Tip's body and mind were focused. He bound Sanchez's arms and legs together behind his back using the electric cord from a rusty hot dog cart. Tip took great pleasure in stuffing an oily and dirty rag into Sanchez's mouth to gag him.

Securing the door by extending more of the electrical cord from one door handle to the other was the next logical step. Tip's mind was taking in the scene and the body was carrying out the orders. No one should be coming into this room anytime soon, but he didn't want to take any chances. Sanchez remained unconscious on the floor; it would be some time before he would regain consciousness. The game didn't start for another six hours. A luminescent popcorn machine Tip plugged in supplied the only light in the room. The soft hum of the machine was relaxing. Tip once again thought about his parents, Hamilton, Burke and Lisa. "I won't let you down this time," he said aloud.

## CHAPTER 50

"Oh, well, well, well, sleepy head. It's so nice of you to join the party," Tip said to Sanchez as he opened his eyes. "I mean this little get together is in your honor my friend. It's a party celebrating men raping defenseless women and you just so happen to be the president of this esteemed club." Tip's blood was starting to boil and he needed to remind himself to remain focused. A false move here and he wouldn't obtain the information he needed.

Tip leaned down next to Sanchez's left ear and asked him in a small whisper "What's going to happen to the person seated in 9E?" Sanchez's flabbergasted look was a dead giveaway. The initial bewilderment from Sanchez was all Tip needed to confirm his intuition. Tip was correct, which was good, but it was also bad for the unfortunate soul who'd be seated in seat 9E, unless Tip could foil the diabolical plan.

"What's going to happen, Sanchez?" Tip pulled the dirty rag from his mouth.

"Fuck you!" he spat and tried to struggle free from the cord.

"Okay, the rag goes back in the mouth until you have something intelligent to say. Oh by the way, the more you struggle the tighter the cord will become. Which, in turn, will cause your leg and back muscles to cramp up even more. Let me tell you, the pain from the cramps will be excruciating. I should know, since this is how you had me and Lisa tied up in your trunk. It's ironic I'm telling you that struggling will only make matters worse. That is probably what you told the Klein girl before you rapped her, isn't it? And you would have said the same thing to Lisa if I hadn't shown up to spoil your perverse plan.

I feel sorry for you Sanchez, you're the lowest form of coward there is. I mean, how can you live with yourself? A coward who, when required to go one on one with an average Joe, such as myself, is tied up in a knot and lying helplessly on the floor. Besides being a coward, you're a horny pervert who must not be getting enough action. How else could one explain your twisted behavior? You really are pathetic. Now, since you didn't hear me the first time, I'll give you a second chance. I hope you appreciate the fact I'm being so charitable. Now, what's going down today?" Tip removed the rag once again, and Sanchez let out a sinister growl.

"You're going down. Raping that Klein girl wasn't half as much fun as looking at the face of your dying friend Hamilton as he helplessly watched me have my way. She actually enjoyed me being inside of her. It was the first time she'd been satisfied by a real man. She truly died with a smile on her face."

The dirty rag was stuffed back into Sanchez's mouth forcefully. "Good, I was hoping you'd elect to be stupid and do this the hard way." The rag muffled Sanchez's scream as Tip hoisted him off the floor by the locks of his hair, several of which were violently torn from his scalp. Sanchez had made the mistake of painting too vivid a picture of Hamilton's final hours. It was a mistake, because it dramatically increased Tip's rage and strength.

The antiquated popcorn machine was now warmed up and humming. Tip stuffed Sanchez's face inside the cube-shaped Plexiglas popper. The cube contained remnants of stale popcorn and burnt kernels. "See, Sanchez, you are going to tell me what's going on today, only it's going to hurt a lot more now. You could have told me the same thing a couple of minutes ago, but now we're going to do it my way. I'm going to tell you a little something about myself. It's something you probably didn't pick-up while on surveillance with your friend, Garcia. That is his name isn't it? Oh, you're surprised that I knew your dead partner's name? Well you'll probably be joining Garcia in hell real soon, especially if you don't start cooperating. Oh, but I digress, what was I talking about? Oh yeah, I was talking about myself; let's continue shall we?

# CRISIS

I used to work in a small movie theatre near my high school. We had a popcorn machine similar to the one you currently have your head in. However, our theatre had a more elaborate countertop model rather than this "meals on wheels" version. Anyhow, it's a simple three-step process to make melt-in-our-mouth movie theatre corn. You simply add the kernels to the silver bowl up top here, close the lid and then press this button, which will automatically release a pre-measured amount of butter. Not real butter of course, most places these days use canola oil since it's lower in cholesterol.

Anyway, I'm rambling, and I certainly don't want to bore you. I know you're a busy man that's running behind schedule since it's almost noon and you haven't killed any defenseless people today. Since we don't have any popcorn kernels, we'll just have to make due with your large cranium kernel. Oh, yeah, I left out an important feature of this unit. As you're probably aware, the oil is now in a solid form, contained in this large fifty pound barrel below, see?" Tip opened the cabinet doors revealing the large yellow barrel. "This long metal rod here heats the butter in this barrel and turns it into a liquid form. As you can see it's doing a great job." Tip pulled the electrically heated rod out and it was dripping with the translucent substance. Damn, that's pretty hot, huh?"

Tip placed the hot rod into Sanchez's tied up hands and Sanchez wiggled wildly as he sustained third degree burns. "I told you it was hot. But I need to put this back into the barrel for the oil's sake. Tip's left hand held Sanchez's neck forcefully against the flimsy metal bottom grate of the popper, while his right hand hovered over the red oil button. "Now, what's going on today that requires you to be here? And, don't tell me you're just a huge baseball fan?" Once again Tip removed the rag which was now wet from Sanchez's saliva.

"Do you know who you're fucking with!?!!" spat Sanchez.

"YES, but the real question is do YOU?!" Tip pressed the button and used both hands to hold Sanchez's head in position. A hot stream of oil landed squarely on Sanchez's left pupil. Sanchez tried desperately to escape the scalding stream of butter, but Tip's clutches weren't allowing him to go anywhere. His makeshift gag muffled Sanchez's painful scream.

A nearby hammer was now firmly clenched in Tip's right hand. The gag was removed.

"Oh, my Goddamn eye. Are you crazy?" pleaded Sanchez, his left eye swollen shut and red.

"What's going on, Sanchez? I'm growing weary of this game," Tip said calmly.

"What's going on? I don't know what's going on! Valez just told me to be here for assistance purposes. Even if I did know what was going on, I sure as hell wouldn't tell your fuck face. You know, I thought about not taking money for killing your puke little friends back in Michigan, because it was so fun I thought I should be paying someone," slurred Sanchez.

"Are you going to tell me what I want to know, or are you going to take the hard route again?" Tip calmly asked as he tossed the hammer from one hand to the other.

"I'll tell you what I told you before-eat shit," defiantly stated Sanchez.

"Okay, you want to play rough, good. What I'm about to do is for Amy Klein, Hamilton, my parents, Fred Weeks and for Burke. Tip's mind was starting to blend the two instances together.

"You don't deserve to die Sanchez, that would merely rescue you from your pathetic life. But I need a guarantee that you won't rape anyone anymore," and with that, Tip forcefully swung the pronged end of the hammer into Sanchez's exposed groin area.

"Now, Mr., or is that Ms., Sanchez? Who are you supposed to kill today? Or, would you like me to restock the wienie cart over there, because it looks fresh out to me. Although this model is a "jumbo" cart and you sure don't measure up to that standard.

"Gasp," "groan".... Okay, okay. Ahhhh, shit, okay I'll talk, oh...You were right, we're murdering the person in that seat."

"Oh, so now you're finally ready to join the party and cooperate. Well I guess it's better late than never. Exactly what do you mean? Specifically, how is it going to be done? How is this person going to be killed? Is it another bomb?"

"The chair is supposed to be booby trapped I'm not sure exactly how."

"How is it going to happen? Who's sitting in the seat?" pressed Tip.

"I don't know, I swear, that's all that I know...ohm"

"Someone's got to know, who hot wired the chair?"

"I don't know...Valez took care of it with a guy he's never seen. The guy only deals via grocery lists."

This information helped explain to Tip why there was an existing note that had accidentally made its way into Hamilton's hands.

"Where is this guy that receives the notes and carries out their requests? Is he here today?"

"I already told you, I don't fuckin' know, I don't deal with him."

"All right then, see that wasn't so bad now was it?"

Tip forcefully re-stuffed the oil rag into Sanchez's dry and now unconscious mouth.

## CHAPTER 51

Wrigley Field had filled up substantially since Tip had entered the cramped room. The mingling crowd paid no attention to him as he exited the room. He made a quick stop in the men's room to wash the blood off his knuckles. Fortunately none of it had splotched his clothing. All the vendors were set up and ready for the masses to pour in. Some of the more intriguing T-shirts were screaming "Windy City World Series" and "Win it for Ernie." The later item was in reference to Cubs great, Ernie Banks, whose stellar career didn't include a World Series crown.

The hallway floors were still clean but soon they would acquire a movie theatre-type sticky feel, courtesy of excited fans spilling soda pops, beers, popcorn and Cracker Jacks.

A twelve-ounce can of Old Style beer was going for that special World Series price of nine dollars. Quick math would put a case of beer at a monopolistic price of two hundred and sixteen dollars.

A cute girl in pigtails ran past Tip and did a cartwheel to the delight of her little brother. The girl couldn't have been more than 9-years-old and was adorned with a navy blue jumpsuit with a supportive "I Love USA Gymnastics" printed on the back. Tip watched the girl and remembered reading in the *Chicago Tribune* that the US Gold Medal Women's Gymnastic team was going to sing the national anthem tonight. Following the game, some of the fans would be venturing down to the United Center to watch the gymnastic team perform a special post-game show.

The girl's little brother attempted a cartwheel of his own, but it was more like a summersault, and the older sister squealed with glee. The mother wore a face that indicated she knew her body and mind were in for a long and tiring day. The father, having already conceded victory to the kids, knew just how to prepare for the long day. To the beer tent he went.

This family scene, coupled with the smell of the ballpark and thoughts of Lisa and his little sister reminded Tip that life, at times, could be rather pleasant.

A pleasant life, just as it had been when he could hang out with Hamilton.

"Don't turn around, just do as I say. I don't miss at this range." The unmistakable stench of pastrami, onion and cigar accompanied the deep and raspy voice. The sharp nudge in Tip's right kidney felt like the nose of an automatic. It wasn't necessary for Tip to turn and see his enemy; it had to be the one and only Ricardo Valez.

With encouragement from the gun, they made their way up the backstairs to the newly built upper level skyboxes. Valez made Tip open the white doors to suite number forty-five. The skybox was expansive and the new carpeting made it smell like a model home. The photographs of the Merchel Corporation Headquarters indicated this was their company box.

The trays of brightly colored tapas and ample supply of liquor indicated that Merchel was undoubtedly planning on entertaining some prominent clients during tonight's ballgame. You could almost smell the bullshit and ass kissing that would be flowing almost as freely as the food and booze.

"You've been a pain in my ass much too long. I'd have thought you'd get scared off and run away, perhaps you should have. But, if it's any consolation, I'm certainly glad you decided to keep sticking your nose where it didn't belong. This way, I can watch you die, correction, watch you die painfully. Who knows, maybe you did give up and you're just here to enjoy the baseball game. If that's the case, than I'm one lucky son-of-a bitch, or conversely, you're the unluckiest person I know. Whatever the case may be, I'd love to waste you right now, but I need some information before we do that. Unfortunately, I've got to go meet Mr. Corrigan and don't have time to chat with you right now. Don't worry, I'll send up some men to keep you company. I believe that you already know one of them, and I think he'll be happy to see you again. He wasn't too thrilled about what happened to his friend Garcia," said Valez.

Little did Valez know that Tip had already seen Sanchez and that, at the moment, Sanchez was too preoccupied with an anatomical problem to pay them a visit.

A small smirk began to curl at the corner of Tip's lip at the thought of Sanchez. This smirk didn't go unnoticed by Valez. Excruciating pain echoed at the base of Tip's skull as Valez struck him with the butt of his gun. Tip was surprised at how strong Valez was. Stars flickered in front of his eyes, but he quickly shook them off. He'd been hit harder in hockey before, but not by much.

Valez wrapped several layers of duct tape around Tip's ankles and some more just above his knees. Valez also tightly strapped two layers of tape around Tip's upper body, effectively rendering his arms useless.

"Oh, since I won't be here to see you die, I wanted to leave you something to remember me by," breathed Valez. Tip's eyes stayed unwavering on Valez's brown bean-teeth.

An inch separated Valez's face from his. Tip knew something unpleasant was coming. Stay focused, don't give him any satisfaction, thought Tip. Valez grabbed Tip's little pinky finger and bent it back. "Crack!" The discomforting sound of the bone snapping happened before the warm rush of pain rapidly flowed through his entire body. Tip couldn't tell whether his finger was still attached or whether it had been ripped clean off. He knew it served no purpose to look at it. What was done was done.

Tip tried to hide any signs of pain. "This is a luxurious suite you have here. Is the reason you have it because your fat ass doesn't fit into the regular seats?" Tip asked nonchalantly.

Valez's fat fingers pushed down on Tip's head and shoved him face first into the small coat closet. Tip's face broke his fall. Fortunately, he landed in the corner of the closet, so both cheekbones took most of the impact rather than the nose. Running his tongue across his teeth confirmed that all of them were still there, including his porcelain bridge. The cosmetic bridge was compliments of an old hockey injury.

Valez slammed the closet door and locked it. There was no need to do this, Tip certainly couldn't go anywhere the way he was currently tied-up. The little closet was not conducive to a tall frame, and Tip's head was almost perpendicular to the coat hanger shelf. Needlelike tingles were already running through his neck and back; impinged nerves voicing their discomfort. Tip could hear Valez exit the suite. The useless finger throbbed in pain.

There was no access to a pointed stone this time to poke through the duct tape and bail him out. The only items in the closet were, by Tip's best count, five hangers. Unfortunately, they sounded plastic and would be of no use to him even if he could somehow manage to reach them.

The adhesive on the back of the duct tape tasted awful, much worse than licking postage stamps. His intent was to keep moistening the tape with his tongue in the hopes of loosening it to the point where he could yell for help before the goon squad arrived. The taste of the adhesive was a small price to pay if it worked. There was also a remote chance, if he could free his mouth, of being able to bite through the tape around his legs and chest. These were both long shots, and his mouth was quickly drying out, but it was his best play at the moment; the game clock was quickly ticking down to zero.

The sound of the outer suite door opening was not music to Tip's ears. He thought it could only be more trouble; the patter sound of feet made its' way toward the closet.

The game was up; he'd failed in his mission. Hamilton's name would be muddled forever. The Klein's would win their lawsuit and the Hamilton's would be the villains in the public's eye. Everyone that Tip cared about would lose, the bad guys would triumph again.

Tip thought about his little sister and about who would take care of her. He guessed that she'd just take care of herself as she always had. How would she be without anyone? Sure the Hamiltons would take care of her, but with what money? The lawsuit would surely clean them out of everything. What really would become of her? Tip's only hope was that the authorities would somehow be able to use the documents he'd compiled to piece things together.

But, he knew all too well that much of the evidence was soft or based on hearsay and wouldn't hold up in court against high-paid defense lawyers.

The footsteps came to an abrupt halt outside of the closest, and someone now was trying to turn the doorknob on the closet, but it wouldn't rotate. There was rummaging that sounded like it was coming from the bar area but it was difficult to tell. Didn't Valez give his henchmen the key? It also sounded as if there was only one person in the suite. From the weight of the footsteps, the person was not very big.

Whoever it was came back to the door again, jimmying something in the lock. The lock clicked and the door swung open. Tip's eyes automatically squinted in reaction to the contrasting bright light. When the pupils finally adjusted, he saw a saintly figure standing in the doorway.

Before him in the door frame, with effulgent light behind her, was Lisa's beautiful face. The tape stung, a good kind of sting, as she forcefully ripped it away from his mouth. Her face was inches from his. He felt the urge to lean forward and kiss her.

She slapped him hard across the face. "You're very lucky, you stubborn bastard. The only reason I'm saving your ass is that I happened to be tailing Valez, when I saw him snare you. Let's get something straight; I'm doing this for me and not for you. I didn't want to feel that I owed you anything. Obviously you felt the same way, since you abandoned me."

"Lisa, listen, if this is about me leaving Virginia hastily, I'm sorry but.."

"Tip, I don't care, you did what you had to, and like I said we don't owe each other anything anymore. We're even. We can act like we never met, which suits me just fine."

Not in his mind, thought Tip. How could he let himself care

about this girl? She should mean nothing to him, and the feelings he had for her irked him. Tip knew he had to stay focused. He knew Lisa would only wind up hurting him if he let his emotions guide the way. Tip knew he had to stay focused and finish the task at hand.

Lisa was removing the last strip of tape from him when the door to the suite slowly opened. She slid into the closet and was facing Tip. She closed the door without a sound.

Her tight body was flush against his; the contours of their bodies were a perfect match. Her flawless bust was pressed just below his chiseled pectorals. Their collectively firm nipples couldn't have been more than a couple of inches apart. Her breath was cool and refreshing against his cheek. Despite the precarious position, he couldn't prevent his body from becoming physically aroused. Lisa couldn't help but notice Tip's manhood pressing against her.

Tip hadn't felt this type of affection and attraction toward anyone since, well, since ever. He'd never had this type of sensation captivate every inch of his body and soul. How could this be? Two sets of footsteps closed in on their tiny door. Focus, dammit, thought Tip. He was going to will his way to succeed or die trying. Death didn't scare him; failure was the only thing he feared. The keys jiggled their way toward the lock.

Now was the time. Tip's feet hit the door with tremendous velocity and the force of the swinging door sent Valez's man sprawling. A nasty looking gash on his face started to bleed profusely.

The other assailant steadied the silencer on his gun. A swift karate-like-kick from Lisa sent the weapon flying. As this thug fumbled for his weapon, the other attacker gathered himself, and Lisa and Tip bolted out the door.

"Go that way," pointed Lisa "It'll be more difficult for them to find us if we split up."

Tip's brisk walk in the opposite direction was his sign of agreement. Running through the crowded corridor would cause a scene, so it was best to keep a moderate pace. There were scores of secret service agents and undercover police in the stadium, and Tip paid particular attention not to raise their suspicions. While Tip briskly walked he painfully grabbed his finger and reset it – the pain almost causing his knees to buckle.

Valez and his entourage were also aware of the high level of security, and Tip was banking on them being smart enough to not risk running either. He periodically glanced over his shoulder, just in case the enemy was closing in.

The last look spotted Valez's men exiting the skybox a good forty yards behind. The corridor began to curve sharply and Tip kept close to the interior wall and out of site of his assailants.

On the left was skybox twenty-four, a good omen, since, twenty-four is Tip's favorite hockey jersey number. He developed an affinity for this number after respecting the aggressive play of former Detroit Red Wing, James Darling. Tip slid casually into the suite, thankful the door wasn't locked. Inside the suite were about twenty people, mostly men and a few women.

Most of the skybox occupants were in their mid-forties, properly dressed in business casual attire. Thus, a lot of Ralph Lauren and Calvin Klein dress shirts were mingling. Tip was glad that no one paid particularly close attention to his presence. A couple of women gave him the once over and were not impressed by his casual attire. A sharply dressed man made his way toward Tip; it turned out he was the host of this little shindig.

Above the gourmet cheese and cracker tray was a DDB Needham logo sign. Needham was a large advertising agency based in Chicago. Tip was familiar with Needham, as they'd recently appeared in *BrandWeek* Magazine. Needham had recently won the prestigious Best Advertising Agency Award on the heels of garnering two Clio Awards for producing the best advertising in differing categories. Tip recalled from the article that one of Needham's largest clients was Anheuser-Busch. Tip also suspected that the host probably didn't know everyone that had been invited to the suite this afternoon.

"Welcome, welcome. Come on in, you sure look like you're thirsty. What's your drink of pleasure son, I'm Dan Jacobie Account

Director of Needham's North American Operations," he graciously extended his tanned hand.

"Paul Tipton, nice to meet you. As far as the drink is concerned, I'd love bottled water. Do you know if my father has stopped by here yet? He told me to meet him here around this time."

Jacobie, to avoid an embarrassing situation, took the question in stride and hedged, "Well, Paul, I don't believe he has stopped by just yet, but I'm sure he'll be here any moment. Feel free to stick around if you'd like. In the meantime help yourself to the food and refreshments," Jacobie said turning to some of his top brass clients. Jacobie was a smooth talking high-level account director and he would spend every inning mingling and handing out drinks.

The door began to open and Tip positioned himself strategically by the sink. It was one of Valez's men. His eyes took in the whole scene and began to pan from left to right and his gaze was rapidly approaching the sink. He couldn't see Tip, however, because he was bent down near the sink and hidden by the open door of the mini-refrigerator. Before Tip were dozens of cans of Budweiser, Bud Light, Bud Ice, Bud Dry, Michelob, Michelob Light, Ziegenbock, Coke and Diet Coke. The cool air of the refrigerator was causing Goosebumps to form along Tip's forearms and chest.

"Excuse me sir, can I help you?" The gracious Jacobie asked.

"Oh, no. This must me the wrong suite," mumbled the thug.

With no one now chasing him, Tip decided to enjoy a refreshing Coca-Cola. It was two hours before the game and the park was really beginning to fill up and come alive. Players from both teams were beginning to warm up on the field. Kids of all ages and kids at heart clamored on the railing near the teams' dugouts in hopes of an autograph. The players on the field were too focused and nervous to notice all the adoring fans. From his hockey playing days Tip knew that once you were on the field, no matter how big the stage, your body just played the game like you were in your own backyard.

The tops of the adjacent apartment roof buildings were filled to the hilt at this point. The building owners rented out these rooftop parties to groups, generating a tremendous amount of revenue. A typical roof held upwards of eighty people, and for a regular season game a patron could enjoy sitting on the roof for an admission price of seventy-five dollars. This was probably the best deal going. The roof admission cost included all your food and liquor, as well as a pretty good seat for the game. Most of these roofs were equipped with the same green wooden bleachers that are found in the stadium. And just like the bleacher creatures, the game was an afterthought for these rooftop partygoers.

Large corporations for client entertainment purposes had rented out most of the rooftops for this marquee match-up. A local Lincoln Park newspaper, *The Reader,* estimated that the price for today's rooftop was running close to two thousand dollars per head.

Tip drained the last of his soda and pitched it into the plastic lined cardboard box before discretely leaving the suite. He blended back into the crowd and began to make his way toward section one-twenty-seven.

# CHAPTER 52

Valez was furious when he caught news that Tip had escaped. It also sounded as if Lisa Appleton had made her way to the Windy City as well. The news about Lisa he liked, he would enjoy killing her, yes, he would like that very much. He would enjoy killing her much more than he'd enjoyed killing her younger brother. Valez didn't have too much against her brother because he didn't really know him. The brother merely had to die since he knew too much information.

Lisa on the other hand deserved what was coming to her. She had tricked and intentionally betrayed him. Killing her was also going to be much more enjoyable than bagging his old secretary, Barbara Fernandez. Life and hope still abounded in Lisa, whereas Barbara was old and weak. It would be a tragic loss to society for a youth to have their candle of life extinguished so soon after being lit.

Valez also was going to enjoy killing two of his incompetent mercenaries. These men had failed him in a simple request. Valez knew he wouldn't have to worry about this type of incompetence after Corrigan was elected President. Valez would assume his rightful place in the Presidential Cabinet, and he would have the best and brightest the country had to offer at his disposal. The real kicker was that the taxpayer would be paying for his hired help. This thought humored him to no end.

Several fans looked in Valez's direction but didn't dare stare too long at this hideous monster. A deep sinister laugh that sounded more like a rolling growl resonated from his gut.

———

Tip bided his time by walking patiently behind a 9-year-old boy dressed from head to toe in Chicago Cubs paraphernalia. The boy was concentrating on stepping on the heels of his younger brother's shoes. His little brother was also wearing a complete Chicago Cubs baseball uniform.

Tip wondered how much Lisa had figured out on her own. He also wondered if she'd received the Fed-Ex package. He ruled the Fed-Ex package out however; she was here much too early to have received the package. It may have been possible if the package arrived a few hours earlier than the normal ten-thirty delivery time, but odds of that were slim. Tip was still befuddled about her presence.

Whatever the case, she was here and he wondered if they would both be intently watching the same seat: 9E. Maybe she just knew something was going down during the game and wasn't aware of the significance of the seat. Whatever the case, Tip kept a watchful eye out for Valez and his men. He also kept on the lookout for Corrigan. Corrigan wouldn't know Tip from Adam if they crossed paths. Tip wasn't concerned about Corrigan; rather, he was merely bemused. Tip wished he had a third eye to make sure Lisa was okay. There was no need for her to suffer any more than she already had.

As Tip drew closer to section one twenty-seven, he overheard a conversation between an attractive younger couple. From their chic dress and erudite mannerisms it was evident that they were affluent and more than likely lived in the upscale Gold Cost area of downtown Chicago.

"I can't believe we got these seats, they're better than I could have ever imagined. We really need to do something special for Dave and Connie. Perhaps we can take them to dinner at Les Nomades next Friday," she said. Les Nomades was one of the premier restaurants in Chicago and it was reflected in their prices. Their restaurant selection indicated that they didn't need to worry about money.

"Yes, we do owe them. Next Friday, hmm let me see, don't we have tickets to *Ambrosia* at Second City?" queried the husband.

"Oh drat, you're right. Hey, why don't we try to get two more tickets and make it an evening out on the town with them? Do you think you could get two more tickets from work?" she asked.

"Yea, I think I can pull it off. I'll see what I can do on Monday," the husband said smugly and they both embraced and kissed.

"This will be great. I can't believe we're sitting two rows behind her. And, I think it's wonderful that Vince Carry is coming down from his booth to sing with her during the seventh inning stretch. Do you have your camera with you?" The wife asked eagerly.

"Yes, although I've forgotten it in the past, I made damn sure I'd have it today," said the husband who seemed to be on his game today and as a result had a good chance of having sex for the first time in weeks.

"Splendid, we've go to get a shot of us in the foreground when they start singing," the wife said.

"Oh, certainly we must. I'll make sure the camera is all set and idiot proof and we'll have someone nearby take it-maybe even a secret service agent," he said facetiously and they both laughed heartily at such a witty remark.

"You know it was kind of exciting to be frisked for the first time," said the husband.

"Oh you liked that did you? It wasn't a pleasant experience for me-having that big hairy guy touch me. But if you behave, maybe you can show me how it's done tonight," said the wife in a very soft, barely audible, libidinous tone.

The woman wrapped her arms around her husband, holding the two tickets in her hand. Tip inconspicuously read the tickets just as if he were glancing at a stranger's watch to get the time, and the seats were situated in section one-twenty-seven.

Upon reaching section one-twenty-seven, Tip saw no sign of Valez or Corrigan. The ushers, donned in their blue blazers, looked much younger than the other ushers throughout the remainder of the ballpark. These ushers also had tiny earpieces for two-way radio communication. Thus, these guys were probably undercover secret service agents.

Tip knew his plan of attack would probably be futile, but he needed to make an attempt. He confidently strode between the two agents posing as ushers. The smaller of the two men stuck out his arm effectively obstructing Tip's pathway into the stadium. The move by the agent was quick and strong, yet politely done.

"Sir, can we see your ticket stub please," said the taller black man. It was more of a statement rather than a question.

"Oh, I just came back up here to take a leak...um, I mean, to use the facilities, you know all that beer and all," Tip stammered this on purpose to appear weak and disoriented.

"Yea sir, we know what you mean. But we still need to see your ticket stub to let you in here," replied the shorter agent.

"Well, that's going to be a problem, because just like a bunch of other people, I sold it to a guy inside the stadium that wanted them for his grandson's scrapbook-I mean the guy gave me forty bucks! I hope that doesn't stop me from being able to get back to my seat-because he promised me that it wouldn't," Tip lied.

"It should have been made perfectly clear at that gate that you'd need to retain your stub in order to enter and exit your seat for this particular game," said the tall agent.

"No one said anything of the sort to me. I'm a season ticket holder and I've never had to show my stub before. Where are the guys that normally work here, Jim and George, they'd recognize me," Tip played a hunch and hoped it paid off. He would be screwed if these were in fact the regular ushers, or worse yet if the regular ushers were at either of the adjacent gates and these secret service agents could go grab them for verification.

"Sir, I'm sorry. I'm sure what you're saying is true, but we have to take more precautions today due to the heighten security for obvious reasons. What we can do is take your seat number and if it's vacant we'll be able to accommodate you. Are you with anyone today?" asked the agent.

"Oh, no, I had enough trouble getting this ticket for myself, let alone my boyfriend," Tip said off the cuff. Tip figured it was best to always keep people's minds on numerous variables when you were trying to deceive them; give them a smokescreen.

Both ushers gave each other a look after the mention of the boyfriend. One of them almost allowed a smile, or at least he almost showed his teeth-which is considered a fit of laughter by secret service standards.

"It was seat fourteen B, B as in boy (Tip was really laying on the effeminate touch now). It's located in aisle thirty-eight," Tip gesticulated.

The taller agent wrote the number down on his pad of paper. "Thanks sir, I suggest moseying back around at game time and we'll see what we can do. Or you can try and find the guy you sold the ticket stub to. Unfortunately, we can't have you hanging around the entrance here. I hope you understand," said the agent.

"Oh I understand perfectly, I just *loovve* a man with authority." Out of the corner of his eye, Tip spotted Valez's entourage. The one man's facial wound from the closet door had stopped bleeding, but it was still quite an eyesore. Neither of the men looked too pleased, however the least pleasant looking of them all was Valez.

The secret service agents eyed the three men suspiciously and it appeared that they were relaying some information via their transmitters. Perhaps they had gotten the Federal Express package and were on the look out. Tip had talked with Rathman this morning. Rathman's buddy in the FBI indicated that Tip's package was one of seventy packages reviewed relating to some aspect/ conspiracy revolving around the game. The Bureau, along with the secret service had been planning the World Series security once the possibility of a game seven in Chicago was remotely plausible.

In the minds of the Bureau and Secret Services, no stone had been left unturned. As far as any unexpected bombs in the ballpark, well this was considered highly unlikely since they combed the park twice during the week. Rathman told Tip that the FBI was slightly pompous about their security-but he also said they had the right to be since they had a very good track record.

Tip was quite sure that these agents were probably transmitting their lunch order or something of less importance back to their boss. Tip was treating outside help just like he did Social Security. Social

Security money would be a welcomed surprise come retirement, but he wasn't banking on it. Lisa's assistance this morning was one such surprise payoff however.

Tip attempted to enter the sections adjacent to section one-twenty-seven, but was told the same story by the ushers manning those respective entrances. Although the attendants appeared to be genuine ushers, Tip didn't push his luck trying to gain access to their sections. It wouldn't be prudent to raise people's curiosity throughout the ballpark. The bad guys were already giving him enough trouble. The last thing needed was to have the good guys chasing him as well.

Tip ascended the concrete stairs to the upper deck, to section two-twenty-seven, perched on top of section one-twenty-seven. A loud roar sprang from the crowd and the stadium began to jump. This was in response to Mr. Cub himself, Ernie Banks, taking the pitchers mound to throw out the traditional first pitch.

The Yankees were heavily favored to win this game. The Yankees had rookie sensation Pedro Fernandez from the Dominican Republic starting as their pitcher. Pedro had already led the Yankees to victory over the Cubs in games one and four of the series. Pedro recorded a shutout in the opening game of this series. However, he topped that shutout performance by pitching a no-hitter in game four. By doing so, Fernandez became only the second player in history to pitch a no-hitter during the World Series.

By the looks of things, security was still tight on the upper level, but it was definitely a little more lax than the sections below it. Still, it was obvious that in order to gain access, Tip was going to need to somehow get his hands on a ticket stub.

The game moved rapidly into the bottom of the fifth inning. The game was much higher scoring than the sports analysts had predicted. The score was already four to three in favor of the hometown Cubs. The Cubs had the lead and were currently trying to increase it. Wrigley Field was at a fever pitch. Valez and Corrigan were savoring the fact that it was such a tight contest, because that meant more television viewers would stay glued to the boob tube.

Valez and Corrigan wanted the largest audience possible to witness their fireworks display.

Tip pondered what kind of plan they had in store for the nation. It couldn't be another bomb, could it? Another bomb didn't seem plausible at this venue. The dogs and FBI would easily detect it-if Corrigan's hit men were fortunate enough to sneak it in.

Tip waited patiently in the corridor trying to be as inconspicuous as possible. He whittled away a majority of his time in the first stall of the latrine. He wasn't about to argue with the logic that man does some of his best thinking in the bathroom. The first stall was always his preferred selection since studies indicated that it was by far the least used toilet in multiple stalled bathrooms. Tip couldn't remember where he'd read such an outlandish research article (probably *Maxim*), but he firmly believed in their findings. Mother nature wasn't calling at this time, Tip just thought it was the best place to hideout.

As long as the game remained close, his task of getting into the stadium would get more difficult by the inning. There weren't many fans descending on the beverage and food vendors anymore, only the beer cart. Nobody wanted to risk missing any of the action. Also, no fan was about to leave early in an attempt to beat traffic, everyone knew that there was no beating traffic tonight. Tip retrieved what he needed from the stashed gym bag and made the necessary preparations before concealing the materials.

A rather agitated man was waiting impatiently in line for another foamy Old Style beer. This was the sixth inning, which meant it was the last inning that the stadium was allowed to serve any alcohol. This sixth inning policy was instituted years back in an effort to curb drinking and driving. Some believed that this policy only encouraged binge drinking up until the sixth inning and didn't assuage the drinking and driving problems. In fact, some believed this policy increased the likelihood of drunks being behind the wheel.

These were sound arguments against the sixth inning policy and the gentleman in front of Tip looked like he'd had more than his share of Old Styles this afternoon. More importantly, protruding from the back right pocket of his undersized jeans was a glorious ticket stub. A couple of other anxious beer drinkers stood in line and the line began to grow as more drinkers poured out from the bathroom and headed to refill their respective bellies with another cold one. Steadily, Tip paced up the line and excused himself for cutting through the line on the way to the nacho stand. Turning toward the agitated man, Tip brushed up against his flaccid flesh and with a flick of the wrist, deftly swiped the ticket stub.

## CHAPTER 53

The stadium was really beginning to rock and sway as the Cubs were threatening in the bottom of the sixth. The Cubs had runners on the corners (first and third base) and only one out. The fans were all standing and clapping in unison for their all-star first baseman as he confidently strode to the plate. It was difficult to get a clear look through the enormous crowd and Tip strained and contorted his body to get a clear shot through his binoculars. Fortunately, the first baseman popped out on the first pitch squelching the fans' vivacity for at least the moment. Adjusting the binoculars, Tip now had a clean shot of the unfortunate person sitting in seat 9E.

Thankfully, the binocular strap was around his neck. Out of pure astonishment, the binoculars fell from his hand and dangled in the air. Tip didn't know whom he expected to see, but he certainly didn't expect it to be the Vice President of the United States!

This latest revelation made an already intricate task that much more difficult. It would be difficult enough to get close to Charlie Duke, let alone remove her from her seat. Tip pondered several options in his mind and concluded that rash times called for rash actions. Tip quickly looked around. The idea was a long shot, but it was the only shot that he had.

An insert in the game's program had highlighted that Cubs announcer Vince Carry would be making his way down from the broadcast booth at the bottom of the seventh inning to sing the traditional Chicago version of *"Take Me Out to the Ball Game."* He was making this voyage in order to sing a duet with long time Cubs fan Charlie Duke. Charlie Duke, the consummate politician was outfitted in a baseball uniform that was half New York and the other half Chicago. The pinstriped and brilliant blue outfit was quite becoming. This spirited outfit epitomized Duke's loveable flair and was one of the reasons the American Public considered her a national treasure. Singing this duet would also be a natural for Duke, she'd received a minor in music during her undergraduate years at The University of Texas.

The next batter struck out on three successive pitches and to the disappointment of Chicago fans, the Cubs stranded the two base runners. Tip made his way back toward section one-twenty-seven. The forthcoming plan ran through his mind, so many things could go wrong, he knew it was truly insane, but what other option was there? Failure certainly wasn't an option, and if he didn't do something soon, that surely would happen. Approaching the FBI for help was definitely not an option. If they hadn't found anything before the game, Tip knew there was no way that they were going to believe him now. Aside from that, by the time he'd explained who he was it would be too late. More than likely he'd be carted off before having a chance to explain himself and then Charlie Duke would be doomed. But what if Sanchez was full of a load of crap, then what? He knew he would be probably be charged with attempted assault or murder of the Vice President.

Zar Kumbadi sat patiently in the left field section of the bleachers, giving him a clear view of seat 9E. Unlike Tip, Zar was delighted to see that 9E's occupant was Vice President Charlie Duke. In Zar's country, women had their subordinate role clearly defined, and a woman's role certainly didn't involve leading the country.

Only in the U.S., Zar thought, could that woman ascend to where she is-what a joke. He'd probably be doing the U.S. a favor by killing Charlene Duke and that thought bothered him. He despised the United States and all its citizens.

Zar didn't know his employer but he was beginning to respect him more and more with each passing job-he/she must also hate Americans. Zar knew his employer more than likely was a man, because no woman would ever want to eliminate the heroine, Charlie Duke.

# CRISIS

Zar suspected that this last job was going to be a big name. The money was almost quadruple that of his previous hits and his highest payoff ever, assassin money not terrorist money. Zar was impressed with the magnitude of the job, knocking Charlie Duke off would solidify him amongst the great killers of all time. His name, if he decided to eventually make it known, would be mentioned along with legends Lee Harvey Oswold, Sir Han Sir Han, John Wilkes Booth, Osama Bin Laden and others of note.

Zar cheered periodically for the Cubs so that he wouldn't appear suspicious by his subdued behavior. The Wrigley Bleachers were famous for their fans. The Cubs historically fielded low caliber teams, yet the fans always came to the park year after year, losing season after losing season.

The reason the fans came to watch mediocre teams through all these years was because the fans were always able to fabricate their own fun, regardless of the development of the game. The bleachers were generally a large cocktail party for the twenty and thirty something yuppies of the city. The crowd today was composed of a few more blue bloods than normal, but the crowd was still raucous. Zar was doing a good job of fitting in. He was wearing a nostalgic Cubs hat and an old Ryan Sandberg throw back spring training jersey. His fake red hair flared out from beneath the royal blue cap.

The strapping fan seated to the left of him was extremely hyperkinetic and had the bad habit of always wanting to high five him after every good play the Cubs performed. Zar was contemplating staying around after his job was done to kill this obnoxious sandbag, for no other reason then simple, pure, pleasure. If the guy hugged him, then he was definitely going to slit his throat after the game. Zar didn't know why silly stupid Americans thought that everyone on the street or next to them was somehow their buddy-he hated it!

Zar knew he was getting cocky by remaining inside the stadium, but he wasn't getting careless. He could easily be relaxing at a nearby hotel to perform this job but he wanted to be here. The camera just didn't quite capture the human drama and suffering that one could experience live. There was also the possibility that the networks wouldn't show such a horrifying scene.

There wasn't much need for concern anyway; there were too many people he could hide among at the stadium. Zar kind of chuckled at the idea of hiding; there was no need for him to hide. No one knew what he looked like.

Zar thought this simpleton probably believed that the Cubs winning the World Series was as good as it could get. Not so thought Zar, that was nothing like the high of causing mass destruction. Ecstasy is knowing that you have the power to control the destiny of others' lives. Zar was called "Big Ben" among the terrorist and assassin communities because, similar to the famous clock in London, he determined when someone's time was up.

"Big Ben" caressed the small black control in the palm of his hand. The time was drawing near and he calmly waited. His employer had specifically stated that Zar needed to wait until the conclusion of the top of the seventh inning. Zar wasn't familiar with the rules of the American game of baseball. However several hours reading about it on the Web gave him a good understanding. Zar was surprised at how long and boring each individual inning was and was happy that he wouldn't have to sit through all nine of them.

Zar was to set the show in motion thirty seconds after the last out of the inning. He thought about doing it earlier than this since he didn't like being told how to do his job. And this particular employer was starting to give him a little too much direction. Zar thought he might need to send a message to his employer as a signal to who was in control of the situation.

He almost wasted Charlie Duke in the fourth inning when the expression on her face was just too damn perky for him. The only thing that stopped him from killing her earlier than planned was the fact that he had a reputation to uphold. He was Big Ben, and every operation he had ever performed worked like clockwork. This precision enabled him to demand top dollar and earned the respect of his peers. The underground community knew to give Zar his space. At the same time they knew he remained cool and calculating during the most stressful of jobs. Zar's mix of sagacity and tenacity was a scary and deadly combination.

Zar didn't have the opportunity to test his death contraption prior to the game, but testing wasn't necessary. He was confident in the device he'd built; he didn't have a Masters in electrical engineering for nothing. Zar's design was simple, yet brilliant at the same time. The two shafts running up the back supports of the chair looked like all the other steel rods in all the other stadium seats. The difference being, the one's he inserted into Charlie Duke's chair could conduct electricity. Having enough electricity to fry the occupant was not difficult at all. The ballpark had to generate power for the lights and scoreboard. Zar's death chair would just divert this electricity for a split second.

The difficult part was transferring and harnessing the power into the seat. Fortunately, a water pipe ran below these particular seats, and Zar had infused a two-inch pipe connecting the conductors he'd inserted. The water would act as a conduit, funneling this enormous amount of electricity and sending it coursing through the Vice President's veins. Using the water stream would lose some of the electric strength, but there would still be enough to cook Charlie Duke well done.

Zar knew that nothing would look out of the ordinary when the FBI and Secret Service performed their customary inspections. The Feds were always looking for wires and visible plastics. What damage could water do? Well, they weren't dealing with your average dime store bomb maker this time; they were dealing with the best.

For added effect to the spectacle, Zar had rigged the chair so that it would glow a bright red. It was going to be a beautiful display he thought, the lights would slightly dim and then over the murmur of the crowd you'd hear the horrified screams of thousands. Zar knew that only the lucky few seated by Duke would experience the erotic smell of burning flesh. It was a shame that not everyone would be able to experience that sensation, thought Zar.

---

Upon reaching section one-twenty-seven, Tip quickly noticed the gentleman from whom he'd borrowed the seat ticket. It was a shame that he had to ruin this gentleman's day, but it was for the greater good. Tip loitered about the area, keeping a close eye on the progress of the game. Tip knew that he wouldn't be able to sit in the seat too long without raising suspicion. Tip had no idea whether this guy was with friends or family. All of the seats surrounding the borrowed ticket were occupied. Settling in the seat when the Yankees had two outs would probably be his best bet to go unnoticed.

Unluckily, this never occurred. The Yankees started to rally, putting both of the first two batters on base. The Cubs decided to make a pitching change, which further prolonged the inning. The Cubs wanted a left-handed pitcher to face the right-handed batter. The next batter after that was left handed, so it wouldn't be surprising if they made another pitching change. That would mean another five minutes while the pitcher warmed up. In the last game of the playoffs, managers had the luxury of using all of their pitchers including their starters, in relief pitching roles. This was possible because there weren't any more games that the manager would have to rest each pitcher's arm.

Fortunately for Tip, the batter grounded into a double play, taking out the two lead runners. The stadium was rumbling and the crowd was chanting in unison, "Go Cubs! Go!" Now was the time, and Tip's adrenaline was pumping at full capacity. He hastily flashed the usher the ticket. The legitimate ushers were caught up in the excitement of the game as well as being preoccupied with the enraged fan before them (the one Tip had swiped the ticket from) and paid little attention to Tip.

Tip quickly skipped down the small cement steps of the stadium to his borrowed seat. It was an aisle seat in the front row of the second deck; his luck was beginning to take a change for the better. He glanced down to the level below. Charlie Duke's seat was only two seats to the left of Tip's and hence for all intents in purposes was a straight shot down below. He didn't really have a plan at this point of how to get her out of her seat, but at least she was in shouting distance.

"Hey mister, what are you doing?" questioned the rosy-faced eight grader in the seat next to Tip. "Where did my Pa go?"

"Oh, I work here and am just securing the proper equipment to hang a championship banner in case we (we meaning the Cubs) win. If we win, make sure you're smiling, because you're probably going to be on national television," Tip couldn't help embellishing the story.

"Mom, mom did you hear that, if we win, we're going to be on TV-I'd be the bomb at school!"

"What? Oh, that's great honey," half heartily replied the frail and heavily perfumed mother, "Excuse me sir, why are you sitting in my husband's seat, where is Jerry anyway?"

"Mom, if you were listening you'd know that he works here and that he's putting up the necessary supports for the Championship banner in case we win, then we'll be on TV," replied the kid who gave Tip a look like he was embarrassed for his mother's ignorance.

"Well where the hell is Jerry? It's not like him to be missing the best part of the game," said the mother. The mother needed to generate a tremendous amount of momentum to allow her the strength to pry her frail limbs from the seat.

"Oh, I'm sorry ma'am. If your husband was the man sitting here, a jolly old fella wearing a Ryan Sandberg jersey I believe. He was in the beer line, which was pretty long considering it was the last inning that they are allowed to serve. He should be here any moment. He said it would be a good time for me to set things up since he didn't want to be bothered."

"Oh yeah, that's my husband all right," replied the lady. "And they say you can't judge a book by its cover, baloney."

Tip snuck a peak at the game action. Time was running out. The mother was satisfied for now, but that wouldn't last much longer. The ball count on the batter was full, and there were two outs. If this guy didn't get out soon, the plan was in trouble. Tip couldn't stall much longer. The crowd was too loud at this point for Charlie Duke to be able to hear him.

The husband was in view and still arguing profusely with the ushers, although it appeared that his blood pressure had dropped somewhat. Perhaps he was becoming calmer because he could see the game now. At any rate, if he could see the game than it wouldn't be much longer till he spotted the intruder in his seat.

The New York Yankees took a mighty swing and sent the foul ball into the seats along the third baseline. "Damn, just strike out," Tip couldn't restrain himself from yelling.

"Yeah, damn! Just strike out," echoed the kid.

"Georgie, watch your language!" snapped the mother who gave Tip a crossed look and then looked up the aisle to see her husband. Tip's goose was cooked.

"Crack!" The ball sprang off the batter's bat and was sailing foul right at their section. Instinctively, Tip reached over, leaned down, and with one hand grabbed the errant ball. It was an unbelievable catch and the loud roar of the crowd showed their appreciation. Tip handed the ball to the kid next to him. The kid's face lit up like a Christmas tree and he was so happy that he couldn't speak.

"Thank you," said the mother.

"My pleasure," Tip was on the new stadium jumbo screen and he had to chuckle at the thought of Valez's astonished fat face.

"Excuse me sir, that was a great catch, but can I please see your ticket," asked the usher who was politely tapping Tip's shoulder.

"That guy's in my seat I tell you, honey tell these guys that that's my seat!" boisterously yelled the irritated man.

"Dad, dad, did you see the ball I got? This man gave it to me. It was an awesome catch. This guy works here Dad-you missed it," yelled the kid over the excitement of the moment.

"Ohhhh, you work here huh, we'll see about that. Your ticket please sir," tersely stated the usher.

"I must have dropped it, just a second," Tip bent down and eyed up the large banner in front of him on the railing. It was a huge banner that was tied down by one long and thick bungee cord

# CRISIS

due to the prevailing winds of the city. Tip eyed up the cord and a thought, albeit a very crazy one, crossed his mind. He continued to act like he was searching for his ticket as the racket and commotion continued around him. He sized up the cord one more time and quickly grabbed the end that was already loose. He strapped this end tight around his left ankle.

In high school, when Tip was bungee jumping off of bridges all through the summer, he had developed quite an eye for distance and his calculations were usually within a couple feet of the actual distance. Of course, they would still do a sandbag run beforehand to determine if the calculations were correct, because he knew that a foot too long in bungee jumping wasn't a good thing. Also these jumps were usually over forgiving water. There would not be the luxury of running a sandbag test run today. Tip would serve as the day's sandbag. The only thing is his favor was this jump wasn't long at all compared to what he'd do during the summers.

He glanced down below one last time. The cord had purposely been made a little shorter than his estimated calculations. It would be better to air on the short side as opposed to having it be too long. Tip couldn't afford to crash head to head with Charlie Duke from a fall of this level-it would kill both of them. And if he missed it may cause enough of a stir to have Charlie Duke removed from the seat.

The crowd erupted into the loudest cheer all game. As Tip bent back up he noticed that the batter had struck out. It was onto the bottom of the seventh.

"Sir, please show me your ticket now or I'm going to have to politely escort you out," stated the usher.

"Oh, the ticket is immaterial anyway sir. You can have your seat back, I was just leaving," said Tip.

# CHAPTER 54

"Ladies and Gentlemen, please direct your attention to section one-twenty-seven. Our own Vince Carry is down there right now to sing his traditional seventh inning stretch *Take Me Out to the Ballgame*. Accompanying Mr. Carry for tonight's rendition is Vice President Charlie Duke," boomed the golden voice of the public address announcer in a loveable Chicago accent.

The crowd let out a roar of approval, which was highly unusual for a politician in the United States. For any politician, no matter how popular, there were usually a few dissenting boos to be heard. If there were any boos for Charlie Duke on this night, they were overpowered by the resounding cheers. It would also be difficult to tell if people were booing, because many times when Charlie was introduced the crowed would elongate DUUUUUUUUUKE!

Zar was really beginning to like this particular job. The world was going to see his fabulous talent on center stage. He glanced at his watch; there were only twenty seconds till the show began. All the cameras would be in perfect position to film his glorious moment. Unlike 9/11, the best cameras the world had to offer would be filming this historic event from every angle. Zar couldn't believe his eyes, what the hell was that, was that a body hurtling down toward the Vice President!?

Meanwhile, one section above, to the usher's and family's astonishment Tip casually hopped up onto the railing and jumped into the night air. Tip arched his back as far as possible and kept his arms loosely locked in the iron cross-position. This was the best way to maintain balance and to keep in a straight line to the target when bungee jumping. He was descending rapidly, but a peaceful calm came over his entire body. He couldn't hear the crowd; all he was focused on doing was getting Charlie Duke out of her seat. He could feel the cord begin to tighten around his legs and his speed was beginning decelerate; the cord was doing it's job.

Fear swept over his heart, as he thought the tightening was happening too soon. Perhaps he'd been too conservative. The cord may not be long enough and he wouldn't be able to reach Charlie Duke. If that was the case, Tip knew that he'd be blamed for any catastrophe that ensued.

Tip stretched every muscle in his body and strained to grasp onto Charlie Duke. He was right on target, and he was barely able to reach underneath her arms and lift her from the seat with quite a jolt. The secret service agents dove and clamored in an effort to stop Tip, but were just a second too late. They were never trained for something as ludicrous as what they just witnessed.

Tip and Vice President Duke bounded back up rapidly. Charlie Duke was lithe and her one hundred and twenty-pound frame slowed their ascent, but not by much. Surprisingly, she hadn't let out a scream. Duke was renown for making sure that she'd taken in the whole situation, whatever it may be, before taking any kind of action. However, when she took action it was fast and furious. Tip with the Vice President in his arms bounded up and down jerkily a few times, before finally starting to slow and maintain a steady position.

"It's okay, Madame Vice President. Although it may not seem like it, my intent is not to harm you. You will only be doing yourself a disservice by trying anything rash at this point. We are roughly 25 feet off the ground and a fall from this height would cause serious harm not only to yourself but also to anyone that you landed on. That didn't sound very nice. You're actually very light, it's just the law of gravity."

"If you don't intend to harm me, than what is your intention?" she said calm and collectively.

"To save you. Hopefully, that will reveal itself in the next few moments."

All of the secret service agents, FBI agents, and local policeman had their guns pulled and pointed directly at Tip. Tip had moved the adjustable clasp to around his waist so that he wasn't dangling precariously upside down. Tip's arms were tightly clasped around Charlie Duke's body. Her body was serving as a shield to deter any thoughts of some John Wayne in the group trying to play hero by putting a cap in Tip's head. Tip also twisted randomly and periodically for the same reason. He didn't need some sniper from the backside taking a crack.

Tip doubted that anyone would take a shot. If they did, it would certainly not bode well for Charlie Duke as she would plummet from his grasp.

"Please put your guns away. I have no intention of hurting Vice President Duke. There's no need for anyone to get hurt here," Tip calmly commanded.

"Yes, do as he says," echoed Charlie Duke. Maybe she believed Tip, but not likely. What she did know was that she didn't want to be dropped.

Tip could see Corrigan trying to vacate the area as soon as possible, but was having a difficult time managing his way through the now crowded aisle.

The bungee jump was the most difficult part, but Tip was far from being out of the woods. He was hoping that whatever death contraption the seat was booby-trapped with couldn't be stopped at this point. Tip could tell from his interrogation of Sanchez that little was known about the actual execution. It was his hunch that someone, most likely an expert in explosives, had already rigged the area to explode or do whatever insidious action was to come and had left the scene. Yet, there had been no explosion, no fireworks. Perhaps Corrigan himself had the detonator. Tip had trusted hunches in the past and they'd never let him down, now would not be the best time for a first time.

Dozens of Secret Service agents and law enforcement officials descended on the sections above and below Tip. The players were quickly shepherded into their collective dugouts and the local police formed human barriers in front of them.

Over the loud speaker Vince Carey was imploring that fans remain calm as a palpable hysteria was starting to sweep across the entire stadium as well as the nation.

Tip looked up at the bungee cord and could see the strain at the top. He didn't have much time.

"Mr. Corrigan, would you mind sitting in the seat that the Vice President just vacated," shouted Tip in an authoritative voice.

"Pardon me," Corrigan replied.

"Would you kindly have a seat in 9E? It's the one that the Vice President was sitting in a moment ago."

"What for?" asked Corrigan playing dumb.

"I don't think now is the time to ask such questions. You have a very important person in a very precarious situation right now. I would think with your past track record of bravery, that my simple request to sit in a little old chair wouldn't be too difficult of a task," Tip couldn't allow Corrigan to stall any longer. If the chair blew up before he got Corrigan to blow his cover, he was doomed. It would look like Tip planted the bomb, "It's a simple task for a real man, aren't you a real man Corrigan? But perhaps you're bark is bigger than your bite, I think deep down you may be a little bit of a coward."

Corrigan loved being in the spotlight and the situation right now presented one bigger than any in Hollywood. Corrigan didn't like to be upstaged, it never happened. He wasn't about to let some young punk do it either. Corrigan was enraged.

"I'm no coward. You are the true coward. Attempting to hurt or maim innocent people like Charlie Duke. No, I'm not being a coward. I'm being smart. If my sitting in that chair would save Charlie Duke then surely I'd do it. However, I'm not going to sit in some chair that you obviously rigged, so the whole nation can watch me be electrocuted," smugly and passionately delivered Corrigan. He was so captured in the moment that it took him a moment to realize his drastic error.

Zar didn't know quite know what to make of the scene that he was witnessing. He couldn't believe that a man had just lifted the

# CRISIS

Vice President out of the electric chair via an improbable bungee jump. The bleachers were a sea of confusion around Zar, but he remained poised and quickly sent his mind to work. Zar glanced at his watch. There were five seconds till he was supposed to activate the chair. Was this entire spectacle a plan of his employer all along? It didn't seem rational, too much could go wrong with the bungee jump. And, if it was part of the plan, why wasn't he informed about it? He'd definitely worked on double operations in the past, but one of this magnitude should have at least had some level of coordination.

Judging from the Vice President's reaction, she obviously wasn't expecting it. Maybe that was his employer dangling from the bungee cord. Perhaps the plan was for this other guy to be made to look like a hero, by saving the heroine. Perhaps Zar had been set up. Whatever the case, Zar didn't like dealing with amorphous situations and realized that he'd better get the hell out of there. However there was one minor detail he had to perform before he evacuated the building. Big Ben was always on time, whether there was someone in the seat or not…Dong…Dong…

Thankfully, Tip's hunch had been correct. "Excuse me Mr. Corrigan, who said anything about electrocution? I certainly didn't mention anything about it."

At that moment, the lights of the entire stadium dimmed slightly and seat 9E began to glow a bright red. The entire crowd let out a synchronized "AWWWW at this unbelievable sight. The patrons seated around the chair quickly bolted from their respective seats as they could feel the forceful electric current, but fortunately nobody was seriously injured. Charlie Duke's umbrella was in the seat and everyone watched the metal instantly spark and the material shoot up into flames and fizzle. The crowd let out even louder yells this time. Persons near the chair scatter about frantically.

The chair slowly returned to its normal shade of green. The lights of the stadium returned to normal and the charred umbrella continued to smolder in the chair. Everything was being streamed live across all the major networks and the jumbo screen at the game.

Many of the fans in the other parts of the stadium also started to panic and there was mass pandemonium as they scrambled toward the exits.

When the lights were restored, Corrigan stood near the chair alongside Valez with a sinister grin on his face. In-between both of them was Lisa. Valez had a gun to her left temple while Corrigan had one sharply on her right temple. Lisa, being the fighter that she was, stood there as if unfazed by the entire situation, but clearly she was worried.

"Oh, you think you're so clever. Yeah, I knew about the electrical chair because I was behind it. That's right, that's what you want me to say isn't it! Well, there you have it! I was going to do this country a great service by frying that stupid bimbo!!" yelled Corrigan. The crowd let out a huge gasp in disbelief. Curious players were attempting to get out of the dugout to see what was going on, but mounted policeman had quickly barricaded the dugouts in a protective maneuver.

Several of the secret service agents at this point looked like they may be getting anxious. Tip hoped that none of them got trigger-happy and hurt Lisa in the process of taking down Corrigan. More than half of the guns were trained on Corrigan and Valez now, the remainder stayed pointed at Tip.

"Everybody put your fucking guns away, or I swear to God this sweetheart's brains will be splattered all over this park. And the blood will be on your hands for not listening. You all are pathetic, protecting a female Vice President." The microphone in Vince Carry's hand was picking up Corrigan's words. The network cameras covering the game had also turned their attention to the commotion so that Corrigan's diatribe was being broadcast to the nation.

"How can you look yourself in the mirror like a man having to take orders from someone physically and mentally inferior!? I know you're also too weak to shoot me, because you're concerned for this girl's life, a meaningless life at that. When are you people going to learn that you need to make some sacrifices along the way and not always do the fucking politically correct thing! You've got to do what's the greatest good for the greatest number of people and mourn the necessary casualties along the way.

I was going to lead this country back to its glorious past. The United States would be the economical and military monopoly of the world for years to come. Crime would cease to exist, because I wouldn't tolerate it. I would rule with an iron fist-something this country has lacked for a long time. Politicians are always concerned about doing what will be perceived as right and not what's in the best interest of the country and its people. Also, these civil lawsuits would be cut in half; I've had enough of these faggot lawyers weakening our society. The homeless and people on welfare would also be eliminated, because only the strong should survive. This is supposed to be a capitalist society. I don't remember handouts to the lazy and weak being in Adam Smith's *Wealth of Nations*. This tact on the homeless would also help eliminate the weak; the none pure. Everyone is going to speak English in this country, not whatever language they want to speak. No wasting good money putting on Special Olympics for the retarded and the lame. That money should be used to train our real athletes so we can ensure we totally dominate all Olympic competition. That is just the tip of the iceberg.

But, it's not to be. You pathetic losers can thank your quasi hero here for allowing the U.S. to continue in mediocrity for the next millennium," some spittle flew from Corrigan's mouth as he was attempting to broadcast his ludicrous sermon to the entire stadium and his eyes increasingly widened with each passing moment. I'm sure you will celebrate him as a hero and the media will welcome it with open arms! I'm the one you should be applauding. I'm the one that can give this nation hope. But you all are too pathetic to see it," accused Corrigan.

"No, you're the pathetic one. Look at yourself. You're picking on a defenseless woman. If women are so weak, than why do you need a gun against a young woman that is unarmed? Let's just put the gun down David, there's no need for anyone to get hurt here" said the Vice President in a loud clear voice that at the same time was commanding. Duke was still dangling precariously on the bungee cord with Tip.

Tip could hear the Vice President having a muffled side conversation via a small two-way radio attached somewhere on her clothes. "No, I'm okay – there is no need to point your guns toward my captor. Aim them at Corrigan. Do not shoot as long as that girl is in harm's way that's a direct order. They aren't going to be able to go anywhere, so there's no need for anyone to get hurt. If the guns come off the girls temple and you have a clean shot that will take both the aggressors down, do it," whispered Charlie Duke underneath her breath.

"You're right Madam Vice President, or I'm sorry your highness, Charlie Duke. Whatever the case, there is no reason for anyone to get hurt. But I'm sick of listening to your tiresome prattle!" bellowed Corrigan and he raised the gun in his right hand while keeping the one in his left still flush to Lisa's skull. "The only one that is going to get hurt here today is you!"

Tip nimbly reversed positions with Charlie Duke before she had time to argue.

Corrigan pulled the trigger twice and the loud shouts echoed off the overhanging rafters.

The wind left Tip's body as both shots landed squarely in his chest. Lisa let out a loud scream. Tip mustered as much strength as possible to hold Charlie Duke for as long as he could. But the inevitable finally came and his grip on her loosened and she dropped.

Horrific screams and shouts came from the surprised crowd. They were stunned by the real life drama that was unfolding in front of their eyes. The Secret Service hadn't been idle this whole time, they had formed a human net situated below Charlie Duke with everyone's arms intertwined. About ten of these men deftly caught Charlie Duke with their human net just like male college cheerleaders. Charlie Duke only sustained a minor cut from someone's wedding ring.

The crowd was in pandemonium, and the secret service wasn't

able to get a clean shot at Valez or Corrigan without risking the safety of several innocent bystanders. Besides, the aggressors still had Lisa close to their sides. Corrigan and Valez were also retreating from the scene, so the Vice-President's life was no longer in danger. Now that the Vice President's life wasn't in danger, the Secret Service couldn't justify firing wildly.

Tip hung loosely from the bungee cord swaying and twirling back and forth. Charlie Duke looked up fondly at the man who just saved his life and a gripping pain clenched her heart. Tip's head was slumped into his chest and his body was limp. Hysteria was raining all around the stadium.

To everyone surprise, Tip shook his head slowly clearing the cobwebs and casually felt where the two bullet holes had landed. His wind was slowly returning. The bulletproof jacket Tom Rathman had supplied had done its job. The velocity of the bullets still stung like hell however. Tip was lucky to just have the wind knocked out of him. His faculties were almost all the way back when he saw Valez and Corrigan making their get away with Lisa in tow.

Everyone was concerned with following Corrigan and Valez or with checking on Charlie Duke's condition and safety. Thus, Tip casually attached an ancillary bungee cord to the main one and slowly began to lower himself down. The crowd was in disbelief at his original movements. This disbelief turned into a momentous and spontaneous cheer as they realized that Tip, but more importantly Charlie Duke, was all right. Tip made sure to steer clear of Charlie Duke and her entourage. Despite his best efforts, a welcoming committee awaited him. It was a mix of well-wishers and Secret Service agents. It quickly became all agents as they thoroughly frisked him. They released him after they were satisfied that he wasn't armed.

"Thank you so, much. I am indebted to you. You saved my life young man," said Charlie Duke who was inches away and it appeared that she was fighting back tears. She gave Tip a great big hug, the kind of hug that wasn't just for show, but rather one from the heart. The crowd roared its approval. Aside from the stern Secret Service agents, there didn't appear to be a dry eye in the ballpark.

"Duke, Duke, Duke," the mixed crowd of Cubs and Yankees fans chanted in harmony.

"Is there anything that we can do for you sir, heck I don't even know your name," blushed Duke.

"Oh, I'm Tip. Yes there is something you can do for me; did you see which way those guys went? They've got my girlfriend. It surprised Tip that the word girlfriend rolled of his tongue, but it didn't feel that weird after all.

# CHAPTER 55

Several of the pedestrian cops directed Tip, along with an army of agents, toward the El train stop in Wrigleyville. The traffic was at a standstill. The police had stopped all traffic around the stadium when they got word of the developments inside. Stopping the traffic wasn't difficult, since it was only at a crawl to begin with. The downtown street grid was a cluster of vehicles. Everyone in the city was out tonight, and travel by car was nearly impossible on the city streets. That's why Valez and Corrigan were heading for the El.

Valez and Corrigan were again spotted at the top of the escalator inside the station. A train had just pulled in. There was no way that Tip and the agents would be able to reach them before the train took off. It was amazing how quick on his feet Valez was for a man his size.

"This is Jack Webber of the FBI. Whoever is in charge of this station must make sure that the train up there does not leave. Do you understand!" The agent yelled at the top of his lungs with his badge held high for everyone to see.

"Sir, the train has received the orders. It's not going anywhere. Let me know what else I need to do. I'm Cedric Watson station controller sir," proudly stated a short man.

"Thank you. Just make sure that train doesn't go anywhere," said Webber.

"Alright men, I want all the exits covered. Two men underneath the tracks and the rest scour the place for these three. No one is too shoot unless fired upon. They have one hostage and access to many more on the train. I don't want any casualties!" ordered Webber

It didn't take long to find the three fugitives in the first car of the four-car train. Corrigan and Valez weren't making much of an effort to hide, they knew there wasn't much sense in it. They were safe as long as they had at least one hostage.

"Get this thing out of my face," snapped Webber as he shoved a WGN cameraman out of his way.

"This is Webber, open the doors to the train," Webber relayed his demand over his palm sized transmitter.

"Don't take another step Jack. If you want to see this pretty girl stay alive and everyone else on this train remain unharmed, then you'd be smart to stay right where you are," stated Corrigan who revealed his gun for effect as did Valez. At the sight of the guns, most of the car's occupants scrambled to the back of the car. "Nobody gets off the train. Do I make myself understood people." The silence from the train passengers indicated that they understood, although a few stifled whimpers could still be heard. "Nobody needs to get hurt here, so nobody panic. Just remain in your seats as you were and be quiet. If Mr. Hot Shot FBI guy here is smart, then everyone will be getting to their intended destination soon," assured Corrigan.

"I'm not moving any closer David. Look, this doesn't concern these people or the girl, so why don't you just let them go," requested Webber. It was evident that Webber wasn't comfortable with making deals. If Webber had his way he'd probably take a chance with his snipers putting a bullet in the head of both Valez and Corrigan. Webber had met Corrigan twice before and didn't particularly care for the man. Webber didn't know why he originally felt disdain for this man, he just remembered getting a bad vibe from Corrigan. In this business, it was often wise to trust one's intuition.

"You're right, it doesn't concern these people. But it does concern our lovely girl here. You see, she along with Captain America there (Corrigan pointed the gun in Tip's direction), were the ones who had to play nosey detectives. They were the ones who figured out my brilliant little scheme. Yeah, two punk college kids figured out the riddle, not the great Jack Webber and his entourage of overpaid suits. I had you all fooled. I had the whole country fooled except these two. So, yes, she is involved and I've got plans for her," said

Corrigan as he grabbed Lisa's face and gave her a long lick with his tongue on her cheek.

It took four of Webber's men to hold Tip back from rushing forward. They forcefully carried Tip far from the scene, but still remained within earshot. These agents didn't want to miss any of the action anymore than Tip did. They relaxed their grip when they felt they were far enough away. They maintained a human box around Tip.

"Now, start the fucking train or people start dying!" shouted Corrigan, "No tricks either."

"I'd start the train if I could, but they shut the power grid down for this whole sector. It's going to take another fifteen minutes before it powers up again," bluffed Webber.

"I don't have fifteen minutes and I'm tired of playing your games." Corrigan with Lisa and Valez in tow headed for the driver's seat. Corrigan forced one of the guns into Lisa's hands and physically forced her to pull the trigger. The driver's blood sprayed all over the small windshield.

"Congratulations Webber, you just helped our precious Lisa here commit her first murder. I tried to stop her, but you know kids these days. They just don't listen.

The color drained from Webber's face and he motioned for the power to be restored to the El.

"These controls seem to look like they're all fired up. All aboard," sadistically shouted Corrigan.

The train rocketed out of the station as Corrigan pushed the throttle full speed ahead.

"Get the chopper's ass on that train. Update me every minute on its position. Find me any local police near the next few stops of this train immediately. I want Robinson and Calloway to somehow get their asses to the next train station before the train does, over," coolly ordered Webber.

Tip knew from announcements on the train earlier that morning that due to excess capacity the train would only be stopping at select stations and not taking its usually route. The next stop would be at

Fullerton in the heart of Lincoln Park. This was roughly four miles away.

The human box around Tip relaxed and two of the agents quickly dispersed. Tip deduced that they must be Robinson and Calloway. In fact, now that he thought about it, he remembered the younger agent being called Robinson earlier.

The agents didn't seem too concerned with Tip anymore, so he hastily followed Robinson and Calloway down the escalator. Traffic was almost at a stand still outside the stadium. Apparently, after a long delay and much debate they had agreed to resume play and the game was knotted at four apiece heading into the ninth inning. All the cars had their radios tuned to the game and most of the drivers had stepped out of their cars to enjoy the game with their Chicago brethren.

"I want someone to get a hold of whoever is in charge of that train and have it shut down when it gets to Fullerton station. How many police do we have in that area?" asked Webber to a faceless voice on his wireless.

"There are only three patrolmen that will be able to get there in time sir. As you are aware, most of Chicago's public security is around the vicinity of the game tonight," replied the flinty female voice.

"Make sure they cover as many exits as possible then, there should only be four exits at that particular stop. Make sure they all have a description of the assailants and try not to harm the girl, but if necessary they can shoot to kill," said Webber. There was no telling how many people Corrigan and Valez could kill if the mood struck them. One innocent person was already dead. Webber knew he'd have to sacrifice the girl's life for the greater good. These were the types of decisions that kept him awake at night.

Agents Robinson and Calloway sprinted into the crowd and out of site. The least of the FBI's worries at this point was Tip's location, which was good. Tip found what he was looking for instantly. Propped up against a poll was a policeman's motorcycle. The cop was stationed in the middle of the street to direct traffic.

With traffic at a stand still, the cop was trying to listen to the action of the game being broadcast from the speakers atop The Cubbie Bear Bar & Grill. Tip sprinted for the motorcycle and was glad to see that the keys were in the ignition. The keys were probably always in the ignition, because nobody would be crazy enough to steal a cop's bike with him standing twenty feet away.

The bike fired up right away. "Hey, what the hell do you think you are doing!" shouted the incensed cop. The cop's shouting was in vain; he could only see taillights as Tip rode into the night.

Tip snaked his way in and out of traffic and prayed that no one opened a car door. In the congestion, he didn't have time to figure out how to get the police lights and siren to work. Besides, he didn't know if he wanted to attract any more attention. Tip knew of a shortcut to the Fullerton station. He made it to a side street and really opened the bike up. It was difficult to concentrate on the choppy road and he knew the speedometer had to be approaching one hundred miles per hour. Meandering through the congested car traffic was dangerous as hell, but it was the only chance of making it to the station in time. Tip would rather die trying than get there too late.

Tip slowed the bike down as he approached Fullerton station. Traffic was again extremely heavy in this area. He was roughly six hundred yards from the station when he heard the hard clicky-it-tee-clack of the train as it sped along the rails overhead and directly into the station.

―――

Valez was sweating profusely from being confined in the stuffy driver's cockpit. Corrigan held Lisa tight against him with the gun pointed up to her temple. He was growing weary of having to keep this feisty and strong girl under wraps. He'd be able to waste her soon enough, but he still needed to use her as a safeguard, for a little while longer anyway.

Corrigan glanced out into the mobs of waiting people. He didn't see any cops waiting for him, but there could be some agents amongst the crowd. He covered his head with a black hat he'd taken from a passenger and switched into another borrowed raggedy coat. Lisa was forced to change into a new coat with an accompanying navy blue scarf wrapped about her head.

"Valez, you know we have to part ways here. Otherwise they will surely catch one of us," said Corrigan.

Before Valez had a chance to respond, Corrigan leveled the barrel with the silencer and put two rounds into Valez's thick skull. Blood splattered against the glass of the train. Valez's big body fell backwards with tremendous force.

Lisa, bent her head sideways and closed her eyes from the vivid image. She rapidly regained her composure and wiped the flecks of Valez's splattered blood from her face. She had to get away from this animal soon, because if Valez was expendable to Corrigan, there was no question that she was as well.

Corrigan released the automatic train doors and the crowd poured out from the cars, most yelling and screaming frantically. Many patrons got off the train, even though it wasn't the stop they wanted. Others were making quite a commotion warning the oncoming passengers to get the hell out of there.

With Lisa by his side, Corrigan ducked both of their heads and joined the frantic crowd scrambling for the exits. Uniformed Chicago policemen covered three of the four exits. Corrigan steered his and Lisa's way toward one of the guarded exits, he liked to fool people by the unexpected tact. He also assumed that the FBI and Secret Service agents would be manning the fourth exit and Corrigan liked his odds better against the Chicago police than the Feds. The train passenger that Corrigan had borrowed the coat from kept a close eye on him and chased frantically after him. The passenger was an off duty postman and was heroically trying to catch-up to Corrigan. Dragging Lisa slowed Corrigan. The postman lunged at Corrigan and grasped his shoulder, but part of the panicked crowd turned at the same instance knocking the postman's grip from Corrigan's shoulder. The force of the postman's grip spun around Corrigan, but once the postman's grip released Corrigan once again held the advantage. He squared his gun at this would be hero and killed him instantly.

Trying to stop this frenzied crowd to check each person individually would only cause the cops to be stampeded. The mob was streaming down the narrow stairs and the cops had no choice but to quickly scan the faces as they streaked by. News from the dispatcher instructed the cops to keep a keen eye out for a gigantic body (Valez) and they were doing just that. And most would recognize Corrigan easily if he weren't in disguise.

The policeman was short but stocky. He was around thirty and one could tell that he normally had a friendly face to him. This man's normal patrol was on the nearby DePaul campus. The most action he'd seen down there was someone pulling a gun over a dispute on the basketball court.

Right now, the policeman's face was firm and showed strain from the intense concentration it was undergoing. The crowd spilled past him faster than he could fathom. An occasional hysterical person would approach him looking for help and protection. This only caused distraction and put these people in greater danger.

The policeman spotted Corrigan and Lisa as they bounded off the last step. The recognition was too late, Corrigan expertly pumped three bullets into the policeman's heart. The already hysterical crowd was now at a fever pitch, some people were so frightened that they couldn't move. Others had fainted and no longer had to endure the horror film that they had involuntarily played bit roles in.

The nearest cop to the scene turned when he heard the shooting. The large and portly Polish policeman turned just in time to see the eyes of Corrigan as he sadistically executed another blue uniform. The third policeman had time to pull his gun, but couldn't get a clean shot at Corrigan as people still streaked back and forth in an unbridled panic. Corrigan of course had no regard for these pedestrians and callously sent bullets spraying in the direction of the last policeman. The policeman took a shot in the knee and went down hard on the pavement. To the cop's credit, he was able to fight the pain and squeeze off a couple of shots as Corrigan sprinted into the night. Unfortunately, both of these shots missed their intended target.

# CHAPTER 56

Tip dropped the motorcycle on the fissured asphalt of Lincoln Avenue and began sprinting toward the station. His legs were driving hard and he effortlessly sprang over the hood of a 1977 Chevy Nova. Now within two hundred yards of the station, he could sense Lisa's presence, and he knew she needed him. There were three-uniformed policeman manning the entrances as frantic patrons poured down the stairs. A tremendous amount of commotion was occurring at one of the exits and one of policeman crumpled over into a heap. "Aha!" There were Corrigan and Lisa! Corrigan had just shot the young policeman. But, where was Valez? Tip scanned the area in a hurried fashion looking for any sign of the Valez. He had to be somewhere Tip thought, but where?

Tip's hatred for Corrigan began to make his blood boil as he witnessed two more cops get dropped. Tip was about one hundred yards away and gaining fast. He watched Corrigan duck down an alleyway with Lisa. Tip sprinted through the paranoia and turned down the alley. To his dismay, the alley was dark and dank and there was no sign of either of them.

# CHAPTER 57

Corrigan and Lisa exited from the stolen automobile in the inner circle of Lincoln Park. Corrigan eagerly hurried into the protective darkness of the Lincoln Park Zoo. There were only a few street people milling about inside the grounds. The free zoo was normally packed on sunny days during the summer. People wanted to either see the animals, or it was a convenient thoroughfare to North Beach. Tonight the zoo was calm. The city's residents were watching the exciting drama of the World Series unfold.

"As I hope that you are soon beginning to realize, your use to me is becoming less and less by the minute my dear. Valez didn't tell me about you and I can see why, you're quite a gem. He must have been hoarding you for himself. What a hedonistic slob he was," stated Corrigan.

Lisa sneered back at him with her eyes. She was too tired to waste any words on this pitiful animal. Although she was scared, her hatred and detest for the creature before her suppressed any fear.

"Oh, yeah, I like that. You're beautiful when you're angry-show me that hate. That hate gets me off. Unfortunately, my dear, despite your beauty, I'm still going to have to kill you. The shame being, there is really no reason other than for my own personal joy. I could just as easily let you go free never to worry about seeing or hearing from you again. Or, I can just as easily kill you.

You see I'll be hiding in some foreign land in a few hours. I will never be heard from or seen again, but believe you me my presence will still be felt. As long as I'm alive, Charlie Duke's life will not be safe. But, oh I'm sorry, you won't be around to see any more of my handy work, I forgot, how silly of me. You see, you and your Boy Wonder had to go and spoil it for everyone. Because of you, the United States will continue its downward spiral into mediocrity, just like the fall of Rome. Oh, people will rejoice when Marshall is re-elected and then there will be festivals galore when Charlie Duke is eventually elected President four years from now. But, that weak little airhead will lead this great country into ruin. It'll be a feminists' and faggots' heyday. Congratulations on contributing to the downfall of the industrial world's greatest empire. As a prize for your outstanding efforts we offer you a very cruel and unpleasant death."

Corrigan pulled out a very long and jagged bow knife with a white ivory handle. "On second thought, I'm in kind of a generous mood since it's such a beautiful night, perhaps I will let you live. So that you never forget our precious time together, I will remove your eyes very delicately so that you won't be tempted to look at another man. That's not enough for someone like you, someone that's, so special to me. We'll need to remove all of your fingers as well. We wouldn't want you to touch anyone ever again now would we my dear," said Corrigan. His eyes had become completely black and it seemed as if they were starring not at Lisa, but rather directly at her soul.

"So, what would you like to start with, eyes or fingers?" nonchalantly drawled Corrigan.

Lisa attempted a swift punch at Corrigan. Corrigan easily clasped her wrist and twisted it violently backward causing Lisa to let out a slight screech. "Ah, good choice, fingers it is. That way you won't be tempted to reach up to your eyes sockets out of sheer pain," tersely stated Corrigan between clenched teeth. Rather, they will just be bloody stubs beating against your head. If you're lucky, you'll have passed out from the pain and blood loss before I get to your eyes."

The zoo was black except for the faint walking lights lining the cement path every hundred yards. The path winded its way through the zoo and adjacent park until it reached the North Avenue walking bridge. Lisa and Corrigan were currently situated in a dark enclave of the park. No lights were stationed in this area. The silhouette of a

Siberian Tiger gracefully pacing back and forth in the mock jungle below could barely be made out.

The heavy foliage inside the zoo fences offered relief from the streetlights of Clark, which lay two hundred yards to the West. Automobile horns began to honk simultaneously all across the city. The city was jubilantly rejoicing. After an hour delay at the game, officials decided it would be best to play on once security was cleared.

Cub's first baseman Scott Mueller had knocked in the winning run in the bottom of the ninth inning with a sacrifice fly, scoring Steve Tynes from third base. The beloved Cubs were World Champions for the first time in their storied history. The town was going to be up all night celebrating. Several taverns and restaurants were serving free drinks until midnight in honor of the historic achievement. Corrigan knew that pandemonium in the city streets would make his getaway that much easier.

"Oh, do you hear those horns in the background honey? I was going to hear horns like that on my inauguration. They'd be much more meaningful than a meaningless World Series victory for the stupid Cubs. It's a shame that all that racket is going on, because even if you were stupid enough to scream for help no one would hear you," said Corrigan.

She knew that screaming would do her no good. Especially since it appeared as if Corrigan had managed to escape the authorities. It pained her to know that Corrigan would silently sail off into the darkness on nearby Lake Michigan. She knew that she was dispensable at this point. She'd have to make a move quickly, even if it resulted in her death. She'd rather die than give Corrigan the satisfaction of torturing her.

"I would've been the best President this country has ever seen. America would become strong again under my leadership. It's sad to have to sit here and watch such a great dynasty painfully erode. The country is rotting at the core as a result of idiots like you. Simpletons who think they are doing a good deed by meddling where they don't belong. People like you make this country weak," repeated Corrigan.

"And you suggest making this country stronger by killing the innocent, deceiving the public and forming partnerships with known criminals?" prodded Lisa.

"Lisa, Lisa, Lisa. This is exactly what I'm talking about. Your viewpoint is so myopic in nature that I pity you. These evils that you mention are just a necessary means to an end. If it took us ten percent of the population to test a cure for cancer, don't you feel that it would be selfish to not go through with the test? Of course you would conduct the test. Hell, we could just use the entire homeless and handicap population, that's about ten percent right there. Ultimately what you should always focus on is, the greatest good for the greatest amount of people," logically concluded Corrigan.

"What makes you think that you have the right to play God? Who is to say that you're the one that gets to pick and choose who survives and who will perish? America is based on democracy, not a Hitler-like dictatorship," spat Lisa.

"America is weak. I'm the only one that had a chance to raise the Phoenix from the ashes. Too many faggots, women and minorities have been given too many breaks in the form of college applications, job opportunities and welfare. This is the cancer of society. There would be no homeless, crippled or uneducated foreigners in a Corrigan run country. These people are parasites on a healthy nation," said Corrigan.

"Whatever happened to the meek shall inherit the earth?" quipped Lisa.

"Well, why don't we conduct a little experiment right now. Seeing that you're a woman-you're meek, but the only thing that you're going to inherit is a freshly carved epitaph. However, being the sport that I am, I'll at least give you a fighting chance," said Corrigan. She was shoved away from him so hard and unexpectedly that she nearly flipped over the nearby fence. The waist-high fence lined the Siberian Tiger exhibit.

There were two options for Lisa: hop the fence into the tiger pit, or head back toward the clutches of Corrigan. The tigers, nocturnal by nature, had been aroused by the excitement occurring above them. There were three tigers, one male and two female; male Siberian Tigers couldn't coexist with other males. She would have to jump into the moat surrounding the manmade habitat. She was a good swimmer, but she also knew that Siberian Tigers were very adept in the water. Siberian Tigers always bit their prey on the nape and dragged them close to water. The largest living cat in the world, the Siberian Tiger was capable of eating over one hundred pounds of meat in one sitting. They were also able to drag prey that would take more than a dozen men to move. A wicked hiss rumbled from the darkness.

Her other option wasn't much better. Corrigan was much stronger than she and also had the power of the pistol and knife on his side. She decided her best option would be to stall as long as possible and hope that another option presented itself.

"Tell me, how is a person so used to power and being in the limelight going to survive running off to a desolate region of a small foreign country? Wouldn't that be like death itself to you?" asked Lisa.

"That's the first intelligent thing you've said my dear. Perhaps I'm starting to rub off on you. You are correct in saying that I won't be in the limelight, which won't be fun. However there will not be a lack of power as you so prophesize. I will still be able to pull the necessary strings from behind the scenes to instill my will on the outcomes of events in this country. Who knows, after a few years and through the wonders of plastic surgery, I may be able to resurface as a totally new identity. Yes, I like the thought of that," answered Corrigan.

"How are you so certain that you will have persons willing to pull the strings? After all, you did just kill your top man in cold blood. Word travels fast, and I'm sure that you aren't the most popular person right now in your tight little circle. In fact, some of your hired guns may start looking for you since you didn't deliver with your promised election win," said Lisa.

"With Valez dead, the foot soldiers have no leader. None of these small timers will bother tracking me down, nor will they have the necessary skills to do so if they desired. As far as having people pull the strings for me, new people can be bought," wielded Corrigan.

"Least we forget, that you no longer have the pipeline of cash pumping in from Rodriguez, your drug lord sugar daddy," said Lisa.

"Least you forget that I have plenty of funds stored in a Cayman Bank account. You should know that there is enough there to get anything that I want. Now your questions are becoming more mundane and tiresome. It's that time of year to do some pumpkin carving, and you are my little pumpkin," he sneered.

Corrigan began to methodically approach Lisa, the long knife glistened in the dark. She wasn't going to let this animal gouge up her body. She leapt up onto the waist high railing. He closed in fast and went for her leg. He didn't want her to cheat him out of his fun by jumping into the tiger pit. As he reached out, she sprang from the railing, doing a back flip landing behind him.

A swift kick with her left leg caused the pistol in his hand to fall harmlessly into the tiger pit. This allowed her the opportunity to run. The only weapon he had left was the knife. Incensed by being duped by a woman, Corrigan darted after her with the knife raised above his head and ready to strike. There was no need for Corrigan to waste his time chasing after her, she was of little importance in the whole scheme of things now, but he wanted revenge at any cost.

Lisa was weak and tired from the emotional draining day and it was all she could do to muster up enough strength to sprint away from the pursuing madman. Running back to the entrance at Clark Street was her best means of escape. The poor lighting in the zoo made it difficult for her to find the way. She didn't have the time to get her bearings and forged ahead full speed in what she hoped was the right direction.

Her athleticism was enabling her to maintain a twenty-foot

cushion on Corrigan. He was in good shape, but he was also a little older. However, he wasn't getting tired chasing after her, rather he was having fun, and the horrified look on her face every time she turned around inspired him. She in turn ignored her burning lungs that were screaming for her to stop.

She should have been out of the park by now and into the public safety on Clark Street. She'd obviously made a wrong turn and was still on the general walking path inside the zoo, whizzing by the anaconda and crocodile exhibits. Realizing this drastic error, she reminded herself not to panic.

The path was beginning to narrow and it appeared as if there was some construction ahead. She was almost on top of the chain-linked fence before she noticed it. Glancing about her, she quickly realized that she was trapped. The only hope for escape was up and over. Lisa dug into the flimsy fence and began to climb. The climb was analogous to those she'd performed as a child playing sand volleyball. An occasional errant shot would send the ball sailing over the fence and rather than take the long walk through the swim club, she'd simply climb the fifteen-foot fence.

She hadn't gotten very far when Corrigan forcefully pulled her down. Landing hard on the unforgiving asphalt, a pain shot sharply up her hip. Before she knew it, he was on top of her and had her arms pinned down with his knees.

"Looks like I have my giant pumpkin. This is good, because it's time to do some carving," said Corrigan.

## CHAPTER 58

Tip had anticipated that Corrigan would be heading toward Lake Michigan to make his getaway. By taking a boat across Lake Michigan, Corrigan could avoid the high surveillance of the airport. The airport was probably already crawling with police and FBI agents. Thus, Tip followed the quickest route to the water. This brought him through the zoo. As he approached the entrance to the zoo from Clark Avenue, two silhouettes in a frantic chase passed before him. He was a good two hundred yards behind the commotion when he began pursuit. It was difficult to see the bodies in the dimly lit zoo. Fortunately, he was able to quickly make up ground and he could now see the figures more clearly. He hoped that it was Corrigan and Lisa and not just some teenagers horsing around. Corrigan didn't hear Tip due to his own heavy breathing, and Tip's effortless strides didn't make much noise on the pavement. Drawing closer, Tip could now discern that the two bodies where that of Corrigan and Lisa. His pulse and stride quickened.

Corrigan now had Lisa pinned and wore a truculent grin on his face. Just as he was about to plunge the knife into her left eye socket, he looked up in response to Tip's rapidly approaching hoof beats. Tip crouched low and sprang.

Corrigan diverted the knife from Lisa and turned it in Tip's direction. The knife glanced off Tip's shoulder and clanged onto the ground as he separated Corrigan from Lisa. He landed on Corrigan with all of his weight and purposely drove Corrigan's head into the ground. Unfortunately, they landed off the path and in some soft dirt, so the impact wasn't as damaging to Corrigan as Tip had hoped.

Tip had underestimated Corrigan's madman strength and they

began to tussle on the ground. They rolled violently back across the pavement, as each one vied to gain the upper hand. Their journey came to a sudden halt as they crashed into the cement barrier that housed the Nile Crocodile exhibit. Tip was on top. With the deaths of Hamilton and Burke etched in his mind, Tip unleashed a fury of ferocious fists onto Corrigan. Four ribs crunched under the impact of a hard punch to the abdomen. The cacophony of sound emanating from Corrigan's mouth was short lived as the other fist hammered five teeth out.

Corrigan was hunched over on the ground holding his mouth. Tip didn't want to let up and sprang toward him. Corrigan anticipated this and drove the knife he'd surreptitiously picked up from the ground into Tip's chest. Fortunately Tip was still wearing the flak jacket and the Knife just pricked him slightly.

Imagining what Corrigan would have done to Lisa fueled Tip's motivational fire. Temporarily insane at this point his strength had more than doubled. Tip hoisted Corrigan up by the neck and then over his head. Without hesitation he tossed him twenty-feet below and into the Nile Crocodile exhibit. If Corrigan didn't drown from his sustained injuries, his fresh blood would surely attract the attention of the adult crocodiles. The Nile crocodile is the largest crocodile in Africa growing to twenty-five feet and weighing up to fifteen hundred pounds. The Nile Crocodile accounts for more human deaths than any other animal in the world. Using its strong jaws, the crocodile drags its victim underwater until it drowns. Not being able to chew, the crocodile wedges its prey beneath a tree trunk in the deep depths of the water until it rots. Corrigan's soul was already rotten, so to be drowned in this manner was a condign punishment.

## CHAPTER 59

Lisa clung tightly to Tip's sculpted chest as they comfortably relaxed on the soft sand of North Beach. Lake Michigan peacefully waited at their feet. Lisa's warm breath felt good on Tip's bare chest. Both had suffered through some difficult times over the past several years and it was good to have someone who understood. Through fate, their lives had become intertwined surrounding events that would not soon be forgotten. The late Mr. Tipton once said that everything in life happens for a reason, both the good and the bad. Tip, for the first time, was beginning to believe his father's words. Although his life would never be the same, he wanted the girl currently in his arms to be with him for the new one. A star glistened in the clear night sky. Deep down, Tip knew this star was one of his loved ones letting him know that everything was going to be all right.

# EPILOGUE

Zar tore out the newspaper article and stuffed it into his pocket. He had just been shuttled across the water to a small island off the coast of Thailand. Zar figured he would lay low here for a few weeks. The newspaper article described Corrigan's death, and Zar easily determined that Corrigan was the one who had hired his services. Zar was glad that Corrigan was dead since he didn't care too much for incompetence. The reason he was really saving the article was because it had a detailed picture of Tip. This was the first time that Zar hadn't gotten his target, and Tip was the person responsible for foiling his plan.

---

The ice felt good tonight. It was weird how some nights it felt like one was fighting the ice while on other nights, such as this, it felt a part of you. Becoming tired wasn't an option for Tip tonight. He was going to skate through four overtimes if necessary. Tip was in the zone. Hopefully overtime wasn't going to happen, thought Tip, winning the game in regulation was his only intention.

Play had stopped for the moment as the result of an icing penalty. An icing penalty occurred whenever someone shot the puck more than three-quarters of the ice without anyone else touching it. This rule was designed to prevent teams from stalling. This respite allowed Tip the opportunity to soak in, and for the first time, truly appreciate the scene surrounding him.

It seemed out of place to Tip that they were playing against their arch rival, Michigan, in Boston's Fleet Center. Munn, Joe Louis and Yost Arenas were more familiar backdrops for this intense rivalry. Yet, a different venue made sense, since this was a different game.

This was the most important game in the series' storied history. This game would determine the Collegiate National Hockey Champion. By the looks of the crowd, it was evident that many folks had made the ten-hour drive from Michigan.

The clashing of maize/blue against green/white was a familiar palate of colors. The crowd had been standing in anticipation since the five-minute mark in the third period. Included in this cluster of fans was Tip's personal cheering section.

Tip looked past, or rather through, the University of Michigan Coach. This was the coach that had revoked his scholarship four long years ago. Holding a grudge against this man was a waste of energy and thus wasn't in Tip's best interest. He understood now that it was best to take things in stride and accept the responsibility to deal with them accordingly. This fortitude coupled with four years of intense rehab enabled him to be on center stage, or ice, at the moment. There may not have been a grudge, but Tip was not about to let the opportunity to stick it to his rival pass him by.

Seated beyond the enemy's bench was where Tip's focus resided. The Hamiltons appeared nervous, which was their normal state whenever they watched him play. Wrapped around Mrs. Hamilton's legs was his younger sister, Allison. Draped on her tiny body was one of his old game jerseys. Allison had to constantly hold the bottom of the jersey to keep it from dragging on the ground.

Allison was holding hands with Mrs. Hamilton and Charlie Duke. Charlie Duke had been a positive force in Tip's life since their chance encounter last fall. It would have been easy for her to fall by the wayside following the formal presentation in Washington honoring the unlikely heroes, Tip and Lisa. To everyone's surprise, they had kept in touch and Tip had to admit that everything printed about Charlie Duke was true-she was bright, beautiful, charismatic and above all, caring. He could only hope that the relationship would continue for years to come. Little did he know that she wished for the same thing. In a mere four years, Charlie Duke was destined to become the first female President in the history of the United States.

## CRISIS

One person that would remain a big part of Tip's life for sometime to come was adjacent to Charlie Duke. Although they knew their lives would be forever changed from the recent events, Lisa and Tip knew that life without each other wouldn't be worth living. Tip didn't know what would become of him if Lisa were no longer a part of his life. A radiant glow exuded all around her. Looking at her laughing eyes was the only thing he needed for motivation. Her eyes were even more inspiring of late as she was encouraged by the improving health of her mother.

Enjoying her first hockey game was Lisa's mother. It was her first public appearance since being released from the institution a month ago. Her attendance was just the latest step in a dramatic recovery. Despite doctors' protests, Lisa divulged to her mother the whole sordid story about the murder of her son, Eddie and everything inbetween. This revelation helped bring some closure for her mother. Her mother decided it was time to put the past behind her and to start a new life. Eddie's new life wouldn't be as pleasant, as he was now confined to a wheelchair and was admitted to an alcohol rehabilitation center. Eddie's father was removed from the Office of Governor, once his dirty tactics became know to the public. It didn't hurt to have the Vice President in your corner.

Tip's eyes refocused on the two beads in front of them. Looking deep into those irises, he could see a glimmer of fear. This was understandable. A great hockey player stood before Tip, but the player knew he was no match for Tip in a face-off. Tip led the nation in face-off winning percentage and had set a new NCAA record in the process. This All-American hockey player had already lost five of the six face-offs against Tip tonight. It was Tip's intent to make it six loses.

The opponent also knew that this was the most crucial face-off yet. Michigan State was in Michigan's zone with fifteen seconds to play and Michigan State aggressively removed their goalie even though the game was tied. Hence Michigan State would have one extra man to fire on goal if Tip won the face off. It was a risky coaching move, but Michigan State's coach had the utmost confidence that Tip would win the face off. Tip wasn't about to let him down. He vowed to never let anyone down again.

The referee dropped the puck and it slowly descended to the ice. Playing the puck's bounce off the ice perfectly, Tip skillfully backslapped the puck back to his teammate.

Waiting patiently for the play to develop, Tip casually skated toward the seam in the left part of Michigan's trapping defense. The puck glided smoothly along the ice back in his direction, a perfectly executed pass and play. Bringing the stick from behind the ear, Tip's banana blade stick struck the puck true and launched it off the ice. The Michigan goalie only saw the puck after it was engulfed in the netting of his goal and the red flashing light twirled rapidly. Lying at the bottom of a mountain of joyous teammates was ironic since Tip was on the pinnacle of life.

Post-Game Press Conference: "My father said that everything in life happens for a reason, no matter how cruel. It is up to each individual to handle what life throws at them. Doctors, too many to mention, said I would never play hockey again. It would have been easy to take this advice and accept defeat. That would be the easy way, but it's not my way. I thank the few that did believe in me and helped me through my painful rehab.

I also don't know why so many of my loved ones had to suffer so much; that's not for me to decide. It's my job to deal with this suffering as best as possible and try to make sure it doesn't happen again. We cannot go back to make a new start, but we can start now to make a new ending."

## ABOUT THE AUTHOR

Diving with Great Whites, running with the bulls, skydiving, playing in March Madness against Duke, singing at Oktoberfest, dancing at Carnival, being an uncle, glacier climbing, enjoying Mardi Gras, reporting directly to a CEO and bungee jumping are some of the author's real life adventures. These various experiences help supply his characters with rich depth and enlivens the story telling.

The proceeds from Erik Qualman's various works help support numerous charities including the 9/11 and Hurricane Katrina Relief Funds. The author enjoys hearing from readers and can be reached at equalman@gmail.com.

*Crisis* by Erik Qualman

When terror attacks again strike the United States, two ordinary citizens—Paul Tipton and Lisa Appleton—join forces to uncover a web of conspiracy reaching the highest levels of government. Their task is difficult, for while trying to prevent the assassination of the first female vice president, they must also confront feelings about their past and a possible future together.

After our nation was attacked on September 11, 2001, one would expect there to be a surplus of Tom Clancy-meets-Tom Ridge inspired novels to follow in the wake of this tragedy. Fortunately, Crisis, the new novel by Erik Qualman, avoids not only sensationalism but nearly every possible pitfall in suspense fiction, while also addressing the tragedy of terrorism with empathy and understanding.

Crisis is brilliantly written, with a plot that, despite its complexity, succeeds in moving at a brisk and compelling pace. Qualman's ease with language—from realistic dialogue to near cinematic descriptiveness—is the hallmark of a truly talented writer. This is a novel for those who want more than spies and explosions in a political thriller; it was written for more discriminating readers and it certainly does not disappoint. Qualman powerfully delivers one of the most insightful and enjoyable reads of the year...expect to see more from him soon.

-New York Times Best Selling Author, Ellen Tanner Marsh